BEAR NO MALICE

ALSO BY CLARISSA HARWOOD

Impossible Saints

BEAR NO MALICE

CLARISSA HARWOOD

PEGASUS BOOKS
NEW YORK LONDON

BEAR NO MALICE

Pegasus Books Ltd
148 West 37th Street, 13th Floor
New York, NY 10018

Copyright © 2018 by Clarissa Harwood

First Pegasus Books hardcover edition January 2019

Interior design by Sabrina Plomitallo-González, Pegasus Books

ISBN: 978-1-64313-052-1

10 9 8 7 6 5 4 3 2 1

Printed in the United States of America
Distributed by W. W. Norton & Company, Inc.

For Michael

kedves férjem

The shackles of an old love straitened him,
His honour rooted in dishonour stood,
And faith unfaithful kept him falsely true.
—Alfred, Lord Tennyson, "Lancelot and Elaine"

LONDON: OCTOBER 1907

When Tom first opened his eyes, he didn't recognize his surroundings. Instead of his own bedroom, with its simple, tidy chest of drawers and washstand, he was in a hotel room with heavy, dark upholstery and burgundy velvet curtains. And, most startling of all, Julia lay next to him. It was the first time he'd spent a whole night with her, and he instantly regretted their recklessness.

He slipped out of bed as quickly and stealthily as if a wild animal were lying next to him. Gathering his clothing, which was strewn about the room, he began to dress.

Behind him, he heard Julia stirring. Tom froze, hoping she would go back to sleep, but instead she murmured, "What time is it?"

"Six o'clock." He kept his back to her as he answered and began to button his shirt.

"So early? Why are you getting dressed? Don't you want to stay in bed with me a little longer?"

"I have a meeting at the cathedral to prepare for." The meeting wasn't until nine, but Julia didn't need to know that.

Tom went to the window and pulled the curtain aside. The hotel fronted onto a quiet street, and at this hour few people were about, but he noticed a man standing across the street, looking up at the hotel windows. There was nothing particularly strange about his appearance or demeanor—he was probably just waiting for someone—but Tom quickly stepped away from the window, letting the curtain fall back into place.

He heard the swish of the bedclothes behind him, and a moment later Julia stood before him with the bedsheet loosely wrapped around her. Her auburn hair spilled over her shoulders, a riot of color setting off the creamy white of her skin. He knew from the way she was looking at him that she wanted him to touch her, but all he could think about was getting away and being alone. Last night she had been Julia, the woman he loved. This morning she was Charles Carrington's wife, the mother of three Carrington children, a symbol of Tom's failure. He let his hands fall to his sides and looked at her with what he hoped was a neutral expression.

Julia tucked the sheet more securely around herself and reached out to finish buttoning his shirt. He could feel her warmth and smell the jasmine scent she used in her hair.

As she fastened the top button, she said, "Sometimes I think you hate me."

"I do hate you," he said. In spite of himself, he caught her hands and kissed them.

"I hate you, too." She raised her face to his, closing her eyes.

He kissed her, but only briefly, then held her away from him with his hands on her shoulders. "Julia, we have to stop this."

She sighed and stepped back, out of his reach. "Not that again."

"I mean it. There are so many risks—"

"To your career?"

"To both of us."

"Really, Tom, you ought to marry." She turned away and sat on the edge of the bed.

He raised his eyebrows. "Do you have someone in mind?"

"Any of the girls who are always making sheep's eyes at you will do. You'd better marry someone soon, if you want to quell the cathedral gossip."

"What gossip?"

"Oh, I'm sure you've heard it." Julia altered her tone, sounding like a querulous old woman. "How strange that a handsome man like Canon Cross, established in his profession and already in his mid-thirties, seems to show no interest in marriage. It doesn't help that most clergymen look like horses."

"People actually say that most clergymen look like horses?"

"No, that was my contribution."

"I don't care what people say."

She laughed bitterly. "If you truly believe that, you don't know yourself."

"People of your class can act on their whims and avoid serious consequences. I don't have that luxury."

"Oh, Tom. Spare me the sermon about the dissipation and corruption of the upper classes. It seems to me you act on your whims often enough, and you seem to have no trouble avoiding the consequences."

She had gone too far. "It's over, Julia," he said, turning away.

"Very well. But don't expect me to take you back if you change your mind."

He walked away without another word, picking up his coat on the way out. The hotel room door closed behind him with a decisive thud.

"My wife will be leaving later this morning," he told the hotel clerk in a brisk, authoritative tone when he stopped at the counter to pay the bill.

"Yes, Mr. Harlowe." The young, narrow-faced man had a respectful manner, but there was something a little too keen about his eyes.

Being called "Mr. Harlowe" startled Tom, although it shouldn't have—it was a false name he had used before. Once inside the hansom cab that took him to the cathedral, he mentally rehearsed the name most people knew him by: Thomas Cross. Although it hadn't happened before, he was worried he would revert to "Harlowe" by mistake.

He was grateful for the long ride in which to sort out his thoughts, alternating between berating himself for his stupidity in meeting Julia at a hotel and blaming her for seducing him months ago. In any case, he needed to free himself from this entanglement in order to regain some self-respect. As gratifying as it was both mentally and physically to be with her, the risk of people finding out about their relationship was too great.

Tired of listening to his spinning brain, Tom called to the cabdriver to stop, deciding to walk the rest of the way to the cathedral. It was only autumn, but the air whispered icy warnings of winter. He pulled his coat collar closer around his neck, feeling his lungs expand with relief now that he was out of the stuffy confines of the cab.

He arrived at the cathedral an hour later, with a few minutes to spare before his meeting, and he paused at the baptismal font, noticing that the hairline crack at the base of the marble structure still hadn't been repaired. As he strode down the aisle to his office, he glanced up at the roof trusses. He couldn't see where they were rotting, but he knew only too well what repairs were needed and how much they would cost. The building was an aging courtesan whose beauty was more trouble and expense than its maintenance was worth. He knew others came to the cathedral to find God, but he'd never done so. He found God in people, not buildings.

His meeting that morning was with a parishioner, Cedric Jenkins, a bereaved husband whose wife had died of puerperal fever three months earlier. As the two men sat in Tom's office, Mr. Jenkins alternately raged against God and begged Tom for words of comfort. Tom let him talk as long as he wanted to, saying little at first.

"Maria was everything to me," Mr. Jenkins declared. "We were married only five years, but I've been in love with her almost all my life. Her family and mine were neighbors, so we knew each other as children. When she told me she loved me, it was the happiest day of my life. Are you married, Canon Cross?"

"No."

"I ought to envy you. You're not in any danger of feeling your very soul ripped out of your body. My wife was my best self. Now I have nothing left," he said, dropping his head into his hands.

Another clergyman might have disputed this last statement or quoted Tennyson: "'Tis better to have loved and lost than never to have loved at all." Perhaps others would have assured him his wife was in heaven or, most offensive of all, that God needed her more than he did. Tom knew better than to do any of those things.

"I'm sorry you've lost someone you loved so much," he said quietly.

Mr. Jenkins raised his head, staring at Tom with hopeless eyes. "Why did God take her from me?"

"I don't know."

"I've tried to be a good man. I've kept the Ten Commandments."

That's better than I've done, Tom thought. He had broken every one of them at some point in his life, aside from the injunction not to commit murder, and there was still time for that.

"I haven't attended church as regularly as I ought, but surely I'm not being punished for it."

"I don't believe God is punishing you," Tom said. "I understand why you might feel that way, but your wife's death has nothing to do with anything you've done or not done."

"Then why? Why did she have to die?" Mr. Jenkins's look was desperate.

"I wish I had an explanation for you, but I don't."

He said nothing more profound than this, but by the end of the conversation, the bereaved husband was comforted. It almost always happened this way. Whether he spoke much or at all, Tom had the gift of making others feel that he sympathized deeply with them. He didn't know if it was the look in his eyes or something about his presence—the clerical collar alone was a comfort to some people—but it was rare that he left anyone in as much distress or anguish as he found them. On his worst days, knowing he could help people in this way was all that kept him going.

As soon as Mr. Jenkins had left, Tom went to the chapter house for a meeting with the dean and the three other canons. Every chapter meeting was the same. The dean's opening remarks always made it seem as if he were in charge, but by the time the meeting was really under way the dean would be asleep, and either Paul Harris or Tom would take over. Dean Whiting was in his eighties, partly blind, mostly deaf, and generally in ill health. It was only a matter of time before he died and the deanship was available. The cathedral gossip had it that Harris and Tom were the primary rivals for the post. A high churchman, Harris was only seven-and-twenty, from a wealthy family, and rumored to be the bishop's favorite. In Tom's opinion, Harris was a prig who had never experienced hardship in his life and was incapable of understanding the needs of the parishioners. But he didn't hesitate to dictate what should and should not be done regarding the daily affairs of the cathedral.

"We need to make a decision regarding Mr. Narbridge's request," Harris was saying. The dean, true to custom, was already asleep, but the other two clergymen, Canon Martin and Canon Johnson, were listening attentively.

"What request is that?" Tom interjected. William Narbridge owned a railway company and was the wealthiest member of the congregation. He also made no secret of his preference for Harris as the next dean.

"I'm certain I showed you his letter—don't you remember?" Harris gave Tom a supercilious look.

"Be so kind as to remind me."

"He wants his wife to be buried in the crypt."

"Obviously that's impossible, unless she can be surgically flattened and propped up against the door," said Tom. "The crypt is full. Nobody has been buried there for at least a century."

"I'm aware of that," Harris said, irritation creeping into his voice. "But Mr. Narbridge has been one of our most generous benefactors. Last year alone he donated two thousand pounds to the cathedral."

Tom raised an eyebrow. "Perhaps he'd like to pay for a larger cathedral to be built, then, with room in the crypt for every wealthy sinner and his family."

Narbridge employed former prison inmates, and Tom had clashed with him three years earlier over the brutal treatment of his workers. Tom had been interested in prison reform ever since he'd worked as a prison chaplain when he was first ordained. When he became a canon at the cathedral, he was also appointed to the Prison Commission, which required him to assess the condition of prisoners during and after their sentences. Three years ago he'd learned that the former inmates who'd found work with Narbridge's railway company didn't last more than a year, either having been too severely injured to work or having died on the job from easily preventable accidents. Tom had opened an investigation into Narbridge's business practices, but the magnate had received only a fine and a warning. As far as Tom was concerned, Narbridge was no better than a murderer, but the man had too much influence to be treated with the contempt he deserved.

Harris ignored Tom's barbed comment and appealed to the other canons for their ideas.

After a brief discussion, Harris said, "Well, I think that's all the business we need to discuss today. Ah, wait, there is one more thing. Tuesday evenings are most convenient for the lecture series, so they will begin next month."

"Tuesday evenings?" Tom exclaimed. "That's impossible. The Temperance Society meets here on those days. As you know."

Harris shrugged. "Surely you can find another place until the lecture series is finished. The bishop has agreed that it's the perfect way to address the problem of our dwindling numbers. The topic of the relevance of God and the church in the modern world, with the lecturers some of the foremost thinkers of our time, will certainly attract more people to the cathedral."

Tom was furious. Harris knew perfectly well how important the Temperance Society was to the community, and the fact that it was flourishing under Tom's direction annoyed Harris enough to try to undercut it at every opportunity. Using the bishop to bolster his argument was just another slap in Tom's face.

"Instead of talking about the relevance of the church, we need to prove its relevance by being involved in practical reform," Tom said, struggling to keep his temper. "Choose another day of the week to have the lecture series or find another place for it. I won't have the Temperance Society meetings moved."

Harris gave Tom an icy stare. "We are speaking of what is best for the cathedral."

"We're speaking of what's best for the people," Tom snapped.

The argument ended in a tense silence, as the arguments between Tom and Harris usually did. Tom left the meeting with a resolve to speak to the bishop about the Temperance Society meetings. Harris rarely represented the bishop's concerns objectively, being too caught up in his own interests.

After such an encounter, despite whatever annoyance or anger he felt, Tom was always more confident about his own prospects for the deanship. He had more experience than Harris, as well as a wider variety of leadership roles in church work, and aside from the bishop's apparent preference for Harris, Tom expected the deanship to be his. He wanted it desperately, though sometimes he admitted to himself that he wouldn't want it quite so much if Harris didn't want it too. In any case, becoming dean would allow him greater influence. His many plans for social reform would be heard by more powerful people and more readily accepted.

It was a busy day. After the chapter meeting, Tom finished some paperwork, went to another meeting—a Prison Commission committee meeting—and then to London Hospital in Whitechapel to visit patients.

It wasn't until late that night that Tom left the hospital, but his physical weariness was worth the mental relief he had gained. The affair with Julia no longer loomed large in his mind, and he had administered a palliative, if not a cure, for that sickness by visiting people who were truly sick. He no longer despised himself. He was doing some good in the world, which he hoped would outweigh the bad. It might be poor theology, but it assuaged his guilt.

A cab was waiting near the front doors of the hospital. Assuming the driver was waiting for someone else, Tom began to walk past it, towards the cabstand down the street, but the driver made a sign that he was disengaged.

Gratefully Tom climbed into the cab and called out his address through the trapdoor in the roof, then sat back and closed his eyes. Normally he walked nearly everywhere he went, but after such a long day it was a welcome relief to take a cab. And his lodgings near the cathedral were a long way from Whitechapel.

The cab rattled down the street at a pace Tom thought was unnecessarily fast, but he was too tired to care. He supposed he'd get home sooner that way. Despite the jolting of the vehicle on the cobblestone streets, he found himself nodding off.

He awakened with a start, surprised the cab was still moving after what seemed like a long time. It was too dark to check his pocket watch, but when he pulled aside the heavy curtain and looked out, his confusion turned to alarm. Instead of the familiar landmarks lit by lampposts near his lodgings, he saw fields and hedgerows in the moonlight. The cab had left London.

"Driver!" he called out. "What the devil is the meaning of this? Stop at once!"

The driver neither answered him nor slowed the cab, which was now wildly careening around curves in the road.

Tom tried the doors on either side, but they were securely fastened. He rapped loudly on the ceiling of the cab with his walking stick, shouting at the driver, but all his efforts were in vain. What could the man be thinking? Had he lost his mind? Had he mistaken Tom for someone else?

Just when he was considering trying to shatter one of the windows, the vehicle halted so abruptly that he was thrown against the front window. An eerie silence followed in which Tom righted himself. He heard the driver release the doors, and Tom burst from the cab in a fury.

He had only a second to notice that the cab had stopped on an isolated country road before he saw the silhouettes of two burly men advancing upon him. He hadn't time to think; he could only act. His body remembered the fighting techniques he'd learned years ago at Nate Cowan's boxing club, and he punched the taller man in the stomach hard enough to make him stagger and fall back. The shorter man swung at him, but he deflected the blow and directed a powerful jab to his opponent's jaw. What he hadn't counted on was a third man behind him. He sensed the man's presence a split second before he felt a blow to his head and a sharp, searing pain.

As Tom lashed out blindly, he felt one more blow, this time to the side of his leg with what felt like a metal rod. The excruciating pain was accompanied by a cracking sound, and he fell to the ground. Then he lost consciousness.

2

SURREY: OCTOBER 1907

Miranda had been running full tilt through the crisp morning air for at least a quarter of an hour, so when she burst through the front door of the cottage, she was gasping for breath and couldn't speak.

Her brother, who had been reading a newspaper in the parlor, jumped to his feet. "What's happened, Mouse? Are you all right?"

She nodded, one hand on her chest and the other struggling to push back her hair, which her mad dash had shaken loose from its knot at the nape of her neck. Simon started to guide her towards the sofa, but she resisted.

"There's a dying man in the wood," she finally managed to say. "We need to fetch Dr. Mason."

"A dying man? In our wood? Are you certain?"

Simon had the look in his eyes that she had learned to dread, and she bit her lip to prevent herself from uttering a sarcastic retort. Yes, finding a dying man in the wood was strange, but it wasn't impossible. And she didn't make a practice of telling people unbelievable things. Not anymore.

"I'm certain. I thought he was dead at first, but then he groaned and moved his arm. He was so cold he must have been lying there all night. We've got to help him."

"What were you doing in the wood?"

"Walking. I heard an unusual birdcall, so I was looking up into the trees, and I nearly tripped over him."

Her brother gave her a diagnostic look.

"I'm going for the doctor. You don't have to come," Miranda said.

"No, wait here and rest. I'll run to the village and get him." The wood and Dr. Mason's surgery in the village lay in opposite directions.

"Very well. But do hurry, Simon."

It seemed like forever before Simon returned with Dr. Mason in the doctor's trap. Dr. Mason was a tall, craggy-faced man who was kinder than his habitually stern expression implied, and he listened to her explain how she'd found the injured man. Soon the three of them were in the trap and on their way down the hill and into the little wood. As she directed them to the spot, Miranda uttered a silent prayer that the man would be exactly where she left him.

The man was still there. His clothing was torn and bloodied, and he looked as though he had been beaten: there were bruises on his face, and one eye was swollen shut. Some personal items that had presumably been in his pockets were strewn on the ground: a pocket watch, a handkerchief, a crumpled note. If he'd been carrying money, it had been stolen. He wasn't moving.

Miranda knelt down beside the man as the doctor examined him. Simon stood several feet away, his face taking on a greenish tinge. He'd always been squeamish in the presence of physical injuries, especially if they involved the spilling of blood, and there was quite a lot of blood, even on the fallen leaves surrounding the man's body.

Dr. Mason felt for the patient's pulse at his wrist. Then, frowning, he tried again, this time at the man's neck.

Miranda took the injured man's left hand in hers. It was the only part of his body that seemed unscathed, and she thought it might comfort him a little, though she didn't know if he was aware of her presence. At one point he seemed to be, for his fingers tightened around hers.

She hoped he wouldn't die, for her sake as well as his. It was good to have someone besides herself and Simon to focus on for a change. Someone she could help. The bruises and scrapes didn't hide the fact that he was relatively young, probably in his early thirties. Who was he and where did he come from? He wasn't wearing a coat, which was odd for the season, but perhaps his attackers had taken it. He was a gentleman, too—that much was evident from the fine white cambric shirt he was wearing, despite the blood and dirt that marred it, and from his interesting hands. He had long, tapered fingers and spotlessly clean fingernails, but his ring finger was crooked and had a flatter knuckle than the others. There was also a long scar on his palm. She wondered what story lay behind these hands.

She watched Dr. Mason poke and prod the patient, muttering under his breath. Finally, he turned to Miranda and said, "This fellow's in a bad state. He must have been lying here for hours after being attacked. He seems to have put up a good fight, but either his attacker was stronger than he was, or there was more than one. I can't be certain about the extent of his injuries until he regains consciousness, but I suspect his leg is broken, and probably some ribs, too."

"We shouldn't stay here," Simon said, still standing at a distance. "For all we know, the people who attacked him could still be nearby."

"Let's take him to our cottage," Miranda said. "We'll look after him, won't we, Simon?"

"I suppose so," her brother said, clearly not overjoyed by the prospect.

"I don't think you're in danger," Dr. Mason said. "Your cottage is so isolated that it would be hard to find if someone comes looking for him. Besides, his attackers probably think they killed him and won't risk coming back."

The three of them did their best to get the man into the doctor's trap without jostling him overmuch. He groaned and muttered something incoherent during the process, but he didn't seem aware of them or his surroundings. When they reached the cottage and lifted him out again, his face was drained of color. They put him in Simon's bedroom, and Dr. Mason promised to check on him the following day.

"He isn't an injured bird or rabbit, Miranda," Simon said as they conferred in the parlor that evening. "You can't nurse him back to health and then release him into the wild—or keep him here—without consequences."

"I know that." She frowned at her brother, who seemed determined to misunderstand her intentions. "What do you propose we do with him? Drop him back in the wood where we found him and hope he survives? You know as well as I do that he needs someone to care for him."

Simon sighed. "This man could be a murderer, for all we know. Nobody is beaten that badly just to be robbed—if he was robbed—and what was he doing in such a remote area, anyway? He was probably attacked by people who had good reason to be angry with him."

"So he deserved what he received, then?" Her frown deepened, and she placed her hands on her hips.

"I didn't say that. Mouse, try to be reasonable. He could be dangerous to us. After everything we've done to create a safe place to live, do you want to throw it all away just because of some stranger who may not deserve our kindness?"

Dangerous to me, you mean, she thought. Instead of saying it aloud, she said, "You're making many assumptions about this man. Whatever he deserves, we may be the only people who have ever shown him kindness. Could you really turn him away?"

Her brother was silent, but the look on his face communicated his concerns clearly enough. Ever since they had moved to the cottage, he had been overly solicitous of her, as if the slightest upset would bring on an attack of nerves or aggravate the hysterical illness her former doctor had diagnosed her with a few years earlier. But Miranda was tired of being treated like a child—after all, she was seven-and-twenty—and although she knew Simon loved her, he didn't really understand her.

She went to her brother's side and linked her arm through his, leaning her head on his shoulder. "I do appreciate all you've done to ensure my safety, but please don't allow your worries to make you insensitive to the suffering of others."

He kissed the top of her head. "Very well. I surrender. I hope he's worth your concern. But as soon as he is well enough to move about, we must send him on his way. You won't argue with me on that point, will you?"

"I won't."

With a rush of affection, Miranda watched her brother leave the room. His loping gait and tousled dark hair made him look like an undernourished bear. He had inherited their father's tall, thin frame and dark coloring, while she was a pale imitation of her beautiful mother, who was small and fair. When Miranda was a child, she had been subjected to frequent sorrowful looks followed by loud whispers: "What a pity she doesn't look more like her mother!" She thought herself just as small, drab, and insignificant as the mouse that was Simon's affectionate nickname for her.

She entered the room in which the stranger lay and sat down in the chair closest to the bed, finally allowing herself to think about the consequences of what she and Simon had done. When this man regained consciousness, he would want to know where he was and who had taken him in. Even the simplest explanation would be risky if he couldn't be trusted to keep their names and location a secret.

Miranda and Simon didn't know many people in Denfield, the nearest village, only the parishioners of the small local church and Dr. Mason. She felt guilty about Simon, who missed the company of others more than she did, and she worried that his choice to live with her in such seclusion was too much of a sacrifice. Soon, she hoped, it would be safe to live openly in the world like ordinary people. Surely the injured stranger would respect their desire for privacy, if not because he was a good man, then because of his gratitude to them for saving his life.

She lost track of time as she kept her vigil by the injured man, inventing stories about him that became increasingly outlandish with the lateness of the hour. She imagined he was the eldest son of foreign royalty who had been plotted against by an evil younger son who wanted the crown for himself. Or perhaps he was a seductive Byronic hero, destined to be an outcast in the world. Her favorite story, suggested by his olive skin and the hint of the exotic in his features, made him a combination of Heathcliff and Svengali, a gypsy wanderer with the power of mesmerism, a tormented lover and musical genius. As was her wont, she wasn't interested in the mundane truth of who he really was.

Her life before she and Simon went into hiding had been full of incident, but it was too ordinary these days to offer much scope for her imagination. Simon often cautioned her about what he called her "dream world," but he didn't understand that she had full control over her fantasies. Her dream world was a place in her mind that she could choose to enter and leave whenever she wished. Besides, she needed that place whenever painful memories of the past threatened to overwhelm her.

3

My first thought was, he lied in every word.

—Robert Browning, "'Childe Roland to the Dark Tower Came'"

Though Tom had hoped that Hell wouldn't be his final destination, he hadn't been certain. The physical pain wasn't a surprise, but he hadn't expected it to be worse in specific parts of his body—his head, his left leg, his ribs. He also hadn't expected it to be so much like his childhood. The terror. The helplessness. The knowledge that the brief moments of calm would end without warning.

Eventually, he came to understand that he wasn't in Hell, because his surroundings were peaceful and he was lying in a comfortable bed. He heard whispered conversations, felt gentle hands arranging his pillows and bedclothes, and smelled the subtle scent of lavender instead of sulfur.

When he finally awoke fully and opened his right eye, sunlight was flooding the room. His left eye wasn't working properly. When he raised his hand to touch it, he felt the puffiness of his swollen eyelid.

The room was small but cozy. The walls were covered with drawings of plants. A large vase of daisies and other late-season wildflowers stood on a side table, and books overflowed the small desk by the window as if they, too, were alive, spilling untidily onto the floor in a heap. The iron bedstead on which he lay was covered with a bright patchwork quilt. The only inhabitant of the room that wasn't colorful was the pale young woman sitting in the chair by the bed. She reminded him of a faded painting, as if the sunlight had drained her of the warm golds and pinks that ought to have been her natural coloring. The black dress she was wearing didn't help—the best that could be said of it was that it was modest and neat.

"Oh, you're awake. We were starting to wonder if you'd ever enter the land of the living," she said with a smile. She had a low, soft voice and unusual eyes. They were such a light blue as to be almost translucent, making the dark pupils and outline of the irises stand out.

Tom's mouth felt horribly dry. He tried to ask for water, but his words came out as an indistinguishable croak.

His companion seemed to understand what he wanted, since she reached for a glass of water on a side table and held it to his lips, slipping her free hand underneath his head for support. He took a few gulps and then lay back, surprised by the pain that shot through his left leg and the general soreness of his whole body.

"Thank you," he said, wincing as he shifted in the bed, trying to find a better position for his leg.

"You'd better not move too much. Your ankle is broken, and the rest of you isn't much better off."

"What happened to me?" he asked.

"Don't you remember?"

"No." An image of two menacing figures on a dark, quiet road came to him, but nothing more.

"I'm afraid I don't know." She hesitated, as if unsure of how much to tell him.

"Where am I?"

"We're in Surrey, but our cottage is in the middle of nowhere, really. I found you in the wood, and my brother and I brought you home. The nearest village is an hour's walk from here."

He digested this for a moment. "How long have I been here?"

"Three days."

"I was left in this sorry state in the forest, and you fished me out?"

"Yes."

"I'm obliged to you. What's your name?"

"Miranda."

"'Admired Miranda,'" he said slowly, "'worth what's dearest to the world.'"

"You know your Shakespeare," she said with a smile. "What's your name?"

"Tom." He closed his eyes as a wave of dizziness passed over him.

"One ought never to quote Shakespeare on an empty stomach," she said. "May I fetch you something to eat?"

He felt the light, warm pressure of her hand on his arm and was absurdly, desperately grateful for the comfort it gave him. He opened his mouth to decline her offer but then realized he was ravenous. "Yes, please."

She left, and Tom heard distant sounds of dishes and cutlery clinking. He felt too disoriented to think clearly, and the mysterious circumstances surrounding his injuries, combined with the kind but ghostly presence of the woman who called herself Miranda, made him wonder again if he were experiencing some version of the afterlife. It was strange enough to be bedridden and in need of help for something as simple as a glass of water. He had always been on the other side of the bed, the one who helped others.

He almost hoped it was a hallucination, so he would not have to endure this humiliating situation. If he had the strength to drag himself out of bed and into a cave somewhere like an injured animal, he would have done so.

But he had no such strength, so he had to accept the fact that he was completely dependent on the kindness of this young woman. When Miranda returned with a bowl of soup, he accepted her help, as he had with the glass of water, without showing his uneasiness. Or so he thought. After he had finished the soup, she took the bowl and sat back in her chair with her head tilted to one side and a thoughtful look on her face.

"It won't do," she said after a moment, as if they had been in the middle of a conversation.

"What won't do?" he asked, worried that they had indeed been conversing and his disturbed mental state was as apparent as his physical injuries.

"You can't force yourself to recover any faster than your body will allow. As much as you hate being taken care of, you may as well accept the necessity of it."

"How do you know I hate being taken care of?"

A fleeting smile crossed her face. "Every nerve in your body is screaming it."

"There are people who depend on me—"

"They'll have to wait until you feel better. Please, just rest."

He couldn't reply, concentrating on beating back a wave of nausea. Miranda was gazing off into the distance as if she had gone somewhere else in her mind. Tom wasn't used to silence, either in other people or in his environment, but in his weakened state he was grateful for it. His head was throbbing painfully, and he closed his eyes.

He must have fallen asleep, for the next time he opened his eyes it was evening. A lamp was lit in the room, and the dying light outside the window was a suggestion more than a reality. Miranda was nowhere to be seen, and this time a young man wearing an old-fashioned farmer's smock was sitting by his bed.

"Who are you?" Tom asked, startling the man, who had been reading a book.

"I'm Simon Thorne. My sister tells me your name is Tom. Have you a surname?"

Tom paused for only a second. "Jones."

"Tom Jones?" A flicker of amusement crossed Simon's face. "I hope you're nothing like your literary namesake. We live a quiet life here and don't need the kind of excitement Mr. Fielding's Tom Jones would create."

Interesting, thought Tom. These siblings lived like rustics but obviously had some education. He silently congratulated himself on the cleverness of lying about his surname. It had given him valuable information about the people who had taken him in. It didn't really feel like a lie, anyway— Cross was no more his real name than Jones or Harlowe, so what did it matter? Besides, he'd worked too hard to escape his past to let his true name come out.

"I have no desire to create excitement," he said. "I've had more of that lately than I can bear."

"Yes, I can well believe that. My sister says you don't remember anything about the people who attacked you."

"I didn't see them clearly. I remember now getting into a cab that was supposed to take me to my lodgings in London. Instead, the driver took me out into the country. When I got out of the cab I saw two men coming towards me in the darkness, but the next thing I remember with any certainty is awakening here in this bed."

"Do you have enemies, Mr. Jones? Do you have any idea who could have done this to you?" Simon was looking at Tom probingly, if not quite suspiciously.

My father, was his first, illogical thought. His father was most likely dead, and even if he was still alive, he hadn't the power to hurt Tom again. Not physically, anyway.

"Call me Tom, please. We all have enemies, don't we?"

Simon's eyes narrowed at this evasive response.

"I can't think of anyone who'd want to kill me," Tom went on, "but there are certainly people I have offended, people who have enough power and influence to arrange for my demise if they wish to." He surprised himself by telling the truth, vague as it was.

Simon was silent for a moment. Then he said, "It would help if you could remember something specific if you wish to prosecute a claim. If there was a witness to the attack, that would help, too. My sister and I can be of no help to you if you choose to take legal action. We have no desire to draw attention to ourselves."

What was Simon hiding? For all his apparent suspicion of Tom, he clearly had secrets of his own.

"I promise not to involve you in any way if I do take legal action," Tom replied. "What you've done for me already is far beyond what most people would do for a stranger. You could have left me to die in the wood."

"I wanted to, but my softhearted sister wouldn't allow it."

Tom stared at the other man in astonishment, but Simon was smiling. "You're welcome to stay here until you're fully recovered."

"Thank you. I won't tax your hospitality any longer than is necessary."

Simon rose from the chair. "I've kept you talking long enough, Mr. Tom Jones. Get some sleep." He spoke brusquely but kindly, and Tom felt a twinge of guilt for lying about his name.

In the days that followed, Tom's primary challenge was learning to graciously accept the help of Simon, Miranda, and their doctor, who visited every day. He could wait to decide whether he wanted to find out who had beaten him or not. Tom was skilled at putting out of his mind problems that would eat away at others of a weaker disposition. Although this walling off of whatever concern he wished to ignore at the moment was always temporary, it was a convenient way of allowing himself to get on with whatever he needed to get on with. And what he needed to get on with right now was his recovery so he would not be as dependent as a child on these kind strangers.

As soon as he was able to think clearly, he dictated a general letter to Miranda to be sent to a friend at his club in London, asking him to inform Tom's superiors that he had fallen ill suddenly and was recovering in the country. Tom did not identify his superiors in the letter—his friend would know whom he meant—and Dr. Mason had obligingly provided a letter confirming Tom's "illness" without being specific or asking inconvenient questions. At least there was no danger that the bishop would consider Tom's unexpected absence a black mark on his character. Until this incident, he hadn't missed a day of work in the four years he had held his canonry.

Tom wasn't ready to reveal where he worked to Simon and Miranda, though even he didn't understand why he felt the need to hide his profession. Perhaps it was merely a relief to be treated like an ordinary man instead of a priest: his clerical collar always seemed to provoke strong reactions, both positive and negative.

Tom achieved his goal of joining the Thornes at the dinner table a week after they found him in the wood. Dr. Mason had fitted his lower left leg with a brace, and Tom had learned how to maneuver himself around the cottage in a wooden wheelchair. He would have preferred crutches to the chair, which sometimes stuck in doorways, but his ribs were still too bruised to bear any pressure. He refused Simon's and Miranda's offers of help, determined to wheel his chair to the dinner table by himself. The effort took all his energy, so he didn't contribute much to the conversation, but he was content to listen to the friendly banter between the siblings and to enjoy the delicious stew and fresh, hot rolls Miranda had made.

"I won't draw more plants for you until you find a place for the existing drawings," Miranda was saying. It wasn't the first time Tom had heard her complain about the disorganized state of Simon's bedroom, where Tom slept. The cottage had only two rooms in addition to Miranda's and Simon's bedrooms—a small kitchen and the combination dining room and parlor, where they were now eating. Simon had been sleeping on a battered old sofa by the front door and refused to consider exchanging places with Tom until he was completely recovered, despite Tom's protests.

"You don't mean that," Simon replied. "I'll find a place for the drawings when you're finished. Drawing only some of my plants is like planting half a garden. It's got to be done completely or not at all!"

"That's ridiculous. If you keep trying to force me to draw those plants without organizing the drawings I've already done, I'll start drawing non-sense botany just like Edward Lear's." She jumped up and plucked a thin volume from a nearby bookcase, opening it and plopping it down beside Simon's plate.

From his vantage point, Tom could see Lear's "Manypeeplia Upsid-ownia," a tree with a long branch from which hung several human forms by their feet.

"Brat," said Simon, giving Miranda a menacing look, which didn't fool Tom for a second. If there was anything he'd learned in the short time he had spent with these siblings, it was that they adored each other. They were different from the people he knew in London. There was something inno-cent and pure about them, as if they belonged to a happier, simpler time, a fairy-tale world where virtue was rewarded and vice punished.

Miranda looked at Tom. "Simon wants to become a famous naturalist. He's going to write a huge tome that chronicles every species of vegetation native to England, which would be a worthy goal if he didn't also expect me to provide the illustrations for said vegetation and take all the credit for himself."

"Liar!" cried Simon, and turned to Tom. "She's the one who wants the credit. She's already corrected some of my descriptions when I wasn't looking, and she told me herself it would be a fine thing for her to be known to the world as a woman naturalist and artist."

Ignoring Simon's challenge, Miranda said, "I do love Edward Lear. We used to read his nonsense verse all the time as children. Did you read it as a child, too, Tom?"

"No," Tom replied. He didn't want to tell her his family didn't own any books besides the Bible. Instead, he asked Miranda, "Do you draw other things besides plants?"

"Yes. I love to draw people. They're far more interesting than plants."

"May I see your other drawings? I'm no judge, but if they are as finely detailed as your drawings of plants, I'm sure they're very good, indeed."

"I don't know."

He felt, rather than saw, her retreat from his question.

"Miranda doesn't usually show her drawings to anyone," said Simon.

"I certainly understand if you wish to keep them private," Tom assured her.

Miranda gave a little shrug. "I'll think about it."

There was an awkward silence.

"This stew is delicious," Tom said finally. "If my landlady in London cooked half as well as this, I'd be very happy. And fat."

Miranda smiled.

"Do you have family in London?" Simon asked.

"No. I grew up in Yorkshire. My parents and sister died years ago." The lie rolled off his tongue smoothly as it always had, but for the first time in years, he felt guilty about it, just as he'd felt guilty when he'd lied to Simon about his name.

His guilt only intensified when Simon and Miranda, with almost identical looks of sympathy, said in unison, "Our parents died, too."

"I'm sorry," said Tom. The only thing that would make him feel better would be if they were also lying. But their sincerity was reflected in their faces. Tears came to Miranda's eyes, and she looked away quickly before they could spill over, and Simon's lips tightened.

Miranda was the first to recover. "Then you understand how we feel," she said, laying her hand lightly on Tom's arm. "Our parents were killed nine years ago in a railway accident."

Tom allowed Miranda's hand to remain on his arm for a few seconds longer, but his guilt about lying to her was so intense that he had to pull away. He did so as unobtrusively as he could, and she seemed to take no offense at his withdrawal. Perhaps she thought his loss was simply too painful for him to discuss.

The hot roll that only a moment earlier had melted in his mouth now stuck in his throat, and he braced his hands against the table, pushing his wheelchair back.

Simon and Miranda looked at him in surprise.

"I think I'll lie down for a bit. Thank you for that delicious supper," he said, managing a grimace that he hoped passed for a smile and turning away. Both Simon and Miranda rose from the table, and she reached out her hand as if to push his chair for him. But Simon shook his head at her, and Tom was allowed to make slow progress alone to his room.

As he maneuvered himself out of the wheelchair and lay down on the bed, he found to his intense irritation that he was trembling, whether from physical or mental causes he didn't know. What was the matter with him? Why, after so many years of lying to people about his family and his past, did he suddenly feel so guilty when he lied to these two strangers? Perhaps his injuries had turned his brain to pulp. Or, more likely, he reasoned, his unwonted physical weakness had spread to his brain, allowing his mind to wander in places it shouldn't and giving way to feelings he normally suppressed.

Perhaps the explanation was simpler. Seeing a brother and sister who were so close made him think of his own sister for the first time in years. Kate had done nothing to deserve his abandonment. There was something of her sweetness and modesty in Miranda's manner, and he missed having a sister who treated him like a hero. Perhaps he hadn't lied and she truly was dead. The same could be said of his mother, who hadn't been at fault any more than Kate had been, and whose reproachful dark eyes sometimes haunted his dreams.

Tom believed he would never have risen to his current position in the church if his past were known. Even his affair with Julia, though less justifiable than his other sins, had begun innocently enough. She had come to him for spiritual guidance, as so many of his parishioners did, but at some point he had let his guard down, hadn't preserved the necessary distance. He had learned to lie as a method of survival, and it still worked.

He would have liked to tell Simon and Miranda the truth about his life, but they would surely regret caring for him then, and he would feel like even more of a burden than he already was. He was the villain who existed in their story merely to be found out and then destroyed by some ingenious method. Perhaps he would be killed by drowning in a trough of water, or being attacked with an ax like the wolf in the "Little Red Riding Hood" story. Simon and Miranda wouldn't be the ones to destroy him, of course. The fairy-tale hero and heroine never wreaked revenge on the villain with their own hands.

The room started to spin, and he felt light-headed. Was there a higher concentration of opium in the medicine Dr. Mason had given him than there ought to be? He buried his face in the pillow and pretended to sleep. After a few minutes, he no longer needed to pretend.

4

So long as men believe that women will forgive anything they will do anything. Do you see what I mean? The mistake from the beginning has been that women have practised self-sacrifice, when they should have been teaching men self-control.

—Sarah Grand, *The Heavenly Twins*

NOVEMBER 1907

"May I see what you're drawing?" Tom asked as he shuffled into the parlor. He had progressed from the wheelchair to crutches. It was too soon for him to be moving around so much, in Miranda's opinion, but she and Dr. Mason had already remonstrated with him, to no avail. Tom was maddeningly stubborn.

Miranda was at her easel by the window, adding shading to a charcoal drawing of Dr. Mason's ten-year-old daughter, Anna. "Not yet. It isn't finished."

"Very well," said Tom, pivoting on his good leg, then lowering himself to the sofa. "But you'll never become a famous artist if you don't show anyone your work, you know."

"What makes you think I wish to be famous?"

"You said something at dinner last week about wanting to be a famous naturalist and artist, didn't you? And don't all artists want some sort of public recognition?"

"I was teasing Simon. I don't want to be famous."

"Perhaps not, but your drawings—the few of them you've allowed me to see—are so good that it would be a great pity to deprive others of the pleasure of seeing them."

She couldn't tell if he was being sincere or simply flattering her. She did think some of her drawings were good, but they were not to everyone's taste.

Before she could reply, she noticed the box in which she kept her smaller drawings teetering on the edge of the side table beside the sofa. She ran to save it just as Tom reached out to do the same, and their sudden movements from either side caused it to fall to the floor. Loose sketches scattered everywhere.

Miranda tried to gather them up quickly, before Tom could see them, but he reached down to help her. There were several half-finished sketches of him—far too many, given the short time she'd known him—and she blushed to the roots of her hair, imagining only too well what he must be thinking. She'd been careful to sketch him when he wasn't looking because she lacked the courage to ask him to sit for her, but now her secret was out.

"I don't need help," she said, her voice sharp with embarrassment.

He let her finish gathering the loose pages and sat back without comment.

She turned her back on him under the pretense of looking for more papers, waiting for her face to cool.

"I think I understand now why you don't like to show your drawings to people," he said after a moment.

"Oh? Why?" she replied shakily without turning around.

"You expose what your subjects think they're successfully hiding."

She was surprised enough to turn around and meet his eyes.

"That one, for example," he said, pointing to the drawing on the top of the pile. It was a sketch of him she'd made stealthily one evening when he and Simon were talking. "It's a good likeness of me, but it's more than that. The way you've placed the crutches at that angle, in the middle of the painting, makes it look as though I'm in prison. And I don't think there's a word for that expression in my eyes. I'd like to say I don't look like that, but I suspect you see more than I do. You have real talent, Miranda."

"Thank you, but I struggled with that drawing. I'm still not happy with it." She did like the way she'd captured the wary, wounded look in Tom's eyes, but the rest of the drawing wasn't quite right.

"Of course you're not. No true artist is happy with his work, no matter how good it is. 'A man's reach should exceed his grasp,' and all that."

"I suppose so." She put the last of the drawings back into the box and said, in what she hoped was a casual tone, "I hope you don't mind that I've sketched you. Living in such an isolated place, I have few human subjects to choose from, and Simon is tired of sitting for me."

"Naturally. I don't mind at all."

She started to turn away, but he said, "You've forgotten this one." He was holding out a sketch of the old church in Smythe. She didn't remember drawing it, and she was surprised she'd kept a reminder of the worst years of her life.

"You don't usually draw buildings, do you?" Tom said as he handed it to her. "What's special about this church?"

She considered evading his question, but something in his eyes reassured her. For all his own evasions and secrecy, she sensed she could trust him. "I drew that a long time ago. That church was my haven after my parents died. Until it became my torment."

"What happened?" Tom asked. He had a way of listening intently, as if he didn't want to miss a single word of what his interlocutor said. She'd seen him do it with Simon too, so it wasn't something he did only with her. Still, it was immensely flattering.

She sat down beside him and said, "Simon and I were raised in that church. It's in a village called Smythe, not far from Birmingham. Not long after our parents died, a new vicar was installed there. He was a mesmerizing speaker, and he was sympathetic to our loss. He had four children of his own, all younger than we were—at the time I was eighteen and Simon was twenty—but he invited us to live with his family and treated us as his own, knowing how much we still needed the care and advice of a guardian."

Miranda paused and swallowed hard, remembering how she had clung to the Morris family in her grief. How trusting she'd been. How wrong she'd been.

"Things were fine, for a while," she went on, "but I became increasingly dependent on this man. Simon had withdrawn from me in his grief over losing our parents, and I spent most of my time in church, praying and asking for spiritual guidance from the vicar. I saw him as a father figure, and he treated me like a daughter. At first. I don't know if you're a religious man"—Miranda paused, but Tom didn't speak or move, so she continued—"but it's easy for those of us who have been taught to respect religious leaders to trust them too quickly and to be duped into doing wrong even when we sincerely believe we are doing right."

"Religious leaders can be the very devil," Tom said.

"Amen to that," Simon said from across the room. He was standing in the doorway, and Miranda didn't know how long he'd been there or how much of the conversation he had heard. He and Miranda had never told anyone the story of their ordeal in Smythe, and she knew he wouldn't approve of her telling someone they hardly knew.

Simon came into the room and sat down in the armchair across from the sofa. "What are you talking about?" he asked. His gaze fell on the drawing of the church, and he stiffened.

"I'm telling Tom a little about what happened after Mother and Father died."

"Those experiences are best forgotten," Simon said brusquely.

"You have my word that I won't share what you tell me with anyone else," Tom said, "but of course you needn't say more."

"We don't like clergymen very much," Simon said. "That's all you really need to know."

"That's not true," Miranda objected. "It's just one clergyman we don't like."

"I understand," Tom said with a nod. "I'm not terribly fond of them myself."

Simon took the drawing of the church from Tom and looked down at it, frowning. "Why did you keep this, Mouse? Doesn't it bring back bad memories?"

"I'd forgotten about it," she said. Reaching for the drawing, she ripped it in half, then turned to the grate and threw it in the fire. All three of them watched the heavy paper turn black at the edges and curl in on itself.

Miranda looked at Simon, and they conducted a silent argument with their eyes.

"It's more your story than it is mine," Simon said finally. "If you want to tell it, I won't stop you."

After a brief pause, she said, "Since I was a child I've had unusually vivid dreams, and many of them had a spiritual element. I've always been fascinated by the saints and mystics, fancying that I had a kinship with them. I got into the habit of telling the vicar my dreams, and he would tell me that God was speaking directly to me through them. He had me teach the young girls in the parish and constantly praised me as an example for them to follow. I felt important and . . . loved. But his interpretations of my dreams became more about him and less about God. Even though he was married and much older than I was, I believed what he told me, that I was . . . his true wife."

She couldn't go on. She had already said more than she intended, and she stared down at her lap, her face burning. What if Tom didn't believe her? What if he thought less of her?

"Miranda has left out my part in this," Simon said. "I knew what was happening and did nothing to stop it."

"You were as much his victim as I was," she said, raising her head to meet her brother's eyes.

But Simon had averted his face. Tom was looking at her, though, and to Miranda's surprise, there were tears in his eyes. As little as she knew him, she knew he wasn't the sort of man who revealed his emotions easily.

"I went a bit mad afterwards," she continued. "'Religious mania,' the doctor called it. Simon came to realize the vicar was the cause of my suffering—though he still doesn't see how he was also a victim—and he fought back, trying to protect me from further harm. The vicar retaliated by publicly denouncing us both as immoral. As highly as he had praised me before, now he spread lies about me, claiming that I was corrupting the girls I was teaching. It went so far that I couldn't go out in public without being the object of suspicion and even, in a few cases, threats of violence from a couple of extremists in the parish. It was as if we were living in the sixteenth century instead of the twentieth."

"That's why we left," Simon interjected. "But we didn't move far enough at first. In every new village, people seemed to know and believe the vicar's version of the story. Finally, last year, we came here. I chose this place because I thought the solitude would help Miranda's nerves to recover, and it's also far enough from our old village that nobody knows us or is likely to have heard of us. We're hoping the scandal will be forgotten and we'll be able to start over."

"You must hate the man who did this to you," Tom said.

"Not exactly," Miranda said. "Hate" was too simple a word to express what she felt towards Richard Morris.

"Well, *I* hate him," Simon said. "Before he entered our lives, we were grieving for our parents, but we had friends, we were part of a close-knit community, we had a nice house, a couple of servants, and all the material comforts we needed—"

"And peace of mind," Miranda put in quietly. "That's what I miss most."

"Yes," Simon agreed, "but living here is not so bad. Our life is simpler and quieter now. We don't need servants or fine things, but I still hate what that man did to Miranda."

"I'm much better now," Miranda said reassuringly, no longer as aware of Tom as she was of her brother and his pain. "I don't trust people as quickly as I used to, and I'm careful not to get carried away with strange ideas. I am under strict orders from Simon not to pray for more than thirty minutes a day."

Tom looked at her in surprise. "Are you tempted to pray longer than that?"

"Sometimes," she said. He didn't need to know that in the past she had lost herself in prayer and contemplation for hours at a time, that she had not been aware of time passing or of missed meals. Once she hadn't noticed the transition from night to day and back again. She didn't know if Tom prayed or believed in God, but even those who did would likely find her behavior strange.

"Thank you both for sharing a story that must have caused you much anxiety to tell, much less to live through," Tom said. He leaned forward, his elbows resting on his knees, looking so fierce that his dark eyes seemed to give off sparks. "That man will rot in hell if there is any justice in the afterlife."

Miranda appreciated his sympathy, but she was surprised by his vehemence. It was odd. Odd enough to make her wonder if perhaps he had experienced something similar. Even though he hadn't mentioned his religious beliefs, she had sensed from the beginning that religion was anathema to him. Perhaps some religious leader had hurt or disappointed him, also.

That night, Miranda was awakened by a strange sound. At first she thought it was an injured animal outside the cottage making the half-strangled, smothered cry, like a wolf caught in a trap. But as she awoke fully and her mind cleared, she realized there couldn't be any wolves or traps near the cottage.

She sat up, listening carefully. Had she only dreamed the sound? But there it was again, coming from Tom's room. Hastily she got out of bed and put on her wrapper and slippers, then went to his door and knocked softly.

There was only silence at first, and she turned away, but then she heard labored breathing and another smothered cry. This time it sounded like a name: Kitty? Kate? Tom's voice was filled with such terror that it sent chills up her spine.

She opened the door and went in. The curtains were open, allowing enough moonlight in for her to see Tom thrashing about under the bedclothes, as if trying to push something or someone off his chest. His eyes were closed, and he was muttering incoherently.

Worried that he'd cause further injury to himself, she went to his side and spoke his name, placing her hand on his shoulder lightly, then, when he didn't respond, more firmly.

He opened his eyes and stared at her. "Who—" he began, then went silent.

"I'm Miranda," she said. "You're in our cottage—Simon's and mine—near Denfield, remember? I think you've had a bad dream."

"Oh. Of course." He raised his hands to his temples and rubbed them, taking a deep breath.

"You were calling out in your sleep. I was worried you'd try to walk without the crutches and injure yourself more."

"Thank you," he said, raising himself to a sitting position. "I'm sorry to alarm you."

She could tell he was still trying to awaken fully and shake off the nightmare.

"Would you like me to stay with you for a while?" She saw only as she asked the question that he might take it the wrong way. A lady ought not to be in a gentleman's bedroom at night, even if he was still an invalid and her brother was sleeping in the next room.

"Yes, if you don't mind," he replied. "You're not part of my dream, are you?"

She smiled. "No, I'm not." She drew a chair close to the bed and sat down. He looked so bewildered that she reached out to take his hand, thinking only of comforting him. But she stopped in mid-gesture, realizing how intimate a setting it was, with him awake and not really an invalid at all.

Before she could withdraw her hand, he took it and held it firmly. His fingers were warm, almost hot.

"I thought I was drowning," he said. "Are you certain I'm alive and you're not an angel, robed in white as you are? Even touching your hand doesn't convince me—it's inhumanly cold."

"I'm certain. I'll light a lamp, if you wish."

"No, it's not necessary."

"You spoke a name in your sleep," she said hesitantly. "Kate, I believe. Is she your wife?"

"I have no wife. Kate is—was—my sister."

"Oh, I'm sorry," she said, remembering that he'd said his sister had died. "Would you like me to say a prayer for you?"

"A prayer?" He sounded so shocked that she was taken aback. But then he said, "Yes, if you wish to."

"I shouldn't have assumed anything. It's just that I find it comforting to pray when I have bad dreams."

"Go on."

Feeling self-conscious, she began, "Thou, O Lord, that stillest the raging of the sea, hear, hear us, and save us, that we perish not. O blessed Saviour, that didst save thy disciples ready to perish in a storm, hear us, and save us, we beseech thee."

When she'd finished, he said, "Why did you choose that one?"

"It's from the *Book of Common Prayer*, for a storm at sea. You said you were drowning, so it seemed fitting."

He was silent long enough that she thought she'd offended him, but then he squeezed her hand and said, "You *are* an angel."

"No." She pulled her hand out of his grasp. "I don't like to be called that."

Richard had called her an angel. Later, he had called her a witch, and then other names, too, cruel ones. But she didn't want to dwell on thoughts of Richard—that way madness lay.

"Very well," Tom said. "Not an angel. You remind me more of something . . . someone else, anyway." He ran a hand through his hair.

"Who?" she said with some trepidation.

"The Lady of Shalott. You often have a faraway look in your eyes, as if you're in another world, just like in the Waterhouse painting. An artist in an isolated place who never sees the outside world because she's under a mysterious curse."

She was surprised how apt the comparison was, more than he could guess. She did indeed feel as though there was a curse on her, one that kept her bound to the past and unable to imagine a future.

"There's some truth in what you say," she said, "though I wish it were otherwise. I'd rather be an ordinary person. But you're not ordinary, either, are you? I think I've figured out why you say so little about yourself."

"Have you?" He sounded a little worried.

"Yes. I think you're the eldest son of a foreign king. Your younger brother wants the crown for himself and paid someone to murder you. That's why you were attacked."

He smiled. "That's a romantic story, but I'm hardly that interesting. The people who attacked me must have mistaken me for someone else."

Miranda hoped he was right, but she wasn't convinced. He didn't sound as certain as his words implied, either. Tom might not be foreign royalty, but he was far from ordinary.

"I've stayed long enough," she said. "Try to get some sleep."

"Good night, Elaine. And thank you."

The name startled her until she remembered that the Lady of Shalott was Elaine of Astolat in the Camelot legends. But had it occurred to him that he was in the role of Lancelot? She hoped not.

She bid him good night and went back to her room.

5

I hate the dreadful hollow behind the little wood,
Its lips in the field above are dabbled with blood-red heath,
The red-ribb'd ledges drip with a silent horror of blood,
And Echo there, whatever is ask'd her, answers "Death."

—Alfred, Lord Tennyson, *Maud*

A few days later, Tom awoke to the smell of sausages frying and the sounds of doors opening and closing. The clock on the mantel showed that it was only half-six, and the Thornes usually didn't stir until seven.

He performed his morning ablutions and dressed as quickly as his still-recovering body would allow, then left his room in search of Simon and Miranda.

Miranda was in the kitchen cooking, and she waved at him with a wooden spoon as he lurched past on his crutches. Simon was polishing what looked to be his best black shoes by the front door. He was dressed in a faded black suit.

"Good morning," he said with a smile as Tom approached.

"Good morning. You and Miranda are up early."

"It's Sunday. We're going to church."

"Oh." Tom hesitated. "I thought you don't like churches."

"We don't like clergymen. We have nothing against churches in general."

"I see. In that case, may I join you?"

Simon's hand, which had been vigorously rubbing his shoe with a cloth, stopped mid-swipe. He stared up at Tom with a look of utter shock.

"You . . . want to come with us? To church?"

Tom raised an eyebrow. "Yes. If that's all right."

"I thought you were an atheist."

Now it was Tom's turn to stare. He probably wasn't the first clergyman to be mistaken for an atheist, but it was the first time it had happened to him. Of course, the Thornes didn't know he was a clergyman, but what could have led Simon to believe such a thing? It was a relief that Miranda chose that moment to call them for breakfast.

"You must be looking forward to wearing your own clothes," Miranda said to Tom as they ate. "Are you certain you don't wish to send for them?"

Tom looked down at the tweed suit he had borrowed from Simon. It was out-of-date and nothing like the clothing Tom wore in London, but it was neat and clean. He wasn't particular about his clothing and usually dressed simply when he wasn't wearing his vestments, though he did have a fine woolen greatcoat of which he was especially proud.

"This may sound strange," Tom said, "but I find Simon's clothes more comfortable than my own—though mine are a better fit, of course."

Simon gave Tom a thoughtful look. "Perhaps you're merely enjoying this respite from the pressures of your ordinary life and all its trappings."

Tom heard what was beneath Simon's words: an invitation to reveal something about his life. But all he said was, "Yes, you're probably right."

"Tom is coming to church with us," Simon told Miranda.

"Really?" She didn't look quite as shocked as Simon had, but her surprise was enough to make Tom uncomfortable all over again.

"On second thought," he said, "if the church is in Denfield, I'll only slow you down if I try to walk with you. Besides, I don't think I'm ready to go out in public."

To Miranda's credit, she recovered quickly. "We'd be happy for your company, but I do think the walk is too far for you to attempt on crutches. If you'd like to come with us next week, we can hire a horse and trap in advance."

"I'll think about it," Tom said. "I must say I'm still surprised you attend church at all after what you experienced in Smythe."

"God hasn't changed," Miranda said gravely, "and it isn't His fault that some of His ministers fall into error."

"Some people would disagree with you. Some people wouldn't understand why God didn't protect two young, defenseless people from a monster like the man who hurt you."

"Is that what you think?" Miranda asked, looking puzzled.

"I think it would be understandable for you to distrust God because of what happened, and I think a clergyman who misuses his power in such a way ought to be hanged," he said. "But it so happens I do believe in God."

He heard the defensiveness in his voice and wondered what was wrong with him. Was it really so surprising for them to think he was an atheist? He had avoided all talk of religion, spoken harshly of the vicar who took advantage of them, and reacted with shock the night Miranda woke him from his nightmare and asked if she could pray for him. None of these actions made him look like a man of faith. In truth, he'd been shocked by her offer only because nobody had ever offered to pray for him before. And Miranda's prayer had touched him deeply.

Once the siblings left for church, Tom went for a walk to the edge of the wood where Miranda had found him. He had a morbid fascination with it, but it was a long walk for a man on crutches, and the Thornes would have stopped him if they knew he intended to go that far. In fact, he'd been removing the brace on his left leg for short periods every day and walking without the crutches, though he kept them close. It didn't pain him to walk slowly and carefully, and he thought it was time to build up his strength. After all, he'd been at the Thornes' cottage for nearly a month, and he couldn't afford to avoid his responsibilities in London much longer.

He managed the first part of the walk on crutches, then sat down on a large rock to remove the brace. His left leg was no longer swollen, but it looked thinner and weaker than it used to. Taking the crutches but leaving the brace behind, he walked on, into the wood. It was a warm day for November, and the fallen leaves crunched satisfyingly under his feet. He rested his hand against the trunk of an oak tree, took a deep breath, and stared up through the leafless branches at the bluest of blue skies, listening to the far-off song of a lark.

Contrary to what he'd told Miranda, he suspected his attackers hadn't mistaken him for someone else. They could have killed him if they wanted to, so they must have intended only to scare him. Tom thought Charles Carrington was the most likely person behind the attack if he suspected Tom's affair with his wife. And if Tom stayed away from Julia from now on, he would likely not be attacked again. But what if it was someone else? Perhaps Little Roy or Smiling Joe from Nate Cowan's boxing club—though Tom hadn't been a regular member of the Club, nor had he fought for money, since his youth. Nate's fighters didn't usually cause trouble for anyone unless money was involved.

He wanted to tell Simon and Miranda more about his life, even about his past. When they had told him their story, he had recognized the gesture as an invitation to a deeper friendship. It was also a courageous act of trust from people who had many reasons not to trust others. He was troubled that he couldn't respond in kind to this invitation. He knew his secrecy puzzled and frustrated the Thornes, but he had never told a living soul about his past, and he wasn't sure he was capable of doing so after all that time.

He had an idea of the relief it would bring him to tell somebody—all he had to do was think of the many people he had counseled who had found release in confessing their sins to him—but the gulf between this idea and its realization was too wide to be bridged. Even to admit to the Thornes the simple fact that he was a clergyman seemed impossible. After hearing their story, he expected they would probably put him in the same category as the man who had deceived them. He was already too aware of his own failure to live like a Christian, much less to meet the higher standards demanded of a clergyman.

Tom stayed in the wood, walking and thinking longer than he'd intended. When he returned to the cottage, he was surprised to find that Simon and Miranda had a visitor, a pretty young woman introduced as Gwendolyn Sifton, who had vivid blue eyes and dark curls that framed her heart-shaped face. She had walked back with them from church that morning. It was the first time anyone besides Dr. Mason had come to the cottage since Tom had been there, and he was curious about the connection between Miss Sifton and the Thornes. As the necessary introductions were made and Tom sat in the parlor to take tea with the others, he sensed tension in the air that couldn't be entirely explained by his presence as a stranger among them.

"Miranda and Simon have told me how they met you," Miss Sifton said to Tom, "and they've sworn me to secrecy about it. But eventually people will find out about you, and they're bound to be curious. Since I live in the village, I'll have to bear the burden of people's questions."

"I'd hate to think of myself as the cause of such trouble for you," was his gallant response. "You have my blessing to invent any story about me that you think will appease their curiosity."

"How kind of you."

Only a hint of a smile appeared on Miss Sifton's lips, but there was defi-nitely a playful look in her eyes as she glanced at him. She was just the sort of woman he enjoyed flirting with—not only pretty but also lively and quick-witted. But he was mindful of the fact that at least one of the wit-nesses to their lighthearted exchange was not amused. Miranda was unmis-takably giving him the evil eye, and he thought it best to rein himself in.

Tom didn't need to do much to deflect the conversation away from himself. The talk naturally turned to local gossip, which just as naturally didn't interest him. He contented himself with observing the interactions among the others. Miss Sifton's energetic manner and rapid speech con-trasted with the Thornes' slower, more thoughtful responses. Simon was quieter than usual, but his eyes rarely left Miss Sifton's face. Miranda spoke enough to keep the conversation going, but her manner betrayed an uneas-iness that Tom hadn't seen in her before.

"Did you see Josiah Griffith asleep during the sermon this morning?" Miss Sifton said. "I don't think that man has stayed awake for a sermon these three years."

"It's probably the only time the poor man gets any peace and quiet," Simon replied with a smile. To Tom he added, "Josiah lives with his mother, who keeps him hopping with endless tasks around the house. She lives by the adage 'Idle hands are the devil's handiwork,' but only if those hands are her son's. She usually feels too unwell to do any work herself, or so she says."

"Simon thinks Mrs. Griffith's complaints are imaginary," said Miss Sifton. "I, for one, think he's being unfair. Mrs. Griffith may be working her son too hard, but that doesn't mean she is well when she says she isn't. Miranda, you agree with me, don't you?" She gave Miranda a chance only to nod before speaking again. "We women must band together against the prejudices of men."

"I'm glad to hear it," Tom said. "I like to hear women defending other women instead of tearing them down."

"Indeed," said Miranda stiffly. "If our sex can't expect support from one another, we have little hope of being treated with respect by men."

"You may be right," Tom said, "but most men have a natural impulse to protect and support women. Only a powerful reason to the contrary can check this impulse."

Miss Sifton beamed at Tom, but Miranda looked grave. "There are many such powerful reasons, I fear," she said. "Women can't depend on men in general to behave kindly or even respectfully."

Tom said, "Has it come to that? If that's true, I am sorry for it on behalf of my sex. I hope we can find a way to redeem ourselves."

The gravity of Miranda's expression deepened. Miss Sifton looked at Tom as though she had some specific ideas about how he could redeem his sex.

Simon, not seeming to notice the unspoken messages that were passing between their guest and Tom, returned to the subject of Mrs. Griffith and her son.

"I fear we're boring you, Mr. Jones," Miss Sifton said after a while. "Our village gossip must be very dull to a London gentleman such as yourself."

Before Tom could reply, Miranda broke in. "No doubt we *are* too dull for Mr. Jones. I can offer him an escape." Turning to Tom, she said, "On our way back from church, we stopped to look at the view of the valley. It was so warm that I took off my gloves and put them on a fencepost, but I forgot to bring them back with me. It's not a long walk. Would you fetch them for me?" She gave him a look that threatened dire consequences should he refuse.

"That's a cruel request to make of a man with a broken ankle," Miss Sifton put in.

"He tells us he's quite recovered now," Miranda said, "which must be true, for he's no longer wearing his leg brace."

Everyone looked at Tom's leg, which was indeed devoid of the offending device. He had forgotten to put it back on after his walk in the wood.

Tom preferred to be the one giving orders rather than taking them, but he was curious to find out why Miranda was so anxious to get rid of him, and he thought of a compromise. "I'll go if you'll come with me," he said. "I'll need help finding the path you took."

She assented, and they left Miss Sifton and Simon alone in the parlor.

Tom and Miranda were well along their walk before either of them spoke again. Despite Miranda's petite stature—the top of her head was barely level with his shoulder—she walked so quickly he found it difficult to keep up with her, especially on his crutches.

"Do have some pity for an injured man, won't you?" he said finally, half in jest.

She looked at him, startled, as if she had forgotten he was there, and slackened her pace. "Forgive me," she said. She didn't seem inclined to say anything more, yet she looked troubled.

"Have you known Miss Sifton long?" he asked.

"Since Simon and I moved here last year. Her family was the first to welcome us."

"I was surprised to see you with a visitor. I thought you and Simon don't mix with others very often."

"We don't. Perhaps we're overly cautious, but we don't want anyone from our former village to know where we are. Miss Sifton is one of the few friends we have here."

She came to a sudden halt and faced him, looking serious. He stopped too and waited.

"May I be frank with you?" she asked.

"Of course."

She looked uncomfortable, keeping her eyes fixed on one of his coat buttons. "I hope you'll forgive me for speaking to you the way I might speak to my brother. Even though you've said so little about yourself, I know you're a gentleman, and I'm taking a liberty that would be unpardonable in some circles—"

"Nonsense," he interrupted in a quiet, firm voice. "I'm not in any way above you, I assure you. Since our first meeting, you have treated me as an equal, and if you treat me as a brother, that's far more than I deserve. Please tell me whatever is on your mind."

"Very well." She met his eyes, but only for a second, her gaze returning to his coat button. "When Miss Sifton is with us, I'd like you to behave in a more . . . circumspect manner."

He understood at once that Miranda was objecting to his mild—very mild, in his opinion—flirtation, and he was momentarily at a loss for words. When an unmarried woman objects to a man's flirtation with another unmarried woman, the man may be forgiven for imagining that the reason for the objection is a personal inclination. Did Miranda have a romantic interest in him?

Although he was accustomed to being the object of feminine interest, he set Miranda apart from other women. For the first time in his life, he was enjoying a friendship with a woman that had none of the usual manipulations and complications that had always accompanied his relationships with the opposite sex. He couldn't imagine Miranda engaging in any sort of flirtation—she was too serious and too ingenuous. He wasn't tempted to flirt with her himself, not after knowing she'd been treated so badly by another clergyman. Even if he tried, he was certain she'd shut him down with one of her unsettling stares.

Tom finally said, "I apologize if I've offended you."

Miranda looked up at him and, as if she had read his thoughts, color flooded her face. "You mistake me," she said. "What I said was only for Simon's sake."

He remembered the way Simon had looked at Miss Sifton. He usually thought of himself as highly observant, but he'd completely missed the signs in this case. "Of course. Simon is in love with her."

"Yes." Miranda began to walk again, and Tom matched her pace. "He wants to marry her," she went on, "but he tells me he hasn't the courage to propose because she's given him no sign that she would welcome his courtship."

"Do you believe that's what holds him back?" Tom was anxious to listen carefully, in order to make up for his earlier lack of insight.

"That may be part of it, but I think our circumstances are what really keep him silent. Miss Sifton is the daughter of a banker with a comfortable fortune and a good reputation in our community. Simon is merely a farm laborer with no past, from others' point of view."

"He is no ordinary farm laborer—anyone can see that. From the first words you and Simon spoke to me, I knew you must be educated people."

"Thank you. But such observations are not enough when combined with the reality of our life and the mystery surrounding our past. Gwen knows some of what went on in Smythe, but not everything. In any case, Simon's position makes it difficult for a respectable banker's daughter to seriously consider him as a husband."

"Does she love him?" Tom had his doubts, based on his admittedly brief acquaintance with Miss Sifton. Surely a woman in love would not flirt with another man in the very presence of the one she loved. On the other hand, perhaps she was trying to make Simon jealous.

"I'm not certain. She seems to enjoy his company, but she doesn't tell me her secrets."

"Do you think she's worthy of Simon?"

Miranda gave Tom a grateful look. It was a question that a casual observer would doubtless think ought to be asked the other way around. "I haven't met a woman yet who I think is worthy of Simon," she said, "but I'm naturally biased. Gwen Sifton is as good a choice as most, I suppose. What matters to me is that Simon loves her, and I want him to be happy. He'd be happier in a city, working with people as he used to do as a solicitor's clerk. The only reason he's lowered himself to do farm labor is on my account."

"He's fortunate to have a sister who cares so much about his happiness."

"He cares about mine just as much."

They had reached the fence post where Miranda's gloves lay. Tom was surprised she had told the truth about leaving them behind. As soon as he had realized why she wanted to talk to him, he had assumed she had merely invented an excuse to speak to him alone.

She took the gloves and they resumed their walk. Tom glanced at Miranda's face, wondering if he had fallen a great deal in her estimation.

"I hope I haven't caused trouble for Simon," Tom said. "I didn't mean to."

"I doubt you've caused any permanent damage to his chances."

"I didn't mean to imply that," he said quickly. "I don't think as highly of myself as you seem to assume." His leg had begun to ache, but he didn't want her to know he'd pushed himself too far that day, so he tried to focus on matching her pace.

"I don't assume anything of the kind. I don't think you like yourself very much at all."

He stopped abruptly, shifting his weight to his good leg. What was it about this odd, sometimes shy, sometimes brutally frank young woman that made him so anxious that she think well of him? She wasn't particularly attractive, witty, or charming, and in any circumstance but the one that had brought her into his life, he wouldn't have given her a second thought.

"You speak as though you know me," he said with an edge in his voice.

"I know enough," she replied. She had walked ahead a few paces, and now she turned and gazed at him with an impassive look.

"What does that mean?"

"You're afraid people won't like you if you show them who you truly are, but you're wrong. I like you."

"Is that so?" His defensiveness dissipated at once. She had said the words in such a matter-of-fact way, like a child, as if their meaning could be taken only in the innocent sense she intended. "I fear I'll sound like I'm looking for a compliment if I ask what you like about me, but I can't help it."

"I like the way you listen so carefully when Simon and I talk. I like that you know Shakespeare and Tennyson by heart. I like your strength. Is that enough?"

His strength? He had never felt weaker, both physically and mentally, than during the month he'd spent with her and Simon, and he'd been ashamed of that weakness.

She began walking again, and he joined her.

"It's more than enough. Thank you. I like you, too, Miranda. Very much."

"Why?"

"Your thoughtfulness. Your imagination. The fact that you know prayers for peril at sea from memory."

She smiled.

"You also don't seem to hide behind masks as most people do," he added.

"I do have masks, but I suppose I don't always wear them. We all need people with whom we can remove them."

"With whom do you remove yours?" he asked.

"Simon."

"Only Simon?"

"Yes. With whom do you remove yours?"

Tom thought for a moment. Julia had come to his mind, but he suddenly realized he merely played the role of the perfect lover with her. He certainly knew the appropriate words and actions, but was that who he truly was? He had removed his masks with Osborne Jay, the clergyman who saved him from living on the streets and sent him to university, but he'd been too young and too desperate to dissemble then. And he had lost touch with Jay long ago.

"I can't think of anyone," he said.

6

There she weaves by night and day
A magic web with colours gay.
She has heard a whisper say,
A curse is on her if she stay
To look down to Camelot.
—Alfred, Lord Tennyson, "The Lady of Shalott"

Miranda surveyed the drawings she had laid out on the parlor floor. There were several of Simon, who often complained that she had too many drawings of him. He was a good subject, though, with his angular face and open gaze. He was also more likely to sit still than most of her other subjects, who were usually children or animals. Simon had asked her to draw Gwen, and she'd tried, but she could never get it right. Miranda refused to show any of her half-finished efforts to Simon, claiming that he wouldn't be satisfied with any drawing of Gwen because in his eyes she was perfect. Miranda's private opinion of the difficulties she was experiencing was that depth couldn't be represented in a drawing if it didn't exist in the subject.

There was no question that Tom was a fascinating subject, but she didn't want to risk repeating the embarrassing situation when he'd seen how many drawings she'd made of him. She'd stopped sketching him for a while.

The day after Gwen visited them, when Miranda and Simon were alone together, he asked her abruptly, "Do you think Tom is good-looking?"

"Yes," she said with a smile. "Very."

"I mean objectively speaking. Would most women consider him handsome?"

Poor Simon. He was so transparent. "I think most women would," she said carefully. "But I also think most women wouldn't consider a man's physical appearance as important as his character . . ." She was about to add *and his ability to support a wife*, but stopped herself. It would have been cruel to say such a thing to Simon, who most certainly could not support a wife.

He regarded her thoughtfully, then said, "You're not going to fall in love with him, are you?"

The question surprised her, since she had assumed Simon was thinking of Gwen, not herself. "You know my heart isn't free," she said quietly.

She expected Simon to accept this reminder the way he always had, but instead he said firmly, "Sam isn't real, Miranda."

Once she had dreamed that she was a deer shot by a hunter. She'd felt the impact of the bullet in her chest and the breath leave her body all at once. Gasping, she'd awakened in real physical pain. Simon's words made her feel the same way.

"How can you say such a thing?" she cried. "Sam is more real to me than you are."

"I'm sorry." He reached out as if to pat her on the shoulder, but she stepped away, out of his reach. "It's just . . . I want you to be happy, and as long as you hold on to him like this, I don't see how you can be. I thought you might be starting to forget him."

"I'll never forget him, and I'll never stop loving him."

"Very well." Simon raised both hands in a gesture of surrender, then turned and left the room.

When she had recovered from the shock of Simon's words, Miranda was able to see them as motivated by concern for her rather than malice. But there was much that Simon didn't understand about her heart. He also didn't realize that Tom was a welcome distraction for her. The aura of mystery around him was a large part of his fascination, and she hadn't stopped constructing outlandish explanations for it. She'd decided against the possibility of his being an Italian prince and decided that he was the illegitimate son of a Catholic bishop who had fallen in love with a gypsy girl in his youth. The bishop didn't know he had a son who was raised by gypsies until recently, and he needed to silence Tom in order to keep his position in the church. Miranda knew this story was as ridiculous as the others, but it kept her amused—and protected her from developing real feelings for Tom.

Besides, if it hadn't been clear that Tom had no romantic interest in her before, it certainly was after seeing him with Gwen. He had never made any attempt to flirt with Miranda, and it was clearly his nature to do so with women he found attractive. She didn't expect or wish to be attractive to men, so Tom's lack of interest in that way didn't trouble her.

As she was sorting through her drawings, Tom walked into the parlor and asked, "What are you doing, Elaine?"

Miranda didn't answer him at once. She sensed that he liked to think of her in the role of the isolated, enchanted artist, but she didn't like all the implications of her new name. She'd be damned before she'd die of love for anyone and float in a barge down to Camelot—or anywhere else.

"I'm trying to decide what my subject ought to be for my next drawing," she said finally.

Tom approached her and glanced at the papers strewn around her. Even though she'd been careful to keep the sketches of him well hidden since the incident that had embarrassed her, she was still nervous about his seeing something she didn't want him to see.

He picked up one of the sketches. "Is this your mother?" he asked.

"Yes. I did that a couple of years ago. From memory, but I think it's a good likeness."

"She was beautiful," he said.

"She was. Thank you."

"Her eyes in the drawing are very like yours. I want to look away because she sees too much." Tom looked from the drawing to Miranda, studying her face as intently as he had studied the drawing. "Have you ever tried your hand at painting?" he asked.

"I used to paint, before my parents died." She had painted while living with Richard and his family, too, but she didn't want to talk about that. "My parents were supportive of my art, and they even paid for art lessons for a few years. But since they died I haven't wanted to do anything but draw. Painting just doesn't feel right, somehow."

"I hope you'll pick it up again. I have the feeling your paintings would be impressive. I say," he added, "have you ever done a self-portrait?"

"I've attempted it, but I'm not happy with the results."

"May I see an attempt, or am I encroaching upon private territory?"

"I suppose you may."

She rifled through a pile of drawings, pulled one out, and handed it to him. In it, she was curled up in an armchair in the cozy drawing room of the old house she'd lived in as a child, gazing out the window. She was an adult in the drawing, but everything else was just as she remembered it from when her parents were still alive, from one of her father and Simon's perpetually half-finished chess games on a side table to the assortment of potted plants.

Her mother loved to bring the outdoors inside; there were so many plants that visitors were always tripping over them.

Tom looked at it for a moment, then said impatiently, "You've revealed nothing about yourself. Your face is turned away. It's not even in profile. And you're so small in relation to the surrounding objects. I haven't seen furniture and ornaments in your other drawings. Usually the face is dominant and there's nothing else to take the viewer's eye away from it."

"It isn't easy to represent oneself in one's art," she said, more amused than troubled by his criticism.

"What I don't understand is whether you truly see yourself this way—as a tiny, blank figure of no importance—or whether you're choosing not to show yourself and your secrets, preferring to expose others instead."

Of course he wouldn't realize that she had tried to reveal herself through her favorite room and the things that represented the people she loved most. Still, she was pleased that she was at least momentarily as much a mystery to him as he was to her.

"Don't look at me like that," he demanded, his tone changing from real to mock frustration. "If I were an artist, I'd draw you exactly as you are—I'd reveal everything."

"An artist must look closely at his subject," she said. "I don't think you've observed me enough to be able to draw me, certainly not to represent me 'exactly as I am,' whatever that means."

"Well, perhaps that claim was a bit grandiose," he admitted, "but I suspect I've seen more than you realize. For example, if I made a drawing of you—no, I'd paint you, for I need color—there are a few things I'd include that a casual observer might not notice. I'd paint you in sunlight because some strands of your hair turn to gold when the sun shines on them. I'd have you avert your eyes, lest you intimidate the viewer with that piercing gaze. And I'd include the little crease that appears between your eyebrows when you're concentrating very hard, or when you're anxious about something."

He reached out to touch the spot with his fingertip. His touch was light as a breath, but it cut through her like a sword. As if on cue, the lines from the Tennyson poem echoed in her head: "'The curse is come upon me,' cried the Lady of Shalott."

It wasn't a curse in the way that the burden of her past was, but it was still a curse. Miranda had told Tom what she liked about him, and she'd kept to herself the things she didn't like—his secrecy, his stubbornness, his irritability. But in that simple, devastating moment when his finger touched her forehead, she knew that her heart was no longer only Sam's.

Simon chose that moment to enter the cottage, which allowed Miranda time to recover her composure. Throwing off his coat, Simon took a chair near Miranda and Tom in the parlor, looking tired but pleased.

"You ought to see the pile of wood outside, Mouse," he said. "It will see us through the whole winter, I'll wager. Our friend has regained his strength. I could hardly keep up with him."

Miranda gave Tom a quick glance. "You were chopping wood?"

"Yes, but Simon has exaggerated my usefulness. I really didn't know what I was doing."

"You've used an ax before, that's certain," Simon put in.

"Yes . . . a long time ago."

"Well, if you ever choose to change your vocation, you'd have no trouble finding work as a laborer."

Miranda was worried Tom would be insulted by Simon's words, but he didn't seem so.

"It felt good to do something physical after being an invalid for so long," he said. "After all the good care I've received here, it shouldn't be a surprise that I've recovered so quickly. I'll need to return to London soon, probably next week."

Next week! The words came as a shock. It was too soon. He couldn't possibly be well enough to return to London, could he? If he was able to chop wood with Simon, that was a sign he felt better, of course, but it didn't mean he was fully recovered. On the other hand, now that Miranda was aware of the danger to her heart, it was best for him to leave.

Her skill at hiding her feelings stood her in good stead now. She picked up one of her drawings and examined it as if her life depended on finding the one tiny detail that needed changing. Simon took the news in stride, telling Tom what he knew about the train schedule from Denfield to London. Simon and Tom then spoke of the work they had done together that day in and around the cottage, fixing a broken chair leg and mending a fence in addition to chopping wood.

Miranda listened to their conversation without taking part in it. She preferred to stay in the background for the time being, still too unsettled by her reaction to Tom's touch. Simon seemed to enjoy Tom's company, and Miranda was glad her brother had another man to talk to. One needed a confidant of one's own sex. Gwen was the only woman in Miranda's life now who could be considered a friend, but she found Gwen difficult to understand, and the feeling seemed to be mutual. Gwen's endless talk of shopping trips and the superficial details of other people's lives was tedious to Miranda. She preferred to discuss ideas or feelings, but such discussions didn't seem to interest Gwen.

"I need something to drink after all that hard work," Simon said, rousing her out of her reverie.

"I can make tea," she said, rising to her feet.

"No, I think I'll have some beer. There are still a few bottles left in the larder, aren't there?" Simon rose and made his way out of the room, saying over his shoulder, "Would you like some, Tom?"

"No."

Tom had spoken so vehemently that Miranda looked at him in surprise. Simon had already left the room, so he may not have noticed anything odd about Tom's response, but it seemed strange to her.

A fleeting expression of something like rage crossed Tom's face—it was out of place and therefore startling. When he realized she was looking at him, he looked away as if embarrassed.

Amid the noises of Simon banging cupboards and utensils in the kitchen, Miranda kept watching Tom. He finally said, "I don't drink. I've seen it ruin too many families."

"Yours, too?" she asked.

He met her gaze, and something in his face changed again, a softening of expression, a little crack in his façade. "Yes, mine too."

"I'm sorry." She wanted to ask more questions, but Simon was returning with his bottle of beer and the moment was lost. It didn't really matter. She was used to Tom's way of closing up like a clam as soon as he shared even the slightest bit of personal information, so she likely wouldn't have learned anything more from him.

Miranda decided to excuse herself and spend some time alone in her room. She didn't feel like engaging in light conversation, and she was disturbed by the sadness she felt at the thought of Tom's departure. Of course he would go back to London, to his own world, a world she knew nothing about, and she and Simon would remain where they were. Their lives would go on as usual.

Whatever she was feeling for Tom was nothing compared to her love for Sam. She was no longer angry with Simon for what he'd said earlier, but he didn't understand what made one person real and another imaginary. Miranda knew Sam—she'd touched him and kissed him and felt his heartbeat. Tom, on the other hand, was largely a creation of her imagination. He lived in her mind, and she was resolved he would die there, too. There was no Tom Jones except in the pages of Henry Fielding's novel. There was no illegitimate Italian prince or wandering gypsy musician. There was no Lancelot. The man who had been beaten and left in the wood—who had recovered under Miranda's care, and who was now in the parlor talking with Simon—was a stranger.

Two days before his departure for London, Tom awoke to something he'd never heard before: Miranda and Simon arguing. He'd heard them engage in friendly sparring matches and whispered disagreements, but now their voices were raised enough that he could hear them in the parlor from his room. Although they weren't shouting—indeed, he couldn't imagine either of them doing so—there was enough emotion in their voices to carry through the closed door of Tom's room.

"It's a terrible idea. Surely you can understand that," Simon was saying.

"Whether it's a good or bad idea is immaterial. I must go."

"Why? What possible purpose can it serve? And what if someone sees you and recognizes you?"

"Simon, we have the same argument every year, and you still expect me to give you logical reasons for my decision when I keep telling you I'm compelled to do it. My heart doesn't need reasons. Besides, the risk of my being recognized is not very great."

"What of the risks to your well-being, your peace of mind? Don't worry—I won't repeat what I said the other day. But how can this be good for you?"

"I don't go more than once a year. You have no idea how difficult that is for me when I wish I could be there every day. One visit won't destroy me."

"Let me go with you, then. I can't let you go alone."

"What will Tom think?" Miranda lowered her voice, but Tom could still hear her. "He's leaving in two days. Wouldn't it be rude to leave him here alone all day?"

"It would be more rude if I'm here worrying about you to the point that I can't even speak to him."

"Very well. You can come with me. Let's not argue anymore."

Tom's curiosity was piqued. Where were Simon and Miranda going, and why was this trip such an emotional subject?

When Tom emerged from his room a quarter of an hour later and went into the parlor, the Thornes were engaged in final preparations for their departure. Simon, holding his best overcoat and felt hat, was wearing his Sunday suit. Whether because of the trip he was about to take or the large, stiff collar he was wearing, he looked uncomfortable. Miranda, who had been buttoning her boots, straightened up when Tom entered the room. She was wearing a black dress and large black hat with a heavy lace veil that she hadn't yet pulled over her face. They both looked as though they were going to a funeral.

"Good morning," Miranda said, pleasantly enough, but her face was pale, and there was a feverish look in her eyes.

Tom had never seen her this way before. Her manner was usually so quiet and placid, at least on the surface, that the contrast was surprising.

"Good morning," he replied. "I see you're going somewhere."

"Yes," said Simon. "We have business in Birmingham."

"That's a long way from here." Tom couldn't help hoping they would tell him more.

"Your breakfast is on the table," Miranda said. "I've also prepared a lunch for you—it's in the larder."

"Thank you."

"We'll return later this afternoon," Simon told Tom, and with that, the Thornes left the cottage.

Tom spent a restless day. Having few of his own belongings to pack for his trip back to London (only the contents of his pockets, minus his coins, had survived the attack), he went for a long walk, made himself tea, and worried about what was happening in his absence at the cathedral, the prison, and the hospital. He had written to Canon Martin, a colleague at the cathedral, to ask him to take over Tom's duties while he was away, but Martin had written back, "I'll do my best, Cross, but even if there were two of me, I couldn't keep up with your usual punishing schedule."

Tom also thought about where Simon and Miranda could have gone. If they truly had gone to Birmingham—and there was no reason to suppose Simon would lie about that—perhaps they were visiting their parents' graves. It would certainly explain the way they were dressed. But then why would Simon object, and why would Miranda want to go alone? Instead, perhaps their trip had something to do with the vicar who had caused so much trouble in their lives. But why would Miranda want to see him or anyone connected to him? She had spoken as if she were desperate to make this trip, as if it were torture to stay away. Was there a man she loved, someone she couldn't be with, or someone Simon thought was bad for her? Miranda didn't seem like the sort of woman who would be involved in a secret romantic liaison.

Tom decided his own secrets were making him imagine that the Thornes' trip to Birmingham was more mysterious than it really was. Very likely they were merely visiting a relative whom Miranda cared about and Simon didn't. Perhaps they would even tell Tom the whole story when they returned home. Yet he couldn't forget the emotion he'd heard in their voices, especially in Miranda's.

Tom was in the parlor reading a book late that afternoon when Simon and Miranda returned. She was the first to enter the house, and Tom laid down his book to greet her. But she didn't pause to speak to him or even to remove her boots. Instead, she rushed past him in a flurry of skirts, her face a white mask. He heard her bedroom door close a moment later, then silence.

Alarmed, Tom rose to his feet just as Simon walked in. Simon made no dramatic entrance, just smiled wearily at Tom and said, "Have you had your tea yet?"

"Yes, but—"

"I'm famished, but I've got to change out of this infernal suit first. Is there any bread and cheese left in the larder?"

Tom waited uneasily for Simon to change his clothes. When he heard shuffling and clattering sounds in the kitchen, he went to investigate. He leaned against the kitchen doorframe, watching Simon tear off a large piece of bread and slice some cheese.

"Is Miranda all right?" he asked, keeping his voice low.

"She will be," Simon replied just as quietly, concentrating on the cheese knife as if he were a surgeon performing a risky operation.

Tom wrestled with the many questions he wanted to ask Simon about the trip. He didn't want to pry, and he knew better than most people what it felt like to be questioned about subjects he didn't want to discuss, but he was worried about Miranda.

He finally settled on, "Is there anything I can do?" It was a vague offer, but also the least intrusive he could imagine.

"She just needs a bit of time alone." Still standing at the counter, Simon crammed a large piece of bread into his mouth and stared blankly at the wall in front of him.

Tom retreated. It was obvious that Simon didn't want to talk.

After Simon had finished his tea, he invited Tom to join him outside to look at his vegetable garden. The garden was Simon's pride and joy, and his afternoon visits to it were a well-established ritual, though Tom was mystified about what needed doing in late November. In fact, Tom thought of the garden as an imaginary one: though he'd never been in it, he could see it, such as it was, through the cottage window, and to him it looked like a barren rectangle of dirt. Nevertheless, he was aware of the honor of being actually invited into the garden, so he didn't hesitate to accept.

Simon visibly relaxed as soon as his feet touched the frigid soil. He paused from time to time to prod a lump of dirt with the toe of his boot or crouch down to stare intently at the ground, putting Tom in mind of a fortune-teller reading tea leaves.

Just when Tom was thinking of returning to the house to fetch a muffler—he'd expected to be outside for only a few minutes, so he wasn't dressed for the cold—Simon stood abruptly, beamed at Tom, and proclaimed, "This one is ready to harvest!"

What Simon meant by "this one" was a mystery to Tom, for he still saw nothing that looked remotely like a plant. Bending down and looking more closely, he noticed some greenish-white shoots protruding from the ground.

"What is it?" Tom asked.

"What is it?" Simon echoed, looking shocked. "You'll see. Wait a moment."

He went to his tool shed and returned with a spade. He began digging in the soil around the dead-looking shoots, which was no small feat, considering the mostly frozen state of the ground. Tom offered to help, and after several minutes of exertion, Simon gratefully handed over the spade. Tom jabbed it into the soil at a safe distance from whatever it was they were harvesting. It took them at least twenty minutes to dig a hole large enough to remove what turned out to be a large parsnip.

Tom didn't know what he was expecting, but it wasn't this. Simon lifted the vegetable out of the ground and brushed the excess dirt away. He nestled the parsnip in the crook of his arm and gave it a loving pat, almost a caress.

"This," Simon said reverently, "is a Tender White Jewel."

Tom couldn't suppress a snort of laughter, but he covered it up by turning it into a cough.

Simon didn't seem to notice. He waxed eloquent on the quality of his Jewel's skin, color, and size. Tom found it odd that Miranda believed Simon would be happier living and working in a city.

When Tom was able to keep a straight face, he said, "Is it edible when it's harvested so late in the year?"

"Is it edible?" Simon repeated Tom's words again, looking just as shocked as he had the first time. "It will be *delicious*. Parsnips always taste better after the first frost."

Before they left the garden, Simon poked and prodded a few other lumps of dirt, still cradling his precious parsnip. "This time of year isn't the best time for most vegetables, of course. In the spring I'll be able to really watch them grow. I like to talk to the little ones: some encouragement helps them grow as big and strong as their fellows."

Tom smiled. "You'll be a good father someday."

"Me?" Simon looked astonished. "I'd need a wife first. What woman would have me?"

"You're too modest. What should prevent a woman from marrying you?"

"My lack of means, for one thing. For another, I can't think of anything intelligent to say in the presence of a woman I admire."

"The first is a problem, I'll admit. The second can be easily remedied."

"That's easy for you to say. I'll wager you've never been at a loss for words with a woman in your life."

Tom hadn't, but he thought it best not to say so. "I suggest speaking to a woman the way you'd speak to a male acquaintance who is a little above you in station. Then, once you've mastered that, you can compliment her eyes or her hair, or merely just look at her a little longer than is necessary—upon my word, not like that!" he exclaimed at the sight of Simon's attempts to practice looking at an imaginary woman. "An admiring look is what I meant, not the look of a sheep being led to the slaughter."

Simon laughed. "You see? I'm hopeless."

"Not at all. You just need some practice. Miss Sifton would perhaps be a good person to start with." Tom observed Simon's face blanch a little at this, but he wanted to make up for whatever damage he might have done when he flirted with Miss Sifton himself, so he continued, "Would you object to putting in some effort to interest her?"

"Object? No, I'd make a great deal of effort if I thought it would do any good," Simon replied, staring down at his parsnip as if it could inspire him with courage.

"Then the first thing you must do is build up your confidence and stop assuming she has no interest in you. Have you any evidence for her feelings one way or the other?"

"No, not really."

The wind had picked up, and Tom pulled the collar of his coat more closely around his neck. "When Miranda and I went to retrieve her gloves that Sunday, did Miss Sifton go home at once?"

"No. We talked for a while. She told me that her father has an acquaintance in London, a solicitor, who is in need of a clerk. It's my old line of work, and the salary would be better. Gwen—Miss Sifton—said she'd ask her father to recommend me."

"Well, I'd call that evidence of warm regard, at least," Tom said. "Isn't it possible that she might enjoy your company?"

"Perhaps."

"I'm not telling you Miss Sifton is in love with you. I have no idea if she is or not. I'm simply saying you have reason to believe she isn't indifferent to you, and if you follow my advice, she may very well find you fascinating before long."

"Good heavens. This whole business is frightening." Simon sighed, then looked meditatively at Tom. "Why do I have the feeling you've given other men similar advice?"

Tom shrugged. "I may have done."

"I also have the feeling these strategies have worked well for you."

"That depends on what you mean by 'worked well.' I can talk to women easily enough."

"Have you ever been in love?" Simon asked.

Tom hesitated. He had been in love many times, if "in love" meant the excitement of pursuing an attractive woman until she returned his interest. Until Julia, that was as far as most of his encounters with the opposite sex had gone. He enjoyed the attention he received from flirtations, and he didn't think beyond that. When he saw the spark of interest in a woman's eyes, he was content, and his interest in her would gradually fade away. But Julia had become an obsession that he couldn't shake off until they'd gone to bed together.

"I was in love with someone," he said finally, "but there were barriers that prevented us from marrying."

"Oh?" Simon seemed to be waiting for more information, but Tom had no intention of discussing Julia.

"What of Miranda?" Tom asked abruptly. "Has she any suitors?" He instantly regretted asking the question; it seemed too transparently designed to discover her secret.

Simon didn't seem to find the question suspicious, but a bleak expression appeared on his face. "No, and there will be none. She'll never marry."

Tom was surprised by the finality of Simon's statement. "Are you so certain of that? Sometimes young women claim a lack of interest in marriage, but it's only because they haven't yet met the right man."

"Yes, I'm certain. You know she was treated badly in the past by the vicar we told you about. That would be reason enough for her to avoid men. But she has her own reasons for her decision, and they're not for me to tell you."

"I didn't mean to pry."

"No, I'm glad you asked. You're the first person in a long time whom Miranda has allowed herself to form a friendship with. I think it's good for her to learn to trust people again." Simon stamped his feet. "It's freezing out here. Let's go inside."

Simon turned back to the cottage, still cradling his Tender White Jewel, and Tom followed, wondering about the things his friend had left unsaid.

7

[L]ife is made of ever so many partings welded together . . .
—Charles Dickens, *Great Expectations*

DECEMBER 1907

Tom groaned, forcing his eyes to open in the early-morning darkness and cursing himself for agreeing to accompany the Thornes on their mysterious errand. It was his last day with them—he was returning to London on the afternoon train—and they had been so importunate about a secret place they wanted to show him that he hadn't the heart to refuse. But it was difficult to struggle out of bed. He peered at the thin layer of ice in the pitcher of water on the washstand. His lodgings in London were modern enough to have hot water pipes fed by a boiler, so he hadn't had to wash in ice-cold water since his childhood.

He broke the ice and splashed the water on his face, gasping. A flash of memory imprinted itself on his closed eyes. He'd been fifteen or sixteen, and just as the icy water he was washing with hit his face, he heard Kate scream. Throwing on his clothes and rushing into the front room, he saw his sister cowering on the floor. His father stood over her, his hand raised, shouting something about his breakfast being cold.

Tom had shot across the room and shoved his father hard, so hard the man staggered and fell back against the wall. It had been the first time Tom realized his own strength. The shock in his father's liquor-clouded eyes showed that he realized it, too.

"If you lay a finger on her again, or on Mam," Tom snarled, "I'll kill you. D'ye hear me?" He'd meant it, every word.

His father didn't beat him again after that, nor did he strike his mother or sister, as far as Tom knew. But he didn't know what had happened after he left home. He hoped his father had either died or been sent to prison. He'd had violent altercations with men at the pub; he'd stolen money. Tom's youthful threat would have lost its power eventually, and for that he felt immense guilt. Now, as he finished his ablutions and got dressed, the memory faded, but the feelings it evoked remained vivid, both the satisfaction of besting his father physically, and the guilt of leaving his mother and sister behind.

The Thornes were waiting for him by the front door, Simon in his warmest winter coat and hat, and Miranda in a thick hooded cloak. As Tom put on his own coat, he mumbled an apology for keeping them waiting.

"It's no matter," Simon said. "Let's go."

They opened the front door to darkness and a blast of cold air. The Thornes had to be mad to go out in such weather. Snow had fallen overnight, muffling the sound of their footsteps. The best place to be on a day like this was in bed under a warm quilt or in front of a roaring fire. But Tom set his teeth and didn't complain aloud—indeed, it would have been unmanly to the worst degree to complain when Simon and Miranda, both as thin and unsubstantial as willow branches, were gamely pushing on through the frigid air.

They walked in silence towards the wood and away from the village. Simon had a lantern that he held aloft to light their way, and Miranda followed him, with Tom bringing up the rear. They walked past birch trees shining eerily white in the darkness. Miranda's cloak was a shade lighter than the sky and enveloped her so completely that she might have been a phantom. And Simon, a dark figure with a lantern, looked like the man in the moon. All he lacked was a bundle of sticks on his back. Tom felt as if he were entering a dream world.

Once past the wood, Simon took a path that veered to the east, one Tom hadn't noticed before in his wanderings. The ground was no longer level, and it became clear they were climbing a hill. The wind rose, and Tom pulled his muffler over his nose, hoping their destination wasn't much farther.

At one point, Miranda paused to look back at Tom. "Are you managing?" she asked, her breath forming a frosty cloud in the air. "We needn't go on if you're in pain."

"I'm fine," he said, despite the fact that his bad leg was already aching from the chill.

"We're almost there," called Simon from above.

When Simon reached the top of the hill, he set down the lantern and snuffed it out with a sigh of relief, sitting down on a large flat stone. The sky had lightened a little, but it was still too dark to see anything in the valley below. Simon moved to the edge of the stone to make room for Miranda, and she huddled close to him, beckoning Tom to join them. The only way he could do so was to sit pressed against her in a way that would have been inappropriately intimate had they not been wearing heavy winter clothing.

"Where are we?" asked Tom.

"You'll see," said Miranda. Since the Thornes' trip to Birmingham, she had been quieter than usual and seemed depressed. But she sounded brighter now, and there was a lilt in her voice.

They waited. Nobody spoke. And then, just when Tom felt he couldn't wait any longer, a fiery yellow semicircle appeared on the horizon, and streams of golden light slowly spread across the field below them. Tom held his breath as a deep silence settled on the landscape.

After a few minutes, Miranda whispered, "There's someone I'd like you to meet. Will you come with me?"

It seemed like a strange time and place for such a request, but Tom answered, "Of course."

As Miranda rose, Simon said, "I'll stay here. Three of us might scare him away."

His curiosity piqued, Tom followed Miranda rather stiffly down the slope to the field, marveling at the beauty of what he would normally consider an ordinary landscape. Frost sparkled on seed heads. Cow parsley shimmered like strands of gold. Even the brambles looked like exotic plants in the early dawn light.

When they reached the field, Miranda stopped and looked about her, then made a chirping sound. A moment later, Tom saw a small yellow bird perch sideways on a stalk of cow parsley about ten feet away.

"There he is," she said softly.

"Is that a finch?"

"Yes, a siskin."

"Does he live here in the field?"

"I think so. Siskins usually travel in a flock, but he seems to have been separated from his. I've never seen any other bird with him. And they usually live in the woods, where there's more food for them. I've been feeding him until he can find his friends again."

"I suppose the female siskin is drabber looking."

"Yes, though they're still yellowish. They don't have the black crown."

"I always think it unfair that male birds are more attractive than female ones."

"I don't. The females don't have to go to all the trouble of primping and preening. They get to choose."

Tom smiled. "Good point."

Miranda took a step closer to the bird, but it fluttered away to a more distant stalk of parsley.

Turning to Tom, she said, "Can you move back a bit? You're much taller and bigger than I am, and he's not used to you."

He took a few steps back, then crouched down so as not to disturb the bird. Miranda took a folded handkerchief from the inside of her cloak, then unwrapped it to reveal a small assortment of seeds and nuts. She took off her gloves and pushed back the hood of her cloak, holding a handful of the seeds towards the bird.

The siskin flew to her and perched on her hand, then began to eat the seeds. Now that he was close enough to see clearly, Tom marveled at the beauty of the bird's markings: its black crown gave it a serious, almost worried, expression, contrasting with the green on its back and the yellow on its wings and cheeks.

Miranda's hair was in a loose plait reaching nearly to her waist. The angle of the sunlight on her hair and on the bird made them both glow with a golden light. Tom could have watched them forever, as if they were a painting: *Woman Feeding a Bird at Sunrise*. The rolling hills and hedgerows beyond them gave him a sense of limitless space.

He remembered the first time he'd gone to church as a young boy with his mother and sister. They'd been late for the service, and his mother had tried to slip unnoticed into a pew at the back, but Tom had stopped in the middle of the aisle, dazzled by the way the sun shone through a stained-glass window. He no longer remembered what the window depicted, but the awe and reverence it evoked in him returned now as he looked at the scene before him. He'd forgotten that he'd felt this way for the first time in a church.

After a few minutes, the siskin flew away. Miranda turned and approached Tom. "Isn't he lovely?" she said. There were tears on her cheeks.

Tom realized he was kneeling on the ground, and he struggled to his feet, feeling foolish and very cold, despite his hat, muffler, and heavy gloves. And here was Miranda, bareheaded and gloveless, with her cloak open at the front, exposing her neck.

"You're going to catch your death of cold," he said, reaching behind her to pull the hood of the cloak over her head, then removing his muffler and arranging it around her neck. She said nothing, merely waiting like an obedient child until he was finished.

"Where are your gloves?" he asked. Without waiting for an answer, he went to where she'd been standing, found the gloves on the ground, and returned, handing them to her.

She put them on in silence, the tears still on her cheeks. Tom removed one of his own gloves and gently brushed away the moisture with his thumb. She met his eyes and went still, even more still than she'd been with the bird.

Anyone who could hurt this woman, Tom thought, *must be a monster.*

Then Miranda turned away and said, "Simon is waiting for us."

Tom had forgotten Simon. He had forgotten himself, too. Reluctantly he followed Miranda as she made her way up the hill.

Simon had left the flat rock on the crest of the hill and was standing a short distance away, staring at the ground.

"What are you looking at?" Miranda asked him.

He looked up as if surprised to see the others. "I'm trying to identify this strange plant. What do you think it is?"

He and Miranda bent to examine the plant and were soon engaged in a discussion of what it might be. Tom stood apart, not listening. The spell was broken, and the light had changed. They were standing on an ordinary hill on an ordinary day in early December, among dead grasses and plants.

It was another reminder that he didn't belong in this fairy tale with these innocent, adult versions of Hansel and Gretel. His place was elsewhere, among the dirt and noise of the city, among the ugliness of poverty and illness and people who had lost hope. The gates of the paradise he'd glimpsed during the sunrise were closed to him.

Miranda didn't look at Tom or speak to him as they walked home.

At the cottage, they had a quiet breakfast of eggs and fried parsnip: Simon had sacrificed his Tender White Jewel to prove to Tom that it was as delicious as he'd said. It was indeed tasty, but Tom wasn't very hungry. After breakfast, he packed his few belongings and prepared to leave for Denfield to catch his train. When he went to the parlor to say his goodbyes, only Simon was there.

"Are you off, then?" Simon asked.

"Yes." Tom glanced around the room. "Where's Miranda?"

"I don't know." Simon called her name, then checked her room. He returned with a shrug. "I think she's gone somewhere. Probably for another walk."

"I'll wait for her."

"There's no point. She hates goodbyes and avoids them whenever possible. She'll come back after you've left."

"Oh." Nonplussed, Tom paused, then said, "I hope you'll convey to her how much I appreciate everything she's done for me, then."

"Yes, of course. We've certainly enjoyed your company in our isolated situation." Simon shook Tom's hand and added, "Hopefully you'll carry some of the peace you said you've found here with you to London."

"Thank you. I hope so, too. I can't help thinking of Wordsworth, you know: 'But oft, in lonely rooms, and 'mid the din of towns and cities, I have owed to them, in hours of weariness, sensations sweet.'"

"Indeed." Simon smiled. "Have a good journey, Tom."

Tom left the cottage and began to walk down the path that led to the main road, wishing he could have said a proper goodbye to Miranda.

A few minutes later, after he had rounded a bend that took the cottage out of his sight, he heard footsteps on the path behind him and turned to see Miranda running towards him. There were wisps of hair escaping her plait, and her cloak was not properly fastened, as if she'd thrown it on as she ran. At least this time she was wearing her gloves.

"I forgot to give you something," she said as soon as she stopped in front of him.

She held out a small box, and he took it and opened it. Inside was a simple gold cross on a chain. It looked very old and was surprisingly heavy for its size. Looking closer, Tom saw scratches on its surface.

"It was my grandfather's," Miranda said, struggling to catch her breath.

"I can't accept this," he said. "It's too valuable."

"It isn't valuable, not in the sense of being costly. It isn't solid gold."

"That isn't the sense I meant. It's important to you."

"What's the point of giving meaningless gifts?" she countered, meeting his eyes.

"I'll accept it, then. Thank you." Mindful of Simon's words about Miranda's hatred of goodbyes, he said carefully, "I hope you and Simon will visit me if you come to London."

"I don't want to go to London."

Daunted by her words as well as her flat tone, he said, "Well, then, I'll just have to come back and visit you."

"As you wish." She turned away without meeting his eyes, behaving not in the least like someone who had just given him a heartfelt gift. It was very provoking.

"Miranda, wait."

She made a half turn back to him, gazing at the horizon.

There were so many things he wanted to say. That his time with her and Simon had changed him. That his work was no longer the most important thing in his life. That she made him want to be a better man.

Instead, he said, "May I write to you?"

"Of course you may write to us."

Was it his imagination, or had she emphasized the word *us*?

"And you'll write back?"

"Perhaps."

This was provoking, indeed. He opened his mouth to make some sort of protest, to force her to respond properly, but she looked up at him with the tiniest hint of a smile. Then she turned and ran away as abruptly as she'd come.

8

Unhappy men, who went alive to the house of Hades,

so dying twice, when all the rest of mankind die only once . . .

—Homer, *The Odyssey*

Tom spent his trip back to the city in an uncomfortable state of mind. As soon as he was on the train, all the problems he had avoided while he was in the country hit him with a vengeance. His primary concern was what to tell the bishop about his mysterious illness and long absence. He didn't want anyone to know he had been attacked. If his attackers were connected to his past, whether distant or recent, his sins would come out and it would jeopardize his position at the cathedral. On the other hand, if the attackers were just random thugs, there would be no negative repercussions if he told the truth. Still, he was also worried that his six-week absence would damage his chances for the deanship. Who knew what Paul Harris had been doing while Tom was away? Tom would have to work hard to remind everyone that he was the more logical choice. If the dean had died during Tom's absence, perhaps Harris had already been appointed to the position. Tom tried not to think about that possibility.

He had put Miranda's gift in his pocket. Now he took it out, fastened the chain around his neck, and slipped it underneath his shirt. The weight of the cross felt reassuring against his chest.

Canon Martin had written to say he hadn't been able to manage Tom's hospital visits or Prison Commission meetings, so Tom resolved to go to the hospital as soon as he arrived in London, even before going to his lodgings, to offer reassurance to the people who depended on his comfort and support. He was worried that a few of the seriously ill patients had gotten worse, or even died, in the interim.

Death seemed to be everywhere. This trip to London was a transition from his own near-death to what he hoped was a new life—a life he would live with more integrity, devoting himself to his parishioners, telling the truth more often, and avoiding the temptations of women, especially Julia. During his time with Simon and Miranda, he hadn't felt the need to communicate with anyone from London aside from the bishop and Martin, and the thought of whatever other letters might be piling up hadn't troubled him even after he was well enough to care. He wanted to think of himself as Odysseus in the underworld, traveling back into life with a new perspective, leaving the old things and people behind.

When the train stopped at Waterloo Station, Tom took the Underground the rest of the way to Whitechapel. Once aboveground, he found the noise of the city deafening: street sellers hawking their wares, the clattering of carriage wheels, the mechanical whirr of motorcars. The sounds and bustle of the city used to energize him, but he felt jolted by the modern world after his pastoral idyll. It made his time in the country seem even more remote, as if he had traveled fifty years back in time and had forgotten how to live in the present.

He pushed aside the sense of unreality as he entered the hospital, where he was welcomed, if not like a returning hero, then with as much warmth and interest as he could have hoped. He told everyone who asked about his absence that he had been ill, giving vague answers to the few people—a doctor and two nurses—who asked more specific questions.

After Tom had finished his visits and was on his way out of the hospital, a commotion in the front foyer caught his attention. A man was trying to carry an unconscious young boy into the hospital while another man was attempting to hold him back, amid the raised voices of medical workers and onlookers.

"What's happening here?" Tom asked a nearby nurse.

"The boy is Jack Goode," she replied. "He works at the textile factory. He's been injured there before. The man carrying him is one of the workers. The other man is the boy's father—he wants to tend to the boy's injuries himself and doesn't want him here."

Tom had never been one to stand by passively when something needed to be done, so he entered the fray without hesitation. One glance at the pallor of the boy's face and the blood-soaked rag wrapped around his arm convinced Tom that the hospital was the right place for him, and he stepped between the man carrying the boy and the boy's father.

"Mr. Goode, your son needs a doctor," Tom said.

"Nah, he dasn't," was the gruff reply. The man was short and wiry, with greasy-looking hair and a shabby coat. He smelled strongly of liquor, a smell that instantly curdled Tom's insides with bad memories.

"He does. Come with me," Tom said firmly, grasping the man's arm and hauling him none-too-gently away from his son and towards the front door.

Mr. Goode tried to resist at first, but he was no match for Tom. Hoping the cold air outside would knock some clarity into the man's head, Tom escorted him out, blocking the entrance to the hospital with his body. The inaptly named Mr. Goode let fly with a string of curses, the only effect of the blast of wintry air apparently being a loosening of his tongue. Tom withstood the barrage silently, waiting for him to finish.

"Who the bloody 'ell are you?" Mr. Goode demanded. "You got no right to throw me out of the 'ospital."

"I'm a clergyman."

The man regarded him with narrowed eyes. "You don't look like one." He was probably right, since Tom was still wearing Simon's clothes, which after the train ride to London were a little the worse for wear.

"I am one, nevertheless. What happened to your son?"

"Eh? The lad'll be fine. 'E's just clumsy, gets 'imself in the way of the machines at the factory all the time."

"Go home, Mr. Goode," Tom said. "Your son will be well cared for here."

The man protested, but Tom remained firm and repeated himself when necessary. When Tom decided not to budge, few people tried for long to budge him. He'd learned many years ago from his mentor, Osborne Jay, how to use his natural stubbornness and air of authority to gain the upper hand with unruly or violent people. Having an imposing physical presence didn't hurt, either.

When Mr. Goode finally walked away, Tom went back inside. Although he was tired, and his stomach was reminding him that he had missed his dinner, he wanted to know more about the boy and his condition. He found Jack in the crowded ward reserved for urgent cases, where the pungent odor of the room, a mixture of antiseptic and bodily fluids, assaulted Tom's nostrils. A nurse was in the process of bandaging the boy's right hand and arm, and the man who'd carried him into the hospital was looking on.

"How is he?" Tom asked.

The nurse glanced up from her work. "He'll live."

"What happened?"

"Caught his arm in one of the machines at the factory," said the man. "I say, mate, don't I know you from somewhere? My name's Bert Gunn."

Tom had been too concerned about the boy to pay much attention to the man, but now he turned to look at him, feeling a sliver of foreboding. Gunn was young, probably in his early twenties, as tall as Tom but so powerfully built that he appeared to have no neck. Tom didn't recognize him or his name.

"I don't think so," Tom said. He turned back to the boy, who was now awake, staring with unfocused eyes at the bandage being wound around his arm. Jack Goode had a thin face, a shock of thick, dark hair, and gold-flecked brown eyes. Unless he was unusually small for his age, there was no doubt Jack was too young to be working in a factory. Tom was also troubled by what looked like bruises on the boy's other arm.

Bert Gunn was still studying Tom too closely for his liking, so he decided to find out what the man knew about Jack. Tom gestured to a corner of the room where they could talk privately. Once they'd moved out of earshot of the boy, Tom asked him, "How long has Jack been working at the factory?"

"I'm fairly new, but others say he's been there at least a year. Bloody foreman has no heart, makes the lad work long hours."

"What do you know about his family?"

"You saw his da, loutish drunken bastard. Same old story: too many little ones, the da spends his wages on drink, so the kids are sent out to work."

"Jack can't be thirteen yet," Tom said.

"You won't hear him admit that, but if I had to guess, I'd say he's ten."

Tom knew that the law required child workers to be at least thirteen years of age. He started to turn away, intent on talking to Jack himself and avoiding the keen eyes of his interlocutor.

"Aha! I know where I've seen you," Bert Gunn exclaimed, loud enough for Tom to wince and turn back to him. "You were one of Nate Cowan's fighters."

A queasy feeling settled in Tom's stomach. "No," he said coldly. "I don't know anyone by that name."

"It was maybe four, five years ago. I was still a youngster, but I saw you flatten a bloke twice your size. 'The Dagger,' they called you—"

"As I said," Tom interrupted, losing his patience, "you're mistaken."

"Steady on, mate. I'm not going to fight you."

Tom's hands had curled into fists at his sides. Loosening them was as difficult as turning rusty gears.

"I'm going to check on Jack," he said in a calmer voice. "Thank you for bringing him in."

He waited, trying to decide what to do should Gunn prove persistent, but the other man simply nodded and left.

Tom took a deep breath and returned to Jack. The nurse had gone, and the boy looked very small and alone as he lay in the hospital bed.

"Jack, I'm a clergyman," Tom said. "Can you talk to me for a bit, or are you in too much pain?"

The look in the boy's eyes was guarded, but he answered politely enough, "I can talk, sir."

"Have you been injured before while you were working?"

The boy hesitated, then said, "Yes, sir. Just one or two times. It was my fault—everybody says I'm clumsy."

Tom frowned. "It's not easy working with those big machines when you're so small."

"It ain't so bad, sir. I don't mind the work."

"Where did you get these bruises? At work or at home?" Tom asked, reaching out to indicate the bruises on the boy's left arm. Although Tom hadn't touched him, Jack flinched. There was a brief flicker of fear in the boy's eyes, though it was quickly replaced by an impassive look. Tom's heart sank—it was as he had feared, and he knew at once the boy was being abused.

"I don't remember," Jack replied. "I'm always runnin' into things. Like I said, I'm clumsy."

"I'd like to help you," Tom said. "Do you know St. John's Cathedral? The big white church with the dome and the cross on top of it?"

The boy nodded.

"If you ever want to talk to someone or just go somewhere safe for a while, you can come to the cathedral and find me. I'm Canon Cross—will you remember?"

Jack nodded again, but his guarded look had returned, and Tom knew the boy wasn't likely to take him up on his offer.

There was nothing more Tom could do at the moment, so he left the hospital and made his way home, feeling exhausted. Too much had happened that day, and the conversation with Bert Gunn had been the last straw. He couldn't let himself think about it.

Fewer letters than he had expected awaited him at his lodgings. There were none from his friends, a group of men at his club who had been fellow students at Cambridge. They didn't seem to have noticed his long absence. There was one letter from the bishop, asking Tom to visit him at the palace as soon as possible—this he had expected. There were two letters from Julia, the first dated a fortnight earlier. She wanted to know why he had been absent from Sunday services at the cathedral. She ended the letter with, *You will, I know, not hesitate to reassure me if you are all right, despite the way we parted. Although I'd hardly call us friends, you can't expect me to be indifferent to you if you are in some sort of trouble.*

Julia's second letter, dated a week after the first, was shorter and importunate:

Dear Tom,

I am worried something has happened to you. I must speak with you on a matter of the utmost urgency. I don't care where we meet, but I must see you. Don't keep me waiting.

Julia

Tom couldn't help feeling a little pleased that Julia had missed him enough to write to him twice. He wasn't too concerned about the urgency upon which she had insisted. It was her wont to urge others to act hastily merely because she felt impatient. But another part of him wished she hadn't written.

Tom tossed the letters onto a side table and went into his bedroom. When he removed his clothes—or rather, Simon's clothes—he realized he was still wearing Miranda's gold cross around his neck. He left it on. It was a comforting reminder that he hadn't imagined his time in the country at the Thornes' cottage.

As he lay down in bed and curled his fingers around the cross, he remembered curling them into fists earlier that day. Then older memories surfaced, from a time when that motion was accompanied by a rush of energy that electrified his nerves. A time when he would fight any man who would take him on.

The next morning, Tom arrived at the bishop's palace precisely at nine o'clock, clothed in his customary black morning coat and clerical collar, feeling uneasy. He had decided to make a clean breast of things, at least as far as the attack and his subsequent recovery in the country was concerned.

Bishop Chisholm would have looked like a bishop even without his purple apron or other clerical accoutrements: he was a dignified, silver-haired, noble-looking man. When troubled or angry, he never looked stern, only sad, and he had the enviable ability to cause anyone he looked upon to quake, not with fear but with the sense of having disappointed someone who had his best interests at heart.

The bishop received Tom cordially and listened to his story without moving or interjecting. He looked sad as Tom spoke, and Tom accordingly felt himself quaking internally, as if he were responsible for his own injuries.

Tom ended his story by saying, "I beg your pardon for my long absence, my lord, but I hope you understand that the circumstances were beyond my control."

"I do understand, Canon Cross. I only wish you had provided these details in the letter you sent me while you were still recovering. I could have begun legal proceedings on your behalf."

"With all due respect, I don't wish to take legal action. I didn't see my attackers well enough to describe them, and since I don't know them, it would be a waste of the police's time to try to find out."

"You have no idea who might wish to hurt you?"

"No."

Yes. Charles Carrington. Or one of Nate Cowan's fighters. Tom clenched his teeth. Despite his best intentions, it seemed he couldn't talk to anyone for more than a quarter of an hour without lying.

"In the course of your work, especially with the Prison Commission, you naturally come into contact with people who have a rough way of life," Bishop Chisholm mused, "although perhaps the people who pose the greatest danger are the more powerful ones who are opposed to the reforms you are working for."

Most of the prison inmates tolerated Tom's visits and inquiries, and some even welcomed him once they'd learned to trust him a little. It was the others—the prison governors, the wardens, and employers like Narbridge who depended on the cheap labor of former inmates—who were Tom's real enemies. He'd considered the possibility that Narbridge was behind the attack on him, but the investigation Tom had begun into Narbridge's company had no discernible effect on the magnate's business. Besides, the investigation occurred three years ago: if Narbridge really wanted to hurt Tom, he would have done so then.

Tom nodded mutely, feeling he didn't deserve the kindness in the bishop's voice.

"Are you quite recovered now? Can you return to work?"

"Yes." Tom saw no reason to mention that his bad leg wasn't quite back to normal. He was perfectly capable of carrying out his usual duties. "I stopped at the hospital yesterday when I arrived in London. I haven't been to the prison yet, nor have I had a chance to speak with Canon Harris about the Temperance Society meetings. Is there anything pressing that you'd like me to take care of today before I do those things?"

"Canon Harris is away from the cathedral today, so if you can spend a few hours there overseeing the usual Advent chaos, I'd appreciate that. None of the other clergy can organize people as well as you can."

"Of course. I'll go at once."

"Don't overdo it, though, son. You probably still need more rest than you think you do."

The bishop had never called Tom "son" before. It threw him off-balance, and he struggled to suppress his emotion.

As Tom rose to leave, he offered to write to Dr. Mason for further corroboration of his injuries, but the bishop waved him off.

"There's no need for that. I am satisfied with the documents I've already received from your attending doctor and with the information you've given me. If you were given to mysterious absences or irresponsible behavior, it would be different. However, you are as reliable as clockwork and the hardest-working member of the cathedral clergy, as well as a model leader. I have no reason to question your report of what happened, and I am only sorry you don't wish to pursue the matter legally. If you remember anything about your attackers or change your mind about taking legal action, let me know."

Tom nodded. This time tears actually did come to his eyes, so he took his leave hastily. He chose to walk the half mile or so to the cathedral from the bishop's palace in order to calm himself enough to begin his duties for the day. While he knew he was a hard worker and a good leader, he felt the bishop's praise was undeserved—and he hated this new weakness.

It seemed as if some unpleasant emotion was always threatening to burst out of him. It felt dangerous, uncontrollable.

He was a little calmer by the time he arrived at the cathedral, and the cathedral staff was clearly relieved to see him. He spent the rest of the morning sorting out the various problems they brought to his attention: a disagreement among members of the altar guild regarding the proper way to clean the sacred vessels, a misunderstanding between two of the other canons regarding who would be preaching the next Sunday, and a flat-out refusal from the organist to play a well-known Advent hymn required by the precentor. In all but the last situation, Tom solved the problems by listening and pointing out the most logical solutions. In the case of the Advent hymn, he used a mild threat, telling the organist, "The congregation has heard this hymn every Advent for at least fifty years. If you don't play it, it will be your job to answer the many letters of complaint we'll receive when the season is over." This was enough to change the organist's mind.

Later that afternoon, Tom left the cathedral to meet Julia. He'd sent her a brief letter first thing that morning to inform her of the time and place. Choosing the location had been difficult. He had resolved never to return to her house, and she certainly couldn't come to his lodgings or see him privately at the cathedral. The only option that seemed safe and private enough was to talk with her in a cab. He had asked her to take a cab to a quiet street in Camden that he chose mainly because it was far from both of their neighborhoods.

When Tom reached the location he had specified, he was ten minutes late, but the cab was there, the drawn curtains making it look more conspicuous than he'd hoped. There was also a man across the street watching the cab: something about his posture looked familiar. It wasn't clear if the man was waiting for someone and his gaze happened to rest on the cab, or he was watching it on purpose, but Tom was suspicious.

He stepped back, behind a tree, and waited another few minutes until the man walked away.

The cabdriver opened the door as Tom approached, and a moment later he was alone with Julia inside the dim, confined space. It was the first time Tom had been inside a cab since the night he was attacked, and he felt additional anxiety on that account. He issued a curt order to head north to the cabdriver through the trapdoor in the roof, and they set off.

Julia neither moved nor spoke until he gave her his full attention. She was wearing a black cloak lined with white fur and a matching fur hat set perkily at the back of her head. Julia eschewed the current fashion that called for large hats, presumably because they would hide her flawless skin and hair. Even in the dim light, her beauty stunned him, and he stared at her in silent admiration, amazed that such a woman had been his, if only for a short time.

"This is a strange place to meet, Tom, even for you," she said, her light tone at odds with the serious expression on her face. "I feel like Madame Bovary."

"It was the only way we could speak privately that I could think of."

"Where have you been?" she said, her voice low, but urgent. "Why didn't you answer my letters sooner?"

"It's a long story. The short version is that I was attacked and left for dead in the countryside. Some kind strangers found me and took me in while I recovered. I returned to London only yesterday."

"Dear God!" Julia caught his hands in hers and looked wildly into his face. "Are you all right now? Oh, Tom, if I had known . . . I could have come to you and cared for you myself."

"You know that would have been impossible," he said.

Her tender concern for him was harder to resist than the touch of her hands and her proximity. He hadn't expected to have to steel himself against her after everything that had happened between them.

"Do you know who attacked you?" she asked.

"No, though I have my suspicions. Your husband, for instance. Is there any possibility he's found out about our relationship?"

She stared at him. "You think Charles attacked you?"

"Of course not, but he may have paid others to do it."

"I don't think he knows. But if he does, I suppose he could hide his knowledge from me if he wished to. We have very little to do with each other anymore."

"You mentioned in your last letter that you had an urgent matter to discuss with me. What is it?"

Julia's manner changed. She looked down at their clasped hands and took a deep breath before saying, "I'm pregnant."

He stared at her, stunned. Even as he formed his question, he knew what the answer would be: "What does this have to do with me?"

"You're the father." She raised her head to meet his eyes.

"Are you certain?"

"Of course," she said sharply, releasing his hands. "Who else could it be?"

Tom didn't speak the name of Julia's husband, but it hung between them in the silence.

"I haven't let Charles touch me since you and I have been together," she added.

"Bloody hell!" he exclaimed, in a flash of white-hot rage. If Charles found out about Julia's relationship with Tom, it would mean the end of Tom's career. The deanship would never be his, and he would be defrocked.

Her eyes widened. He had never cursed in front of her—indeed, he didn't remember the last time he had cursed in front of anyone.

The cab came to a halt, forcing Tom to think more clearly and control his anger. He opened the trapdoor and ordered the driver to keep moving.

"Where to, sir?" was the response.

"Keep heading north. I'll tell you when to stop."

Tom sat back and sighed as the cab began to move again. "I don't understand how this happened."

"I believe it happened in the usual way," she said, a hard edge to her voice.

"You know what I mean. We were being careful."

"I don't see what good it will do to talk about how it happened. Instead, we must think of what to do now."

"Could you go away for a while? Tell Charles you need a long holiday and visit your sister in Italy."

"I'd need to go away for seven months. Charles would never agree to a holiday as long as that without him." She pulled the edges of her cloak more closely around herself.

"You could suggest it anyway. Perhaps he'll surprise you."

"It won't work." She stared straight ahead.

He tightened his grasp on his walking stick. "Julia, our relationship can't become known publicly. I'd lose everything I've worked so hard for."

"Yes, I know. It doesn't seem to have occurred to you that I'd lose my reputation as well. Not to mention the damage it would do to my children. You'd probably be relieved if I threw myself into the Thames like some poor unfortunate."

"Don't be ridiculous. We'll just have to think of a solution."

She looked down at her lap and smoothed her skirt. In a low voice she said, "I know of a doctor I could see."

Tom had always felt pity for the women who took such drastic measures and hated the men who drove them to it by failing to own up to their responsibilities. Yet here he was, feeling a sense of relief—and despising himself for it.

"Is this doctor reputable?" he asked. "So many who . . . do what you are suggesting have dangerous and . . . unhygienic practices."

"I believe he's one of the best. Would you like me to see him?" She looked at him. He expected to see a mocking look in her eyes. She knew what a hypocrite he was, and she was in a position to twist the dagger. But she merely looked lost and unhappy.

He couldn't answer her question. In fact, he couldn't speak at all. Instead, he took her hand and squeezed it, wanting to give her some comfort but feeling maddeningly helpless.

After a few minutes, Julia bit her lip and looked away, pulling her hand out of Tom's grasp. "I didn't know it was possible until now to love and hate the same person with equal intensity," she said bitterly.

Tom understood how she could hate him. The love was far less comprehensible. The close, dark interior of the cab was beginning to feel like a coffin. He rapped the ceiling with his walking stick. The vehicle stopped, and without another word to Julia, Tom paid the driver and got out. Not knowing or caring where he was, he walked away without looking back.

9

Young men in such matters [of love] are so often without any fixed
thoughts! They are such absolute moths. They amuse themselves
with the light of the beautiful candle, fluttering about, on and off,
in and out of the flame with dazzled eyes, till in a rash moment
they rush in too near the wick, and then fall with singed wings
and crippled legs, burnt up and reduced to tinder by
the consuming fire of matrimony.

—Anthony Trollope, *Framley Parsonage*

LONDON: FEBRUARY 1908

The fish fork was the last straw. Specifically, the ivory-handled fish
fork. Miranda had been patient—excruciatingly patient—during the
long hours of shopping with Simon and Gwen, but even a saint would
have screamed in frustration after being forced to weigh the merits and
demerits of what seemed like hundreds of fish forks: silver fish forks, bone-
handled fish forks, ceramic-handled fish forks, fish forks with pierced
designs, fish forks with shell motifs, fish forks with beaded borders. Gwen
had exclaimed delightedly over almost every fork she saw, and when she
insisted that Miranda look at the ivory-handled one, it was one fish fork
too many.

"What do you think, Miranda? Would it match our dishes?" Gwen asked.

Miranda took a deep breath, walked over to the counter where the beaming shopkeeper stood holding the offending item, and forced herself to look at it.

Without waiting for Miranda's answer, Gwen turned to the shopkeeper and asked, "Could we have it monogrammed?"

All Miranda could think was how pleasant it would be to take the fish fork and stab Gwen, then herself, with it. MURDER-SUICIDE BY FISH FORK, the next day's headline in the *Times* would scream. Simon's life would be spared. As cloying as his starry-eyed devotion to his fiancée had become, he deserved to be happy, and Miranda hadn't the heart to do away with him, even in her imagination.

Gwen and Simon had become engaged shortly after he accepted a post as a law clerk at the firm of Keating and Merryman in London. Keating was an old friend of Gwen's father and had mentioned Simon's name when the post became vacant. Simon had known that moving to London would be difficult for Miranda, but she had assured him she would become accustomed to city life. His protectiveness had eased a little now that he had new people and events in his life to engage his attention, but at times he still treated her as if she were wrapped in cotton wool. Despite Simon's doubts, his passion for Gwen had prevailed, and he'd assured Miranda they'd be safer and more anonymous in the city than they'd been in the country. Miranda didn't protest. It was time to stop hiding and try to live a normal life.

Everything happened very quickly after Simon's trip to London for the successful interview and his equally successful proposal to Gwen. He'd hinted to Miranda that Tom's advice about women had helped him win Gwen's heart. Despite her curiosity about what that advice might be, Miranda had spent the past two months trying to put Tom out of her mind, so she thought it best not to ask.

The wedding was only a week away, and this interminable shopping trip was one of the flurry of pre-wedding activities in which she was inevitably included. Miranda had kept her mixed feelings about the marriage to herself, but she wasn't convinced that flighty, self-centered Gwen would be a good wife to Simon. On the other hand, if Gwen was willing to marry a poor day-laborer-turned-law clerk, she must have cared for him. The trouble was, judging from the purchases she had made that day alone, Gwen seemed to think she was marrying a member of the nobility. Simon was too much in love to even notice what she was spending, and the efforts Miranda had made to draw Gwen's attention to modestly priced items had met with no success.

Miranda couldn't remain in the shop a moment longer. She took another deep breath, looked up at Gwen and Simon, and said, "It's a lovely fork. I'm going to go for a walk. Why don't we meet at St. James's Park in an hour and a half?"

Simon looked worried. "Are you all right, Mouse?"

"Yes. I'd just like some air."

"We'll come with you," he said.

"But, Simon, we have ever so many more shops to visit this afternoon," protested Gwen. "We don't have time to take a walk."

Simon looked from his sister to his fiancée. Then, with a beleaguered expression, he agreed to continue shopping, as Miranda knew he would.

"Do you really want to go alone? You won't get lost?" he asked before Gwen could draw his attention back to the fish forks.

"I'll be fine," Miranda assured him. She only barely restrained herself from adding that nothing would please her more than to get lost alone in London.

As soon as she had made her escape, Miranda's homicidal urges abated slightly. She had tried to explain to Gwen and Simon that they needn't include her on this shopping trip, but neither had listened. Gwen insisted she needed Miranda's help and that no woman of her acquaintance would miss the opportunity of spending an afternoon at the London shops. Simon had said it would be good for her to leave the house for a change and see the city. It was no use telling them that she hated shopping, or that she would be happy to see London as long as she wasn't forced to see its shops. It pleased them that she should accompany them, so she had.

It was a frigid winter day, and she walked quickly to stay warm, trying to avoid the main roads where the noise and fumes of motorcars were the worst. She knew nobody wealthy enough to own a motorcar and had never been inside one, nor did she have the desire to be. But even on the side streets in the city there was far more noise and many more people than she was used to. The world in her head was noisy enough, clamoring for her attention, so to have the external world doing the same was inexpressibly fatiguing.

All she needed now was a little peace and quiet to restore herself. A sanctuary, though where she might find one, she didn't know. She headed towards St. James's Park, then, worried that Simon and Gwen might meet her there before the appointed time and rob her of her coveted solitude, she stopped and looked around. Suddenly, the answer was right in front of her—only a short distance away stood St. John's Cathedral, the cross above the great dome like a beacon to show her the way to the peace she sought.

When Miranda entered the cathedral, she paused for a moment to let her eyes adjust to the dim light. Then she slipped noiselessly past the verger, who was deep in conversation with another cathedral worker. Moving away from a group of American tourists who were speaking far too loudly for a place of worship, she kept walking until she found a quiet spot at the side of the nave. She gazed admiringly at the vaulted ceiling, the marble columns at each side of the nave, the intricately carved pulpit, and, from afar, the rich crimson and brass of the chancel. She'd never been inside the cathedral before, having only passed by on her few previous trips to London, and its grandeur and beauty took her breath away.

Her artist's eye was particularly drawn to the stained glass window closest to where she stood. It was a medieval depiction of the Annunciation, with a green-robed Gabriel pointing to the Virgin Mary, whose long dark hair cascaded over her blue robe. Mary's face was fascinating—not as serene as she was usually depicted, but with a mixture of astonishment, fear, and hope. It was an amazing accomplishment for an artist to render such subtle emotions in stained glass. As Miranda continued to gaze at the window, she felt a deeper longing for quiet both within and without, and she slipped into the nearest pew and knelt to pray.

She didn't know how long she remained there. She lost track of time in the quiet joy of knowing she was exactly where she needed to be. Although her surroundings were new to her, the experience was thrillingly familiar. For the past couple of years, she had starved herself of all the beauty and ritual of her faith, but this was a feast she wouldn't deny herself. After a long, delicious silence had settled on her, making her forget all the frustration she had felt in the shops, she opened her eyes and rose to her feet, ready to face Simon and Gwen again.

As she made her way back towards the narthex on her way out of the cathedral, she was dimly aware of a man walking towards her. Then he stopped in front of her and spoke her name. Surprised, she looked up.

It was Tom, and he was wearing a clerical collar. The shock rendered her speechless.

She remembered Simon telling her that he thought Tom was an atheist. And Tom saying, "Religious leaders can be the very devil," when she and Simon told him about their experiences with the vicar in Smythe. And then there was his shocked reaction when she asked if she could pray for him after his nightmare.

"I'm glad to see you," Tom said. "What are you doing here?" Although he did look pleased, he seemed—understandably—quite uncomfortable as well.

"I've been at the shops with Simon and Gwen."

"Ah, yes. Their wedding is next week, isn't it? Simon sent me an invitation."

She knew that Simon and Tom had exchanged a few letters, but she hadn't written to Tom herself. She'd been disappointed by his first letter, which contained a brief expression of gratitude to her and Simon for their care of him and a fifty-pound note to repay them for that care. It might have been a business letter for all the warmth or personal detail it contained.

Miranda had no patience for small talk, especially when more important matters needed clarification. "Why didn't you tell us you're a clergyman?"

He looked away, a slight flush discernable beneath his olive skin. "I don't know," he replied. "I suppose it was partly what you told me about what happened to you in the past. I thought you'd hate all clergymen after that."

It wasn't a convincing explanation. He knew she and Simon still went to church and had nothing against clergymen in general.

"I suppose your name isn't Tom Jones, either," she pressed.

"No. People here know me as Thomas Cross. I'm a canon."

"I ought to address you as Canon Cross, then."

"Only in public. I'd still like you to call me Tom."

Miranda couldn't resist. "So this is your secret? You're not a criminal but a clergyman?"

"Yes. No." Now he looked very uncomfortable. "It was never a secret, just an omission on my part." He met her eyes. "I'm sorry, Miranda. I ought to have told you."

He looked haggard, as though he hadn't slept in days, and she felt sorry for him. Something was clearly troubling him.

After a pause, Tom asked, "Did Simon tell you what I wrote about Isabella Grant, the artist, in my last letter to him?"

"No." Miranda hadn't read the letter, but she knew of Mrs. Grant. Her paintings had been exhibited at the Royal Academy, and King Edward himself had commissioned one.

"She's one of my parishioners," he said. "If you're interested, I could introduce you. I believe she's taking pupils."

"I should like very much to meet her," Miranda said gravely. It was true, but there was no way she could afford to pay for art lessons, especially from such a prestigious artist.

The cathedral clock chimed the hour, and Tom said, "I must go. I have an appointment. But I'll see you at the wedding next week."

She nodded and turned to leave.

"Miranda."

"Yes?" She turned back to face him, startled all over again by the sight of his clerical collar. It was difficult to reconcile the injured man she'd cared for in Surrey with this London priest.

"Why didn't you write to me?"

"We did."

"Simon did. Why didn't *you* write?"

"I wasn't doing anything interesting. I had nothing to report."

"You could have told me your thoughts. Your feelings."

"Did you write to me about *your* thoughts and feelings?"

"Touché." He smiled, but the smile didn't quite reach his eyes. "I'm a terrible correspondent, anyway. I'm glad you're in London now so we can see each other in person."

She murmured a vague assent, then left.

She hardly noticed her surroundings as she walked to St. James's Park, deeply unsettled by her interaction with Tom. It wasn't just seeing him in the cathedral wearing priestly garb. She sensed something was wrong with him, and it was not likely to be as easily fixed as his broken leg and bruised body had been. She wished he would allow himself to be known, though there seemed to be little hope of that if he'd found it necessary to lie to her and Simon about things as simple as his name and his profession, both of which were perfectly respectable.

Later that evening, when Miranda was alone with Simon at their cottage in Surrey—a home that would be theirs for only one more week—she told him about her encounter with Tom at the cathedral.

"Did he mention being a clergyman in any of his letters to you?" Miranda asked Simon.

"No, never. What a strange fellow! I don't understand him."

"Nor do I. He seemed unhappy and very tired."

"Poor Tom. He's certainly done everything he can to repay us for taking care of him."

"He's done too much. It's as if he can't bear to be in any sort of debt to anyone. Simon, why didn't you tell me about Isabella Grant?"

"What? Oh, yes, Tom did mention her in a letter. I must have forgotten."

"I'd like to meet her," she said, quick to add, "not that I'll necessarily take lessons from her."

"Why not? Don't you want to?"

Miranda hesitated. "They'd be expensive."

"That's no trouble. I'm sure we could find the money to pay for them."

"I don't want you to do that, not with all the expenses of moving to London and setting up house there. I'm worried you'll go into debt as it is." It was the closest she had come to expressing her concerns about Gwen and Simon's excessive spending.

"There's no need to worry about that. I'll work longer hours at Keating and Merryman, if necessary. Gwen is coming down in the world by marrying me, and I don't want it to be too much of a shock for her. She's trying to be reasonable about money."

Miranda didn't see any attempt at reasonableness on Gwen's part, but she didn't want to argue with Simon on this point, so she kept silent.

Simon and Miranda were hiding behind a tree in the graveyard at the Church of St. Eustace the Martyr. Simon and Gwen's wedding was scheduled to begin in half an hour, and the church was already filled with Gwen's very large, very noisy family. It had been Miranda's idea to go outside, if not exactly to hide, then to encourage Simon to breathe. He'd been looking increasingly pale during the bustle of activity and conversations in the church, and since his groomsmen, Gwen's two brothers, didn't seem to notice his discomfort, Miranda took it upon herself to rescue him.

"Do you feel better now?" she asked, examining his face. He still looked a bit peaky.

"I don't know. I need a cigarette." He fished around in his pockets. "Where's my cigarette case? And my matches?"

"Here." She took the items from her handbag and handed them to him. He'd forgotten that he gave the contents of his pockets to her when they were at home that morning.

"Bless you, Mouse." He lit the cigarette and put it to his lips, inhaling deeply. "I don't know if this is a good idea."

"What? Smoking?"

"No. Getting married."

Miranda raised her face to the sky, closing her eyes. It was a mild day for February, and the sun was shining. She needed the peace and quiet of the graveyard as much as Simon did. Gwen was the youngest of seven siblings, and the others were already married with children of their own. Just before Miranda and Simon had made their escape, Gwen's siblings were arguing about the way the wedding ought to be conducted in the very presence of the officiating clergyman, a bespectacled, impossibly young man with shaky hands. Gwen's nephews were adding to the chaos by running up and down the aisles and shouting at the top of their lungs.

"Shall we run away?" Miranda asked, her eyes still closed.

"What? Now?"

She opened her eyes and smiled at Simon's shocked expression. "We could, you know. If you really don't want to go through with this."

"Gwen would sue me for breach of contract."

She raised her eyebrows. "Is that all that's stopping you from calling off the wedding?"

"No, of course not. I love Gwen." He contemplated his cigarette. "It's just a terrifying thing. Marriage. Not for the faint of heart."

"No doubt you're right." She reached up to straighten his white cravat. "But think of all the people who marry and live to tell about it. You will, too."

"Perhaps." He managed a weak smile. "After all, the inscriptions on these gravestones mention nothing about marriage as the person's manner of death."

"Exactly." She pointed to the nearest one. "*William Gresham, beloved husband*, lived to be ninety, and no doubt he was married for most of those years. Take comfort from that. Shall we go back inside?"

He nodded, flicking what was left of his cigarette to the ground and crushing it with his shoe. Simon looked handsome in his black frock coat and blue silk waistcoat, and Miranda felt a pang of sadness that their parents couldn't be here to see his wedding. No matter how many years went by, that sadness never entirely went away.

They returned to the church, only to find that the noise and chaos hadn't abated. If anything, it was worse. Gwen's little nephews were still shouting and running around the church, two of Gwen's sisters were arguing loudly near the altar rail about whether the wedding breakfast should have been before or after the ceremony, and the young clergyman's face was even paler than Simon's as he stood near the vestry door, listening to a diatribe from a wildly gesticulating groomsman.

Before Simon or Miranda could do more than stare at the unfortunate scene, Rose, Gwen's eldest sister, hurried over to them.

"There you are, Simon!" she exclaimed. "Do come with me, will you? Gwen's in the vicar's office in a hysterical fit. We need your help to calm her down."

Simon hesitated.

Miranda asked, "What's the matter? May I help?"

Rose rolled her eyes. "Oh, she's just upset about her hair. She doesn't like the way the hairdresser arranged it, but I see nothing wrong with it. All she needs is for Simon to tell her she looks beautiful. She'll be fine."

Simon, looking like a soldier mustering up the courage for battle, turned to go with Rose.

"Oh, there *is* something you can do," Rose said over her shoulder to Miranda. "John seems to have his hands full—there's some problem with the ring—so the children need to be watched."

"Yes, of course." The children needed more than watching, given what Miranda had already witnessed. The only trouble was that she couldn't remember which of the children were Rose and John's. She'd met Gwen's siblings and their families a few times, but they'd always been together in a large group, so she hadn't been able to tell which children belonged to which couple.

Miranda took a deep breath and decided she'd better find out about the ring first, as that problem seemed more important than childcare. But before she could start down the aisle towards the front of the church, a boy of about eight in a naval style hat careened past her, nearly knocking over an elderly woman on her way to a pew. As Miranda sprang to the woman's rescue, she saw Tom striding towards them just in time to catch the boy and haul him up by the armpits so he could look him in the eye.

"Ahoy, captain!" Tom said to the startled child. "That's no way to behave in a church."

"I'm not a captain," the boy said.

"Just a common sailor, then?"

"No. Wait. A captain."

"A captain needs to set a good example for the other seamen. No running or shouting in church. Do you understand?"

"Yes . . ." The boy glanced at Tom's clerical collar and added, "Reverend."

"Apologize to the lady, then. You nearly knocked her down."

The captain did as Tom bid him, and the elderly woman grudgingly accepted the apology.

"Stay with me," Tom ordered as the boy started to wander away. The boy stopped immediately—and wisely, Miranda thought, given Tom's uncompromising tone.

"I'm sorry I'm late," Tom said to Miranda. "Why hasn't the ceremony started yet?"

"It's a disaster," she said shakily. "There's some problem with the ring, Gwen is crying in the vicar's office, and the children . . . well, you can see for yourself." She gestured to the middle aisle, where two other boys had collided with each other. The bigger one stood over the wailing smaller one as if contemplating murder, as the congregation looked on. Miranda was certain that the parents of these children must be nearby, but if so, they were not stepping in to help.

Tom scanned the chaotic scene for a few seconds. Then, in a calm, determined voice, he said, "Don't worry. If you can look after the little boy who fell, and the girl by that pillar who looks as though she's about to cry, I'll take care of everything else."

"Thank you," she said, so relieved that she was near tears herself.

Tom strode down the aisle with the captain at his side, crouched down so he was at eye level with the older boy who had murder in his eyes, and spoke to him. The boy paused, nodded, and continued down the aisle with Tom and the other boy. They made their way to the front of the church, where the groomsman was still in conversation with the vicar, gesturing frantically.

Miranda went to the smaller boy and picked him up. He was only a toddler, and his sobs subsided as she held him close and spoke soothingly. Then she turned to the little girl who stood in the shadows by the pillar. Miranda hadn't seen her, and was surprised Tom had noticed not only her presence but also her emotional state. It was Amy, her favorite of Gwen's nieces, a dreamy, quiet girl with black ringlets. Her lower lip was quivering.

"Amy," Miranda whispered, bending down awkwardly because of the weight of the boy in her arms. "Would you like to sit with me? I have a pretty handkerchief for you."

"Yes," the girl said, and followed Miranda to a pew near the back of the sanctuary. Once settled there with the toddler on her lap and Amy close beside her, examining the lace-trimmed handkerchief, Miranda sighed and again turned her attention to the front of the church.

The captain was leading three other children to a pew with an air of authority. The murderous boy was nowhere to be seen. Tom was speaking to the vicar and the groomsman, the former looking relieved, the latter looking cowed. Gwen's two sisters, who had been arguing vociferously, were now sitting at opposite sides of the sanctuary.

Even though Miranda couldn't hear what he was saying, everything about Tom's bearing and gestures showed that he was in complete command of the situation. He guided the groomsmen to their places, helped the vicar find the correct page in his prayer book, and went to the vicar's office to fetch Simon and bring him to the front of the church. She was still worried about Simon's nerves, but Miranda couldn't stop watching Tom. It was as if he were conducting a symphony, though one made up of people instead of musical instruments.

When the ceremony finally started, Tom came to sit beside Miranda and her charges.

"Is he too heavy for you?" he whispered, indicating the boy now asleep in her arms. "I can take him."

"No. I'm fine." Her arms tightened involuntarily around the child. His head was indeed heavy against her breast, and one of his shoes was digging into her side, but it was a pain she welcomed, a pain that filled her with bittersweet memories.

When the ceremony finally started, all went smoothly, which couldn't help but surprise Miranda. Simon didn't faint or run away, and Gwen's hair was a perfect cascade of dark curls underneath her lacy veil. The ring was produced at the right moment and placed on Gwen's finger. The vows were spoken in strong, clear voices.

The boy in the naval hat wandered to the back of the church and asked Tom if he could sit with them.

"Of course. You've taught your men very well, Captain. I'm going to promote you to admiral, if that's acceptable to you."

"Yes, sir." The boy squeezed in beside Tom, who shifted closer to Miranda to make room. She could feel the warmth of his arm against hers through the sleeve of his coat. There was enough room in the pew for her to move away from him, but she didn't. The toddler was asleep in her arms and she didn't want to disturb him; Amy was leaning contentedly against her other shoulder. Most powerful of all, though perhaps not as good a reason, was her desire to be as close as Tom as possible.

When the ceremony was over, Simon and Gwen marched back down the aisle to the front foyer and were immediately mobbed by well-wishers. Nobody seemed to notice Tom, Miranda, and the three children in the shadows of the back pew. Miranda was glad of it. Amy seemed to have fallen asleep against her shoulder, and the newly promoted admiral had done the same on Tom's other side, so they were well and truly hemmed in.

"How did you do it?" Miranda whispered to Tom.

"Do what?"

"You solved all the problems in a matter of minutes. You calmed everyone down and made them do what they were supposed to."

He smiled. "You forget I'm a clergyman. I'm used to the madness that goes along with weddings."

"*This* much madness?"

"Well," he admitted, "this was more than usual. But the children just needed to use their energy for good instead of evil. The groomsman had merely forgotten which pocket he'd put the ring in. And it was the first wedding the officiant had conducted, so he just needed some guidance."

"And Gwen's horrible sisters? What did you do with them?"

"Some people need to stay away from each other. I gave them a strongly worded suggestion to sit at opposite sides of the sanctuary."

"Thank you." She looked up at him, risking the possibility that he'd see more than just admiration in her eyes.

"You're welcome," he said. "I like solving problems. The most important thing is that Simon and Gwen are married and nobody has been seriously injured in the process."

"Yes. And Gwen's hair looked perfect to me, even though she was upset about something the hairdresser had done to it. She looks beautiful." Miranda glanced at her new sister-in-law through the crowd of people in the front foyer.

"So do you," Tom said.

Miranda glanced at him in confusion. He was definitely looking at her, not Gwen, and his eyes were warm. "I've never seen you wearing anything but black or gray."

Not knowing how to respond, she looked down at her rose-pink silk dress. It was relatively plain for wedding attire, but it did have lace trim and a velvet sash. "Gwen forbade me to wear black. She said she didn't want anyone to mistake her wedding for a funeral."

"That seems like a reasonable request from her perspective. I thought you'd be in the wedding party."

"No, Gwen has so many sisters there wasn't room for me. I don't mind." She lowered her head to breathe in the warm, sweet scent of the sleeping child.

Their conversation was interrupted by the vicar, who approached them and said to Tom, "Sir, you didn't tell me your name. I'd like to thank you properly for your help. I'm glad you brought your wife, too. What a lovely family."

Miranda was in an agony of embarrassment. She didn't dare look at Tom. Of course they must look like a perfect family tableau, the parents sitting close together with the two older children leaning against their shoulders and the youngest one asleep in the mother's arms.

Tom and Miranda spoke at the same time.

"No, they're not—"

"He isn't—"

Rose saved them by swooping in to fetch her children. It turned out that the admiral and Amy were hers, but the little one in Miranda's arms belonged to another sister. In the ensuing confusion and bustle of people collecting their children and the vicar apologizing for his mistake and thanking Tom profusely for his help, Miranda slipped away.

She went into the graveyard again and stood by the same tree where she and Simon had hidden before the ceremony. There was a chill in the air, and the sun had gone into hiding. Her arms and back ached from having held the little boy for so long. She realized that she didn't even know his name. She stared at the inscriptions on the gravestones. Near "William Gresham, beloved husband" was "Sarah Stott, safe in the arms of Christ" and "Our Darling Jane, gone too soon," whose dates indicated she had died at the age of four.

She felt guilty. She had no right to be shocked by the vicar's assumption when she wanted so badly for it to be true. Not for Tom to be her husband or for those particular children to be hers, but for everything they represented. All she had ever wanted, even as a child, was to have a family of her own. She had grown up dreaming of a loving husband and five or six adorable children. Even when she was old enough to laugh at herself for imagining that perfect family, she still wanted it.

She was glad her younger self couldn't have guessed how her dreams would be crushed later. Richard had destroyed that innocent girl. And then there was Sam, who made up for everything she'd lost, but he had been taken from her, too. After the operation, she'd still held on to her desire for a family, despite what the doctor told her. She remembered very little of the immediate aftermath of Sam's birth, only that she seemed to be drowning in a sea of blood. Later, the doctor used clinical words to explain what had gone wrong, words that masked the fact that her life was changed forever. *Postpartum hemorrhage. Hysterectomy.* "You nearly died," he'd added. "You ought to be grateful." She hadn't been grateful then, and she wasn't grateful now.

She hoped Tom hadn't sensed what she was feeling. She could tell from watching him at the wedding that he'd be a good father: he'd treated Gwen's wild little nephews with exactly the right balance of warmth and firmness.

Whatever had happened with his own father, he was naturally good with children.

"You idiot," she said aloud. It didn't matter what sort of father Tom would be if or when he married. It had nothing to do with her. She would never have what she wanted most, and she ought to have learned by now that the pain of forcing herself back to reality wasn't worth the few minutes of joy she received from her fantasies.

She made herself return to the church with a smile on her face to congratulate the happy couple.

10

After all, what would life be without fighting, I should like to
know? From the cradle to the grave, fighting, rightly understood,
is the business, the real, highest, honestest business of every son of
man. Every one who is worth his salt has his enemies, who must
be beaten, be they evil thoughts and habits in himself or spiritual
wickednesses in high places, or Russians, or Border-ruffians,
or Bill, Tom, or Harry, who will not let him live his life in
quiet till he has thrashed them.

—Thomas Hughes, *Tom Brown's School Days*

If that isn't the finest cigar you've ever had, I'll eat my hat!" exclaimed
Alastair Bourne.

"It's very good," Tom said, smiling at his friend's exuberance.

"The finest. Admit it, Cross," Alastair insisted.

"Very well, then, the finest, but I'm only saying so because I'd hate to see
a good hat go to waste."

Alastair made a grimace that may have been meant as a smile and leaned
back in his chair to savor his cigar. He was an aristocrat with mild blue
eyes and fair hair that was thinning on top despite his mere thirty years.
The two men had been part of a group of friends at Cambridge who still
kept in touch with one another, though their career paths had diverged

substantially. Bourne dabbled in politics, but his true passions were hunting, gambling, and smoking cigars, not always in that order.

Tom and Alastair were in the smoking room at the Athenaeum, Alastair's club. Alastair had insisted that Tom be his guest that afternoon. Tom would rather have met elsewhere because the Athenaeum was also Charles Carrington's club and Tom, naturally, preferred to avoid places where Julia's husband might be. The smoking room was an oasis of masculine privilege, with its mahogany tables and chocolate-brown leather chairs, the leather as soft and supple as a woman's body. "Nearly all the pleasures of feminine company with none of the annoyances," Alastair often proclaimed. It was difficult not to succumb to the sensuous pleasures of taste and touch offered by this room, but Tom had too many things on his mind to be swayed by them today.

Alastair set down the stub of his cigar on the nearest ashtray and sighed. "That was my last 'Romeo y Julietta.' I've had my valet order more, but the shipment's been delayed for some unknown reason. I'll have to bear the loss bravely, don't you think? I say, Cross, you look like the dog's breakfast. What's the matter?"

"It's nothing," Tom lied. "I've had some trouble sleeping lately, that's all."

"Working too hard, as usual, I assume."

"No, I don't think so."

"Nevertheless, you ought to step back from time to time and let others do some of the work. You can't reform the whole world single-handedly. Besides, it's been months since you've spent an evening with your old chums—why do you think we didn't even notice you were away for so long?"

"I know. But the old dean isn't expected to live much longer, and I need to impress the bishop if I want the deanship. That means more work."

"You've already impressed him, haven't you? And look at your competition. That pretentious Paul Harris doesn't have a chance. He's too young, not to mention too out of touch with reality, to be a threat."

"I don't know about that," Tom said grimly.

"Well, you'd best enjoy that cigar, as it's the only pleasure you seem to allow yourself. You know, sometimes I forget you're Anglican, with your determination to abstain from everything enjoyable in life, from liquor to gambling to women. You're not turning Methodist on me, are you, old man?"

Tom merely raised his eyebrows and smiled. He was used to his friend's raillery.

After a brief silence, during which both men contemplated their cigars, Alastair said, "Do you know anything about an illegal pugilism club that uses an abandoned factory in the East End?"

"No," Tom said, too quickly. "Why do you ask?"

"My valet, Henry, has gotten himself into some sort of trouble with this club. He admitted to placing bets on the fighters, but he's denied doing any of the fighting himself. I don't know if I believe him, since he's had some suspicious injuries in the past few weeks. He's tried to hide them, of course, but it's not easy to hide black eyes and bruises on the face."

"Why would I know anything about it?"

"Because of your work with inmates at the prison. Most of the lads involved in the club have been locked up at one time or another, if what Henry says is true."

"There are probably several illegal clubs of that sort in the East End," Tom said.

"Well, it's no matter. I just thought if you knew where the club might be, I could find out if Henry is lying to me or not. He's a good valet, so I'd hate to see him get mixed up with these toughs or even get himself killed."

"I'll keep my ears open the next time I visit the prison," Tom said. "If I hear anything useful, I'll tell you."

"Thank you."

"I ought to go," Tom said, shifting in his chair and eyeing the door.

"Already? You haven't even finished your cigar. Stay a little longer, for God's sake—er, sorry—and tell me what you've been doing lately. Working for the Society for the Prevention of Cruelty to Persons of Diminutive Size? For the Betterment of Badgers? Against the Adulteration of Adulterers?" Alastair laughed heartily at his own joke.

Tom didn't find the joke particularly amusing, but he could afford to be patient with Alastair, who had always been a generous supporter of Tom's reform work. Although he wasn't a religious man, Alastair seemed to believe that the bad things he'd done were canceled out by the money he donated to good causes, despite Tom's oft-repeated reminder that indulgences were not part of Anglican doctrine. In truth, Tom understood Alastair's motives only too well, as his own were the same. He just substituted good deeds for money.

The two men continued their conversation for a short time longer, speaking of people they knew and of Alastair's planned hunting trip at his cousin's estate in Scotland. As Tom left the smoking room and made his way to the entrance hall, he was deep in thought about his plans for the rest of the day and didn't notice William Narbridge and Charles Carrington until it was too late to avoid them. If he had to make a list of people he didn't wish to see, they would be at the top.

"The Athenaeum has lowered its standards lately," Narbridge was saying to Carrington. "If every Tom, Dick, and Harry gets in, I'll be leaving. Oh, look, here's Canon Cross." The railway magnate never missed an opportunity to mock or discredit Tom.

"Good day, gentlemen," Tom said, assembling his features into what he hoped was a pleasant expression.

Unlike Narbridge, whose face looked like it was carved from rock, there was nothing prepossessing about Carrington's appearance—he was of

average height and build, in his late thirties, with slightly stooped shoulders. Tom was likely not the only person who assumed his money was the
only attraction for Julia. He did have a distinctive voice, though, as deep and
melodious as an operatic baritone's.

"I've just come from the cathedral," Carrington said. "I was hoping to
speak with you."

"Oh?" was all Tom could manage in a casual tone. Carrington knew that
Julia had consulted Tom about religious matters, but he had never sought
Tom out before. Had she told her husband about her affair with Tom, or
even about her pregnancy? Tom had to remind himself to breathe.

"Could we speak privately?" Carrington said, with a quick glance around
the entrance hall.

"We'll continue our conversation later, Carrington," Narbridge said.
With a dismissive nod in Tom's direction, he left.

Tom struggled to maintain his impassive expression. "Would you rather
meet at the cathedral?"

"Yes. Would tomorrow suit you?"

"I don't have time tomorrow. Perhaps next week." He had to concentrate
in order to look the other man in the eye.

They made arrangements to meet at the cathedral the following week,
and Tom left the club. His first clear thought was that he shouldn't have put
Carrington off. It would be maddening to wonder for a whole week what
he wanted to talk about.

He told himself it was unlikely Carrington had found out about Tom's
relationship with Julia because he had seen no anger in the other man's
eyes. On the other hand, Carrington might be so mild-mannered that no
betrayal was serious enough to lead him to a public display of anger. Or
perhaps he was cleverer than he looked, crafty enough not to show his true
feelings in order to lull Tom into a false sense of security. If Carrington had

been behind the attack on Tom—and Tom still thought him the most likely suspect—he would have much invested in playing the role of the innocent, trusting husband.

Tom hadn't heard from Julia since their conversation in the cab more than two months earlier, though not for lack of trying. As soon as they had parted that day, he'd regretted his harsh response to the news of her pregnancy, and the next day he wrote to her asking for another meeting. She hadn't responded. She hadn't attended any of the cathedral services since December, either, and he'd been worried enough to make discreet inquiries about her health. Apparently she was well, only visiting friends in the country. Had she visited the doctor she'd spoken of and needed time to recover? Or had she decided to keep the baby? Part of him hoped she had, despite his initial reaction and the many difficulties such a decision would lead to.

When the vicar had mistaken Tom, Miranda, and their charges for a family at Gwen and Simon's wedding, Tom's first thought had surprised him: he wanted it to be true. Why shouldn't he be a father of legitimate children and have a wife like any other man? And Miranda ought to be a mother: she had held that little boy so naturally and lovingly, and her gentleness had clearly made that timid little girl feel safe. But then he'd come to his senses and remembered that such a life was not for him. There was plenty of evidence that he'd be a terrible husband, and given his own upbringing, it was likely he'd be a terrible father as well.

Miranda had disappeared so quickly after the vicar's blunder that Tom couldn't help but think she had been shocked and dismayed to be mistaken for his wife. He knew she was disappointed by his failure to tell her the truth about his name and profession, and she was certainly more distant with him in London than she'd been at the cottage in Surrey.

Simon had said she'd never marry. Tom needed to find out more about that. While he was not the man for her—his feelings for her were those of a friend, not a lover—perhaps her objections could be overcome if he could find a good man among his acquaintances. Though in truth, he couldn't imagine any man good enough for her. She'd been a revelation to him at the wedding, and not only because of her sweet way with the children. Wearing that rose-colored dress and with her hair arranged in a flattering style, she had a unique, ethereal beauty.

That evening, he went to visit the Thornes. He'd been thinking a great deal about Jack, having visited the textile factory where he worked a few times, and he was hoping his friends might think of ways to help the boy. It was the first time he had visited their modest redbrick house in Holborn.

As the foursome settled themselves in the drawing room, Miranda and Tom in armchairs across from each other and Gwen and Simon together on the sofa, Tom wondered how Miranda was adjusting to being relegated to the periphery of Simon's life. He hadn't had an opportunity to converse privately with her since the wedding, and he knew better than to judge her feelings by her placid mien in the presence of others.

"Have you managed to persuade Mr. Goode to take the pledge?" Simon asked Tom. The pledge of abstinence from liquor was one of the mainstays of the Temperance Society.

"No," Tom answered. "I considered it a triumph when he merely attended one of the meetings. At the end of it I asked him if he'd return, but he merely said the society was 'a lot of swells talkin' rot and humbug.' That's all I was able to get out of him." He smiled wryly.

"What a pity," Miranda said, gazing thoughtfully at Tom. "I hoped he would listen to you."

"I may still be able to change his mind," said Tom, "but the process will likely be too lengthy to be of much help to Jack or his other children. I want Jack out of that factory. Of course, his father won't want to lose the wages Jack brings home, but he isn't a strong lad, and he shouldn't be there at all. I've been trying to think of some other way to make the boy's life easier. Nothing has come to mind so far, so I wanted to ask if you have any ideas."

"Could you find Jack some other kind of work, something easier?" Gwen suggested.

"What sort of work?" Tom asked.

Gwen gave him a blank look.

"Perhaps he could go into service," Miranda suggested. "Do you know any wealthy families who might need an errand boy or stableboy? Such a post would certainly be an improvement, especially if the family is kind to their servants."

Tom immediately thought of the Carringtons, but the last thing he wanted was to become further enmeshed with them. There were a few other families he knew, parishioners at the cathedral, who might be looking for servants.

"I like that idea," he said. "Jack would have to be trained, of course, but he's a clever lad, and I have no doubt he could do the work. And his father probably wouldn't object, since the pay would be better. I'll think on it."

The conversation turned to Simon's work, and he described his duties and colleagues with the quiet humor Tom had come to appreciate. If Simon missed living in the country, he gave no sign of it.

"Keating and Merryman are fortunate to have you," Gwen said to her husband with an adoring look that would have melted a man of steel. "You're such a hard worker, and you know far more about contracts than the average law clerk."

"I don't know about that, dearest," Simon replied, placing his hand over hers, which were clasped in her lap. He smiled and whispered something that only she could hear, and she blushed becomingly.

Tom turned to Miranda, who was examining her sleeve. If he felt like an intruder in the short time he'd spent with the newlyweds, he could only imagine how uncomfortable she must feel on a regular basis.

"Have you arranged to meet Isabella Grant yet?" he asked her.

Miranda raised her head to meet his eyes, looking relieved. "We met last week. She's very kind."

"Did you show her your drawings?"

"A few of the best ones. She encouraged me and gave me some useful advice. Best of all, she offered to give me lessons free of charge."

"I'm very glad to hear that."

She looked down again, smoothing the skirt of her plain black dress. "I doubt that a well-known artist like Mrs. Grant would offer free lessons to just anyone. Did you tell her I couldn't afford them?"

"No. Not exactly."

She gave him a suspicious look.

"Well, perhaps I did throw out a hint or two," he admitted.

Her suspicious look changed to a grave one. With a glance at Simon and Gwen, who were gazing blissfully into each other's eyes, she said, "You needn't continue to do favors for me and Simon. Your debt, as you seem to consider it, is fully paid."

"I know, but is it so terrible for me to do a good turn when I can? You're very proud, Miranda. Until now I thought you nearly perfect, with a staggeringly long list of virtues. I'm glad to see you have faults."

"There's nothing wrong with a little self-respect. I wouldn't call it pride. Besides, you're very proud yourself. You have trouble accepting help from others."

"Very well, I admit I'm proud, too. Does that please you?"

"Yes, a little." She gave him a tiny smile. "I was thinking of attending the cathedral services. Would you mind?"

Before he could reply, Gwen interjected with a laugh, "Why in the world would he mind, Mouse? What clergyman wouldn't like people to go to church?"

Tom was startled to hear Gwen use Simon's pet name for Miranda. While she must mean it affectionately, it sounded strange—unearned—on her lips.

Miranda's expression darkened. Ignoring Gwen, she said to Tom, "I only thought you might not want friends at your place of work."

"I'd be thrilled to see you there," he said, hoping she could tell he meant her specifically.

"You see?" Gwen said. "We'll all go as a family."

"Yes, of course," Miranda said, but Tom saw what it had cost her to speak pleasantly: a tiny flinch before assembling her features into a neutral expression. He felt sorry for both women. Gwen clearly wanted her new sister-in-law to like her, but her intrusive, insensitive way of trying to make friends was exactly the method most likely to drive Miranda away.

Before Tom left the Thornes' house that evening, he had a moment alone with Miranda after Simon and Gwen bid him good night.

Standing with Miranda in the front foyer, he asked in a low voice, "Is it very difficult adjusting to your new life?"

"No. Not very." Then, seeing his raised eyebrows, she added, "Yes."

"Give Gwen a chance," he whispered, taking her hand and squeezing it. "She means well."

"I'm trying."

"I know. But I'd hate to see anyone deprived of a friendship as valuable as yours, even if it's her own fault."

She withdrew her hand from his grasp and looked away, whether because of embarrassment or a desire to end the conversation, he didn't know.

11

Women never have half an hour in all their lives (excepting before
or after anybody is up in the house) that they can call their own,
without fear of offending or of hurting some one. Why do people
sit up so late, or, more rarely, get up so early? Not because the day
is not long enough, but because they have "no time
in the day to themselves."

—Florence Nightingale, *Cassandra*

MARCH 1908

Miranda stood in front of her easel, head to one side, considering
the work she had done so far. She was painting the old cottage in
Surrey from a sketch she had made before moving to London. There was
something wrong with the light, both in the painting and in her bedroom.
Miranda's art supplies were crowded into the room, which was small enough
without the easel, canvasses, and paints. Gwen had told her she could set
up her easel in the drawing room, but that room was far too dark to work
in. Besides, Miranda knew if she attempted to paint there, Gwen would
interrupt her every five minutes to ask for help with something, or just to
make conversation.

Painting a picture of her old cottage made her homesick. It didn't help that the painting depicted a summer scene, with a spacious blue sky and lush green trees and grass, in contrast to this dreary, gray day in the city. The homesickness was bearable, though, because it brought back the joy of being in the place she loved so much, with only Simon for company and plenty of quiet.

She pushed a strand of hair away from her face with the back of her hand and made a light brushstroke on the canvas, creating more shadow along a tree trunk.

A quick, sharp knock sounded on her bedroom door, making her jump. Before she could answer, Gwen opened the door—she'd asked Gwen repeatedly to wait for a response first, but she never did—and peered at Miranda, looking dismayed.

"Oh, you're painting," she said, as if Miranda didn't paint at the same time every day.

"What is it?"

"I just received a letter from Mama. Shall I read it to you?"

"Can't it wait until later? I'm in the middle of a painting, and it's difficult to stop and start again."

"But Mama wants to come for a visit next week and I have no idea where we'll put her."

Gwen walked in, plopped herself down on the bed, and began reading. Miranda heard very little, being occupied in trying to resist the impulse to beat Gwen about the face and neck with her paintbrush.

After finishing the letter, Gwen launched into a long monologue about the preparations that would have to be made for her mother's visit and all the household adjustments that would be necessary.

"The spare room is so small, I can't imagine how we can offer it to Mama," Gwen was saying. "I have no idea how I'll be able to clear out the clutter, even with Jane's help, before Mama comes. Oh, how I wish we had a bigger house!"

Or fewer people living in it. Miranda heard Gwen's unspoken words as clearly as the audible ones and was tempted to make a sharp retort. She had been standing motionless with her back to the easel while Gwen was talking, trying to force herself to be kind to Gwen for Simon's sake. Finally, she said, "Your mother may have my room, if it would help."

"I'd hate to put you out," Gwen said, but there was an unmistakable note of hope in her voice.

"It's no matter," lied Miranda. Mrs. Sifton, Gwen's mother, liked to know everyone's business and couldn't be trusted to leave Miranda's things alone. Where would she put all of her canvasses and paints, not to mention her paintings?

"Thank you, Mouse. You have no idea how much it would help. I feel so much better now." Gwen paused. "You look paler than usual—why don't you come with me to Mrs. Reddie's this afternoon? You could probably use some pleasant company. It isn't good for you to be shut up alone in your room so much."

"I like being alone," Miranda said, giving Gwen a direct, meaningful look that would be difficult for her sister-in-law to misinterpret. She didn't want to hear one of Gwen's lectures about the importance of being in society.

"I don't understand you at all," Gwen said, looking hurt. "I try, for Simon's sake—" She broke off, shaking her head.

Miranda's anger threatened to choke her. "I don't understand you, either," she said. She hated conflict, but sometimes she couldn't remain silent. "Perhaps we shouldn't even try to understand each other, but instead merely accept what the other person says is important to her. For example, you could respect my desire to be left alone to paint for two hours in the afternoons. I would be happy to keep you company or help with the household at other times."

"Don't you think that's selfish? Why should the world stop for you every afternoon?" Gwen's tone shifted from self-pitying to sharp.

Miranda took a deep breath. "I don't ask the world to stop for me—I merely ask that it go on without me for a couple of hours."

"Very well. Have it your way." Gwen left the room.

As much as she tried not to let the altercation affect her, Miranda was too upset to paint anymore that afternoon. Even after Gwen had left for her visit to Mrs. Reddie, Miranda stayed in her room, feeling miserable. She didn't think she was being selfish, but perhaps Simon would agree with Gwen. It was always difficult for Miranda to stand her ground if Simon's happiness was at stake.

Later that evening, Simon said, "Gwen told me you and she quarreled this afternoon."

Gwen had gone to bed, and he and Miranda had been reading by the drawing-room fire. He looked rumpled and weary from his long day at the law firm. He seemed to be working longer hours every day, anxious to impress his employers so he could be promoted.

"I merely asked her to allow me to paint for two hours in the afternoons without interruption."

"She said she's willing to do that, but do you think you could be flexible in case she needs help with some urgent matter?"

"Such as what? The house burning down? A burglar in the pantry?" Miranda was too angry to keep the sarcasm out of her voice.

Simon sighed. "Mouse, I know how much you love your solitude, and I know it's a sacrifice for you to have so little time to yourself."

He looked at Miranda sadly, and she felt a pang of guilt.

"If you tried to understand Gwen's point of view," Simon continued quietly, "perhaps it would help. You know she's used to living in a boisterous household with her family, and she doesn't like to be alone. Perhaps you could try painting here in the drawing room. Then she would feel as though she has some company, even if you don't speak."

But she will force me to speak, thought Miranda. *She can't bear to be in the same room with anyone whose attention isn't focused on her.* But she couldn't say that to Simon. He was so completely head over ears in love with his wife that, as far as Miranda could tell, he had never tried the experiment of not giving her his full attention whenever they were together.

"Will you try it, just for a little while?" Simon pleaded. "If it doesn't work, you can return to painting in your room."

"Very well," she said, feeling as if she had just agreed to a long prison sentence for a crime she didn't commit.

With a fervent thank-you and a squeeze of her hand, Simon went off to bed.

Miranda remained in the drawing room, feeling frustrated. It was perfectly natural that Simon would take his wife's side and that Miranda would be expected to adapt to his and Gwen's lifestyle, not they to hers. She was the spinster sister, the burden on the family, and she was only too aware that she was an added strain on her brother's already-strained budget. It didn't matter that Gwen was the reason the budget was strained. Although she had never had a large appetite, nor a taste for fashionable clothing—"Quaker drab," Gwen once said of Miranda's style, with a laugh— she needed food and clothing, too.

Sometimes Miranda imagined herself working and living alone. It was a delicious fantasy she indulged in only when Gwen was particularly trying. She pictured herself living in a small, cozy attic with a skylight, the room full of her painting tools, with only a small bed and table in a corner. She would take pupils two days a week, sell her paintings to obtain the rest of the money she needed, and live out her days otherwise blissfully unaware of other human beings. But then she would think of Tom calling her Elaine, and she'd realize it wouldn't do to be alone quite so much. She had decided to hide her true identity from the world by using the initials E.A. on her paintings (for Elaine of Astolat), but she didn't truly want to be the Lady of Shalott. It was only Gwen who made Miranda long for solitude with such devout energy.

There were two bright spots in Miranda's life every week: going to Isabella Grant's studio for her art lesson and attending the cathedral services. Mrs. Grant was a sweet-faced, matronly woman in her mid-forties who would have looked more at home in a baker's shop than in an art studio. Seeing her for the first time, Miranda had been struck by Mrs. Grant's resemblance to Queen Victoria in her middle years, especially in the roundness of her body. Mrs. Grant surpassed the former queen in other types of rotundity: her face was round, she wore her hair in a puffy Gibson-girl style, and she had round spectacles perpetually perched low on her nose. As if to compensate for the roundness of her person, Mrs. Grant's paintings were insistently angular: the focal points of her landscapes were the angles of trees and buildings, her flower paintings depended for their impact on the angles of the flower stems relative to surrounding objects, and even her portrait paintings emphasized angular facial features.

Upon her first visit to Mrs. Grant's studio, Miranda had been prepared to be tongue-tied in the presence of such a famous artist, but she had been treated like a long-lost relative. Mrs. Grant had plied her with tea and cucumber sandwiches and asked Miranda about her family, drawing her out like an expert hostess and making her forget, for a while, why she was there. But when Mrs. Grant asked to see the sample of Miranda's sketches and paintings that she had brought with her, the artist was suddenly all business, pushing her round spectacles higher on her nose in a gesture that Miranda would soon come to recognize as a sign of the artist's serious, analytical mood.

After what had seemed an agonizingly long few minutes of silence, Mrs. Grant glanced up and said briskly, "These are very good. Very good, indeed. What formal training have you had?" When Miranda mentioned the art lessons she'd taken when her parents were still alive, Mrs. Grant continued, "Your form and composition are excellent. I don't think I can teach you very much, but I'm happy to try. You have so much natural talent that a little instruction will go very far. You also have something many artists lack—I call it spiritual insight."

Miranda had been speechless with pleasure.

And so began a weekly routine that became necessary to Miranda's peace of mind. Every hour spent in Mrs. Grant's studio was an hour of pure, focused joy. The studio was at the top of an upscale lodging house and resembled the attic of Miranda's fantasies, although it was brighter and more spacious. There were two large skylights instead of one—an embarrassment of riches—and although most of the room was a typical artist's studio, joyfully untidy with a profusion of paints, brushes, canvasses, and easels, a small nook near the entrance to the room from the stairs was just as pleasant in its own way. It contained two overstuffed burgundy chairs, a small sofa, and a table, perfect for taking tea or for a brief rest from the serious business of creating art.

From this cozy nook, one could observe the rest of the studio, as well as the entrance and upper part of the staircase if the door was open. Mrs. Grant's pupils would wait there for her to finish with a previous lesson, and sometimes friends of hers would drop by simply to watch her at work. It took Miranda a bit of getting used to—she would think she and her instructor were alone, but suddenly she would notice there were people watching them. After a while, though, realizing these people expected nothing from her, not even small talk, Miranda relaxed and no longer noticed their presence.

The day after Miranda's argument with Gwen, Miranda arrived at Mrs. Grant's studio sure she had successfully hidden her feelings. But after only a few minutes together, Mrs. Grant looked at her and said, "Why don't we have tea first, before the lesson?"

Startled, Miranda hesitated before acquiescing. She had been looking forward to the lesson even more than usual that day because she knew it would take her mind off the tension at home.

"There's something I've noticed about your paintings," Mrs. Grant said as soon as they were settled, she on one of the overstuffed chairs and Miranda on the sofa. "The work you've done since you've begun lessons with me is different from your earlier work."

"Isn't that as it ought to be?" Miranda asked timidly.

"One might expect so, yes, but I actually prefer your earlier work. I think it's better."

"Oh." Miranda felt the heat rise to her face, and she added quickly, "I must not be applying what you've been teaching me."

"I don't place the blame on your ability to learn, nor even on my ability to teach," Mrs. Grant said. "I suspect the trouble has a different cause. Have you enough space and time at your home in which to paint?"

"I usually paint in the afternoons in my bedroom, sometimes in the drawing room. Sometimes I paint in my bedroom in the evenings, too, but only for short periods when I am not . . . needed elsewhere."

"And what was your routine before you moved to London?"

"I used to work on my drawings most of the day. I took breaks, of course, but my brother was often out, or he would just stay out of my way, and I'd work in our front parlor. There was a big window there, so I had lots of light. My bedroom is a bit small, and the drawing room we have now lets in very little light." Miranda felt tears come to her eyes and wondered if Mrs. Grant thought her ridiculous.

But the woman cried, "That's it, then! There is something cramped and dark about your latest work."

"I can't change my circumstances," Miranda said, hoping she didn't sound too mournful. "I've agreed to keep my sister-in-law company, and she insists upon talking to me all the time. I can't paint well and talk at the same time."

"Of course you can't." Mrs. Grant thought for a minute. "Could you paint a portrait of your sister-in-law? Would she sit for you?"

"Yes, very likely. I've attempted to make drawings of her before, but I wasn't satisfied with the results."

"That doesn't matter in the least. What matters is that your sister-in-law will be sitting still and you can insist upon her silence—tell her that if she speaks, it will ruin the painting."

Miranda still didn't see what good this would do. She didn't particularly wish to paint Gwen, and once the portrait was finished, Gwen would return to her usual garrulous self.

But Mrs. Grant was beaming. "Don't you see the freedom this will offer you? The portrait could take a very, very long time. Many days, perhaps even weeks. You will need a great deal of time to get every detail correct. And while your sister-in-law sits there silently, as long as nobody else is in the room, you can paint anything you like."

Slowly, Mrs. Grant's meaning dawned on Miranda, and she smiled, too. It was a brilliant plan. For a while she would indeed have the silence and freedom from interference that she needed. And Gwen would be pleased to consider herself the center of attention for hours at a time.

"I know I'm suggesting a deception, but a little deception is sometimes necessary for a woman to work at what she loves," Mrs. Grant said. "When I was a young girl, I played many such tricks on people. They worked admirably well, considering that both of my parents were opposed to my obsession with art."

"Thank you. I'll try it."

"Good. Oh, one other thing. Are you an early riser, by any chance?"

"Yes," said Miranda, puzzled again.

"I was hoping you were. Do your brother and sister-in-law require any-thing of you before nine o'clock in the morning?"

"Not usually."

"The light isn't very good that early, of course, but it's spring now and the days are getting longer. Also, I'm never here before nine. If you'd like to work alone in the studio any day before that time, please be my guest."

Mrs. Grant fished from her skirt pocket a brass latchkey and held it out to Miranda as if it were merely a household item of no importance and not the key to her freedom. Miranda stammered her thanks and reached out slowly to take it, as if a sudden movement would make it disappear.

Over the next few days, she took the key everywhere she went. Though she had no opportunity to go to the studio, she would frequently reassure herself the key was really in her pocket, waiting to be used. She would slide her fingers over its flat, smooth surface as if caressing the hand of a lover. Even during the cathedral service that Sunday, she was less focused than usual on the beauty of the building and the words of the liturgy, knowing the very next day she would be able to use the key.

It helped that Paul Harris was preaching the sermon. She preferred his sermons to anyone else's—he created beautiful edifices with words, cathedrals with language, and his sermons were intellectual, not in a dry sort of way, but in a dynamic, living one. She had mentioned her impression of Canon Harris's sermons once, in passing to Tom, whose face instantly darkened. She hadn't needed another signal to tell her there was some sort of bad blood between Tom and his colleague, and she kept further opin-ions of Canon Harris to herself. The few times she had spoken to him in person after the services, he was a little stiff and shy, but that only endeared him to her, being quite stiff and shy herself in social situations.

Tom's sermons were satisfactory, but they didn't delve deeply enough into the Bible to please Miranda, and he tended to preach a variation on the same sermon every time. He spoke often of service to others, or, as he called it, "faith in action," but very little about the relationship of the individual to God or even about church doctrine. Miranda felt disloyal to Tom for preferring the sermons of a man he disliked, but she couldn't help it. Besides, Tom was too good-looking. His appearance distracted her from his words, while Canon Harris, though young and pleasant-looking, proved no such distraction.

At six o'clock one morning, when Miranda was just about to let herself into the building that housed the studio, she heard a familiar voice call out to her.

Wearing a clerical wideawake hat and black greatcoat, Tom descended upon her like a dark angel. "What are you doing on the street so early in the morning?" he demanded.

"Good morning to you, too."

"I beg your pardon. Good morning, Miss Thorne," he said with exaggerated formality.

"I'm going to work. Mrs. Grant lets me use her studio in the mornings."

"Does she? And you come and go as you please, I see. I should have told her not to trust you so quickly."

"You're very unkind, Canon Cross."

"I'm always unkind in the morning. I thought you knew that."

She did know it. It was strange to think that only a few months had passed since he'd stayed with her and Simon at their old cottage. Tom and Miranda knew each other's daily habits and moods in a way that only those who had experienced the intimacy of living together could.

"What are *you* doing out so early?" she asked.

"Just walking. I couldn't sleep, so I went out. It's turned out to be a longer walk than I intended."

"You've been walking all night?" she exclaimed.

"No, only part of it. May I see the studio? Do you mind?"

Miranda hesitated. She didn't mind, but perhaps Mrs. Grant would. Miranda didn't want to take advantage of Mrs. Grant's kindness by entertaining uninvited guests in the studio. A visit from an uninvited *male* guest, in particular, might be misconstrued.

Despite her reservations, Miranda couldn't resist the appeal in Tom's eyes. It would only be one visit, anyway. She let him in and led the way upstairs.

"This is very impressive," he said when he saw the studio. "There's much more space here than I would have imagined."

After a quick glance around the room, he turned to Miranda. "May I rest here for a few minutes? I promise I won't interfere with your work."

"I suppose, as long as you don't stay very long. Mrs. Grant might not like it."

He assured her he wouldn't stay long and would keep his coat on to prove it. He sat on the sofa and put his hat on the seat beside him.

Miranda set up her easel and began work on the far side of the studio. She soon became absorbed in her painting and forgot Tom was there entirely, until she heard the cathedral bells chime half-eight. Looking across the room, she saw he had fallen asleep. She went to him and spoke his name, quietly at first, then louder, but he didn't stir. As she gazed at him, the artist and the woman in her united in the desire to let him sleep, though for different reasons. She couldn't resist this rare opportunity—and dangerous indulgence—to study his face as long as she liked.

If there were no consequences, she thought, she would run her fingers along his unruly black eyebrows, then trace the outline of his strong nose and chin, and caress his cheek where the dark stubble looked pleasingly rough. She might even run one finger along the defined cupid's bow of his upper lip. And then perhaps even press her lips against his.

She sat up straight and looked away as if caught in a criminal act. She was too warm, and her breathing had become shallow and uneven.

Once she had composed herself, she reached out to lay her hand lightly on his arm.

He awoke with a start, staring at her in bewilderment. A look crossed his face that she had never seen before—it was a mere fraction of a second, but it was a combination of suspicion and fear that was meant for someone else, not her. The look disappeared instantly and was replaced by a sheepish one.

"Forgive me," he said, running a hand through his hair. "I didn't mean to fall asleep. It's peaceful here."

"You needn't apologize. You were tired."

"I'd better go." He put on his hat and rose to his feet. "I have more appointments than I care to count today."

"At the cathedral?"

"At the cathedral and the hospital and the prison."

"You work too hard."

"It keeps me out of trouble. For the most part." He turned to leave.

"Tom, wait." She bit her lip, unsure whether to tell him what was troubling her. But he was facing her again and looking at her with intent dark eyes, so she went on. "I keep having the same dream about you."

He quirked an eyebrow.

"You're in a lake or pool, but it's not water. It's some dark, sticky substance, like treacle. And you keep sinking deeper into it."

He looked thoughtful. "That sounds unpleasant. Are you in the dream, too?"

"Yes. I keep reaching out to you and telling you to take my hand, but you just ignore me. Every time I have the dream you sink a little deeper. It's nearly over your head now, and I'm afraid you're going to drown."

"Perhaps I just don't want to take the risk of pulling you in with me," he said gravely. "I don't want you to drown, either."

"I don't think I will. I'm stronger than I look."

His eyes were warm as he studied her face. "Do you remember that prayer you said for me that night when I was staying with you and Simon? The one for peril at sea?"

She nodded.

"There's no prayer for drowning in treacle that I know of, but perhaps we could say the one for peril at sea together."

"You're mocking me."

"I most certainly am not." He reached for her hand, then to her surprise, pressed it against his chest, inside his coat. "Do you feel that?"

It wasn't the romantic gesture it seemed at first, for she felt the hard edges of a small metal object through his shirt.

"I still wear the cross you gave me," he said. "I never take it off. Perhaps it will prevent me from drowning."

"Oh," she said breathlessly. She could feel not only the cross but also the warmth of his skin through his shirt, and it made her think of things she shouldn't. She pulled away as suddenly as if he'd set her hand on fire, and turned back to the studio, muttering something about needing to finish her painting.

12

And David's anger was greatly kindled against the man; and he
said to Nathan, As the Lord liveth, the man that hath done this
thing shall surely die: And he shall restore the lamb fourfold,
because he did this thing, and because he had no pity. And Nathan
said to David, Thou art the man.

—2 Samuel 12:5-7

Tom left the art studio feeling strangely refreshed. He had been there
less than an hour, but he had slept deeply and peacefully, unlike the
uneasy half sleep he usually had at his lodgings. He didn't know whether
it was the studio, with only the sound of Miranda's soft brushstrokes as
she sat at her easel, or Miranda herself, that had the more soothing effect.
Whatever the reason, he had felt safe and at rest. And when she related her
dream, he was touched by her concern for him as well as struck by the truth
of it: figuratively, he was indeed drowning in a sea of troubles.

This day was a particular challenge because he'd arranged to meet Charles
Carrington that afternoon. He still hadn't received a response from Julia to
any of his letters, so Tom didn't know where she was or what she might have

told her husband about their relationship. When the appointed time came, he had already lived through many different scenarios in his mind, none of which ended well, and his nerves were stretched as taut as pianoforte wires. Carrington arrived at the cathedral precisely on time, and Tom showed him into his office.

The first thing Carrington said as soon as they were in the room with the door closed was, "Have you and my wife had a falling-out?"

Was this a trick? What did the man mean? Tom was silent.

"I know she hasn't come to see you in weeks, nor have you been to our house. I hope nothing is amiss."

"No, not that I'm aware of," Tom said. How did Carrington know Julia hadn't come to see Tom in weeks? Had he been watching his wife's movements? Or Tom's?

"Julia seemed to find solace in her meetings with you," Carrington said. "I don't want her to lose that. I'm sure you've noticed that she hasn't been to the cathedral services for a while. She's been agitated lately, so much so that I encouraged her to stay with friends in the country to soothe her nerves."

"Have you come here to discuss your wife, Lord Carrington?" Tom asked. He had no wish to prolong what was already an uncomfortable conversation, and since Carrington wasn't getting to the point, Tom thought it best to be blunt.

"No. Well, yes, I suppose I have." Carrington stared at the desk that stood between himself and Tom with unfocused eyes. "I don't expect you to tell me anything she's told you, of course . . . I know a clergyman can't break confidences."

Tom waited. Carrington shifted from one foot to the other. He hadn't taken the chair Tom offered, so they were both still standing, with the desk between them. Tom wished the other man would sit down and stop looking so uncomfortable. Then he wondered if he looked just as uncomfortable.

"It's strange, being here, you know?" Carrington said abruptly, looking at Tom as if expecting him to understand perfectly.

"I *don't* know." Tom's words came out more harshly than he had intended, his anxiety sharpening his tone.

Carrington laughed, a short, nervous laugh. "Of course you don't."

Was this it? Was Tom going to be exposed right here, right now? His hands clenched into fists, as if his body was reassuring him that he could fell this pale, slight man as easily as he could snap a brittle twig.

But instead of denouncing Tom for committing adultery with his wife, Carrington said, "I haven't been inside a church in twenty years." He shifted his feet one more time and finally sat down. "My mother was French, and against my father's wishes, she raised me as a Catholic. I thought I'd be talking to you in a confessional."

Tom sat down also, awkwardly, as if he had forgotten how. He forced his hands to uncurl, then rested them on the table, lacing his fingers in a priestly position.

"I hated church as a boy," Carrington mused, half to himself. "The building was cold and draughty—I remember shivering through every Mass. The priest seemed just as cold, droning on in his monotone voice as if reading the service was penance for some sin he had committed. I never saw any use for the church, although I did believe in God. As I've grown older, I've begun to see the comfort that religious faith offers people. I'm still wary of the church, but I'm willing to reconsider my childish opinions. I can't believe there is nothing beyond this life, nothing more than this world 'with its sick hurry, its divided aims.' I no longer believe I know the best way to live my own life."

Tom's conscience told him not to let the man go any further—it wasn't right to listen to his confidences, not when he was apparently unaware of the injury Tom had done him. But perhaps it was all a trap, an act on Carrington's part to get Tom to betray himself. And Tom didn't know how to stop him without making him suspicious. But something had to be done to bring this interminable conversation to a close. It seemed like an hour since they had entered the room, but when he glanced at the clock on the mantelpiece, he was shocked to see that not even ten minutes had elapsed.

"Perhaps you'd be more comfortable talking with a clergyman at a different church," Tom ventured, trying to sound casual. "The cathedral clergy no doubt remind you too much of the Catholic church of your youth."

Carrington looked startled. "No, I never thought of going to anyone but you. Julia trusts you, and that's enough for me."

Dear God, Tom thought. It wasn't a prayer but an inward groan.

Suddenly, Charles Carrington began to weep. He did not try to hide his face or stifle his sobs the way most people did. He wept openly, unashamedly, like a child, letting his tears run down his face and stain his expensive-looking black morning coat. Tom couldn't watch. He stared down at his hands, assaulted by his own conflicting emotions. Initially, he was merely shocked by Carrington's unexpected breakdown. Then he felt disgust. Carrington was weak, pathetic. No wonder Julia didn't respect him. Then, although he knew he must be insane for feeling it, Tom was jealous—jealous of the ease with which the other man expressed his emotions. It was no trap. He couldn't know about Tom's affair with Julia. Even a consummate actor would not be able to weep in the presence of the man who had cuckolded him.

After a few minutes, Carrington took out his pocket handkerchief, wiped his face, and blew his nose. He offered no apology or excuse for his outburst. "I've lost her," he said, staring dully into space. "I always feared it, but I thought it would be more obvious—I thought she'd leave me and I'd never see her again. I didn't expect it to happen gradually, in such a subtle way that I wouldn't notice the signs. I didn't think she would stay in the same house with me after she stopped loving me."

Carrington leaned forward, his elbows on his knees, and stared at the floor. "Ah, why hide the truth? She never loved me. I sensed it from the beginning of our marriage, but I thought I could win her love somehow—by buying her gifts, paying her compliments, treating her well—I don't know. It seems ridiculous now. I've never been able to understand what would make her happy. The children made her happy, for a while. But then I'd catch her staring out of windows like a prisoner serving a life sentence. And during the past few months I've heard her crying at night in her bedroom." His voice broke and he paused to collect himself.

"Have you asked her what the matter is?" Tom's voice was hollow.

"Yes. She tells me it's nothing, just woman's troubles. I know she's not telling me the truth. She won't let me touch her anymore. I thought for a while she might have taken a lover, but I don't think Julia would descend to that. She's always tried very hard to do the right thing."

As have I, Tom thought. But if that were true, what had happened to him?

A memory came back to him. He'd been seven or eight years old, eating a bowl of soup at the kitchen table. He had been ill and hadn't been able to eat for a few days, so the soup tasted unusually delicious, even though his family was so poor that it was mostly water, with only some limp greens and a few pieces of potato. He hadn't heard his father enter the room behind him, so when the force of his father's hand hit the back of his head, he was completely unprepared. Down went his face into the bowl of soup, and his father held his head down, long enough that he inhaled some of the lukewarm broth, sputtering and flailing his arms in an attempt to right himself. Just as suddenly, his father released him and calmly walked out of the room, while Tom coughed the soup out of his lungs and wiped his face.

That day he made a vow to help people when he grew up. He would be the one to strike down those who hurt others and he would defend the ones who were hurt. He would meet violence with violence and would wipe the tears (and the soup, if necessary) from the faces of the innocent. He was only a boy, but he knew the difference between right and wrong.

Now, his childhood vow mocked him. He had taken another man's wife for himself without a thought of what it might do to that man, or even to the woman and himself. He had injured all three of them, body and soul, and there was no way to undo the injury. He could not even admit what he had done for fear of losing his position in the church. He could not apologize to Charles Carrington.

"I don't know what to do," Carrington said, looking at Tom with despair in his eyes. "I don't want to lose Julia completely, but it seems I already have. She must have shared some of her troubles with you. Will you tell me what I can do?"

"None of us can make those we love return our feelings," Tom said stiffly. "All we can do is treat them kindly and try to think of their needs before our own." He felt like a fraud, but he had to say something.

Carrington looked disappointed. "Can you offer me no consolation, then?"

"I can't tell you what to do to win your wife's heart, but I can offer you God's consolation, if you will accept it."

"Go on."

"God tells us He will be with us in all our troubles. If you repent of your sins, you may rely upon His forgiveness and His peace. In the Gospel of Matthew, Jesus says, 'Come unto me all that travail and are heavy laden, and I will refresh you.'"

These "comfortable words" from the Book of Common Prayer had never felt less comfortable in his mouth.

Would Carrington choose to accept this consolation? Tom found himself hoping the other man would want to say the confession so he, too, could say it aloud. To confess in the presence of the person he had injured, even if the person didn't know of the injury, would undoubtedly do him some good. But Carrington merely looked thoughtful and said, "I don't know if I can believe that. I'll think on it."

Finally, Carrington took his leave. Tom remained in the office a while longer with the door closed and his head in his hands. He couldn't have explained, even to himself, what he was feeling. His heart pounded like he'd competed in a footrace, his mouth was dry, and he seemed to have forgotten how to breathe.

Tom fulfilled the rest of the afternoon's duties mechanically. He had succeeded in temporarily shutting off his brain, and nobody would have noticed any lapse in his competence. When he went home that evening, he was surprised to find a terse note waiting for him in Julia's handwriting. It was neither signed nor addressed to him by name: *I have taken care of the matter we talked about and don't wish to discuss it again.* The note and its implications chilled Tom's blood, and he sat in front of his roast beef dinner, unable to eat.

The dinner hour stretched ahead of him, a dangerously empty slot of time. He thought about visiting various friends—bachelors only, of course, since few men's wives would brook a last-minute addition to the dinner table. But not many of his friends were regular in their habits and trying to locate them would be an exercise in frustration. Paying a visit to the Thornes was another possibility. He was always welcome there. At the same time, he didn't want to face Miranda's piercing gaze. She knew there was something wrong, and he was using so much energy to prove to the world that everything was fine that he couldn't risk her undermining his efforts.

In the end, Tom decided to pay a visit to a place he hadn't been to for a long time. He had once promised himself he would never return, but this time he told himself he was merely doing his friend Alastair a favor.

Checking up on Alastair's errant valet was part of Tom's public role, to reclaim those who had wandered into error.

He changed from his clerical garb into his most casual, nondescript clothes. In the process, he removed Miranda's gold cross from around his neck and put it in the top drawer of his chest of drawers. It was the first time he'd taken it off since she gave it to him, but he didn't want it to be lost or stolen. An ugly brown coat he'd kept for years completed the ensemble.

He took the Underground most of the way. When he finally reached the abandoned factory in the East End, he knew exactly where to go. The door at the back of the building was unlocked and he stepped inside, pausing as his eyes adjusted to the dim light.

At the far end of the building, a group of men were watching two fighters in a boxing ring. As Tom approached the ring, walking past empty crates and stepping over broken masonry, he was enveloped by the smell of old leather, sweat, and an acrid odor he couldn't identify. The two fighting men were unknown to him, but as one of the spectators turned to look at him, Tom recognized him at once.

"Well, well, well. Look what the cat dragged in!" exclaimed Nate Cowan. "It's the Dagger. Where've you been?" He was a huge man with ginger hair and bushy whiskers.

"Nowhere in particular," Tom replied with a shrug. He scanned the rest of the group, looking for Bert Gunn, whose presence would only complicate things. But Gunn wasn't there, nor was anyone else he recognized.

"Wanna fight? God knows we could replace Jimmy with someone who's got some life in 'im." Nate turned abruptly to look at the smaller of the two men in the ring, a pale, skinny youth who couldn't have been more than eighteen. "Jimmy, what the bloody 'ell are you doing? Let's see some action!"

Jimmy didn't look at Nate, but he seemed to have been listening, for he swung at his opponent limply with his right fist. The other man danced away from the blow easily.

"Whaddaya say?" Nate said, turning back to Tom.

"I don't think so. I'm just looking for someone."

"Pity. The Club could use you. Who's the bloke you're looking for?"

Tom was forced to acknowledge to himself the ridiculousness of his reason for being there. He had met Alastair's valet once or twice, but he could hardly remember what the man looked like. "His name is Henry. He's of middling height, a little stout, I think. In his early twenties."

Nate raised his eyebrows, clearly waiting for more information. Tom knew well enough that his description fit many of the fighters in the Club, and few of them used their real names. It didn't matter. He had more important questions to ask, he realized, questions that might help him find out who had attacked him the previous autumn.

The Club had no official name. Unlike the amateur boxing clubs that operated under specific rules and regulations, the Club had begun as a group of young working-class men who needed to relieve pent-up energy after long workdays. Nate, who ran a public house, was the only one with formal pugilistic training and he'd taught the others. The casual recreation had evolved into its current form, and although Nate had toyed with the idea of registering the Club officially, he had a criminal past and didn't want to be troubled with police or legal matters.

Tom had stumbled upon the Club as a youth of seventeen when he'd run away from home. He'd arrived in London with a small amount of money stolen from his father and a vast supply of arrogance about his prospects. He wanted to attend university but had no idea how to get there, and when the money ran out, he supported himself by fighting. By the time he met Osborne Jay a year later, he was ready to give up the rough life of a pugilist, but he never lost his taste for the sport. Even after he graduated from Cambridge and returned to London, the Club had drawn him back.

He used to spend every Friday with these men, feeling more comfortable in this environment, as much as he hated to admit it, than in the middle-class world he usually inhabited. The Club members didn't know he was a clergyman—in fact, they knew nothing about him and didn't ask questions. As Tom achieved higher positions in the church, from curate to vicar to canon at the cathedral, his visits to the Club had become less frequent, partly due to lack of time and partly because he was well aware that pugilism, especially in this casual, lawless, squalid form, was hardly an appropriate pastime for a man of the cloth. It was mainly because of his continued involvement with the Club that Tom had lost touch with Jay: his old mentor would be dismayed to find that his efforts to reform Tom in this respect had failed.

"Are Little Roy and Smiling Joe still part of the Club?" Tom asked Nate. Of all the fighters Tom knew, these men were the most likely to be involved in the attack on him.

"Nah. Little Roy's been in the clink since last summer. Smiling Joe 'ad an unfortunate accident. Why d'ye ask?"

"I had an unfortunate accident myself last October. I was kidnapped and taken into the countryside, then attacked and left for dead. Did you hear anything about that?"

"You know that's not our style."

It was true. Most of Nate's fighters preferred to settle scores openly, not covertly.

"Not even if they were offered money to do the job?"

"'Ow much?"

"I don't know. I'm just guessing."

"I'll keep me ears open if you tell me 'ow to get the information to you. And if you join us and fight today."

"No."

Despite his refusal, Tom felt the old rush of excitement as he watched the fight. He liked the idea of pushing his body to its limits, of using it as a weapon. The sheer simplicity of a physical fight was compelling, too, especially in light of the internal struggle he'd been experiencing.

He focused on the fight and didn't speak for a long moment, as the effort of restraining himself was like trying to rein in an unbroken horse. There were many reasons why he shouldn't fight. The most convincing one was the difficulty he would have the next day at the cathedral trying to explain the injuries he was likely to receive. Another good reason was that he was out of practice and Jimmy's opponent clearly was not. Stripped to the waist, the man was at least fifteen stone of pure muscle.

Nate was watching Tom out of the corner of his eye, grinning. Tom knew what he was thinking, but Nate was too clever to pressure him.

To distract himself, Tom asked, "How's the Club faring these days?"

"Bloody awful. We're down to twenty men, maybe thirty on a good day. They're all joining the official clubs, wanna be famous prizefighters and win lots of money. Nobody wants to fight just for the fun of it anymore."

"I'm sorry to hear that. I'd hate to see the Club close down."

"You can help keep it goin', my boy, if you come back more regular-like. And bring your gentlemen friends with you. Your togs don't fool me for a minute. I don't know what you work at, but it's probably summat important. Politics or government. You're an educated swell, that's clear enough."

Tom didn't reply, watching Jimmy take a vicious pummeling from his opponent. The two fighters clung together for a moment in a parodic embrace, then the larger man shoved Jimmy away. Jimmy fell to the floor of the ring with a soft thud, as if his bones had turned to jelly and couldn't make a solid sound when they hit an unyielding force.

"That's it," said Nate. "Jimmy's done for."

Jimmy lay as if dead until a bowl of water was emptied over his head, when he slowly raised himself to a sitting position. As he was half carried, half dragged out of the ring, the onlookers clapped and cheered for his opponent, who merely shrugged and scanned the room. His eyes met Tom's with an unmistakable challenge.

"Clive's a new member," Nate said quietly so only Tom could hear him. "A good fighter when 'e's on the offensive, but 'e's not as good at defending 'isself, nor is 'e very quick. You'd be a good match for 'im."

"It's been too long since I've fought. More than a year."

"A man doesn't forget 'ow to fight. Not when 'e's as good as you. Clive's already had one fight today. 'E's tired. That should even the odds."

Tom didn't see how Clive could be all that tired after a fight that was so obviously in his favor. He was also at least ten years younger than Tom. Despite these warning signs, the force that set Tom's heart pounding with excitement finally mastered him, and after a few minutes he stripped off his coat and shirt. Then he climbed into the ring with his opponent.

Nobody at the Club wore protective gear. Nate and his friends disdained the Queensberry rules, which had been followed in official fights and clubs since 1867. Among other things, the Queensberry rules required the use of boxing gloves and prohibited wrestling holds. Ignoring the rules obviously meant there was more likelihood of serious injury, but bare-knuckle fighting was true to pugilism's roots, and as Nate liked to say, "If it was good enough for me grandf'er, it's good enough for me."

The fight began slowly, both men circling each other like cats, assessing their opponent's skills before attacking. Tom tried a couple of jabs. Neither connected, Clive deflecting them easily with a bored expression. The larger man's slowness annoyed Tom. He realized belatedly that this was probably what Clive intended. He tried a more aggressive approach, making a direct hit in his opponent's ribs. Clive retaliated with a punch to Tom's head that sent him reeling. He staggered back but managed not to fall.

This success seemed to galvanize Tom's opponent. He came at Tom like a steamroller, but Tom managed to evade him. Tom's speed had always served him well in these fights. Great lumbering oafs like Clive might have more physical strength, but Tom could land more blows by darting quickly in and out of his opponent's range. Which is exactly what he did for some time, foiling Clive's efforts to flatten him.

"That's the Dagger!" Nate yelled in the background. "Y'aven't lost yer touch."

Some of the onlookers echoed Nate's encouragement, but Tom's whole attention was focused on his opponent. The thrill of the fight was in his veins, the lust for blood, the most primitive instinct a man could feel. It was exhilarating.

Despite his belief that his focus on his opponent was complete, Tom was taken by surprise when Clive suddenly charged at him. The bigger man imprisoned Tom in a wrestle hold, nearly squeezing the life out of him. Then Clive hurled Tom to the ground with such force that the breath was knocked out of him. It was an agonizingly long time before he could breathe again, and it occurred to him that the Queensberry rules were not so bad, after all.

On the other hand, the fight would have been over if the rules had been observed, since it took longer than ten seconds for Tom to struggle to his feet again. He straightened up slowly, relieved that nothing dire had happened to his back, and regarded his opponent with narrowed eyes.

"'Ad enough?" jeered Clive.

It was the wrong thing to say. Tom's exhilaration was replaced by a rage that felt like strength, and it drove him towards his opponent again. He was moving more slowly now, but he was still faster than Clive. He pummeled the other man's torso with his fists, four, five, six blows connecting with satisfying impact. Clive's attempts to shield himself from the blows failed, and he swayed on his feet.

Even though Tom's fists were torn and bloodied by this time, he felt no pain. Darting away from his opponent one last time, he narrowed all of his pent-up energy and fury into one seamless attack, with a powerful blow to the side of Clive's head.

The larger man crumpled and fell heavily to the floor.

Tom was too exhausted to feel glad he had won, despite the cheers from onlookers. He slowly turned around to climb out of the ring, but as he did so, he heard Nate call out a warning.

Raising his head numbly, he saw Clive—incredibly—on his feet and lumbering towards him. He heard, rather than felt, the crack of Clive's fist connecting with his nose. Then time stopped.

"Good God," Simon said, his face blanching. "What happened?"

Tom was not in a position to explain his situation because he was trying to prevent his nose from bleeding all over the Thornes' front foyer carpet. The piece of cloth he was holding to his face was already crimson.

"Help me get him into the kitchen," Miranda said to Simon. "Don't look. Just take his arm."

The siblings guided Tom into the kitchen and helped him into a wooden chair. They were both wearing dressing gowns, and he felt guilty for awakening them in the middle of the night. Simon still had his nightcap on and the usual smooth knot Miranda kept her hair in was half undone, the spiky ends standing out like exclamation points.

"You can go, Simon," Miranda said. "I'll call you back in when I've cleaned up the blood."

Simon opened his mouth as if to protest but then closed it again, swallowed hard as if to beat back a wave of nausea, and left.

After Tom had awakened on the floor of the factory in a pool of icy water with Nate and his friends peering down at him, Nate had tried to fix him up, but the Club's medical supplies were limited to a pail of water and some dirty rags. The last thing Tom wanted to do was to attract attention, and he couldn't go to his lodgings in such a state, so he had Nate put him into a cab and direct it to the Thornes' neighborhood. To protect Simon and Miranda, he hadn't given Nate the exact address, but it had been agony walking from the cab to their house.

"I'm sorry to disturb you," Tom said to Miranda.

"Hush. Save your energy. I can't understand you anyway with that cloth over your face. Take this one." She handed him a clean cloth to replace the blood-soaked one he had been holding to his nose. "Thank God Gwen is still asleep. I can only imagine the dramatic scene she'd create if she saw you this way."

Tom closed his eyes and concentrated on breathing through his mouth. When he opened them again, Miranda was looking at him with a troubled expression.

"Did you see the people who attacked you?" she asked. "Could they be the same ones who left you for dead in our wood last autumn?"

"No, I don't think so." The guilt of knowing how different the two incidents were was too much for him. "I wasn't attacked this time. Not really."

Her eyes narrowed. "What do you mean?"

Removing the cloth, he touched his nose gingerly. "I went to a boxing club. I was fighting in the ring."

"You were . . . fighting?" She sounded as though she didn't believe him. "On purpose?"

"I'm afraid so. It was stupid."

"Indeed. Very stupid."

Miranda turned her attention to his hands, swabbing them with a damp cloth and then bandaging them. He thought she could have been gentler, but he would rather grit his teeth than complain. He was in her debt, and they both knew it.

"There isn't much blood now," she said, "so Simon ought to be able to return without turning green again. I'll fetch him."

"Wait," Tom said. His nose had begun to bleed again, and he held the cloth up to it.

She turned, hands on hips, and looked at him, her lips in a straight line.

"I appreciate this, Miranda. Thank you."

She glowered at him. "You seem to enjoy getting yourself nearly killed, Tom, but I don't find it amusing. I wish I wouldn't have been so sympathetic the first time—you probably provoked that attack."

"I did no such thing." It was difficult to argue with her when his nose was muffled in cloth. "It was a mistake to come here. Perhaps I'd better leave." He started to get up from his chair.

"Sit down." She placed her hand on his shoulder and pushed him back into the chair. She was such a tiny woman that her effort was successful only because he was off-balance. In spite of her curt tone, he noticed she allowed her hand to remain on his shoulder longer than was necessary. He took this as evidence that she cared about him at least a little, and he was glad of it.

Miranda left the kitchen, and a few minutes later Simon returned, looking apprehensive.

"Can you breathe?" he asked Tom. "Are you sure you don't need to see a doctor?"

"Yes. I've broken my nose before. It will heal on its own."

"Miranda said you were hurt fighting in a boxing ring," Simon said. "Is that true?"

"Yes."

Miranda returned with a block of ice. She stabbed it violently with a pick and wrapped the resulting pieces in another cloth. Without speaking, she handed it to Tom.

"Thank you," he said.

"Keep your head upright," she said. She didn't meet his eyes.

Simon was observing his sister closely. "Miranda, why don't you go back to bed? I'll show Tom to the guest room."

"Very well. Good night." She stomped out of the room.

Simon and Tom looked at each other.

"She's angry," Tom said. "I'd better not stay."

"She's afraid," Simon countered. "I know my sister. She only flies into a rage like that when she's frightened. When she's truly angry, she's quiet."

"She's almost always quiet."

"Yes, but there's a difference between her ordinary quiet and her angry quiet. It's rather like the ominous stillness in the air just before a storm."

"I didn't mean to frighten her or cause any trouble. I'm sorry."

"No need to apologize. I'm glad you came to us. If a man can't go to his friends when he's in trouble, where can he go? I'm sure Miranda will agree when she calms down."

Despite Simon's reassurance, Tom regretted having troubled his friends. He should have gone home instead with a plausible story for his landlady and hidden in his rooms until he had healed enough to face people. He hoped he hadn't caused any lasting damage to his friendship with Miranda, especially. He didn't quite understand why, but their friendship had become more important to him than any other relationship in his life.

"Besides," Simon added, "women can't be expected to understand the attraction of pugilism. I've watched some matches over the years, and I'd try it myself if I had the nerve—and if Gwen didn't object."

Tom couldn't imagine gentle, unassuming Simon as a pugilist. But even the gentlest men had their fantasies.

"How will you explain this to your superiors at the cathedral?" Simon asked, glancing at Tom's bandaged hands.

Tom had been asking himself the same question. He slowly lowered the cloth from his nose, which seemed to have stopped bleeding. "I don't know," he said finally. "It was stupid of me. If I tell them the truth, they won't understand, and I won't blame them."

"You could explain it as an attempt to practice muscular Christianity, perhaps," Simon offered with a grin.

Tom started to smile but it hurt too much. "I could try. Though clearly I overdid the muscular part."

"You must be exhausted as well as in pain," Simon said. "I'll show you to your room now, if you're ready."

"I ought to go home instead. I've caused enough of a disturbance here."

"Nonsense. We have a spare room nobody is using, though it's small and cluttered. You can go home in the morning."

Tom relented and followed Simon. His legs shook as he ascended the stairs, and he fancied that he could feel every spot where Clive's fists had connected with his body. He supposed he had been in shock and it was only now beginning to wear off. After bidding good night to Simon, Tom sank gratefully into bed without bothering to undress.

Despite his exhaustion, the pain of his injuries prevented him from sleeping. Troubled by his reckless behavior, his mind didn't shut off, either. Fighting was part of his past. It had helped him feel strong as a youth, able to defend himself against men like his father. And the Club had been the source of his livelihood for a while, but it had no place in his life now. Trying to understand himself was as tiring as engaging in another round of fighting, and he eventually fell into an uneasy sleep.

13

I've room for no more children in my arms,
My kisses are all melted on one mouth,
I would not push my darling to a stool
To dandle babies. Here's a hand shall keep
For ever clean without a marriage-ring . . .
—Elizabeth Barrett Browning, *Aurora Leigh*

APRIL 1908—TEN DAYS LATER

It had been a mistake to buy the toy train. Miranda knew this, but she couldn't help herself. As soon as she'd held the engine, sleek with glossy black paint, she knew she must buy it. The deciding factor, strangely enough, had been its weight—although small, it was surprisingly heavy, which made it comfortingly substantial and real.

She had told the shopkeeper she wanted a gift for an eight-year-old boy's birthday. Those simple words had taken all her energy to speak aloud, so when he asked if she wanted him to add a card to the package with the recipient's name, she just nodded.

"What name shall I write?" the shopkeeper asked.

But she couldn't say it. She looked down at the blank card in the man's hand and swallowed hard.

"Would you like to write it yourself?"

She nodded again, and he handed her the card and a pen, glancing at her curiously before wrapping the toy in shiny red paper. She wrote the three letters slowly, painstakingly, and watched the shopkeeper tuck the card into the top of the package.

"It's the perfect gift for a little boy," he said reassuringly. "His eyes will light up like stars when he opens it."

Miranda placed her money on the counter and waited, fixing the shopkeeper with an impassive stare until the transaction was completed.

She knew the brightly colored package would attract attention as she carried it to the railway station, especially in contrast to her gray cloak and the rain-soaked streets. Even so, the comfort of having something heavy to hold was worth the risk, as ridiculous as it may have seemed to anyone else.

She had told Simon she was going to Exeter for the day with Mrs. Grant to see an art exhibit. Instead, she boarded a train to Birmingham. She'd been lying to Simon for a long time about these trips. He thought she restricted herself to one visit per year, but her frequency of visits depended only on whether she could get away unnoticed and how desperate she felt.

The journey seemed interminable. She tried to read a book but gave up after realizing she had been reading the same page for thirty minutes. She wished she could sleep, but there was no point trying. Occasionally she closed her eyes to rest them and to avoid conversation with other passengers, but most of the time she stared out the window, clutching her package as if it would save her from some horrible, nameless fate.

When the train finally reached Birmingham, Miranda disembarked and walked for another forty-five minutes to reach the school. She hoped the term hadn't ended early for the Easter holiday. But as she drew near to the squat yellow brick building, she was relieved to see a group of boys running about on the playground. Despite the rainy weather—or perhaps because of it—the boys were clearly enjoying themselves, red-cheeked and yelling good-naturedly. Some weren't even wearing coats, and Miranda repressed a vicarious shiver.

There was a bench under an oak tree at the perimeter of the playground where she and Simon had sat on their visit last winter. She returned to it now, close enough to the boys to see their faces but far enough away that her presence wouldn't be too obvious. She didn't recognize any of the boys, but she saw a few more emerging from the front door of the school, and she settled back to wait.

The deep male voice seemed to come out of nowhere. "It's a cold day, madam. Would you like to come inside to warm yourself?"

Miranda gave a violent start and looked up through her veil at a squarely built man about her own age who stood only a few feet away.

"I beg your pardon," he said. "I didn't mean to startle you. I merely thought you must be cold. I'm George Higgins, a schoolmaster here. Are you a relative of one of the boys?"

"No," she replied. "I . . . I appreciate your concern, but I'm fine. I'm just resting here awhile."

"Very well." He paused a moment longer, peering at her concealed face, then glancing at the gaily colored package in her lap. Miranda was glad she had worn her veil.

"Good day, then," he said.

"Good day."

He walked away, and a few minutes later she saw him enter the school.

She realized she had been holding her breath, and she tried to breathe normally again. Would he tell someone he had seen her? She hadn't caused any trouble. Anyone could sit on a public bench. But what if Richard heard about the heavily veiled woman watching the boys and guessed who it was?

Miranda looked from right to left, wondering if she ought to find a different spot to wait, somewhere less conspicuous. But in the next moment, she forgot all other concerns. All she saw was the blond boy wandering by himself along the perimeter of the playground, throwing a small blue ball in the air and catching it as he walked along. He was still at least thirty feet away, but she knew his frame and his walk, and she devoured him with her eyes, begging him silently to come closer.

When he was perhaps fifteen feet away, another boy called out, "Sam! Come here!" His ball was in mid-flight, and as he turned towards the other boy, it fell to the ground. He walked away to talk to the others, and Miranda's heart sank.

Sam. Samuel. The boy dedicated to the service of God. Wasn't his very name proof that God's hand was in this situation? Or was she deceiving herself? Perhaps his name was proof that she ought to have stayed away. But how could it be a coincidence that this secret name she had cherished in her heart was the same name Richard had given him when he and his wife decided to raise him as their own?

After several minutes, Sam returned, this time clearly intent on finding his ball and just as clearly having forgotten where he dropped it. Hardly knowing what she was doing, Miranda rose, set her package down on the bench, and walked slowly to where the ball lay behind a clump of dead grass. She picked it up, careless of the mud on her gloves, and took a few steps towards the boy, holding out the ball.

"Is this yours?" she asked in a voice that didn't sound like her own.

He nodded but approached her warily, and she realized how odd she must seem to him, a strange woman swathed in a black veil with a shaking voice. She crouched down so she was level with him and lifted her veil.

He looked at her with wide blue eyes, an innocent, open stare. He had changed again since the last time she had seen him, though then she had watched him only from a distance. The baby roundness of his cheeks was gone and he was taller. She thought he was too thin, but she comforted herself with the thought that angularity and thinness ran in both sides of his family.

For Miranda, the passage of time was suspended. She didn't move, didn't even blink, for fear of frightening him away. It was a moment of the most painful ecstasy she had ever known.

Sam reached out to take the ball from her outstretched hand. "Thank you," he said in a well-bred, polite voice. Then he turned away.

It took every ounce of strength Miranda possessed not to call him back or run after him. Was this to be their only exchange? It couldn't be called a conversation. She supposed she ought to be grateful to see him at all, to exchange even a few words with him, since she'd promised Richard she would never try to find Sam after those first few months when she'd had him all to herself. If Richard's wife, Lucy, hadn't fought for Miranda during that time, she wouldn't even have been allowed to hold Sam before she was sent away.

Two men emerged from the school and walked in her direction. Miranda jerked her veil back over her face and forced herself to walk away. Seeing the red package that she had left on the bench, she paused. She couldn't leave it there, but neither could she give it to Sam for his birthday. She had been reckless enough that day. If he took it home, questions would be asked. He might be moved to a new school where she would never find him.

Miranda went to the bench and picked up the parcel, then made her way as quickly as she could back to the train station. Her legs trembled so violently that for a while she thought she might faint. But as she went on, her legs became steadier. As if to mock her physical stability, her mind began to waver and lose its bearings.

The weight of her package was no longer comforting but unbearably heavy, a burden. When she reached the train station she saw a woman with two children, a boy and a girl. The woman wore a shabby cloak and had a pleasant, homely face. The boy was younger than Sam and looked a little frightened by all the noise and bustle around him.

Without preamble, Miranda approached the woman and held out her package. "Here. It's a gift for your boy."

The startled woman just stared at Miranda.

"I can't keep it. Please take it." Belatedly remembering the card tucked into the package, she took it out and put it in her pocket, then held out the package again.

Slowly the woman reached out and took it. Miranda rushed away without waiting for the woman's response.

The next morning Miranda was late getting to the studio. She had awakened after a difficult night determined to go on as she always did, despite feeling exhausted and drained. She had done far more crying than sleeping. Yet her looking glass had surprised her that morning. Aside from looking a little paler than usual, her face bore no trace of the trial she'd endured.

It was half-seven when she arrived at the studio, and she had time only to set up her easel and paints before she heard the downstairs bell ring. After a moment's consideration, she decided to answer it. She knew it had to be Tom. Nobody else came to the studio so early in the morning, and until his boxing mishap several days earlier, he'd visited her nearly every day.

When she went down to open the door, she saw that it was indeed Tom, looking better than he had any right to do, given the injuries he'd received during the fight. She had assumed that, as a clergyman, he would have eschewed any form of violence, but apparently she'd been wrong. She still couldn't understand what had possessed him to put himself in such a dangerous situation.

"May I come in?" he asked. "Or am I disturbing your work?"

"Yes, of course you may."

They were both behaving more formally than usual. They had already established an early-morning routine for Tom's visits to the studio: he usually arrived after she'd been painting for about an hour, and she'd take a break to sit and talk with him. Then he'd leave to carry on with his day. Miranda had asked Mrs. Grant for permission to have visitors in the studio and was waved off with, "Of course. Do as you wish." Thus, Miranda was at ease on that score. Nevertheless, it was a little strange. She didn't know what drew Tom to the studio so regularly, especially when his work made so many demands on him.

Miranda didn't feel much like talking, but she led the way upstairs and sat beside him in her usual chair. "Are you feeling better?" she asked.

"Yes, thank you. Still rather sore in places, but I'm on the mend, thanks to your and Simon's kindness the other night."

"I'm glad."

"I'm sorry I upset you," he said quietly. "I was thinking only of myself, not of the effect of my actions on you."

"I'm sorry, too," she said. "I wasn't very kind to you that night, I'm afraid."

"You have nothing to apologize for. You had every right to be upset."

"No, I don't think so. When I thought about it later, I was relieved that you trusted us enough to seek us out for help."

He regarded her for a moment in silence, then asked, "Miranda, are you all right? You seem . . . different. Anxious or sad, perhaps."

"I'm fine," she said quickly. To change the subject, she asked, "How do you reconcile fighting with being a clergyman?"

"I can't, not really. If I belonged to an official athletic club that observed rules and regulations, I could argue that pugilism is a sport." He paused, running a hand through his hair. "But the Club I went to can't so easily be justified, nor can my motives for going there. It's part of my past. I needed it when I first came to London as a youth—it was my only way of making money. But I don't need it now."

Miranda waited for him to continue, studying his face.

"It isn't easy to tell you this, especially with those eyes on me. Perhaps I could be more honest if you looked away." He spoke half in jest, but she obediently averted her eyes.

"The day I went to the Club," he continued, "I had a difficult conversation with someone and I needed to do something that would . . . I don't know . . . release what was inside me. I wanted to hurt someone or get hurt myself—I'm not sure which. I just knew somehow it would make me feel better . . . that physical hurt would make my mental pain go away. Have I shocked you?"

"No." It made perfect sense, especially given what she had been through the day before. She met his eyes and added, "I've felt that way, too."

"You?" He looked amused. "I can't imagine you hurting anyone on purpose."

"What about hurting myself?"

His expression changed from amusement to alarm. "I hope not, Miranda."

"Women do it all the time," she said, knowing she sounded bitter but not caring. "It's unacceptable to hurt others, so we hurt ourselves instead."

He gave her a sympathetic look.

She continued recklessly, "Yesterday I went somewhere I shouldn't have. If I were a man, I'm certain it would have given me some relief to start a fight."

"Would you like to tell me about it?" he asked.

She shook her head. Her visit to Sam was too recent and her emotions too close to the surface. Besides, if she told Tom about Sam, she'd have to tell him everything, and she wasn't ready for that. "I'd rather find out how you explained your injuries to your colleagues at the cathedral."

He looked embarrassed. "I told them I tried to break up a fight at the prison. I'm in regular contact with prisoners in the course of my reform work, so I thought the excuse plausible. I was worried about preaching the sermon on Sunday, but fortunately I was able to convince another canon to exchange dates with me."

"It would look rather odd to see you preaching with a black eye and broken nose." She managed a smile. "Though you could have used your appearance as an example of what happens when one doesn't turn the other cheek."

He smiled back. "I'd prefer not to have such a dramatic illustration. I'm glad you're not too shocked by my behavior."

She rose and said, "I think I'll continue painting now, if you don't mind. I haven't done much yet today."

"Of course not. Carry on."

Miranda returned to the stool in front of her easel.

She lost track of how much time had passed, and she was startled by two things happening at once. One was a tear rolling down her cheek. She thought she had used up all her tears the night before. The other was Tom's hand on her shoulder. She hadn't heard him approach.

She dashed the tear away and stood up, avoiding his eyes.

"You've been staring at that blank canvas for twenty minutes," he said quietly. "Are you sure you don't want to tell me what's wrong?"

She shook her head, then risked a glance up at him. Tom's dark eyes were filled with warmth and sympathy.

More tears came. She couldn't stop them, nor could she resist his offer of comfort as he took a step closer and put his arms around her.

Miranda had imagined many times what it would feel like to be in Tom's arms, but the reality was better. He felt as solid as a brick wall. A warm brick wall. She felt completely protected and safe, and when her tears were spent, she relaxed enough to slip her arms around his waist and rest her head against his chest. She could smell his cedarwood soap and hear his steady heartbeat. She was glad he couldn't hear hers, which was racing wildly.

"I wish you'd let me help you," he murmured, his cheek against her hair.

Miranda shifted a little in his arms, and he winced. She looked up at him in confusion and started to pull away.

"It's only my ribs," he said. "They haven't quite recovered from the fight, that's all."

He pulled her close again, and his lips brushed her forehead.

Miranda went still. If she raised her head, their lips would meet. There were many, many reasons why she must not allow such a thing to happen.

She raised her head.

His lips touched hers lightly, tentatively. Even so, it was overwhelming. Too real.

She pulled away, almost violently, as if he'd struck her. She was mortified to have instigated the kiss, even if he seemed to have no objection to it. She took two steps back, nearly knocking over her stool in the process.

When she gathered the courage to look at him, he was regarding her with an unreadable expression—surprise? confusion? embarrassment?

"You ought to leave now," she said.

"Yes." He hesitated, then said rather awkwardly, "I apologize if I've offended you."

"You haven't," she replied. "It was a mistake, that's all. My past. . . ." Not knowing how to finish the sentence, she tried again. "My life is . . . complicated."

"Mine is, too. And I don't ever want to do anything that could harm our friendship."

"I feel the same way. That's why I'd like to . . . forget this."

He looked relieved. "Consider it forgotten."

She waited as he made his way to the door, but he stopped and picked up something from the floor, looked at it, then turned back to her.

"Is this yours?" he asked, holding out the card on which she'd written Sam's name. It must have fallen out of her cloak pocket.

She snatched it from his hand, her face burning. "Thank you."

He was looking at her searchingly. Tom was an observant man, and he must have recognized her handwriting and noticed the spots on the card where her tears had fallen, blurring the ink. But perhaps he wasn't that observant. The spots could be raindrops.

He left without asking the question in his eyes, and Miranda returned to her easel. When she picked up her paintbrush, she noticed with annoyance that her hand was shaking.

14

You stand outside,
You artist women, of the common sex;
You share not with us, and exceed us so
Perhaps by what you're mulcted in, your hearts
Being starved to make your heads: so run the old
Traditions of you. I can therefore speak
Without the natural shame which creatures feel
When speaking on their level, to their like.
—Elizabeth Barrett Browning, *Aurora Leigh*

Perhaps we should move that armchair a little to the left. No, to the right. Jane, what's that dark spot on the wallpaper?" Gwen cried, observing the offending spot with dismay. "It must be removed at once!"

"Don't know, mum. T'will take time to remove it," Jane replied. The normally placid maid was red in the face from rushing about to carry out her mistress's orders.

Miranda surveyed the scene from the other side of the room. She had been working on her painting of Gwen mere moments earlier when they were interrupted by Jane's announcement that Lady Carrington was at the door and wished to know if Mrs. and Miss Thorne were at home. The announcement had thrown Gwen into near hysterics. She had never had a visit from a noblewoman, and suddenly her drawing room was unfit to receive such a visitor. Miranda collected her painting supplies and took them to her bedroom, which she thought was all the tidying that was necessary, but Gwen had different ideas.

"Miranda, help us move this side table by the wall," Gwen instructed.

Miranda did so, but when she saw Gwen eyeing the sofa, which was far too large for three relatively small women to even consider moving, she said, "Gwen, surely you will be at a greater risk of incurring Lady Carrington's displeasure by keeping her waiting any longer than by having her sit in an imperfectly arranged room."

Gwen frowned, then ran her hands over her hair and smoothed the skirt of her blue merino dress. "I suppose you're right. Show her in, Jane."

With a grateful look at Miranda, the maid left the room. Gwen looked at Miranda, too, but her look was critical. Miranda knew her hair was in disarray, stray wisps having come loose from the knot at the nape of her neck. She had left her painting smock at the studio, so she'd been working in an old gray dress that now had a large smudge of paint on the left sleeve. She also suspected she smelled like turpentine. But none of these things troubled her as much as they obviously troubled her sister-in-law. Besides, peeress or not, any visitor who showed up on a day that wasn't one of Gwen's regular at-homes had to be prepared to see the house and its inhabitants in their natural state.

When Lady Carrington entered the room, Gwen and Miranda rose to greet her. The noblewoman was a dazzling vision of beauty in a magnificent emerald silk gown and matching feathered hat. Miranda felt a pang of regret that she hadn't taken a moment to improve her own appearance, especially when Lady Carrington approached her and gave her a curious look, rather like a beautiful bird confronted with an inferior member of its species.

Miranda had never been formally introduced to Lady Carrington, but one would have to live in a cave not to know who she was. The Thornes and the Carringtons attended the same cathedral services, and the Carringtons' family pew was near the front of the sanctuary, just behind the pew of the ostentatiously wealthy Narbridge family. Lord Carrington didn't attend as regularly as his wife did, but she and her three impeccably dressed daughters were always there. Lady Carrington was active in the Temperance Society and a patroness of several other charitable organizations. She was much talked about by those who envied her beauty, money, and rank. Miranda was always hearing about public events Lady Carrington attended, what she wore to said events, and whom she invited to her dinner parties.

Still, everything she'd heard about Lady Carrington hadn't prepared Miranda to receive an actual visit from her. As the three women seated themselves in the drawing room, Miranda wondered what had prompted this visit.

"We are so very honored by this visit, Lady Carrington," Gwen said, apparently unable to stop herself from talking too much. "Please excuse the state of the drawing room. My husband and I have been planning to make improvements, but we simply haven't had the time. Our days are taken up with a good deal of entertaining. My mother has been here, and of course all our friends from Denfield have come to London to see our new house. We have had visits from some prominent people in London, too, of course."

Gwen's outright lie about knowing prominent people, and her officious manner, made Miranda want to cringe. She felt her eyes widen and had to struggle to keep her eyebrows from rising in shock.

If Lady Carrington was annoyed by Gwen's manner, she didn't show it. "Please forgive me for dropping in unexpectedly. I've intended for some time to visit you, and today I had some other visits to make in the neighborhood, so I thought I'd see if you were at home."

"Other visits?" Gwen repeated. She gave Miranda a significant look, as if to say, *You see what a good neighborhood we live in?* Miranda was afraid Gwen might actually ask Lady Carrington for the names of the people she was visiting, but a fortunate distraction was created just then by Jane entering the room with the tea things.

"Why, Jane, where are the Savoy biscuits?" Gwen asked in an imperious tone. "We always have Savoy biscuits at afternoon tea."

Miranda didn't think they'd had Savoy biscuits more than once or twice before. What they always had was seedcake, but Gwen must have thought seedcake wasn't good enough for a peeress.

"I . . . I don't know, mum," replied the confused Jane. "I don't think we have any left."

"Look again. I'm certain we have some." Gwen gave Jane a severe look, and the maid fled. Turning to Lady Carrington, Gwen sighed and said in a conspiratorial whisper, "I don't know what's the matter with that girl. One simply can't find good servants these days."

Miranda blushed with shame at Gwen's attempt to impress Lady Carrington by sacrificing the dignity of poor Jane, who was a very good maid indeed.

To Lady Carrington's credit, she said, "I don't think it's so very difficult to find good servants. I find when they are treated well, most of them are good workers."

"Well. Hmm. Yes, of course," Gwen stammered.

"May I offer my belated congratulations on your marriage? I understand you and Mr. Thorne were married a couple of months ago." Lady Carrington bestowed a dazzling smile upon Gwen, and Miranda felt the warmth and light of it even though it wasn't meant for her. She felt like a cat irresistibly drawn to a patch of sunlight.

The effect of the smile on Gwen was to loosen her tongue once again, and she poured forth a detailed account of the wedding and the move to London. It didn't include a description of every shopping trip, but it was enough to be painful to Miranda. She assumed it was no less excruciating for Lady Carrington, but the latter was far too well-bred to show it.

Just as Miranda was about to interrupt Gwen in a desperate attempt to save both herself and Lady Carrington from the torrent of words, the peeress herself did the honor, and far more graciously than Miranda ever could have.

"My dear Mrs. Thorne, I am very happy indeed you have found so much pleasure in setting up your new home," Lady Carrington said. Her voice was quiet but so clear it sliced through Gwen's rambling like a knife. "I'm sorry to cut my visit short, but I'm afraid I'll have to leave soon. Before I do, I'd like to speak to Miss Thorne privately for a few minutes."

Gwen looked as shocked as if Lady Carrington had asked to speak privately to Jane. Miranda herself was surprised. She had no idea Lady Carrington had anything in particular to say to her, and she'd been content to stay in the background as she usually did during social calls.

It took Gwen a long time to recover from the shock. She finally stammered, "Ah . . . well . . . of course. If that's what you wish." But she didn't move, looking from Lady Carrington to Miranda helplessly.

"Gwen, perhaps you could check on Jane's progress in finding the biscuits," Miranda suggested.

"Oh. Yes, that's a good idea." Gwen rose and left the room stiffly.

After she had gone, Lady Carrington said, "I hope I haven't offended her."

"She'll be fine," said Miranda.

"I have a rather peculiar request to make of you, and I didn't want to mention it with anyone else present in case it offends you."

Miranda was baffled, apprehensive, and more than a little intrigued.

"You are an artist, are you not?"

"Yes. How did you know?" Miranda had sold a few paintings under her alias only, and she was by no means becoming generally known.

"Isabella Grant told me. She also told me you are reluctant to put yourself forward despite your great talent."

"It was kind of her to say so."

"You needn't be modest with me," Lady Carrington said with a smile. "I disapprove of modesty in all its forms."

You can afford to disapprove of it, thought Miranda. *I can't.*

"I won't keep you in suspense any longer," the noblewoman continued. "You see, my husband wishes to commission a portrait of me, and we've been arguing about which painter to give the commission to, as well as about the style of the painting. He wants a formal painting in the style of Reynolds or Sargent, the sort of thing one sees ad nauseam in people's ancestral homes. I can't bear the thought of posing for such a painting, wearing my silks and best jewels and looking as dull as every other society wife. I want something different."

"Different in what way?"

"I'm fond of religious paintings. I understand you paint religious subjects as well."

Miranda nodded, still confused.

"I wish to be painted as the Virgin Mary, though with a difference."

Miranda was shocked. While she didn't venerate the Virgin Mary or consider her more important than any other Christian saint, it was undeniably presumptuous of Lady Carrington to make such a request. Not to mention the fact that she was too beautiful and sophisticated to be portrayed as the simple, ordinary girl who became the mother of Christ.

"I want this painting to be different from any other of the Virgin Mary, not the frightened girl of Rossetti's Annunciation, nor a serene Botticelli Madonna," Lady Carrington explained. "I want to be her as a symbol of all women, pure and sensual, simple and complex, angelic and demonic . . . I want people to look at this painting and be awed by the way it encompasses every aspect of womanhood."

"Why?"

"You have a very direct way of speaking and looking, Miss Thorne. I can't explain why I want this, not in one brief conversation. Will you visit me at my home another day, so we can discuss it further?"

"I don't think so, my lady. You seem to have a specific, yet all-encompassing idea of what you want me to paint, but I don't work that way."

Lady Carrington held up an elegant green-gloved hand. "Before you refuse my offer, I want you to know I won't give you instructions or meddle with your methods as soon as I'm satisfied that you understand me. I will also pay you five hundred pounds for the portrait."

It was a staggering amount, and the mention of it took Miranda's breath away. The most she had received for a painting to date was fifty pounds, which she'd considered a respectable sum. What a contribution she could make to the household expenses with five hundred pounds! As much as she disapproved of Gwen's spending, she would do almost anything to lift the financial burden from her brother's shoulders.

Yet there was something strange about Lady Carrington's request. What she was asking sounded impossible, far beyond the limits of what the most skilled artists could achieve, and Miranda wouldn't dare to class herself with them.

"The only painting I can think of that comes near to encompassing every aspect of womanhood, as you describe it, is *La Gioconda*," said Miranda. "While I'm flattered that you should think me capable of such a feat of artistry, any attempt on my part to imitate da Vinci would be laughable and embarrassing for both of us."

"I don't want another *La Gioconda*. What I am proposing is something much simpler, and I do think your talents are equal to it."

"You seem to know a great deal about me. How did you come by this knowledge?"

"You are very suspicious, Miss Thorne, as well as very direct." Lady Carrington didn't seem offended, but there was an edge to her voice that hadn't been there before.

"I don't mean to be suspicious, my lady. I merely wonder why you've chosen me."

"I considered other artists, but most of the well-known ones are men, and I don't want a man to paint me. With very few exceptions, men, whether artists or not, see women in only two ways, as angels or whores." Miranda winced, and Lady Carrington added, "Surely I needn't put on false modesty in front of you, Miss Thorne. You're an artist and therefore you must see the truth of things and be willing to call them by their correct names. Am I right?"

Miranda merely said, "Go on."

"Only another woman can paint me as I wish to be painted. Only another woman can see the many facets of womanhood that are not only part of me but part of all of us. My husband wants a portrait of me that will show me off as his prize. He wants to immortalize my beauty—and yes, I see no reason for false modesty about that, either—in the same flat, tedious way as men throughout history have done. It won't do. I will only pose for a portrait if it reveals who I truly am in all my contradictions, all my ugliness as well as my beauty. Do you understand?"

Miranda surprised herself by saying, "Yes, I think I'm beginning to." The other woman's words had a curious effect on her, as if she were standing on her favorite hill near the old cottage watching the sunrise. It was a glimpse of a world where she could be completely free.

Lady Carrington smiled. "Then you ought to understand why I chose you. Last week I went to Mrs. Grant's studio, thinking to ask her to paint my portrait, but then I saw the paintings of yours that were on display. The portrait of the little boy and his mother caught my attention—I stared at it for a very long time. The depth of emotion and intelligence that you were able to portray in both of their faces was extraordinary! I actually wept to see it."

Lady Carrington's voice had become unsteady, and she paused, averting her face.

The painting she referred to was Miranda's favorite, too, and she refused to sell it despite having received several offers. The subjects were strangers to her, a mother and son passing by in the street one day. In an uncharacteristic act of boldness, she had actually pursued them, flying down the street like a madwoman, and convinced them to sit for her.

Lady Carrington turned back to Miranda. "Do you still wonder why I chose you?" Without waiting for a response, she went on, "I must admit, you surprise me. You're younger than I expected. And you dress so"—she paused, as if she were choosing her words carefully—"so plainly and severely. You remind me of a nun from one of the Anglican sisterhoods."

Miranda wasn't offended. Her style of dress was as carefully chosen as anything Lady Carrington would wear at her most lavish party.

The peeress continued, "Your eyes tell a different story, though, as do your paintings. You should know I'm accustomed to getting what I want, Miss Thorne."

Miranda lifted her chin. "*You* should know I'm not easily persuaded if I've decided against a course of action."

"And have you decided not to paint my portrait?"

Miranda's attempt at hauteur deflated quickly. "No. But I'm not convinced that I'm the right artist for you."

The two women looked at each other silently for a few moments. Lady Carrington didn't seem troubled by Miranda's resistance, nor did she look away from Miranda's direct gaze.

"Why do you want it to be a religious painting?" Miranda asked finally. "It would be easier if you merely posed as yourself if you wish to be a symbol of all women. Posing as the Virgin Mary will lead the viewer to see only one type of woman."

"That's where the uniqueness of it would come in," Lady Carrington said. "It will be a Virgin Mary such as nobody has seen before. It will make everyone who views it think about the artificiality of the categories our society forces women into."

In her mind's eye, Miranda caught another glimpse of that sunrise world. What would it be like to live in a society where women were as free as men, where they were thought of as human beings first and women second? It seemed impossible. At the same time, she didn't want her painting to be used to make a political statement. Was Lady Carrington involved with one of the extremist women's suffrage groups that had been in the papers lately?

Miranda said only, "People tend to be very stubborn about the portrayal of beloved religious figures. It would be easy to give offense."

"This will be a private portrait. Although my husband will no doubt want it prominently displayed in our home, it will be possible to control who sees it and who doesn't. I could even arrange to have a curtain in front of it, rather like the one in front of the duchess's portrait in Mr. Browning's poem." She smiled at her own joke.

Miranda wondered if there something more, something potentially offensive in the portrait than what Lady Carrington had disclosed. But there was no polite way to ask.

Catching sight of the clock on the mantelpiece, Lady Carrington rose to her feet. "I've lost track of the time. I must go at once. Will you consider my offer and visit me next week to discuss it further?"

"Yes, I will."

Lady Carrington took her leave after making a gracious apology to Gwen, who was just returning from a fruitless search for the Savoy biscuits.

When Lady Carrington had gone, Miranda remained in her seat in the drawing room, lost in thought.

"Miranda!"

Gwen's voice, loud and close to her ear, made Miranda jump. "What is it?"

"I've asked you three times what Lady Carrington wanted to speak to you about, and you were ignoring me." Gwen returned to her seat on the sofa.

"I'm sorry. I was woolgathering."

"As usual. I hope you didn't do that with her. You must not have offered her any tea—it hasn't been touched."

"I forgot. It doesn't matter."

"So, what did she say? I assume it is not such a great secret that I might not know it."

Miranda restrained herself from pointing out that Lady Carrington had specifically requested a private conversation with her and that Gwen might make what she would of that. "She wants me to paint her portrait."

Gwen's eyes grew wide. "Really? You? What an honor! When will you start?"

"I haven't agreed to do it yet. I need to think about it."

"What is there to think about? You are hardly inundated with commissions at the moment. What did she offer to pay?"

Miranda would have preferred to keep this information to herself, but she didn't want to antagonize Gwen. She also admitted to herself that part of her wanted to throw this tangible estimation of her value as an artist in Gwen's face.

"Five hundred pounds," Miranda said.

"Oh, my word!" Gwen gasped, and sat back with her hand over her heart. "I can't believe it! Why in the world didn't you accept her offer at once?"

"There are other things to consider, things I am not at liberty to discuss."

Gwen tossed her head and began to tap her fingernails on the tea tray. "I don't see why all the mystery is necessary."

Miranda said nothing.

Frowning, Gwen pressed, "I assume she isn't asking you to paint anything immoral or indecent. Though one never knows with members of the nobility."

"Of course not. I would have refused her offer if she had made such a request."

"I'm glad you haven't allowed the artist world to lower your standards, Mouse," Gwen said in what she probably thought was an affectionate tone. She often made reference to "the artist world" in a way that made it sound like a very den of iniquity. "The things one hears about the lives of artists and the sort of people they use as their models . . ." Gwen shuddered. "You are very careful about your models, aren't you?"

"Yes, Gwen."

"You would never paint persons who were . . . unclothed, would you?"

"I might do," Miranda said.

Her words had the intended effect: Gwen was shocked into silence.

15

No one is useless in this world . . .

who lightens the burden of it for any one else.

—Charles Dickens, *Our Mutual Friend*

Tom sighed and rubbed his forehead with the heel of his hand. The Sunday service that morning hadn't gone well. He was standing in the narthex of the cathedral, greeting parishioners as they left and struggling to appear interested in what they had to say. Usually he enjoyed talking with parishioners, but he had been irritated by a number of small mishaps before and during the service, as well as by the sermon, which Paul Harris had preached. A new acolyte had spilled some Communion wine just before the service began; an aged choir member had tripped and fallen on his way up the stairs to the choir loft; and Canon Martin, who had been scheduled to read the Gospel, had taken ill only minutes before he was to read. In each case, Tom had smoothed over the difficulties, taking care of the spill and giving the acolyte a firm lecture on handling the sacred vessels more carefully; determining that the choir member was more frightened than injured and helping him to his seat; and finally, reading the Gospel himself.

Paul Harris's sermon was a bigger problem that even Tom couldn't solve. Harris's sermons were more like university lectures. This one was worse than usual, filled with bizarre mystical fluff and a painstaking (and painful, at least to Tom) exposition of an obscure passage in the book of Ezekiel. Tom had no use for these scholarly flights of fancy, especially in sermons. What the people needed to hear was sound, practical theology, ways they could apply the doctrines of Christianity to their lives. How exactly could visions of cherubim and dry bones and whirlwinds do that?

It was true that some people liked Harris's sermons. Unaccountably, Miranda was one of them. Tom was loath to admit it, but it bothered him that she seemed to prefer Harris's sermons to his own. She hadn't said so, of course, but she had praised one of Harris's sermons so highly that Tom hadn't been able to help hinting at his displeasure. She hadn't said a word about anyone's sermons after that.

In his most charitable moments, Tom admitted that Harris was a good speaker. He had the charisma to infuse his words with drama and passion. Although Tom preached well enough, he hadn't the ability to enthrall his listeners. He told himself he didn't care, that his strengths more than made up for that weakness, if weakness it was. What he did well was solve problems; he knew what to do with things that were broken or spilled or out of place. Even more important, he knew what to do with *people* who were broken. When someone needed help, it was Tom he or she turned to, not Harris, who usually disappeared as soon as a service was over in order to be alone with his elevated thoughts.

Harris was standing at the other side of the entrance to the cathedral, about ten feet away. Of late, he seemed to be making more of an effort to be sociable with colleagues and parishioners alike, and Tom had no doubt that Harris's desire for the deanship was the cause of this change. Tom couldn't help overhearing what Harris was saying as he greeted parishioners, and he found the man's forced, artificial friendliness almost as irritating as his sermon. He was telling people to remember that the Old Testament prophets spoke of final renewal and reconciliation with God, not just doom and destruction.

During a break in the flow of people, Tom approached Harris and said, "Are you really as enamored of the prophets as you claim? Whether the message is of doom or renewal, aren't you more interested in the scholarly minutiae, the more bizarre the better?"

Harris gave Tom a blank look. "What's your point, Cross?"

"It's the intellectual challenge that interests you, not the message."

"I don't see the two as mutually exclusive. Besides, the message is no different from that of the scriptures as a whole. Any priest worth his salt believes that morally corrupt people who refuse to repent deserve punishment. Don't you?"

Tom raised his eyebrows. "Aren't we past the catechism stage?"

"I am, but I'm not as certain about you. Perhaps you ought to brush up on the basic doctrines of Christianity." Harris gave Tom a condescending smile.

Before Tom could reply, William Narbridge inserted himself between the two canons and said, "Another excellent sermon, Canon Harris."

"Thank you," Harris replied. "I'm glad you liked it."

Glancing at Tom, Narbridge said to Harris, "If I had my way, you'd be the only cathedral clergyman allowed in the pulpit."

This was an unusually direct insult, even for Narbridge, and Tom clenched his jaw to prevent himself from making a sharp retort.

To his credit, Harris seemed surprised, too. "We all have our strengths and weaknesses," he said. "I think it's good for the congregation to hear different approaches to the scriptures."

"Certainly," Narbridge replied, "but only from clergymen whose moral character is above reproach. Good day."

He turned to leave, but as he did so he nearly collided with a ragged-looking boy who had just entered the cathedral.

"Beg yer pardon, sir," the boy stammered without looking up.

"What do you want, boy?" Narbridge snapped, a repulsed look on his face. "We don't allow begging in the cathedral."

"On the contrary," Tom objected, putting a reassuring hand on the boy's shoulder, "Everyone is welcome here." The boy looked up and Tom exclaimed, "Jack! I'm glad to see you. Are you looking for me?"

The boy looked frightened. "Yes, sir. I'm not 'ere to cause any trouble. You said I could come and ask fer you if . . ." His voice trailed off.

"You may come here whenever you like," Tom said. With a pointed look at Narbridge, he added, "The purpose of a church is to help people. *All* people." He guided the boy away from the narthex, down a side aisle, and into his office.

It had been weeks since Tom had seen Jack. It wasn't for lack of trying on Tom's part—every time he visited the factory where Jack worked, the boy seemed to be away on some errand. Tom had even gone to Jack's house one evening, a squalid, crowded tenement dwelling in the East End, though there the boy's father prevented him from seeing Jack. Mr. Goode had answered the door, then disappeared inside, keeping Tom standing at the door for a quarter of an hour before reappearing and announcing that Jack couldn't speak to Tom because he was in bed. Mr. Goode's breath had reeked of alcohol, just as it had during their first meeting, and it was all Tom could do to prevent himself from knocking the man down, breaking into the house, and taking Jack away.

As Tom invited the boy to sit down and took a chair himself, he observed with dismay that the skin around Jack's left eye was yellowish-green and there was a long scratch on his cheek. There were probably other injuries, judging from Jack's stiff movements, but the clothing he wore was too big for him, the sleeves reaching past his fingers and the collar of his jacket pulled up high under his chin, so nothing was immediately visible. His unruly dark hair fell over his forehead, partly obscuring his eyes. It looked as if Jack were disappearing.

"What can I do for you, Jack?" Tom asked, leaning forward with his elbows on his knees.

The boy darted a quick glance at Tom as if to assure himself that Tom wasn't about to make any sudden movements, then looked down at the floor. "Could you 'elp me find my sister?"

"Which sister do you mean? Has one of the little ones gone missing?"

The boy shook his head. "Ann's the oldest. She's grown-up. My da said she was dead, but I 'eard the neighbor woman talkin' about her, sayin' she was in a place where bad women go. She called it a pen . . . a pen . . ."

"A penitentiary?"

"Yes."

Tom knew a good deal about penitentiaries. They were charitable institutions, often run by Anglican sisterhoods, that housed unmarried mothers and prostitutes, as well as other women who were living on the streets. Tom and Paul Harris had been commissioned by the bishop the previous year to investigate penitentiaries that had been accused of unduly harsh treatment of their inmates. One such penitentiary, the Whitechapel House of Mercy, had been shut down as a result of the two canons' inquiries. Tom felt strongly about regulating these institutions, and while he believed they generally did some good, he was concerned about the ones that did far more harm.

"Did you overhear the neighbor woman say the name of this penitentiary, or where it might be?" Tom asked.

Jack shook his head, looking mournful.

"It's all right. There are not so many penitentiaries in London that it will be impossible to find her. We'll go to all of them, if necessary." Tom spoke reassuringly, but he hoped they wouldn't have to visit every penitentiary in London. For all he knew, Ann had been admitted under a different name and it would be next to impossible to find her.

Jack brightened a little, meeting Tom's eyes. "If we find 'er, do you think the people at the pen . . . pentery would let me stay with 'er?"

Tom hesitated. Children weren't allowed at any penitentiary he knew of, especially not children who were merely siblings of the inmates. And that was as it should be. He didn't think a penitentiary was the place for children, who could be negatively influenced by the inmates' unwholesome former lives. He wanted to be honest with Jack, but he didn't want to crush the boy's hopes, either.

"I don't know, Jack. I'm sure you could visit her, at least."

The hopeful light died in Jack's eyes. He had a remarkably expressive face.

"Why do you want to stay with your sister?" Tom asked the boy gently.

Jack shrugged. "I don't 'ave anywhere to live."

"Did your father throw you out?"

Jack raised his chin in a defiant gesture. "No. I left on my own."

"Was that just today?"

"No, days ago. Dunno 'ow many."

Tom frowned. "Where have you been living all that time?"

"Different places," the boy said evasively.

Tom had no doubt Jack had been living on the streets. "Why didn't you come to see me sooner?"

"I thought I 'ad to wait 'til Sunday, with you bein' a clergyman."

"I'm sorry I didn't tell you I'm here at the cathedral every day. And if I happened not to be here when you came, someone could have told you where to find me. You'll remember that, won't you?"

The boy nodded.

Tom debated what to do next. There was no way he was going to let the boy slip through his fingers now. If he went back to his father, he might well be killed, and living on the streets was little better. Finding Ann Goode would take time, and there was nothing she could do for her brother from the penitentiary. And if she was close to finishing her time there, she wouldn't likely be able to provide a home for Jack, however simple.

There was still the possibility of finding Jack a position as a lower servant at a home where he would be treated kindly, as Miranda had suggested. But it would take time to make these arrangements, too, and it was unlikely that anyone would agree to employ Jack, especially if they saw him in the state he was in now. He thought of Narbridge's reaction to Jack at the entrance of the cathedral. Tom knew all too well that people didn't want to see bedraggled, dirty little specimens of humanity on their own property.

Thus, temporary provision had to be made for Jack immediately. Although Tom's landlady had a rule prohibiting children from living in her building, he supposed she couldn't evict him for having a child stay with him for a day or two. After that, Tom would find the boy a permanent place. The most important thing was to keep Jack away from his father, at least until all the arrangements were made.

"Jack, what do you think about coming home with me today? You can't stay for more than a few days, but you'll be safe there."

The boy had been gazing around the room during Tom's ruminations, looking less timid than he had at first. Now, he looked at Tom warily. "Will you 'elp me find my sister?"

"Yes, I will."

"All right."

Tom canceled his appointments for the afternoon without a second thought and took the boy to his lodgings, stopping at a pastry shop on the way to buy food for their luncheon. Jack's eyes grew as huge as saucers when he saw the meat pies and jellies that Tom purchased. The simple fare probably looked like a royal feast to the poor child.

Once at Tom's lodgings, Jack didn't say a word, only watched Tom set out the food on the table as if it were a dream he was afraid he'd awaken from at any moment. When Tom said grace and invited the boy to eat, Jack didn't need to be told twice, shoveling in mouthful after mouthful at such an alarming speed that Tom was afraid the boy would choke or make himself sick.

"Slow down a little," Tom said after a while. "It will be a shock to your stomach to get so much in it all at once."

The fork that had been on its way to Jack's mouth halted. He set it down on his plate and hung his head. "Sorry, Mr. Cross."

Tom was alarmed by Jack's extreme reaction to his mild admonition. "There's no need to apologize. I'm not angry. I was only concerned about your stomach. Go on and eat more if you're still hungry, lad."

Jack raised his head, but watched Tom with an uncertain look. Tom had wrongly assumed that Jack would trust him. How stupid of him to forget what it was like to be Jack's age and to be at the mercy of his father's sudden rages.

Assuring the boy once again that he could eat as much as he wanted, Tom excused himself to consult his appointment calendar in the sitting room. As he was doing so, there was a knock at his door. When he went to open it, his landlady stood there, a tall, thin matron of indeterminate age. Mrs. Brown seemed to take great pains to live up to her name. She had brown hair and eyes, and she always wore brown clothing. Only her face was a different color, a bright, feverish red.

"Canon Cross. Is there a child on the premises?"

Tom was amazed she could be aware of Jack's presence within fifteen minutes of his entering the building. The woman must be able to smell children, he thought, like the witch in the story of Hansel and Gretel.

"There is, indeed," he replied, stepping out onto the landing and closing the door behind him so Jack couldn't hear the conversation.

"You know my policy about children," said Mrs. Brown. "How long do you intend to keep the young person here?"

"Only a day or two. He has nowhere else to go, and I'm responsible for him."

"Has he no parents?"

"Mrs. Brown, if the boy goes, so do I. I have no other choice."

She muttered a little, but then said, "Very well. No more than two days."

When Tom returned to his rooms, Jack, still at the table, gave Tom a worried look.

"Must I leave now?" the boy asked.

"No, you can stay here for a few days."

"I don't want to make trouble."

"You're not making trouble. I want to help you, and I'm glad you came looking for me today."

"Why?"

"Why, what?"

The boy suddenly looked older. His eyes were clear and intelligent, temporarily free from fear. "Why do you want to 'elp me?"

"Because I know what it's like to have to work when one is very young," Tom said quietly. "Because I know what it's like to be beaten when one has done nothing wrong. Because I had a father like yours."

"You don't know my da," Jack said with a sudden flash of defensiveness.

Tom wasn't surprised by Jack's reaction. As a child he, too, had defended his father to outsiders, no matter how badly he had been treated. "You're right. I don't."

The next couple of days were a flurry of activity. In addition to his regular duties at the cathedral, the prison, and the hospital, Tom spoke to a few families he knew about the possibility of taking Jack in temporarily. He also visited a few penitentiaries in search of Jack's sister. There was no time for anything else, not even his early-morning visits to Miranda's studio.

Tom took Jack everywhere with him except the penitentiaries and the prison. After a haircut, a bath, and finding clothing that fit him, Jack looked like a perfectly respectable middle-class boy, so much so that some of Tom's parishioners and colleagues mistook Jack for a nephew or young cousin of Tom's.

Although Jack was well-behaved and didn't wander off when Tom told him to wait while he went about his duties, there was still something wild and wary in the boy's eyes, especially when people ventured too near. He was different around Tom—the wary look disappeared, for which Tom was grateful, but the boy remained quiet and uncertain, offering no information about himself or his feelings beyond what he had told Tom the first day.

On the third evening (to Mrs. Brown's displeasure, Tom had not yet been able to arrange a place for Jack to stay), the Thornes invited Tom over for supper. He took Jack with him, happy for the opportunity to take the boy to a friendly household.

Still, Tom was apprehensive about seeing Miranda. They hadn't met since that day in the studio when his attempt to comfort her had ended in the kiss. It could hardly be called a kiss, really, just the briefest touch of their lips, before she had pulled away. He'd been a fool to embrace her without thinking what such intimacy might lead to, but at the time he'd thought only of comforting her. Although he cared deeply for her, he didn't think of her in a romantic way. Yet he was confused by the kiss and had been disappointed when she pulled away. Her hair smelled of lavender, and her lips were invitingly soft.

Tom was also quite sure it had been her handwriting on the card he found on the floor of the studio that day. Who was Sam? What was complicated about her life? He wasn't willing to ask questions that he wouldn't answer himself.

He needn't have worried about his reception at the Thornes' house. Simon, Gwen, and Miranda welcomed Tom and his charge warmly. Except for a momentary reluctance to meet Tom's eyes, Miranda was her usual self, and supper was uneventful until Jack accidentally knocked over his bowl of soup as he was reaching for a roll.

Gwen, who was closest to Jack at the time, leaped to her feet to avoid the soup splashing onto her dress, and Jack fled the room. Tom remained at the table for a moment to help prevent the spill from spreading—it had already soaked the tablecloth and begun to drip onto the carpet. But when Jane, the Thornes' maid, arrived to assist in the cleanup, he went in search of Jack.

Tom couldn't find the boy anywhere. He checked the drawing room, the kitchen (to the alarm of the cook, who disapproved of gentlemen in her inner sanctum), the front foyer, and even the street outside, but Jack seemed to have disappeared. Tom returned to the house in consternation. If the boy had left the house, it would be very difficult to find him. Tom didn't think Jack would be able to find his way back to Tom's lodgings, and he was worried the boy might return to the only home he knew—with his father.

Simon met Tom at the door. "No luck? Don't worry, Tom, we'll find him. Poor lad must have been frightened when Gwen jumped up like that. Do you think he expected to be beaten?"

"No doubt he did," Tom replied. "I think I'd better go back to the street and search a bit further afield."

"I'll come with you."

Just then, Gwen appeared in the foyer and said, "We've found him."

"Where is he?" asked Tom.

"In Miranda's bedroom. He must have run to the farthest room in the house that he could find."

"If you show me the way, I'll fetch him."

"There's no need. Miranda is with him, and she says she can eat later. Let's return to the table before the food is cold."

Tom acquiesced reluctantly. He hoped Jack wouldn't cause any trouble for Miranda.

"Well, that boy certainly gave me a fright, the way he sped out of the room," Gwen said when she, Simon, and Tom had resumed eating. "I had no idea he could move so quickly."

"I think you gave *him* just as much of a fright, dearest," Simon said to Gwen.

"What are you going to do with the child, Mr. Jones?" Gwen asked Tom. "Surely he can't continue to live with you." Although she knew his name wasn't Jones, it was the name he had been using when she first met him, and it seemed to amuse her to refer to him this way.

"I'm looking for a place for him, preferably a home where he can do some light work to earn his keep. I'll admit, I'm having trouble finding such a place. At the moment I'd be happy to find any family who would take him in temporarily. My landlady doesn't allow children, so every day he stays with me is a fresh insult to her, or so she'd have me believe."

"Even if she did allow children, a bachelor's lodgings are no place for a child. You should marry, and then you could adopt the boy." Gwen gave Tom a pointed look. Ever since she and Simon had married, she had taken a few liberties in giving Tom advice on his personal life, as if she were an old matron with many years of experience instead of a young bride.

Before Tom could deflect this unpromising turn in the conversation, Simon stepped in. "Gwen, my dear, Tom can hardly follow your advice instantly, and something must be done about the boy at once. Perhaps we could take him in for a little while."

Tom had considered asking the Thornes if Jack could stay with them, but after giving the matter some thought, he had decided not to. Miranda had hinted that Simon was experiencing financial difficulties, and although one would never know it from the luxurious furnishings in the house, Tom believed her. It was clear enough that Simon was in thrall to Gwen's every whim, and if those whims were expensive ones, his friend hadn't a chance.

All of which made Simon's suggestion more surprising. Judging from the look on Gwen's face, he hadn't mentioned it to her privately first. Shock and displeasure registered briefly in her eyes, but her face quickly assumed a polite mask. The only sign she was still upset was the violent way in which she twisted one of her dark curls around her finger.

"Simon, I don't see how we possibly could," she said. She turned to Tom with a look so innocently appealing that he almost believed in her sincerity. "We'd love to have the child with us, of course, but we don't have a room for him. If we didn't have Jane, the boy could sleep in the kitchen, but as things stand, I'm afraid it isn't possible."

"We do have a small spare room, Gwen. Nobody is occupying it at present."

Tom was impressed by Simon's stubbornness. He had never heard Simon contradict his wife before.

From the shocked look on Gwen's face, apparently she hadn't experienced such an event, either. "That's impossible!" she exclaimed, the polite mask slipping again. "We can't keep a . . . a street child in our guest room.

We don't know what he's capable of." Turning to Tom, she added, "No offense, of course, but children like that can't be trusted in one's home. He might take something that doesn't belong to him without realizing it's wrong—"

"No matter what class they are born into, children have a natural sense of right and wrong," Tom said sharply.

"Perhaps, but what they learn from their parents can quickly change that," Gwen said, refusing to be cowed.

Tom was surprised. His tone had been meant to shut down the conversation, as it usually did with others, but Gwen wasn't backing down. Tom took pity on Simon, who was squirming with discomfort at the direction the conversation had taken.

Although he was angry with Gwen, Tom said evenly, "I'm sure I'll find a home for Jack. I wouldn't want him to stay with anyone who isn't comfortable with his presence. I think I'll see how he and Miranda are getting on."

As Tom rose from the table, Simon rose also and said, "I'll show you the way."

As soon as they were out of earshot, Simon said, "Don't mind Gwen. She's never liked the idea of strangers in the house. It isn't anything personal against Jack."

"No doubt," Tom said, though he didn't believe it for a minute.

Miranda's bedroom was at the end of the hallway on the first floor, and the door stood ajar. As they approached, Tom could hear her voice, steady and calm. He remembered hearing it for the first time when he awoke in the cottage after the attack, and he was again struck by its soothing tone. Jack would have to be beyond human help indeed if he were immune to the effects of that voice.

"If you add some shading there, it looks like the arm is stretched out. You see?" Miranda was saying just as Simon knocked on the door.

"Miranda?" Simon called. "Tom's here with me. How's Jack?"

"Very well, indeed," was the reply. There was no other sound from within, and Tom had the feeling that Jack and Miranda were waiting for them to go away.

"Jack, why don't you come out and finish your supper?" Tom said. "Miss Thorne hasn't had hers yet, and you don't want her to go hungry, do you?"

After a moment, the door opened fully, and Miranda emerged smiling, with a sheaf of paper in her hand, Jack trailing behind her. Turning to look at him, she said, "You can bring the drawings downstairs with you. We can work on them again after supper."

There was a pause while the boy went back into the room, emerging with his own sheaf of papers. There was a dark smudge on his cheek that looked like charcoal.

Looking at his feet, Jack said, "I'm sorry I spilled the soup."

"No harm done, lad," Simon said cheerfully. He reached out to pat the boy's shoulder, but Jack shrank back.

As the foursome made their way downstairs, Miranda lagged a little behind, and Tom turned to give her a grateful smile. "Thank you," he whispered.

"You're welcome," she whispered back. "The poor mite managed to wedge himself under my dressing table. I couldn't coax him out until I started to show him some of my sketches, but we got on like a house on fire from then on."

The rest of the evening passed peacefully. After Jack and Miranda had eaten, everyone reassembled in the drawing room, where the adults engaged in light conversation and Jack practiced the drawing techniques Miranda had shown him. He was clearly more relaxed than he'd been earlier in the evening.

Jack and Tom left a short time later. On the walk back to Tom's lodgings, the boy seemed thoughtful and quiet. Eventually he said, "Miss Thorne said I could visit 'er studio."

Tom smiled down at the boy. "Would you like that?"

"Yes."

"Then I'll take you there later this week."

The rest of the walk home was accomplished in a comfortable silence.

16

You are not a woman. You may try—but you can never imagine
what it is to have a man's force of genius in you,
and yet to suffer the slavery of being a girl.

—George Eliot, *Daniel Deronda*

That's all I need for now," Miranda said, closing her sketchbook. "The painting will, of course, take a good deal of time. Would you prefer to have the sittings here or would you like to come to the studio?"

"It will be easier for you if you don't have to move all of your equipment. I'd be happy to go to the studio," Lady Carrington replied, stretching her arms above her head in a way that was oddly both childlike and sensual.

Miranda had been doing some preliminary sketches in Lady Carrington's private sitting room. It was very different from the other rooms Miranda had seen in the mansion, which reminded her of a museum, with its perfectly placed mahogany furniture, heavy velvet curtains, and long, echoing hallways. In contrast, Lady Carrington's sitting room was a tribute to feminine disarray. The writing table and chair, as well as the sofa, were in the Queen Anne style, with delicate, curved lines. Several small tables overflowed with a jumble of hairpins, jewelry, gloves, and ribbons. Another chair was piled with clothing and delicate silks that appeared to have been carelessly tossed aside.

Even before arriving at the Carringtons' house that day, Miranda had known she would accept the commission. The five hundred pounds was tempting, but even more so was the challenge of painting something unique. Although Miranda still wasn't sure about portraying Lady Carrington as the Virgin Mary, she was intrigued by the idea of a portrait that would express the complexities of womanhood.

Miranda was also intrigued by Lady Carrington herself. She hadn't the arrogant or haughty manner one might expect of such a beautiful woman. She wore her beauty as if it were a medal she had won for fighting in a war she didn't remember—it was her duty to display it, yet she seemed vaguely puzzled by its existence. She was also very frank about things most of the people Miranda knew either used French phrases for or never spoke of at all. Lady Carrington had advanced ideas about everything from women's suffrage to contraception, topics that Miranda knew very little about.

As Miranda began to gather up her tools in preparation to leave, Lady Carrington asked, "I'm told that Canon Cross introduced you to Mrs. Grant—is this true?"

"Yes. He knew about my art, so he mentioned me to Mrs. Grant, and she was kind enough to meet me."

"Is Canon Cross a friend of your family, or did you first meet him at the cathedral?"

Miranda wasn't quite sure how to respond. "My brother and I met him last year when we were still living in the country."

Lady Carrington's green eyes widened. "Oh, you're the ones who took him in when he was attacked."

Miranda was surprised the other woman knew about that, but replied, "Yes."

"You needn't keep the secret from me," Lady Carrington said with a smile. "He told me the whole story."

Miranda had been under the impression Tom didn't wish anyone to know what happened to him, much less the "whole story."

"Canon Cross and I are good friends. I've known him for years," Lady Carrington said, as if to reassure Miranda. "It was very kind of you and your brother to take care of a stranger. Why, you saved his life. It's no wonder he was so grateful to you."

"It was our duty to take care of him," Miranda said, feeling suddenly stiff and awkward. "We couldn't leave him to die in the wood."

"You could have, but you didn't. Few people would have taken on the burden of nursing a stranger back to health with so few resources at their disposal."

Miranda said, too quickly, "It was no burden at all. I was glad to do it."

"Indeed." Lady Carrington smiled again, looking thoughtful.

Miranda felt uncomfortable, sure that Lady Carrington was interpreting her words in a way she hadn't intended. Or as if the other woman knew about the kiss Tom and Miranda had shared in the studio. She hoped Tom had kept that secret to himself.

"Since you and I have a friend in common, I hope we'll be friends with each other, too," Lady Carrington continued. "Besides, one can never truly be friends with a man, can one? Especially one as handsome as Canon Cross. It's much better to confide in a member of one's own sex."

Miranda didn't know what to say. She couldn't imagine confiding in someone as self-assured and confident as Lady Carrington. She took her leave, feeling oddly as if she'd opened a door that could never be closed again.

The next morning, Tom came to the studio with Jack. Miranda had taken an instant liking to the boy. He was clearly troubled, but he tried very hard to please Tom, and he was a quick learner.

Miranda showed Jack around the studio and asked if he'd like to try painting. His face lit up at her suggestion, so she invited him to sit at her easel. She went to the other side of the room to find something for him to wear to protect his clothing. Finding an old sheet that would serve the purpose, Miranda returned to the easel. Jack stood beside it with a distressed look on his face.

"What's the matter, Jack? Do you need help getting up on the stool?" As small as she was, Miranda had no trouble climbing on the stool herself, and she assumed a boy of Jack's age would be more nimble.

He shook his head.

"Have you changed your mind about painting? It's fine if you have." Miranda glanced at Tom, who was sitting on one of the overstuffed chairs by the door with his eyes closed.

The boy stared down at his feet and began to kick at an imaginary object with the toe of his shoe. "Could we move it?" he asked, still looking at his feet.

"Move what?" she replied, puzzled.

"This." He pointed to the easel.

"Where would you like to move it?"

"This way." He made a circular movement with his arm, indicating he wanted the easel turned so the back of it would face the door.

"We could move it that way, but the light is better if it stays here. You'll be able to see your painting better."

Jack said nothing. He looked so small and lost that she wanted to put her arms around him, but she knew better than to try.

"Very well, if that's where you want it," Miranda said, turning the easel and moving the stool in front of it.

Jack climbed onto the stool at once and took the brush she held out to him. The relief on his face was evident, and she felt relieved, too, though she still had no idea why he'd been so distressed.

After Miranda had arranged the sheet over Jack's clothes and offered a little help to get him started, she went to sit down beside Tom, who opened his eyes and smiled at her. She wondered if that smile was calculated to affect her heart as it did, or if he really had no idea. If he hadn't guessed she was attracted to him before the kiss, he must know it now.

"It's kind of you to let Jack use your paints," Tom said. "I hope you didn't give him too much. Paints are not cheap, I suspect."

"I gave him just a little. I don't understand why he wanted the easel moved. Do you?"

"I wasn't paying attention. Where was the easel before?"

Miranda explained.

Tom thought for a moment, then said, "He didn't want to sit with his back to the door. I used to do the same. For years I wouldn't sit down in a room unless I was able to see the doorway clearly. My father liked to take me by surprise—I never knew when to expect a blow from behind."

Tom had never been so frank with Miranda about his childhood, and she was filled with compassion for both him and Jack. She reached out instinctively to touch his arm, but just as quickly reconsidered and withdrew. Since the kiss, Miranda had been uneasy about allowing any intimacies, even the most innocent ones, between herself and Tom.

She assumed that Tom felt nothing for her beyond friendship and a sort of brotherly affection, but surely it had occurred to him that she might misinterpret his intentions. Had he never thought to preserve more distance between them? Miranda knew that marriage was out of the question for her, even if she allowed herself to want it, but he didn't know that. Had he been as gradually and blindly drawn into this intimacy as she had, or was he deliberately playing with her emotions? He had plenty of faults, but she didn't believe he would be intentionally cruel.

Miranda hadn't told Simon or Gwen about Tom's morning visits to the studio, not from any conscious desire to conceal the truth, but from the assumption that they would make more of it than it really was, or even object to it on the grounds of impropriety. It had never seemed improper or even strange to Miranda until recently. Others wouldn't understand that, except for the one embrace and brief kiss, no inappropriate word or touch had passed between them. Her feelings for Tom were another matter.

Forcing herself back to the present, Miranda glanced across the room at Jack and asked in an undertone, "What will you do if you can't find a place for Jack to live?"

Tom frowned. "I must find one. If worse comes to worst, I'll find other lodgings for myself and keep him with me."

"Aren't you worried about his father coming after him? Surely Mr. Goode will seek you out if he wants to find his son, knowing of your interest in Jack."

"He is unlikely to find out where I live, but he could certainly find me at the cathedral."

"What will you do if Mr. Goode demands his son back? You have no legal right to keep him, do you?"

"Legal right!" Tom almost spat the words. Then in a quieter voice he said, "The law is useless to protect children like Jack. Even though children can now give evidence in court, few of them have the courage to do such a thing."

"But Mr. Goode could be arrested for mistreating Jack, couldn't he?"

"Possibly. But how long would he be in prison, and would he treat Jack any better after he was released? The likelihood is that he would treat the boy more harshly for running away." Tom sighed and ran a hand through his hair. "I'm not going to let that happen, even if I'm arrested myself."

Miranda was torn between admiration for Tom's desire to protect Jack and concern that Tom had invested too much energy in helping this one child. He didn't really know Jack, despite the similarities in his and Jack's experiences.

"Shall we see how Jack's painting is progressing?" Tom suggested.

Miranda nodded, glad to think of anything else. They rose and went over to the boy, who was completely absorbed in his artwork. The painting appeared to be a portrait of a woman, or at least a figure with long dark hair. Although Miranda had daubed several colors on the palette she gave Jack, he had chosen to limit himself to black and brown—black for the figure's clothing, brown for her hair, and black again for the space around her, as if she were inside a box.

"What are you painting, Jack? Is it a woman?" Miranda asked.

"It's my sister, Ann. She's in a pentery," Jack said, doggedly reinforcing the frame with ever-thicker black streaks.

In response to Miranda's quizzical look, Tom said, "He means a penitentiary. I've been looking for her, but Jack isn't sure which penitentiary she's at. I've visited a few, but I've had no luck so far."

Miranda knew about penitentiaries. A cold shiver snaked up her spine and a sick feeling settled in the pit of her stomach. She took a deep breath and swallowed hard before asking, "Is she in a penitentiary here in London?"

"I'm not sure, but it seems likely," Tom said.

"What's this dark area by your sister's feet?" Miranda asked Jack, pointing to the painting.

"That's 'er tears. She's sad 'cause she misses me."

Although the painting was crudely executed, something about the enclosed space around the figure of the woman and the way she was bent forward with her long dark hair—or perhaps it was her tears—partly obscuring her face, made the sick feeling in the pit of Miranda's stomach worse. She turned away and bent down under the guise of wiping up some paint spills on the floor, then busied herself with tidying some brushes lying on a nearby table.

"Let's get ready to go, Jack," Tom said. "Miss Thorne has kindly allowed us to interrupt her work, but we mustn't stay any longer. Miss Thorne, will you keep Jack's painting here or would you like us to take it with us?"

"Whatever you like," Miranda said.

She didn't think she had betrayed anything of what she was feeling in her voice, but Tom approached her and gave her an inquiring look. "Are you all right?" he asked in an undertone.

"Yes, of course." She squared her shoulders and smiled. "I forgot to tell you I've received a very interesting commission."

"Oh? From whom?"

"Lady Carrington."

Tom's expression didn't change, but something flashed in his eyes for a fraction of a second, a sharp, bright look that Miranda couldn't interpret.

"Her husband wants a formal portrait of her, but she wants something more unusual," Miranda went on. "She wishes to be painted as the Virgin Mary."

Tom raised an eyebrow.

"I can't really explain what she wants, but it will be a great challenge to express everything she is asking for in one portrait. I'm excited about it. It's my first big commission—the Carringtons are going to pay five hundred pounds for it."

After a pause, Tom asked, "Why did she choose you?"

"She saw one of my paintings in the studio and was moved by it. She wanted a woman artist to paint it, someone who wasn't well-known."

"I see."

Miranda was disappointed that Tom didn't seem happy to hear of her good fortune. His face was grave—no, beyond grave, she realized. He looked downright morose.

"Do you have some objection?" she asked.

The morose look was replaced by an impassive one. "Why should I object? It's a good opportunity for you."

"Lady Carrington said you and she are good friends."

"Did she?" he said coldly. "I wouldn't say that. As the Carringtons' parish priest, I've gotten to know them to some extent. They've both consulted me on spiritual matters."

Mystified by Tom's tone, she had no idea how to reply. Jack came to stand beside Tom, and the tension in the air lessened a little.

After Tom and Jack left, Miranda looked at Jack's painting again. If he wanted to train as an artist when he grew a little older, he had the potential to produce good work. The grotesquely proportioned figure of the woman—the arms and legs too short and the torso too long—didn't mar the emotional impact of the colors and shapes. Miranda could readily believe Ann Goode was in a penitentiary somewhere in London, perhaps sitting in one of the tiny, dark solitary confinement cells, weeping and worrying about her little brother.

17

No evil dooms us hopelessly except the evil we love, and
desire to continue in, and make no effort to escape from.

—George Eliot, *Daniel Deronda*

Tom paced back and forth in the entrance hall of the Carringtons'
house, regretting having come. He was tempted to walk out again, but
he had already been rude to the maid who let him in by refusing to give her
his coat and hat or to let her show him into the drawing room. He would be
the subject of gossip in the servants' quarters if he left before finding out if
Charles Carrington was at home.

The mahogany furnishings and highly polished floors reminded him all
too vividly of his early visits to Julia as her spiritual adviser. He had vowed
never to return to this house. Admittedly, he was there for a very different
reason now, but the house was a reminder of his wrongdoing and only
intensified his guilt.

The maid returned to the entrance hall with a subdued expression. "Lord Carrington isn't at home. Are you certain you don't want to see Lady Carrington?"

Before Tom could reply, Julia herself swept into the hall in a rustle of white silk. "Why, Canon Cross, you are not going to stand here in the hall getting mud on our freshly polished floors and then run off in a churlish fashion without speaking to me. I know you've come to see my husband, but surely there is something I can help you with."

The maid's subdued expression gave way to one of frank curiosity as she looked from Julia to Tom.

"Very well," said Tom through clenched teeth. He reluctantly surrendered his coat and hat to the maid, removed the offending footwear, and followed Julia into the drawing room.

After the maid closed the doors, Julia settled herself on a sofa, half reclining in a pose that looked relaxed to the unpracticed eye, but Tom wasn't fooled. He made no such pretense, pacing about the room just as he had in the entrance hall.

"Do sit down, Tom," she said after a moment. "You're making me dizzy."

He sat down in a chair as far away from her as possible.

"Are you going to tell me what your business is with Charles?" When Tom didn't answer, Julia exclaimed, "For heaven's sake, can you make it any more obvious that you don't want to talk to me? Oblige me by sitting a little closer so I don't have to scream to be heard. I'm not going to attack you."

Tom rose and sat in the chair opposite her, making a mental effort at the same time to modify his attitude. He would not get what he wanted by antagonizing her. "I'm sorry. I wanted to speak to Lord Carrington about finding a situation for a boy."

"What boy?"

Tom explained briefly how Jack had come to be living with him, concluding with, "I thought he might find a place in your household, perhaps as a stableboy or boot boy."

"You ought to speak to Grogan about that," Julia said. "That's the butler's responsibility. I don't think we need any servants at the moment, though."

"Jack is a quick learner. Is there any harm in trying him out? I don't think you'll be disappointed." Tom hoped he didn't sound desperate.

Julia gazed at him coolly. "You must encounter many unfortunate children in the course of your work. Why does this one matter so much?"

"They all matter. Jack sought me out, and I'm trying to help him."

"How admirable of you."

Tom wanted to shake her. "Look, Julia, you may treat me as badly as you like for my past behavior, but don't punish the boy for what I've done. He needs a situation, and you're in a position to give him one."

"I'd forgotten how intense you are when you want something," Julia said. "Is there anything you can't obtain through the sheer force of your will? That intensity was very attractive to me when I was your object, but now it just seems rather frightening. Don't scowl at me like that, Tom. It won't do any good."

"I thought you might appreciate the opportunity to save a child, given what you did to mine."

It took a few seconds for his meaning to dawn on her, but when it did, she sat upright, green eyes blazing. "What *I* did?" she hissed in a stage whisper. "What would you have had me do? Give birth to your bastard and tell Charles it was fathered by the Holy Spirit?"

Tom was tempted to respond with a sarcastic comment about her desire to be portrayed as the Virgin Mary, but he managed to restrain himself. "Don't be vulgar," he said instead. "It isn't becoming to you."

"Oh, yes, of course. I must remember I'm with a clergyman. We must both say and do only what is right and holy."

Tom stood abruptly and strode to the other side of the room. As he stood with his back to her, staring with unseeing eyes at a painting on the wall, he found himself praying for help. The conversation had gone in a direction he hadn't intended, and he didn't know how to repair the damage. For Jack's sake, there had to be a way to turn it around.

Tom took a deep breath and returned to the chair he had vacated. Julia's face was averted, but he saw that she was trembling, and his anger evaporated.

"Julia, I'm sorry for everything that has happened between us," he said quietly. "I take full responsibility for my part in our affair. From the beginning, I knew better than to encourage any sort of intimacy between us, but I did it anyway. And I'm sorry I was no help to you in the matter of the . . ." He stopped. The word *child* was suddenly no longer just a word. For the first time he fully understood the reality of what Julia had done, with his tacit approval, and his throat closed.

She looked at him with tears in her eyes. "Just when I want to hate you, you become human."

Tom struggled to compose himself. "I really did intend to see Charles today, not you," he said finally. "I knew no good could come of further meetings with you." He looked away, then said, "He came to see me a couple of months ago."

He didn't need to see her face to know she was alarmed. "Why?"

"I can't tell you the substance of our conversation. He confided in me as his priest, and I can't break that confidence." Tom knew he sounded like a hypocrite. He met Julia's eyes again. "I believe he loves you. If you could give him another chance—"

"Is that the real reason you came here?" Julia interrupted. "To argue my husband's case? You're hardly the right person to be his advocate."

"No, that isn't why I'm here. I'll say no more about him. Will you please consider my request about Jack and talk to Lord Carrington about it?"

"I'll consider it. Though you do have quite the nerve to come here and ask for favors."

Tom sighed. "I had exhausted all other avenues, and I thought there would be nothing to lose by asking."

She smiled suddenly, giving him the look that used to sustain him for days, sometimes even weeks, between their encounters. "I've always admired your nerve, and you know it. Is there anything you're afraid of?"

He could have listed several things, but he chose to remain silent.

Julia must have seen something in his face that pleased her, for she visibly relaxed. Sitting back and stretching her arm across the back of the sofa, she said, "I met your little friend Miss Thorne the other day."

"She told me you've commissioned her to paint your portrait. Why did you choose her?"

"Why not?" Julia replied airily. "She has talent, and I like to support unknown artists, especially women artists. You men have all the support you need."

Though Julia and Miranda both attended the cathedral services, they moved in such different circles that Tom hadn't expected them to meet. He saw no good coming from Julia's decision to commission Miranda, but he didn't want either woman to know it.

"I like Miss Thorne very much," Julia continued, watching Tom's face closely. "I'm thinking of taking her in hand and making her my new project."

Julia was always taking some younger woman "in hand," as she put it, and turning her into a stylized, watered-down version of herself. The thought of Miranda as a pale imitation of Julia filled Tom with horror. The two women couldn't be more different.

"Don't," he said.

"Whyever not?" Julia persisted. "With some new frocks and a different way of arranging her hair, she'd be quite attractive. Those horrid black dresses and that severe hairstyle remind me of my grandmother in mourning. It ought to be a crime for a young woman to dress that way."

"She'd never stand for your meddling. She may seem meek, but she's actually very strong-willed."

"Is she? I'm glad to hear it. Then she'll have a chance against you, too."

"What do you mean?"

"Perhaps she'll see past your charm and you won't be able to wrap her around your little finger the way you do with most women."

"This conversation is ridiculous. If you wish to befriend Miss Thorne, do so, but you'll oblige me if you don't discuss our relationship with her."

"I understand," Julia said with a look he didn't like.

Tom regretted saying anything to Julia about Miranda. His fear of losing Miranda—or rather, Miranda's friendship—put him too much in Julia's power. His only hope was that her desire to protect her own reputation would also protect his.

Before the conversation could take another bad turn, he rose abruptly. In a more formal tone, he thanked her for agreeing to discuss a situation for Jack with her husband and took his leave.

A few days later, Tom knocked at the door of a modest row house in Kensal Green. After visiting nearly every penitentiary in London in search of Ann Goode, he'd been ready to give up when he received a letter from the Mother Superior of a penitentiary in Upminster. She'd heard about his search and wrote that a young woman named Ann Goode had been an inmate there but had been discharged three months earlier, having found work as a maid in London. The Mother Superior had enclosed the address of Ann's employers, the Smithsons.

During his work on the penitentiary project, Tom hadn't had reason to see the inmates after they had been discharged. He had dealt mainly with the administrators, though the inmates he had seen at the well-run institutions hadn't looked the way he had expected—not like hardened women of the streets, but quiet, sober young women. Most of them were very young, often under twenty, but the spark of life and hope that should have been in the eyes of people so young had been absent. Would this be the case with Ann Goode?

The door was opened by a buxom, rosy-cheeked young woman with dark hair. Although she looked older than Tom had expected—Jack had said she was eighteen, but she could have passed for three-and-twenty—her eyes were the same unusual gold-flecked brown as Jack's. But he needed more information before he could be certain of her identity.

"Yes, sir?" she said, waiting. Her eyes narrowed a little at the sight of his clerical collar, but she lowered them quickly. She returned her gaze to his face and gave him an odd little smile that threw him off-balance.

In a tone that was more severe than he intended, he gave her his name and asked to see Mrs. Smithson, deciding it would be best to speak to her employer before revealing his errand to the girl herself, especially if she wasn't Jack's sister.

Mrs. Smithson received Tom in a small parlor, every surface of which was cluttered with knickknacks. He had to remove knitting needles and yarn from the chair upon which she invited him to sit.

Despite the cluttered state of her house, Mrs. Smithson's person was tidy, and she had a pleasant, unlined face framed by a cloud of silver hair. She would have presented a distinguished and respectable appearance if it were not for the state of her house.

"It isn't every day I receive a visit from a cathedral clergyman," Mrs. Smithson said. "I'm honored."

"Thank you. I'm here because I'm looking for someone. I believe she may be the servant girl who let me in. Is her name Ann Goode?"

"Yes." Mrs. Smithson looked worried. "She isn't in trouble, is she?"

"No, not at all." Tom asked a few more questions about Ann. When he was satisfied that the girl was indeed Jack's sister, he asked to speak with her.

Mrs. Smithson didn't reply immediately, seeming lost in thought. Then she said, "I don't know if it will be good for her to see her brother. She's cut all ties to her family, and wisely so, from the little she's told me about them. The boy will remind her of her old life, and she may fall into sin again."

Tom wasn't surprised by Mrs. Smithson's hesitation, since he had similar feelings on the subject—though on behalf of Jack, not Ann. "I understand," he said, "but the boy is under my care and will have no further dealings with his father, if I can help it. Ann seems to be doing well here, and I don't think a meeting with her brother will hurt either of them."

"Yes. Well." Mrs. Smithson hesitated again. "The girl has been with me only a few months, and I've had . . . difficulties with her."

"What sort of difficulties?"

"She's a good worker, for the most part, but she's had followers, just the sort of thing one worries about with a girl like that. To be frank with you, Canon Cross, I don't think I would hire a servant girl from a penitentiary again. She is too bold with men."

"I see." From his initial impression of Ann, Tom wasn't surprised. "Nevertheless, I'd like to speak with her about her brother."

"Very well."

Mrs. Smithson rang a bell, and Ann appeared at the door. "Yes, mum?"

"Come here, Ann. Canon Cross would like to speak to you."

Slowly, the girl took a few steps into the room, pausing several feet away with a guarded look.

"Do you have a brother named Jack?" Tom asked.

The guarded look changed to one of alarm. "Yes, sir. What's he done?"

"He's done nothing wrong. He has left home, though, and he is under my care. He asked me to find you."

Ann's eyes filled with tears, and she began to search in her apron pocket, presumably for a handkerchief. The search took some time, and Mrs. Smithson didn't make a move to help, so Tom offered Ann his own.

She took it and blew her nose noisily, then turned to him with a tear-streaked face. "Is 'e here? Can I see 'im?"

"Not today. But if Mrs. Smithson has no objection, I could bring him to see you tomorrow."

Mrs. Smithson interjected, "I'm afraid tomorrow isn't possible. I'm having guests for dinner, and I'll need Ann's help all day. The day after would be better, and I think it would also be better if Ann and her brother could meet elsewhere, in a more . . . congenial location. Could you arrange that, Canon Cross?"

Tom felt a flash of irritation. Mrs. Smithson seemed to believe that Jack's presence would lower the Smithsons in the eyes of their neighbors. He wasn't fooled by her careful choice of words.

"Yes, of course," was all he said, attempting to mask his annoyance. He didn't know where Ann and Jack could meet. The cathedral was too impersonal and too public, and Tom's own lodgings were out of the question—a young woman, servant or no, could not be seen visiting him on her own.

"Does my da know you're 'ere?" Ann asked Tom suddenly, looking suspicious. "'E didn't send you, did 'e?"

"No. He doesn't even know that Jack is staying with me, and you needn't fear that I'll tell him where you are."

Ann relaxed a little, tightly clasping the handkerchief again.

Promising to find a place for Ann and Jack to meet in two days, Tom took his leave. Lost in thought and moving quickly, he nearly knocked over a man walking in the opposite direction past the Smithsons' house.

"I beg your pardon," Tom said.

The man didn't speak, only touched the brim of his too-large bowler hat and hurried away.

Tom took Jack to the Thornes' house that evening for a visit. Jack wanted to show Miranda the progress he had made on his latest drawing, and Tom needed advice from his friends regarding a meeting place for Jack and his sister. On the way there, Tom told Jack that he had found Ann and the boy ran in circles around Tom, asking excited questions, few of which Tom could answer. It was good to see Jack happy, despite Tom's misgivings about reuniting the siblings.

At the Thornes' house, Tom made small talk with Simon while Miranda and Jack huddled in a corner of the drawing room with paper and charcoal sticks. Gwen was in Denfield visiting her family for a few days. Tom didn't want to raise the subject of Ann until Miranda could be part of the conversation, so he waited until she looked up from her drawing, then beckoned her to join him and Simon.

Miranda sat on the footstool by Simon's chair, across from Tom. He wondered if she sat there only when Gwen was away. With her hands clasped around her knees, sitting close to her brother, Miranda looked very young and vulnerable, in need of protection.

Tom told Miranda and Simon about his meeting with Ann Goode, speaking low enough that Jack couldn't hear him from the other side of the room.

"I'm so glad you found her!" Miranda said. She spoke quietly, taking her cue from Tom, but her eyes shone with pleasure.

"So am I," said Tom. "The only trouble is, Mrs. Smithson doesn't want the siblings to meet at her house. She's worried, I think, that Jack will somehow be a bad influence on Ann, when I think the opposite is more likely."

Miranda frowned. "I don't understand."

"To some degree it's natural to worry that siblings from such a family could drag each other down," Tom said, "but Jack is only a boy, and Ann is grown-up. And even though she's likely received some good moral and practical training at the penitentiary, that doesn't mean she won't fall again."

He looked at Simon for masculine affirmation. Miranda couldn't be expected to understand the dark side of human nature, even the dark side of feminine nature. But Simon's face remained neutral, and he didn't respond.

Miranda said, "Isn't that true of anyone? We can all fall into error, no matter how sound or extensive the moral teachings we've received." Her ice-blue eyes challenged Tom.

"Of course," he said, feeling uncomfortable, "but a girl like this is . . . in particular danger."

Still the challenging look. "Do you mean morally weaker?"

Tom looked again at Simon, whose expression didn't change. "Yes, I suppose so," Tom said. "I don't think it's appropriate to discuss Ann's past with you."

"I know what sort of past most inmates in penitentiaries have," Miranda replied. "And I know what sort of *training* they receive—though I wouldn't use that word for it."

Simon put his hand on Miranda's shoulder.

Tom was startled both by the emotion in Miranda's voice and by Simon's gesture. "How do you know that?"

"I've done charity work in a penitentiary."

Tom knew there were women who worked with the inmates on a volunteer basis, but he didn't think an unmarried woman ought to do so.

"Does that surprise you?" Miranda asked.

Tom didn't answer. Instead, he turned to Simon. "Did you approve of Miranda's doing such work?"

"I saw no problem with it," Simon replied. Despite his casual answer, it seemed to have cost him something to give it, for he didn't meet Tom's eyes, and he looked anxious and tense.

"*You* seem to have an objection," Miranda said to Tom. "What is it?"

His discomfort increased. Nevertheless, he answered, "I don't think unmarried women from good families ought to associate with penitentiary inmates."

"Do you think the innocent creatures will be corrupted?" There was an unwonted note of sarcasm in Miranda's voice.

Tom resented this. "Perhaps. Surely you can admit it's a possibility."

"Unmarried women ought to be protected from the realities of life. Is that what you think?"

"Some realities, yes. Why should you know all the ugly details of these women's lives? What good would it do?"

"Perhaps it would act as a cautionary tale, to prevent the innocent from wandering blindly into sin."

"Miranda," Simon finally said, a note of warning in his voice. His hand remained on her shoulder.

She ignored him and said, "You men are all the same. You love to label women and keep them in your tidy little categories. Penitentiary inmates, even prostitutes, are still women."

"I'm aware of that," Tom retorted. It troubled him to hear that word on Miranda's lips: *fallen women*, even *bad women* would have been preferable to the stark reality of *prostitute*.

"Charity work is all very well," he continued, "but it doesn't give you a true understanding of where these women have come from or how difficult it is to train them for respectable employment. My work last year involved a comprehensive study of all the penitentiaries in London. I daresay I know more about the system and its inmates than you do."

"Oh, I have no doubt you know more about the *system*," she replied tartly. She rose in one quick movement and returned to Jack at the other end of the room.

Tom stared after her, baffled. She usually took his views in stride, even if she didn't agree with them.

"Don't mind Miranda," Simon said, shifting uncomfortably in his chair. "She feels strongly about penitentiary inmates."

Tom was unconvinced. If Miranda cared so much about these women, why had she never spoken of them before?

"Why not have Jack and Ann meet here?" Simon suggested. "Gwen won't be back for a few more days, so only Miranda and I will be here. We can give Jack and Ann some time alone, but we'll be close by if they need us."

"Are you certain?" Tom asked. "That would work very well, I think, as long as you don't mind the inconvenience."

"No inconvenience at all. I'm happy to offer the house for such a purpose. The little chap deserves a happy reunion with his sister."

"Thank you, Simon. I appreciate it."

Tom had no chance to speak to Miranda again. She remained with Jack until it was time for Tom and Jack to leave, and she said goodbye to Tom with considerably less warmth than she did to Jack. Tom felt she had willfully misunderstood him, and as he and Jack walked home, he tried to forget the exchange, comforting himself with the notion that even his admired Miranda was still a woman, with a woman's unpredictable emotions. But he couldn't stop thinking about what she'd said.

18

"You girls always seem to forget that clergymen are only men after all."

"Their conduct is likely to be better than that of other men, I think."

"I deny it utterly."

—Anthony Trollope, *The Last Chronicle of Barset*

Ann Goode was due to arrive any minute, and Miranda was too restless to keep her mind on her book. After she had jumped up from her chair three times—once to rearrange the ornaments on the mantelpiece, the second time to turn two chairs to face each other, the third to return them to their original position—Simon looked up from his newspaper in consternation.

"Mouse, what's the matter?"

"Oh, nothing. It's just . . . well . . . I'm a little anxious about the reunion between Ann and Jack." She returned to the chair across from Simon's, biting her lip.

"I'm sure it will be fine. What's there to worry about?"

"I don't know. Perhaps one or both of them will be disappointed by how much the other has changed—or perhaps disappointed the other *hasn't* changed. Tom said they haven't seen each other for at least two years. That's a long time for children. Ann isn't a child, of course," she added before Simon could contradict her, "but she's still young, and young people change so quickly."

"They both seem eager to see each other, from what Tom told us. I can't imagine either of them being disappointed. Is that all you're worried about?"

Miranda hesitated.

"You're worried about Tom being disappointed, aren't you?" Simon said.

"No." She frowned. "Not really. It's just that he cares so much about Jack. If the meeting doesn't go well, he'll blame himself."

"Miranda."

"Don't look at me like that, Simon. And don't use that tone."

"You've got to stop worrying about Tom. He's my friend, too, but he's quite able to take care of himself. After your display of hostility the other day, I'm starting to think you're in love with him."

"Don't be ridiculous." She felt her face grow warm. Taking one of the ornamental cushions from behind her back, she tried to smooth the creases in it. "I merely expressed my opinion."

"Yes, far more openly than you do with most people." The smug, knowing look was still on Simon's face.

Miranda threw the cushion at him.

Simon caught it and set it aside, his expression turning serious. "Why don't you tell Tom the truth about the penitentiary?"

"He'd think less of me."

"I mean the complete truth, including my part in it. You would never have gone there if it wasn't for my stupidity. My failure to protect you."

"Oh, Simon. I forgave you long ago for that, and I wish you'd forgive yourself, too. I believed Richard when he said it was the best place for me and Sam." She closed her eyes to block out the memory of the madness that had descended on her when she realized Richard had lied about allowing her to take Sam with her.

"It shouldn't have happened, all the same." Simon shook his head as if to clear it. "But we were speaking of Tom. You ought to give him more credit. He does jump to conclusions sometimes, but he's willing to admit when he's wrong. Besides, I doubt there's anything you could say or do that would knock you off that pedestal he's set you on."

Puzzled, she asked, "What are you talking about?"

He chuckled. "Blind as bats, the pair of you."

Before she could demand an explanation of Simon's provoking statement, Tom and Jack arrived. Jack was clearly struggling to control his excitement—although he didn't speak much, he was as restless as Miranda, fidgeting in his chair and gazing at the door with bright, expectant eyes.

Tom's state of mind was more difficult to determine. He seemed subdued and thoughtful, but as the four of them sat in the drawing room waiting for Ann, more than once Miranda caught Tom looking at her intently, though without animosity. When he saw that she noticed, he looked away. She was still on edge from their argument and hoped he wouldn't try to return to it.

Nobody seemed to be in a particularly talkative mood, though Simon made a few tentative observations about the weather. Although Jack's fidgeting increased as the minutes passed, he was behaving remarkably well, considering his age and the excitement he must be feeling at the prospect of seeing his beloved sister. Of the four of them, Tom seemed to be having the most difficulty. He repeatedly rose from his chair and paced about the room, just as Miranda had done earlier, though he didn't rearrange any furniture or ornaments. Miranda was just about to advise him that he was wearing holes in the carpet when he stopped abruptly and looked at her.

"It's been half an hour. I'm going to try to find her," Tom said. His expression was grim.

"Can I come?" Jack asked.

"No, you'd better stay here in case your sister arrives while I'm gone."

"Don't you think we ought to wait a bit longer?" Simon asked.

"It's been long enough." Tom looked at Miranda again and asked, "Will you come with me?"

She was startled by his request, but she agreed. She went to get her hat and joined Tom outside. It was a warm, sunny day, and the trees had lately burst into full leaf. She closed her eyes for a few seconds, letting the scent of lilacs trick her into believing she was back in the country.

"We'd better take a cab to the Smithsons' house," Tom said. "It will be faster than the Underground."

"Very well." She looked up at Tom's face, searching for some clue to his state of mind. He seemed more agitated than was reasonable under the circumstances.

Once inside the cab, Miranda felt even more off-balance. She'd been in cabs only a couple of times in her life, and never with Tom. They were expensive, and in London it was easy to take the Underground or an omnibus to one's destination. If Tom had been in a more pleasant mood, the experience would have been uncomfortably intimate, given how enclosed and private the space was.

"I'm sure Ann was simply detained," Miranda ventured. "She's probably on her way to our house."

"Or she decided not to go," said Tom grimly.

"You said she was in tears at the mere mention of her brother. Why shouldn't she wish to see him?"

"Who knows? She's evidently a flighty creature."

Miranda compressed her lips to prevent the retort she wanted to make.

Tom was making uncharitable assumptions about someone he knew very little about, but to point out that fact would only invite further argument. She knew he couldn't be reasoned with when he was in this mood.

"Jack has been counting the minutes to this meeting since we arranged it," Tom said, oblivious to Miranda's admirable self-control. "If that girl doesn't have a good reason for not showing up, I'll be sorely tempted to box her ears. I won't have Jack disappointed."

Miranda was alarmed by Tom's attitude. His overprotectiveness of the boy wasn't good for either of them. "Jack has been disappointed many times before in his young life," she said firmly. "One more disappointment, however unfortunate, won't kill him."

"I didn't expect this from you," he replied, turning to her with fire in his eyes. "I thought you'd be sympathetic to Jack's situation."

"Oh, stop roaring at me like an angry lion!" she cried, exasperated. "It's time you looked at Jack clearly instead of through the cloudy window of your childhood. Jack's childhood is not yours. Jack is not you. And even you wouldn't have grown into a responsible adult if you'd been shielded from every disappointment."

Tom stared at her in silent shock.

She raised her chin and met his eyes, ready to stare him down if necessary. But there was no contest. His expression softened into bewilderment.

"Is that what you really think—that I don't see Jack clearly?" he asked.

"Your efforts to help him are admirable, but can you truly tell me he doesn't remind you of yourself at his age? Can you really be objective about him?"

"No," he said quietly. "I can't tell you that." He gazed out of the cab window, seemingly lost in thought.

After a few minutes, he looked at her again. "You're right," he said, sounding surprised. "Of course you're right. How blind I've been!"

"We're all blind to some things."

There was another long pause. Then he smiled, ever so slightly. "So the mouse isn't afraid of the lion, then?"

"No. The roaring is only for show, from what I can tell."

He reached for her hand and squeezed it. "I'm glad the mouse can roar, too, when necessary. Thank you for telling me the truth."

The warmth of his hand on hers sent a tremor through her, and she became too aware of how close they were sitting: her shoulder pressed against his arm, their legs touching. Yet he seemed oblivious to the impropriety of it. Was he like this with other women? Had he forgotten she was a woman? Or did he know perfectly well what he was doing and what effect it must have on her?

Fortunately, they had reached their destination, and Miranda burst out of the cab the moment the driver released the door, hoping Tom would assume she was merely impatient to meet Ann.

A woman was standing on the street nearby, but it didn't occur to Miranda that she could be Ann until Tom alighted from the cab and the woman hurried towards him. She looked considerably older than eighteen, and though she was very pretty, the neckline of her dress was too low and too tight for her ample bosom. Miranda blushed on her behalf, then admonished herself for judging the girl so quickly when she'd only just criticized Tom for his own negative assumptions. Ann likely had only one good dress and didn't realize it was immodest.

Tom introduced Ann to Miranda, but before Miranda could say a proper greeting, Ann turned to Tom and said plaintively, "Where's Jack?"

He looked puzzled. "We were expecting you at the Thornes' house."

"You said you'd bring Jack 'ere."

"I said no such thing."

The lion showed signs of resurfacing, and Miranda decided to interject before the tension in the air could erupt into outright hostility. "Will you give Ann and me a few minutes alone?" she asked him.

He nodded, looking relieved, and, after asking the cabdriver to wait for them, walked about twenty paces down the street. Ann relaxed visibly.

"Will you come to my house?" Miranda said. "Jack is waiting for you there."

Ann hesitated, not looking as pleased by this information as Miranda expected her to.

"Don't you want to see your brother?" Miranda asked, confused.

Ann's lower lip trembled, and she burst out, "Course I do."

"Then why . . . ?"

Ann studied Miranda's face, then jerked her head in Tom's direction. "How do you know 'im?"

"Canon Cross is a family friend," Miranda said. "He can be a little fierce at times, but he's worked very hard to help your brother. He means well."

"I ain't so sure. Looks like a toff, but 'e knows too much about what you gentlefolks call 'low subjects.'"

Miranda had no intention of asking for clarification. And she didn't blame the girl for not trusting Tom. What she must have experienced at the hands of some men would naturally have given her good reasons not to trust others. Miranda also had to admit that Tom wasn't always as charming as he seemed to think he was.

Knowing that a defense of Tom's character wouldn't convince Ann, she said instead, "You needn't talk to him if he makes you uncomfortable, but if you'd like to see your brother, please come with me. I promise you'll be safe, and you can leave any time you wish."

Ann relented and followed Miranda to the waiting cab.

The cab was only meant for two, so Tom offered Ann his place, paid the driver, and said he'd follow them in another. During the ride, Ann peppered

Miranda with questions about Jack, asking about everything from his living situation to his health. Miranda answered as fully as she could, using the opportunity to subtly let Ann know what an important role Tom had taken in Jack's life. The girl didn't make any further comments about Tom, interested only in her brother.

When they reached the house, Miranda entered the drawing room first, followed by Ann, whose eyes lit up when she saw Jack. He jumped up and ran to her, nearly knocking her over with the force of his embrace.

Miranda would have loved to sketch Jack and Ann—the emotional reunion would have made a most appealing painting. She was sorry Tom wasn't there to see the siblings meet, but he arrived not long afterwards and observed the happiness of his charge with a smile. He, Miranda, and Simon stood back so as not to intrude, though Jack was oblivious to the onlookers, imprisoning Ann's neck in a stranglehold. Ann seemed to be trying not to cry.

"Why don't we give Jack and Ann some time alone to become reacquainted?" Miranda suggested to Simon and Tom. "I'll have Jane bring us tea in the dining room."

Simon and Tom agreed. Miranda asked Jane to prepare the tea things, then sat beside Simon at the dining-room table.

"What now?" asked Simon, looking pensive. "Do you think those two will find a way to live together?"

"I don't think so," Tom said from across the table. "Ann's employer didn't even want Jack in her house for a visit. Besides, I've found him a situation."

"You have?" Miranda exclaimed. "Where?"

"Lord Carrington has agreed to take him on a trial basis as a boot boy."

"That's wonderful. You must be relieved," Miranda said.

"I am," Tom said, "but of course it will be more difficult for Jack and Ann to see each other if he's living with the Carringtons."

"Perhaps the Carringtons would be willing to employ Ann as well," Simon said.

"I doubt that." Tom spoke with certainty. "Lady Carrington is very particular about her women servants."

"But she also has a great deal of compassion for fallen women," Miranda retorted, only just resisting the impulse to add, *unlike you*. She wished she didn't feel compelled to defend Tom to Ann and vice versa.

Tom looked at her as if he had heard the unspoken accusation, but he didn't look angry, only thoughtful. "You may be right," he said slowly. "Ann's current employer doesn't have much compassion for her. I confess I don't understand the girl, either. In the two times I've seen her, she's behaved so differently that she might be two separate people. What do you think ought to be done for her?"

Miranda suddenly felt uncomfortable. "I'm sure I'm not the right person to ask."

"I think you're exactly the right person, considering your experience working with girls like Ann. Now that I've come down from my high horse"—a wry smile flickered across his face—"I'd like to learn from you."

Such humility on Tom's part was unexpected, and she wasn't prepared for the way it made her feel. She wanted to throw herself into his arms and kiss him, even with Simon right there.

Miranda rose from the table, said hurriedly, "I think I'll check on Jack and Ann," and left the room.

19

Yet he hath ever but slenderly known himself.
—William Shakespeare, *King Lear*

Paul Harris had a rich, melodious voice, the perfect voice for a clergyman. As Tom listened to Harris read the Gospel that Sunday morning, he wondered why the other canon was speaking more slowly and dramatically than usual. There was no need to give the words added emphasis—the parable of the prodigal son was dramatic enough. But as soon as the thought entered Tom's mind, it disappeared. He had other things to worry about, things that had taken his mind off his duties more than once that morning. Two cathedral employees had already commented on his absent-mindedness, which irritated Tom. Nobody would have noticed the minor lapses in anyone else. It was his usual competence, his flawless performance of his duties, that made any lapse stand out.

His main concern was that the gold cross Miranda had given him had disappeared. The chain had broken about a week earlier, and he was sure he'd put the cross in the top drawer of the chest of drawers in his bedroom, just as he had the evening he'd fought at the Club. He'd bought a new chain for it, but when he went to the chest of drawers that morning to put the cross on the new chain, it was no longer there. It occurred to him that Jack could have taken it, but he didn't want to believe the boy would steal from him, and Jack had gone to live with the Carringtons a few days earlier, so Tom couldn't question him immediately. Regardless, losing the cross upset him more than he thought it should.

The words of the Nicene Creed jarred Tom out of his reverie. He had to get his bearings in time for his sermon, which was, he thought, a particularly good one. Despite how tired he had been lately, he had managed to write the sermon with a fairly clear head. It didn't surprise him that the inspiration for it had come to him at Miranda's studio. Everything good and peaceful happened there. He glanced at the congregation from his position in the chancel, looking for Miranda. She, Simon, and Gwen were near the front of the nave, Simon and Miranda looking sober and decorous in black, and Gwen in a scarlet dress and elaborately beribboned hat.

As Tom's eyes swept over the congregation, which was standing for the recital of the Creed, he saw what he thought at first must be a hallucination. A few pews behind the Thornes stood a man with a shockingly close resemblance to Tom's father. It couldn't be him, of course. But this man had the same dark coloring, the same powerful build, the same way of holding his head. Tom couldn't suppress a shudder. All his other worries vanished as he stared at this man. He was only just close enough that they could make eye contact, and as Tom stared, the older man smiled and bobbed his head in recognition. Tom quickly looked away, as stunned as if a figment of his imagination had taken physical form.

He had expected—no, hoped—the old man was dead. But even though it had been seventeen years since they'd last seen each other, Tom knew the man was John Hirst, his father. How he had managed to find out where Tom worked was a mystery, but he was there. Tom had to do something immediately. The last thing he wanted to do was preach a sermon on the prodigal son with this specter from his past watching him.

The Creed was almost over. Tom turned to Canon Johnson, who was standing near him, and whispered, "Do you see that old man in the shabby brown coat about ten rows from the front?"

Johnson nodded.

"Please have him removed immediately. I'll explain later."

The other canon gave Tom a quizzical look, but he agreed to try, leaving his stall and disappearing into the vestry. A moment later he reappeared in the nave, talking to the verger.

The Creed was over. Even though he felt as if all the blood had drained out of his body, Tom forced himself to assume a neutral expression and walk across the chancel to the pulpit. He nearly stumbled on the first step. The congregation waited in silence for Tom to begin. He didn't remember there being such a silence at this point in the service before—there were always rustlings and murmurings, people dropping their hymnbooks, one or two children crying. But to him it seemed the silence was absolute, as if everyone was frozen in a state of shock just as he was.

All eyes were on him. Canon Johnson had reappeared in his stall, but the old man was still there. Tom looked at Johnson, who shook his head slightly.

Tom took a deep breath, steeling himself, and began to speak.

He spoke of family relationships in general, an introduction that, when he was writing it, had seemed appropriate because it would speak to everyone—after all, who didn't have family troubles of some kind? The last thing he wanted to talk about now was family, but he had no choice. He could hardly improvise when it took all his concentration just to follow his notes.

When Tom began to speak of the parable itself, he was struck by the irony of it—today of all days, to preach a sermon about fathers and sons with his own estranged father sitting in a pew in front of him. He spoke of the love of the father in the parable as an allegory of the love of God, and the different but equally erring sons.

"We must surely see ourselves in one of these sons," he said, knowing he was speaking too quickly, anxious to conclude. "Haven't we all chosen the route of the dissipated younger son or the proud elder son? Some of us have been both at different times in our lives."

"Amen," shouted John Hirst from his pew.

Heads turned.

Tom froze. But the silence was worse than anything else, so he went on without knowing what he was saying except that it was about forgiveness.

He was interrupted by the same loud voice.

"Hear, hear!" John Hirst lurched to a standing position and pointed at Tom. "That'sh my son, everybody! Your old da is proud of you, Tommy!" He started to sway and prevented himself from falling only by grasping the back of the pew in front of him. "Love and forgivenesh indeed! That's exactly what I feel for you, Tommy. Will you give me your forgivenesh?"

Tom couldn't speak or move. It was a nightmare. Things like this didn't happen in real life. For a few moments, nobody else moved, either, all staring—or trying not to stare—at the old man who was obviously in his cups. How strange that this man had been so frightening to Tom when he was a child, so large and menacing. He seemed merely pathetic now, someone who wouldn't merit notice if he wasn't publicly declaring his connection to Tom.

As Tom's eyes flickered over the congregation, he noticed Narbridge crossing his arms and looking disgusted. In the pew behind Narbridge's, Julia was sitting with her three daughters, staring straight ahead, her face white. He couldn't look at Miranda or Simon.

Tom had to do something—it was the only way to end the nightmare. Turning around to face the other canons, he hissed, "Get him out of here!" He was past caring if anyone else heard him.

Paul Harris, Tom's unexpected savior, was the first to move, descending the chancel steps and going over to the old man. Harris and the verger escorted him out. He didn't go quietly, and during the ensuing scene, Tom took advantage of the disturbance to walk out in the opposite direction. Perhaps it was cowardly, but he couldn't remain where he was.

Everyone now knew that Tom was a liar, not only in the obvious sense that he had told everyone his father was dead, but also in the deeper sense that he was not who he pretended to be. It didn't matter that Tom had never taken so much as a sip of liquor as an adult. It didn't matter that he was educated and spoke like a gentleman. It didn't matter that he had stolen money only once, and only from his father, who had found thievery a more lucrative profession than blacksmithing. Tom was a thief and a liar, just like his father, and he knew it. But he didn't want to see that truth reflected in anyone else's face.

Tom didn't remember removing his vestments, putting on his coat and hat, or leaving the cathedral. All he knew was a sensation of slow suffocation, a feeling similar to but more extreme than what he had felt in the cab with Julia when she told him about her pregnancy. He needed to get out, to breathe, to be free from the poisonous, oppressive weight on his shoulders, a weight as heavy as if he were literally carrying his father instead of running from him.

He didn't think—he just walked, all day and most of the night. It rained twice, one half-hearted shower that lasted only a few minutes and one downpour that seemed to go on for hours, drenching him. He was oblivious to his surroundings except for the rain and the gradual lessening of light. At one point he noticed a lamplighter going about his duty. Of the state of his body he was only marginally aware, though it occurred to him fleetingly that he was wet and cold.

He had never felt more alone in his life, not even during the many times he had run away from home as a child. Although his father had always found him eventually, while he was running he had felt free, strong. He would hide in bushes along roads or sometimes underneath bridges, but his surroundings, both animate and inanimate, had encouraged him. It was different now. He felt lost.

The fog in his brain seemed too thick for any clear thoughts to penetrate, but eventually the answer came to him. He needed to see Miranda. Although it was still the middle of the night and he couldn't disturb the Thornes at their house, he could wait outside the studio until Miranda arrived in the early morning. He didn't know when it had happened, but he realized now that the studio was as much his sanctuary as the cathedral was Miranda's.

It was a long way, and because he had been walking for so many hours, his legs were aching by the time he arrived. As soon as the studio was within view, he began to wonder again if he was hallucinating. There was a light in the window. It was the only light in any building on the street.

Hallucination or not, it was worth acting as if it were real. He crossed the street and rang the bell. Nothing happened. He rang again.

As he was about to turn away, he heard the bolt being drawn back and the latch lifted. The door opened a crack, and Miranda's voice said, "Is that you, Tom?"

"Yes," he replied hoarsely. It seemed like days, even weeks, since he'd used his voice.

She opened the door and silently led the way to the top of the stairs. There was only one lamp lit in the studio, and he was grateful for the dim light. He was afraid to look directly at Miranda's face because of what he might see there—disgust, pity, perhaps even hatred.

"I'm sorry it took me so long to get to the door," she said, for all the world as if they had arranged to meet at this ungodly hour.

"Why are you . . . did you . . . were you expecting me?" In his confusion, he stumbled over the words.

"Not exactly, but after the difficult day you must have had, I thought you might need to come here." Her tone was refreshingly matter-of-fact. "Let me take your coat."

She helped him off with his waterlogged coat, and he tossed his hat aside, sinking into his usual chair. His legs were trembling with the long hours of walking.

Miranda drew her chair close to his and sat facing him. She put her hand on his arm and exclaimed, "Your clothes are wet. Let me get you a blanket."

As she started to rise, he caught her hands to stop her. "I'll be fine. Stay with me."

There must have been something desperate either in his eyes or his tone, for she sat down again without hesitation or protest. He gripped her hands hard, and she leaned forward, gazing at him intently.

"Did you see my . . . that man?" Tom asked, unable to acknowledge the connection. Part of him hoped the day's events had occurred entirely in his mind. There would be some comfort even in insanity.

"Yes."

Her answer shattered his hopeful delusion. Meeting her eyes with difficulty, he said, "Do you despise me now?"

Those clear, calm blue eyes met his with disarming directness as she said, "I love you, Tom."

He was stunned. She'd spoken the words so calmly and simply, without prompting, without desperation, without expecting anything back.

Something broke inside him. He slipped to his knees, lowering his forehead against their clasped hands, which rested on her lap. He had forgotten how to weep, and his body shuddered like a ship smashing against rocks. Only a few tears came out at first. Miranda slipped one of her hands out of his grasp and stroked his hair, which seemed to help—the tears came more freely after that. A fleeting image came to him of Charles Carrington weeping naturally, not like his own choking, half-smothered sobs.

When his tears were spent, Tom remained where he was, his face buried in his hands. He began to speak. The words were even more of a compulsion than the tears had been. Or perhaps the tears had blocked the words, damming them up so completely that only after the tears were free could he say everything he needed to say. The last time he had wept was probably as long ago as the last time he had made a full confession to anyone, including God. His words were muffled, halting, illogical. Perhaps Miranda neither heard nor understood half of what he said, but it didn't matter.

He told her about his childhood, both the good and the bad. His mother, loving and affectionate towards him when his father wasn't home. Kate, who followed him everywhere and would join him in his games and explorations in the fields and woods. He told her how everything was different when his father was home—how his mother would become subdued and silent, unresponsive to Tom's questions, how his sister would hide in cupboards. He told her about the beatings.

The longer he spoke, the more his words took the form of a confession. He no longer spoke of the bad things others had done to him. He focused on the ways he had wronged others.

"I abandoned my mother and sister," he said. "I tried to convince Kate to come with me when I ran away, but she wouldn't leave my mother, and we both knew she would never leave my father. I was the one who received most of the beatings, but after I left I wondered if he transferred them to Kate." A bitter wave of guilt washed over him, and he couldn't speak.

Miranda said nothing, but he sensed her alert, careful listening.

He continued, "It took me more than a year to write to my mother and sister. They never answered. I thought my father must have killed them. I don't know why I never went back to Yorkshire to find out for certain." He took a deep breath, then went on. "I've used women to make myself feel important. I've led them to believe I was in love with them and then ignored them when I was tired of them. When I was ordained I told myself I would do no more than flirt with women, but I did have one . . . inappropriate relationship since then. I've caused a great deal of damage to everyone involved."

Tom had never before told anyone all the sins he'd committed. He didn't mention names or delve into the particulars, but he felt as if he'd turned himself inside out. He held on to Miranda's hand for dear life, hiding his hot face against it. His confession had taken on its own momentum and he'd forgotten who his listener was. Now, he was afraid that this pure-minded woman, the only true friend he had in the world, would recoil from the ugly truths he had told her.

"You know the verse in Isaiah: 'Though your sins be as scarlet, they shall be as white as snow,'" Miranda said softly.

Tom nodded, his face still pressed against her hand.

"God forgives you," she said, her voice like warm honey. "And so do I."

Gently, she extricated her hand from his grasp and said, "Tom, you must be exhausted. Go home and sleep. We'll talk more another day."

"Yes. Thank you." It was all he had the strength left to say.

He was amazed that there was no judgment in her voice, no sign that she was repulsed by what he'd said about his conduct with other women. As he left the studio and walked to the nearest cabstand, he realized what an idiot he'd been not to recognize the truth sooner. How long had he been lying to himself about his feelings for Miranda? Or perhaps he simply hadn't recognized them for what they were. She was part of everything he was and everything he did, and his heart was entirely hers.

20

Dear, you should not stay so late,
Twilight is not good for maidens;
Should not loiter in the glen
In the haunts of goblin men.
—Christina Rossetti, "Goblin Market"

I think that's enough for today," Miranda said, setting down her paintbrush.

"I don't mind sitting longer," Lady Carrington said.

"My sister-in-law is expecting me at home. We have guests coming for dinner, and she needs my help."

"Very well. How is the painting coming along?"

"I don't know. It's too early to tell." Miranda never showed paintings in progress to her sitters, and she wasn't happy with Lady Carrington's in its current state. The colors were good, but the expression on her subject's face wasn't right. Instead of expressing all the mystery and plenitude of womanhood, the face seemed blank, vapid. It couldn't have been more different from her real face, which was mobile and expressive.

"Stay for tea, at least," Lady Carrington said. They were at her house instead of Mrs. Grant's studio. Though Lady Carrington had expressed her willingness to sit at the studio, it turned out that the times she was available to sit conflicted with Mrs. Grant's art lessons. Thus, a makeshift studio had been set up for Miranda in a guest room at the Carringtons' mansion in Belgravia.

Miranda agreed to stay a little longer. Tea at the Carringtons' was always delicious. Besides, she was glad to delay her return to what would certainly be a chaotic atmosphere at home. Lady Carrington rang for tea as Miranda removed her painting smock and cleaned her hands and tools in a basin provided for the purpose.

As she washed her brushes, the memory of Tom's emotional confession forced itself into her consciousness. She pushed it back. She knew she'd have to think about it sooner or later, but she'd made a valiant effort to keep her mind occupied since she'd seen him, not ready to consider the implications of everything they'd said to each other.

When the maid arrived with the tea things and the two women began to eat, Miranda asked Lady Carrington if she'd tell her about her youth. Sometimes the key to solving a problem with a painting was getting to know one's subject better.

"My family wasn't as wealthy as you might expect," the peeress began. "Although my father was an earl, he was always in debt, and there was never enough money for the things I wanted. I dreamed of marrying a wealthy man and having beautiful dresses and giving lavish parties. I think I was happiest when I was dreaming about those things. When I actually did marry and received everything I thought I wanted, though, the reality fell far short of my dreams."

Miranda had suspected for a while that the Carringtons' marriage was unhappy. Though she had met Lord Carrington a couple of times and found him pleasant and amiable, Miranda noticed the tension between him and his wife even in the few minutes she'd seen them together.

"Reality always does fall short, though, doesn't it?" Miranda couldn't resist saying. "One can't expect too much."

"Is that how you live your life? It's hard to believe that an artist with a vision like yours could have such meager dreams."

"I have wild dreams sometimes, but I don't expect them to come true."

"Poor Cinderella," Lady Carrington said, but she spoke too kindly for Miranda to take offense.

The peeress set her teacup aside and leaned forward. "Don't you ever want more? Don't you weary of keeping your hopes small?"

"I've been disappointed before," Miranda said slowly. "Keeping my hopes . . . reasonable is better for my peace of mind."

"Spoken like a truly good, modest woman. Perhaps your paintings give you enough freedom so that you have no other longings. Your art is anything but modest and small. But I don't have a talent like that. Everyone expects me to be happy with my lot—after all, what do I have to complain about? But after getting everything I thought I wanted, I was unhappy. I felt empty, unsatisfied."

"What did you do when you realized this?" Miranda put down her own teacup and reached for her sketchbook. There was something in Lady Carrington's face that intrigued her, and she wanted to see if she could reproduce it on paper.

"I didn't know what to do. I tried not to think about it. I tried to be a good wife and mother. I threw myself into charity work. And I discovered that the admiration of men was as effective an opiate as it had been before my marriage. It gave me moments that were almost like real happiness. I saw nothing wrong with it. I never allowed any man but my husband to touch me. Not for a long time, anyway."

Miranda found that listening too closely to Lady Carrington interfered with seeing her—seeing that spark of truth in her face that eluded words.

"Eventually, other men's admiration wasn't enough. I took a lover. He made me happy for a while, but of course, the effects wore off, as they always do." She looked closely at Miranda. "Have I shocked you?"

"No," said Miranda, concentrating on her sketch. Then she looked up and said, "Didn't you feel guilty about your husband?"

"Yes, at first. But my need to feel that false happiness was more important than anything else. I know how selfish that sounds."

"Sometimes people are compelled to do things that make them forget how empty they feel," Miranda said quietly. "It may be selfish, but it's also human."

"True." Lady Carrington turned her head to gaze out the window that faced the front lawn.

"I know you believe in God," Miranda said after a moment. "Has your faith been no comfort to you?"

"Not after this man and I became lovers. I felt I had forfeited any divine mercy at that point. But now . . . I wish I could find comfort in God, but He seems distant. I'm trying to do what's right. Yet I still struggle—"

They were interrupted by Lady Carrington's youngest daughter, a round-faced, golden-haired cherub of about five, who opened the door and peeped around it.

"Rosie, what have I told you about knocking before you enter a room?" Lady Carrington admonished the child, but with no real severity in her voice. Miranda fancied that the firm tone was assumed for her benefit.

Rosie seemed to make the same assumption, for she ran into the room and flung herself into her mother's arms. Miranda had formed a general impression that Lady Carrington wasn't a maternal sort of woman, but the way she wrapped her arms around Rosie and gazed into the child's eyes suggested otherwise.

Miranda turned to a blank page in her sketchbook and made a new drawing as Rosie babbled happily to her mother, who continued to smile into her child's face as if the two of them were alone. The total absorption of mother and child with each other allowed Miranda to work unhindered for several minutes. When she was finished, she looked at the new sketches she had made, realizing exactly what she needed to do next. The old painting of Lady Carrington that Miranda was unhappy with would be discarded, and a new one would take its place.

"You look like the proverbial cat that ate the canary," Lady Carrington said. The little girl had fallen asleep, her curly head nestled against her mother's breast.

"I have an idea," Miranda said. "I'm not certain it will work, but I'd like to start over with the painting, if you don't mind."

"I know better than to interfere with an artist who has such a determined look in her eyes. You may do as you like."

Lady Carrington insisted on sending Miranda home in her Rolls-Royce Silver Ghost, despite Miranda's preference for a less ostentatious mode of transportation. She sat in the back seat, which was luxuriously padded and smelled of shoe polish and leather. The motorcar was quieter than she expected, too: the loudest sound she heard from her vantage point was the clock mounted near the driver's controls.

As soon as she relaxed enough to sit back and think, she burst into tears. The driver was discreet enough to pretend not to notice. Try as she might to blame her tears on her excitement about the painting, she knew perfectly well that her heightened emotional state had several causes. One of them was seeing Lady Carrington with her daughter. The scene had affected Miranda first as an artist, but now it affected her as a mother. It was painful to see another mother who was free to spend as much time with her child as she wished when such an experience of tender maternal care was lost to Miranda forever.

And then there was Jack, who was sorely in need of such care. Once he settled in at the Carringtons', Miranda intended to visit him, worried that he'd be lonely in the unfamiliar environment. She'd hoped that Gwen and Simon might be willing to take him in, but Gwen's resistance could not be overcome. For all Miranda's criticism of Tom's overprotectiveness, her own past colored the way she viewed Jack. She, too, cared too much about what happened to him.

Neither of these children were like Sam, but they reminded her of what she had lost. How ironic that Lady Carrington thought Miranda had no longings apart from her art!

This brought her to another cause of her current emotional state—her relationship with Tom. She hadn't seen or heard from him since that night at the studio nearly a week ago. Deciding what to do about his father must have consumed much of his time. Besides, the old dean had died a few days earlier, so she could only imagine how hard Tom must be working to try to salvage his reputation at the cathedral.

Although Miranda hadn't confessed her misdeeds to Tom as he had to her, telling him she loved him qualified as a confession, and it made her feel vulnerable. She had loved him for so long without revealing her feelings that it had shocked her to hear herself say the words aloud. She didn't expect him to return her feelings, but he hadn't responded to her declaration, hadn't even seemed to hear it. Until that day she'd been fairly successful in channeling her feelings into her art or pushing them out of her mind. But now she was all too aware of her desires and of the hopelessness of the situation.

No longings, indeed! The problem was she had too many competing longings.

As for what Tom had confessed to her, she was surprised by some, but not all, of his misdeeds. She felt only sympathy for his actions as a youth—even leaving his family was understandable, given the abuse he had suffered. But what he had said about his behavior with women was sobering. She realized she was probably fortunate that he didn't return her feelings. It was also gratifying to know she was the only person he trusted with his secrets. Still, she was a woman, too, and she couldn't help wondering why she seemed to inspire no passion in him when other women could.

It had been a relief to Miranda that Lady Carrington hadn't referred to the scene at the cathedral, although now that she thought about it, it was an odd omission. Everyone else who was acquainted with Tom or who was at the service that day had talked of nothing else since. As a friend of his, Lady Carrington would naturally be concerned about him—or perhaps angry that he had lied about his father. Surely she had *some* reaction. Perhaps she was merely being discreet and avoiding gossip.

When Miranda arrived home, the household was in an uproar, as she had expected. It was this way every time they had dinner guests whom Gwen or Simon considered worth impressing. This time the visitors were Simon's employer Mr. Keating, along with his wife and son. Miranda steeled herself to enter the fray and quietly carried out Gwen's orders, thinking wryly of Lady Carrington calling her "poor Cinderella." She certainly felt like Cinderella as she helped Jane fetch and carry and clean for Gwen until her back was stiff and her arms aching. By the time the Keatings arrived, Miranda was in no mood to entertain them, wishing only for the quiet solitude of her bedroom.

Mr. Keating was a rotund man in his middle years with narrow, shifty eyes that gave him a perpetually guilty look. Mrs. Keating was pleasant enough, but she talked too much for Miranda's taste. Her loquaciousness was a blessing in disguise, though, for she and Gwen bore the burden of conversation. James Keating, the son, was in his late teens and had the unfortunate tendency of staring too intently at whichever woman was nearest him, as if he were trying to compensate for his father's opposite tendency. Because Miranda sat across the table from him at dinner, she was the younger Mr. Keating's victim for most of the evening. She tried giving him an icy stare in return, but it made no difference—it was like trying to pierce through a stone wall. The worst of James Keating's rudeness was that his staring wasn't confined to his object's face. Any part of her person was fair game for his scrutiny, and it didn't take long for Miranda to wish she had worn additional layers of clothing. Deciding that her only recourse was to ignore him, Miranda tried to focus on the conversation.

"It's been quite a dramatic week at the cathedral," Mrs. Keating said to Gwen. "Were you there when that horrible man interrupted the service?"

"Yes," Gwen said.

"I wasn't," Mr. Keating put in. "Was he really in his cups?"

"It was awful," Gwen said. "I don't know why nobody threw him out sooner."

"Can you imagine the embarrassment of having a father like that?" Mrs. Keating said. "I wasn't surprised when Canon Cross left the pulpit and walked out."

Miranda remembered how white Tom's face had been and how he had clutched the side of the pulpit when his father first stood and started to speak. She wished Gwen and the Keatings would stop talking about him. Simon looked as uneasy as Miranda felt.

"And the old dean died just a few days ago, did you hear?" Mrs. Keating said. "I know Canon Cross was being considered for the deanship of the cathedral, but this incident is bound to hurt his chances."

"He certainly won't be dean now," said her husband, who couldn't possibly be certain. "The cathedral clergy are the aristocracy of the church. If Cross became dean, it would be like a navvy becoming king!" He snorted with laughter.

"I never trusted him," Mrs. Keating said. "I always thought there was something common about him."

Miranda felt sick. The conversation had spun out of control, but she couldn't think fast enough to figure out how to stop it. She tried to catch Simon's eye, but he was staring silently into his bowl of soup. Surely he wasn't so afraid of his employer that he wouldn't defend Tom.

Gwen set down her spoon and cleared her throat. In a clear, authoritative tone, she said, "Canon Cross is our friend, and he's a good man. Please don't speak of him that way in our house."

Mrs. Keating stared, openmouthed. Mr. Keating's spoon fell into his soup. "Will you allow your wife to speak to your guests in such a way?" Mr. Keating demanded of Simon.

Miranda held her breath.

Simon wiped his mouth with his napkin, then said slowly, "I agree with her."

There was a tense silence that seemed to Miranda to last forever, but was probably only a few seconds.

Gwen turned to Mrs. Keating as if nothing unusual had happened and asked brightly, "Have you seen the new summer hats? They're even bigger than last year and worn at quite a precipitous angle. You could wear them, though: you have such a wonderful sense of style. They'd look lovely on you."

Mrs. Keating hesitated, glancing at her husband, but Gwen's flattery had hit its mark as the two women began a lively discussion of headgear. Miranda started breathing again. She could have hugged her sister-in-law with genuine affection.

Simon and Mr. Keating began to speak of other things, too: politics, social problems, the future of the law firm. James Keating continued to stare at Miranda, taking away what little appetite she had. To Miranda's relief, the Keatings left shortly after dinner.

As she was about to escape to her room, an unexpected visitor rushed into the drawing room, ahead of a flustered Jane. It was Ann Goode, though she didn't look like the same Ann who had been reunited with Jack in this very room. This version of Ann was better dressed, though ostentatiously so, in a gold silk day dress trimmed with lace and a matching hat so laden with feathers and flowers that a bird might be forgiven for swooping down to make a home in it. There was something artificial and hectic about the red of her lips and cheeks.

"I'm sorry, Mr. Thorne," Jane said to Simon. "When I opened the door, she pushed me out of the way."

"Where's Jack?" Ann demanded by way of greeting, looking from Simon to Miranda. "Is 'e 'ere?"

Gwen recovered first. Rising from her seat and drawing herself up to her full height, she said, "Who is this person, Simon?"

"This is Jack's sister," Simon said.

"I'm done with lies," Ann said. "I'm his mother."

Miranda felt her stomach lurch. It wasn't possible. Jack was at least ten years old, and Ann was . . .

Simon was apparently doing the arithmetic in his head, as well. "Aren't you eighteen?" he said. "That's what Jack told us. And he says he's thirteen."

"I'm four-and-twenty. Jack's ten. We've always lied about our ages. An' I've pretended to be Jack's sister since 'e was born. It's not only gentlefolks like you as cares about appearances. But now it's your turn to tell the truth. Where is 'e?"

"I don't know who you think you are," Gwen said sharply, "but you have no right to rush into our drawing room and make demands."

Undeterred, Ann took a step towards Miranda, sitting in shocked silence in the armchair nearest the door. "You'll 'elp me, won't you?" Ann said. "You know Jack loves me. If you just tell me where 'e is, I'll take 'im an' leave an' never trouble any of you again."

Miranda was struggling to reconcile this frowsy, demanding woman with the girl who had seemed to care so much about Jack, and she felt an instinctive desire to hide the boy's whereabouts until she knew more. She also thought that Tom ought to be the one to decide how much to tell Ann about Jack's whereabouts.

"You ought to talk to Canon Cross about Jack," she said. "He arranged—"

"Canon Cross!" The girl spat his name like a curse. "'E's the last person I'll talk to. 'E's the reason I need to take Jack and get away from 'ere."

"What do you mean?" Miranda asked.

"'E's Jack's natural father."

Miranda shot to her feet. "How dare you say such a thing!" she cried, raising her hand as if to slap Ann, despite never having slapped anyone in her life. "After everything he's done for you and Jack—"

"Why d'ye think 'e did so much? Guilty conscience, that's why."

"You've said quite enough," Simon said, advancing towards Ann. "If you don't leave now, I'll throw you out."

Gwen and Jane joined Simon to form a sort of human barrier, and together they managed to herd Ann out of the room, though not without loud protests on her part. The last proclamation Miranda heard was, "You'll see the truth in the papers tomorrow. Then you'll be sorry!"

Miranda collapsed onto the chair she'd been sitting in, trembling from head to toe. Her mind whirled with fragments of words and images that began to form an unpleasant pattern of meaning. Tom's particular interest in Jack. His agitation on the day Ann and Jack were reunited. His judgmental attitude towards Ann. His admitting to Miranda that he couldn't be objective about Jack. His confession that he'd had an inappropriate sexual relationship with a woman.

Miranda used the last bit of strength she had left to take refuge in her bedroom before anyone could see her crying for the second time that day.

21

Who is it that can tell me who I am?
—William Shakespeare, *King Lear*

Tom stared at the books in front of him without seeing them. He was in the chapter house at the cathedral, sorting through his belongings. It was hard to believe his time at the cathedral was over, at least temporarily.

That morning the bishop had summoned Tom to the palace and said, "I want you to take some time away to sort yourself out, Canon Cross. A month at least. Perhaps two."

"Am I being dismissed?" Tom had asked hollowly.

"No. I don't blame you for wanting to hide your past, although I would have preferred to hear the truth from you at the outset of your appointment here. You must know you are in no state to continue your work. You look like you haven't slept in weeks, and the errors you're making are beginning to interfere with the smooth running of the cathedral. You need a rest and some time to think about who you are and what you want. I am offering you that time."

"Thank you," was all Tom could say then. Now he wished he had said more. But what could he possibly have said that would make a difference? He couldn't explain himself—that was the point of being asked to leave. He understood that. But he couldn't help feeling he was in disgrace, and he wished he could prove that he wasn't falling apart.

Of course, the trouble was that he *was* falling apart. The identity he had constructed for himself as a competent leader, someone others looked to for solutions to their problems, *was* disintegrating, and he didn't know what to replace it with. Without his work, he was lost. He'd been asked to take time away from his work on the Prison Commission and his hospital visits as well as his canonry, and he didn't even have Jack to care for anymore.

Furthermore, according to cathedral gossip, Paul Harris had already been offered the deanship. The timing couldn't have been worse.

As Tom continued to sit at the long table in the chapter house, lost in thought, Harris himself entered the room. Despite his colleague's welcome role in removing Tom's father from the cathedral the previous Sunday, Tom felt no warmer towards him than he did before. Harris would never do anything for Tom without some hidden, self-serving motive.

"I need to speak with you," Harris said. He looked uncomfortable.

"What about?"

"It's about what happened when your father—"

"Look, Harris, do you really think I want to listen to your sermon on the subject? Are you here just to gloat? I've said all I'm going to say about it, and you can read anything else you want to know in the papers." It must have been a slow week for news, because his father's outburst at the cathedral had indeed been mentioned in the papers.

"That's not what I'm here for."

"What, then?"

Harris sat down at the table at Tom's left and stared at the wall opposite. "Your father came to see me the week before he came to the cathedral service."

A heavy feeling began to grow in the pit of Tom's stomach. "What are you talking about?"

"He found out I work with you and asked for my help arranging a reconciliation. He told me about the hardships he'd experienced in his past and about your ambitions being beyond his means. I felt sorry for him—"

"Why am I not surprised?" Tom interrupted.

"—and I suggested he attend the Sunday service. I had no idea he would arrive in a drunken state, nor did I expect him to create a disturbance. I was under the impression he wished so strongly to reconcile with you that he would do nothing untoward."

"So you were merely acting out of kindness to reconcile me with my father," Tom said sarcastically.

"You had told everyone your father was dead and you lied about your name. I thought that seeing your father in the congregation would . . . improve your character."

"So you are the person, then, to whom I owe my disgrace," Tom said coldly. "I suppose you orchestrated the attack on me last year, as well."

Harris looked shocked. "What attack?"

Tom gave his rival a wary look. "You must have noticed my long absence from the cathedral."

"I thought you were ill."

"I was driven into the country against my will by a hansom cabdriver, then beaten and left for dead by at least two other men. Did you have anything to do with that?"

"What? Of course not. How could such a thing happen? Did you tell the police?"

"It doesn't matter now."

"But—"

"I don't want to talk about it."

Harris leaned forward with his hands clasped together on the table. "I don't like you, Cross, but I would never sanction a physical attack on another human being."

Tom believed him. Harris was an arrogant snob, but even if he might wish Tom dead in his fantasies, he hadn't the stomach to resort to physical violence, even by proxy.

Tom was finished with the conversation. He pushed back his chair and stood, picking up a pile of papers and tossing them into an empty box.

Harris rose, too. "Regarding your father," he said, clearing his throat, "I was wrong to become involved and wrong to interfere with your personal life, and I'm sorry."

Tom wasn't ready for sincerity from his nemesis. "Well, well. An apology from Canon Harris, of all people. But perhaps you have reason to be magnanimous with the lower orders of clergy these days. Are the rumors that you've been offered the deanship correct? It certainly won't be offered to me now."

"I have, but that has nothing to do with this. Besides, I've declined the offer."

Tom stared at him. "Are you mad? Why? Is your father going to buy you a bishopric?"

Harris said stiffly, "There are many complicated reasons for my decision that I don't wish to discuss at the moment."

Tom shrugged. "Suit yourself."

"I've paid for your father's passage back to America. He leaves next week." Harris turned to leave, but at the door, he paused. With his back to Tom, he added, "I don't know why you and I seem to bring out the worst in each other. I wish it could have been different."

He left the room.

Tom's first thought was to wonder what his father was doing in America. But it didn't really matter. There was nothing he wanted to know about his father's life. Then he wondered why he didn't feel vindicated. Harris had admitted to inviting Tom's father to the cathedral with impure motives. But he had also apologized and offered to make amends. Tom didn't think he could have done that. Harris, it turned out, was the better man. He deserved the deanship. What in the world had possessed him to decline it?

Tom no longer wanted to hide behind his position in the church or any other public role. If he had become dean, he would have had to work even harder to prove to the world that he was worthy of such a position, and he was tired of pretending. He wanted to be himself. Whoever that was.

Tom's only concrete plan was to go to Yorkshire and try to find his remaining family. His father's appearance had brought Kate and his mother vividly to his mind, and he needed to know if they were all right. And though he had no desire to see his father again, he decided he'd better find out when and where the old man was scheduled to board the ship bound for America. It would be good to know for certain that he was leaving the country.

As Tom was on his way out of the cathedral, carrying his box of books and papers, he met William Narbridge on his way in. Setting his jaw, Tom prepared to walk past him without speaking.

But Narbridge couldn't pass up the opportunity. "Leaving, are you, Cross? It's about time." Tom wasn't looking at him, but he could hear the smug smile in his voice. He pushed past Narbridge and kept walking.

"Have you seen the newspapers this morning?" the railway magnate called after him. "If you have any sense, you won't darken any church door again."

This was too much. Tom set down the box and strode back to Narbridge, facing him squarely. "I've had enough of your insults," he said. "Having an alcoholic father isn't a crime, but the way you've treated your workers certainly is."

"Aha, so you do remember. Are you going to fight me, Cross? It won't look good for a priest to knock down a valuable member of the congregation."

"I don't have time to play games with you," Tom snapped. "If you're referring to the investigation I started, that was three years ago, and it didn't hurt your business."

"I have a long memory, and you're wrong about the investigation not hurting my business. I lost out on lucrative building contracts because of the damage you did to my reputation. Was it necessary to defame me in the newspapers?"

"I don't know what you're talking about." Tom didn't remember even seeing any newspaper stories about Narbridge or his company at the time. He turned to leave. Narbridge wasn't worth his time or energy.

The railway magnate called after him, "Now you'll know what it feels like to be talked about, and you won't be so quick to point the finger next time."

Tom shrugged off Narbridge's words. He had more important concerns on his mind. After taking his books to his lodgings, he went out again, this time walking in the direction of the Thornes' house. He couldn't wait any longer to see Miranda. Although it had been a busy and difficult week, she was never far from his mind. And he missed Simon, too. He wanted to apologize for any concern or distress his father's appearance at the cathedral may have caused them. Most of all, he wanted to tell Miranda how he felt about her.

But as soon as Jane answered the door at the Thornes' house, he knew something was very wrong. Her face blanched and she muttered something indistinguishable, then closed the door again. Jane knew him as a regular visitor, so why would she close the door in his face? It couldn't be Miranda's doing. And surely his father's appearance at the cathedral wasn't enough cause for Simon and Gwen to cut off their acquaintance with him, not without hearing his explanation first.

He waited a few minutes, then knocked again. Silence.

Once more he knocked, louder. More silence.

Just when he turned and began to walk away, the door opened. This time Simon stood there, looking haggard. "You'd better come in," he said, not meeting Tom's eyes.

Tom silently followed Simon into the drawing room. The two men sat opposite each other, Simon on the sofa, Tom in an armchair.

"Is Miranda here?" Tom asked. "I'd like to see her, too."

"No, she's not." Simon's voice was firm, not inviting further questions.

"I apologize for lying to you about my father's death," Tom said. "It was wishful thinking, not the truth."

"About your father?" Simon said, looking surprised. "What about Jack? And Ann?"

"What about them?"

"Your lie about your father pales in comparison to your lies about them."

"I don't know what you mean. Kindly explain yourself."

"I can't tell if you're pretending not to know or if you really don't." Simon rose, took a newspaper from the drawer of a side table, then handed it to Tom. "I have no desire to repeat the sordid story. It's here if you wish to read it."

The first thing Tom noticed was that the newspaper wasn't one of the respectable dailies: it was sensational rubbish. He never read such papers and couldn't imagine why Simon would. But then he saw the headline: "Cathedral Clergyman's Sins Find Him Out: Woman Says Thomas Cross Seduced Her at Fourteen and Fathered Her Bastard Son."

A hot, sick feeling spread through Tom's core, and his vision blurred. He didn't want to read the story, but his eyes played the traitor by skimming it anyway. The woman's name wasn't mentioned, of course, but his own was. Over and over again. And even though Tom thought he'd seen and heard everything, he was shocked by the salaciousness of the details in the disgusting story of a sexual miscreant by the name of Thomas Cross. His mind felt stupid and slow: what did the story have to do with Ann and Jack? Eventually the connection became clear, and he flung the paper to the floor. Simon's elbows were on his knees and his head in his hands, so Tom could only stare at the top of his head. Words came to Tom's mind that he had never uttered aloud, but now he had to clench his jaw to prevent them from spilling out.

He took one deep breath, then another. When he trusted himself to speak, he said, "Am I to understand that you believe this filth?"

Simon slowly raised his head. "I don't know what to believe."

"You've spent what, an hour or two in Ann Goode's presence? As opposed to many hours with me. I'm your friend. But you believe her lies." Tom kept his voice clipped, fighting to control his anger.

"I don't even know your real name."

"For God's sake, Simon." Tom stood and began to pace about the room. "It's Hirst. Tom Hirst. What difference does it make? You've spent time with me and learned my character, not from my name or even what I say, but from what I do. How I behave. I have my faults—you've seen my temper, my stubbornness, my pride. I trust I needn't supply a complete list. The point is you *do* know me."

There was a rustle of silk in the doorway behind him. *Miranda.* Tom whirled around, but it was only Gwen, bracing her hand against the door-frame and looking as Little Red Riding Hood might while encountering the wolf.

"What is he doing here, Simon?" she asked. "We agreed—"

"Leave us, Gwen," Simon said. "He won't be here long."

Darting a worried glance in Tom's direction, she obeyed.

"Please tell me Miranda doesn't know about this rubbish," Tom said, prodding the newspaper with the toe of his boot.

"As far as I know, she hasn't read the story, but it doesn't matter. She heard it firsthand when Ann came here yesterday looking for Jack."

"Bloody hell." He wanted to shake the information he needed out of Simon all at once instead of being stabbed with little bits of it like needles. But to alienate Simon was to lose perhaps the only friend he had left, and he needed to stay calm. He took another deep breath.

"Did you tell Ann where Jack is?" Tom asked.

"No."

"Thank God for that. He's safe for the moment with the Carringtons, then."

Simon raised his head, looking with bleary eyes at Tom. "Jack loves her. Whether she's his sister or his mother, you can't deny that. And she seems to care for him, too. I don't think she'd hurt him."

Tom sat down again and forced himself to think clearly. Then he leaned forward, choosing his words carefully. "Simon, Ann's story is a lie. What she says makes no sense. You know how badly I wanted the deanship, how I was so careful of my public image. If I really was Jack's father, why would I so openly and publicly take him under my care? Why would I openly and pub-licly embark on that search for Ann, knowing what she could reveal about me? Only the most stupid of villains would behave in such a way. Thus, if you believe Ann's story, you must believe me both evil and stupid."

Simon nodded once, his eyes closed as if in prayer. Whether he was acknowledging the logic of Tom's reasoning or the belief that Tom was evil and stupid was unclear. Tom held his breath and waited.

Opening his eyes, Simon said quietly, "Ann was dressed well when she came here yesterday. I didn't notice at the time, but Gwen mentioned it afterward. I can't see how she could afford such clothes. It makes me wonder if someone paid her to tell that story about you. Maybe it was the same person who arranged for your father to come to the cathedral and planned the attack on you last year."

"Yes!" Tom exclaimed, relieved that Simon was finally talking sense. "It was Paul Harris who invited my father to the cathedral, but I don't believe he planned the attack, and he definitely wouldn't have paid Ann to tell that story. Someone else could have done both of those things. And it can't be a coincidence that she's told her story now, in the same week that Dean Whiting died."

"You'd better go now," Simon said flatly, extinguishing Tom's spark of hope for their friendship.

"Very well." But Tom was reluctant to leave without speaking to Miranda. "You said Miranda's not here. When will she return?"

Simon merely stood up and pointed the way to the door.

Tom didn't move. He'd just remembered that during his confession to Miranda, he'd told her he had a sexual relationship with another woman. He was thinking of Julia, of course, but after recent events, Miranda could assume—must assume—he had meant Ann. The horror of this possibility was too great to be borne.

"Simon, I need to talk to her. The last time we spoke, I said things she could have misunderstood. Things that could hurt her needlessly."

"Don't you think that meeting her alone regularly at Mrs. Grant's studio has already hurt her?"

Tom slowly rose to his feet and faced Simon. His early-morning visits to the studio were too sacred to speak of, and he was surprised Miranda had told Simon about them.

"She didn't want to tell me," Simon added, "but the truth came out after I told her I heard her leave the house in the middle of the night after your father came to the cathedral. While I can well believe you capable of impropriety, I was shocked that she didn't know better after everything she's endured."

Tom realized that he knew very little of what Miranda had suffered in the past, and he cursed himself for being so caught up in hiding his own past that he hadn't tried harder to find out more about hers.

"Don't blame her," he said. "She's done nothing wrong. I was to blame for not seeing . . . not realizing how my visits to the studio might look to others. I'd rather shoot myself than be the cause of a moment's pain to her."

"What exactly is the nature of your relationship? She was unwilling to tell me."

"I love her."

Simon gave him a suspicious look. "I don't know what that means, coming from you."

"My God, do you think I seduced her?"

"I have no idea. She said you didn't."

"And you don't believe her? Has she ever lied to you before?"

"Yes, many times."

Both Simon's words and his tone shocked Tom.

"But that's not the point," continued Simon. "It's not just her reputation that will suffer. If Richard finds out, he'll make her suffer."

"Who is Richard?"

Simon blinked. "In all your hours of intimate conversation, she didn't tell you? He's the vicar of Smythe, the one we've been hiding from for years."

Tom was confused. "I thought his name was Sam."

"You know nothing, I see. For God's sake, Tom, just go."

Tom walked to the doorway, then stopped, bracing his hand against the doorframe. He knew he was pushing Simon to the limit of his patience, but he was so consumed with worry for Miranda that he couldn't help asking one last question.

"If this Richard is a violent man, can't he be arrested? Can't Miranda be protected from him somehow without having to hide?"

"He's not physically violent. His power over her is more complicated than that. But I have no doubt that she'll be safer if *you* leave her alone. Will you promise to stay away from her?"

"I can't make such a promise. Not unless she makes that request of me herself."

Simon turned away, and Tom left.

21

Wandering between two worlds, one dead,
The other powerless to be born,
With nowhere yet to rest my head,
Like these, on earth I wait forlorn.
—Matthew Arnold, "Stanzas from the Grande Chartreuse"

WETHERBY, WEST YORKSHIRE: JULY 1908

B e off wi' thee, lad! I nivver saw the likes o' thee fer a browl."
The voice came from the street below Tom's window, startling him
out of a reverie. He was sitting at the writing desk in his stiflingly hot room
at the Higby Inn, his shirt sticking to his back. He'd moved the writing desk
directly in front of the open window, but the cooling breeze he'd hoped for
hadn't materialized. It had been an unseasonably hot summer in London,
but he hadn't expected the same in Yorkshire.

A scuffling sound rose from the street, then someone—the offending
boy, it seemed—ran off. The man who had been yelling exclaimed unintel-
ligibly, then walked away, too.

When he'd first arrived a month ago, Tom had been surprised how alien the dialect sounded, despite its having been his own for the first seventeen years of his life. Perhaps by trying to erase his past, he had also erased the language he associated with it. The sounds coming out of these northerners' mouths sounded harsh and grating to his ears. But after a few weeks, he was able to follow the conversation of even the excitable and garrulous Mr. Higby, the innkeeper, and it no longer sounded so foreign.

A knock came at his door, and Tom called out, "Come in."

"Here's the paper tha' asked fer, Mr. Hirst, and thy letters," said Mr. Higby. "Would tha' like summat to eat?" He was a spry, bright-eyed septuagenarian with the energy of a thirty-year-old.

"No, thank you. I'd like a pot of tea, though, if you please."

"Aye. Did I tell thee owt of Dick Rudd? I canna remember."

"I don't think so."

"He's lived in Wetherby fifty years. He knows everybody. I told him about thee, and he remembers a Hirst girl who married a Wilson. Even if that Hirst isn't a relation of thine, mebbe the family will know summat."

"Thank you, Mr. Higby. I'll certainly talk to these people."

Mr. Higby gave Tom the address and left, and Tom tossed the papers on the desk without looking at them. He was grateful for the new opportunity to talk to someone who might know his mother or sister, but he had been following similar tidbits of information since his arrival, and so far they'd led nowhere. His family seemed to have disappeared as completely as he had seventeen years earlier.

He had reluctantly reverted to the name Hirst for his time in Yorkshire. Whenever he introduced himself to people, he hoped to see a light of recognition in their eyes, or perhaps they would say, "Hirst? I know a Hirst in Wetherby. Are you a relation?" Of course, there was also the danger that someone would know his father—and his father's crimes—and Tom would be tarred with the same brush.

Before going to Yorkshire, Tom had stopped in Liverpool, where the *Adriatic*, the ship his father was scheduled to be on, was starting to board. His inquiries turned up nothing conclusive. His father's name was on the passenger list, but Tom didn't actually see him, and there was no proof that he had in fact boarded the ship. He could have sold his ticket to some desperate person for double the price Harris had paid, then gone straight to the pub to celebrate his cleverness. Tom had done all he could, and so decided to let it be.

Tom hadn't done anything during his time in Yorkshire but search for his family and think. He had spent more time alone in the past month, it seemed, than in his whole life so far. He hadn't realized how little used to solitude he was. He did most of his thinking during long walks, mostly at night when the air was cooler and the curious eyes of Wetherby residents were not on him. He thought about whether he could continue to work as a clergyman, much less a canon at the cathedral, and if he couldn't, how he would make a living. He toyed with the idea of staying in Yorkshire and doing some sort of manual labor—even working as a blacksmith as his father had. He had learned some of the trade as a child. But to choose that line of work smacked too much of penance, and he didn't think it was necessary to go that far. He still wanted to work with people, but he no longer wanted a public role. He was afraid of falling into the same trap, being tempted by the admiration of others to think himself invincible.

Tom's thoughts were interrupted by the arrival of Mr. Higby's wife with Tom's tea. When she had left, Tom picked up the three letters and sat down at the desk again. Two of the letters were business-related: one was from the chairman of the Prison Reform Committee, asking for information about some of the inmates Tom had been working with; the other from the bishop, asking when Tom intended to return to London. Reading between the lines, Tom knew the bishop wanted particulars of his spiritual and emotional state to determine if he was fit to return to work.

The third letter was from Julia. He'd had no contact with her in months, and he couldn't imagine anything good coming in a letter from her. He opened it with a feeling of foreboding.

Dear Tom,

You'll be surprised to hear from me, I know, but I'm writing on behalf of another. I hope it's cooler in Yorkshire: God knows we could all use a refreshing change from the suffocating heat of London. We're staying in London for the Season, of course, but I look forward to moving to our country house next month. You'll be interested to know that your little friend Miranda Thorne has been staying with us and will accompany us to Rudleigh.

Tom caught his breath, his thoughts whirling. Why was Miranda staying with the Carringtons? Was she the one who had asked Julia to write to him? He hadn't heard a word from or about her since he'd left London.

By the way, if you're deliberately staying away to avoid the various scandals with your name attached to them, you needn't. Fortunately for you, the Tyne and Bow affair has caused a far greater public stir, and your troubles have been largely forgotten. You, of course, could never be forgotten, and I'm certain you wouldn't wish to be. The general public opinion about you (at least in the circles I move in) is that you are just bad enough to be interesting. That ought to please you!

To get to business, though, Charles has asked me to invite you to stay with us at Rudleigh for a week in August. It's the usual party to mark the beginning of grouse season, and we need a few nonsporting men to entertain the ladies. It will, no doubt, feel strange to both of us after everything that has passed between us, but I think it will seem stranger

*if you refuse to come, especially if you've returned to London by then.
You have an ally in Charles (like it or not), who has defended you to
your critics at more than one social function.*

*If you're still not persuaded, perhaps knowing Miranda will be there
will help. (She and I use each other's Christian names now, having
become great friends.) I am arranging a small exhibition of her paintings
at our house while the guests are there. You likely know how she hates
putting herself forward, but I've convinced her it will be a small party
and that she may play the role of the mysterious artist who is above
the rules of social life we mere mortals must observe. I doubt she'll be
displeased to see you.*

*Let me know as soon as you can. I can't say I'd be displeased to see
you, either, after all this time!*

Julia

Tom frowned. It was an unusually friendly letter, considering the last
conversation he had had with Julia. To think of her audacity in inviting him
to stay at her country house! Even if she was telling the truth and Charles
had prompted the invitation, she could have found some excuse not to offer
it. And the irony of Charles being Tom's ally was too uncomfortable to
ponder. Tom needed all the friends he could find, but for Charles to be the
last man standing by his side was to heap burning coals on Tom's head.

But the invitation was tempting for other reasons. Tom could see Jack
again and find out if he was safe from the scheming of his sister, or mother,
or whatever Ann was to him. He could assess the damage to his reputation
based on the attitude of the Carringtons' guests. And most tempting of all,
he could finally see Miranda. If she and Julia had indeed become "great
friends," as Julia (slyly, he thought) proclaimed in her letter, Miranda must
have no objection to his presence. And Julia had written, *I doubt she'll be*

displeased to see you, so even with the double negatives, he had reason to hope. On the other hand, Julia knew too much, had too much power to influence Miranda against Tom, and she could have issued the invitation merely to torture him.

His feelings for Miranda were becoming clearer every day he was away from her. He had written a cautious but friendly letter to her when he first arrived in Yorkshire, hoping to gauge whether her feelings for him had changed, but to his disappointment, she hadn't responded. This had worried him, though he had told himself that perhaps she simply needed time to think. He wrote other letters too, longer and more intimate ones, but these he didn't send. He could no longer treat her merely as a friend, and what he needed to say must be said in person.

There were so many obstacles. Even if she could look past the damage to his reputation and didn't believe Ann's lies, it would be unfair to ask her to marry him when he was so uncertain about his vocation. And there was also the mystery surrounding the vicar named Richard, and Sam, whoever he was. Simon had told Tom long ago that marriage was impossible for Miranda: was Richard or Sam the reason for this? Was she already married to someone else? Was it some conviction of hers based on her bad experience with Richard, or perhaps on some insecurity about her own fitness for marriage? Such a conviction could be overcome, and Tom intended to do his best to overcome it once he had the chance to talk to her.

He set Julia's letter aside and picked up the *Times.* It was his only link to London now. The first week after arriving in Yorkshire, he had read it with trepidation, worried that his name would be mentioned. One night he had even dreamed that the paper had been full of stories about him, stories that denounced him as a hypocrite and blackguard and presented lengthy lists of his sins. In reality, the *Times* had thus far paid no attention to him at all.

The latest issue was no exception. The front page was dominated by stories about militant suffragettes destroying property and the Tyne and Bow affair. Tyne, a well-known and respected Conservative MP, had been exposed for accepting a bribe from a man named Bow. Tom silently thanked the dishonorable men and the suffragettes for being more newsworthy than he was.

The only other news item that caught Tom's interest was a brief mention of a Royal Academy exhibition: "An unexpected success by a newcomer gathered a great deal of attention: a painting entitled *Wistful* by E.A. was commended by several critics for its unusual and arresting composition. We expect to see more of the mysterious E.A.'s paintings, if not the artist herself, at the Royal Academy. All we know is that she is a woman who prefers to remain anonymous."

Tom knew it had to be Miranda, and he was happy for her success. It made him want to see her all the more. He needed to distract himself before the longing became unbearable. He left his room, deciding to make a visit to the Wilson family that Mr. Higby had mentioned.

It was late afternoon by the time he found the house, about six miles from Wetherby. Tom chose to walk there, but before long his shirt was damp with sweat again and he regretted not hiring a vehicle. He'd also made a wrong turn, which slowed his progress. Finally, he found the Wilson house on an isolated stretch of road, a small yellow brick structure that could have been satisfactory when it was first built, but many decades of wear and poor upkeep had left it with a dilapidated appearance. The roof sagged dangerously in the middle.

As Tom knocked at the door, he tried to beat down the same spark of hope, mixed with anxiety, that arose in him every time he was about to meet someone who might know his family. He had repeated this pattern so often that the hope ought to have been easier to extinguish.

The door was opened by a grimy-faced, wide-eyed boy of about eight.

"Who is it, Freddie?" a harried-sounding woman's voice called from within.

"A gennelman," said Freddie.

"Well, let 'im in! Can't you see I've got my 'ands full?"

Freddie opened the door wider, but only his head showed from behind it, his big eyes staring at Tom as if he were afraid of being eaten.

"Thank you, lad," Tom said, stepping into a tiny vestibule. At the end of a passageway was the kitchen, from which the sounds of cooking and the babble of young voices could be heard.

A woman emerged from the kitchen, balancing a baby on her hip while wiping her hands on her apron. She strode towards Tom with the quick movement of a young woman, but when she came nearer, he saw that her face was lined and sallow. Her graying hair was pulled back tightly, but a few strands had escaped, sticking out at odd angles. She didn't meet his eyes, being occupied with the baby, who was twisting in her arms and beginning to fuss.

"I'm sorry to trouble you, ma'am," Tom said, "but I'm looking for a Mr. or Mrs. Wilson, and I'd be obliged if you can help me."

"Aye, I'm Mrs. Wilson," she said. "What d'ye want?"

"I'm looking for some family members named Hirst, and I was told you might know . . ." Tom's voice trailed off, for she was now looking up at him, and in her eyes was a look of shocked recognition.

"Oh God," she said in a strangled voice.

He didn't know her. She was too young to be his mother, and too old to be his sister. Or was she? Her eyes were very dark, almost black, like his own. And if he imagined her hair without the gray . . . could it be?

"Kate?"

If he thought she would rush into his arms in a paroxysm of joy, rather like Jack and Ann had done with each other, he was mistaken. Once the initial shock of recognition had passed, a hard look came into her eyes and she said gruffly, "You'd better come in."

She half guided, half pushed the boy in front of her as she strode back down the passageway, and Tom followed her with a myriad of thoughts and misgivings whirling in his head. Kate had been only fifteen when he left, two years younger than he was, and certainly she would have changed a great deal in so many years, but it was hard to believe that this exhausted-looking, sour-faced woman was in her early thirties. As a young girl, his sister had had a beautiful laugh—it had bubbled out of her effortlessly when they played together. This woman didn't look as though she was capable of laughter. A creeping heaviness weighed Tom down as he followed her into the kitchen.

His first impression was that he'd been transported into the duchess's kitchen in *Alice's Adventures in Wonderland*. An older woman was stirring a large pot that was bubbling vigorously on the stove, and there were three young children sitting on the floor, too close to the stove, throwing dishes at one another. When his sister—for he was certain now the woman must be Kate—entered the kitchen with the baby and Freddie, the kitchen was crowded indeed. Tom stood uncertainly in the doorway, wanting to rescue the saucers from the children and the children from the stove, but knowing it wasn't his place to do so.

"Katie! Joe! Susan! Stop that this minute. Mam, didn't you see what they're doing? There won't be any dishes left!" Kate stooped to remove the dishes from the children's grasp, nearly dropping the baby at the same time. "We 'ave a visitor," she added.

Tom stood as if turned to stone as his mother turned from the pot of stew to look at him. He knew her immediately. Her dark eyes were sharp, and she was still small and wiry, stronger looking than her daughter, despite being in her sixties.

His mother's reaction to seeing Tom was very different from Kate's. She burst into tears and started towards him, nearly tripping over the three children on the floor in her haste to get to him. Tom moved forward, too, as close as he could without knocking over children or furniture, and his mother sprang into his arms, sobbing uncontrollably.

This reunion had happened so suddenly, despite his long search, that he was too stunned to know what he was feeling. He held her tightly, as if to make up for all the years he was out of reach. In the background, he heard Kate order the children outside to play.

When his mother's sobs had subsided, she took his arm and led him to a nearby chair. He sat down, but when she pulled up a low stool to sit close to him, he protested.

"No, you take the chair, Mam," he said.

"Hush. The stool is fine for me." She sat and leaned on his arm. She looked up into his face, smiling through her tears, and said, "My only son. My Tom. I knew you'd come back. I told you, Kate. Didn't I say he'd come back?"

"Aye," said Kate.

Tom glanced at his sister, who had taken over stirring the pot, still balancing the baby on her hip. She wasn't looking at him. The kitchen had become quieter now that the other children had left and the baby had stopped fussing. The only sounds were the bubbling of the broth and Kate's spoon banging against the pot as she stirred.

"You've become a gentleman, just like you always wanted," said his mother. "And so handsome. Don't you think so, Kate?"

"No doubt," was the cryptic reply.

"Mam, I'm sorry it took me so long to come back," Tom said. "I don't expect you to forgive me. It was wrong of me to stay away."

"I don't blame you, son. I knew what your life was like here. I wanted you to go. Tell me, are you married? Do you have children? What do you work at?"

Tom answered in the negative to the first two questions and told her briefly and generally about his work at the cathedral and prison and his hospital visits.

As he spoke, Kate bustled around the kitchen, banging pots and pans and slamming cupboard doors in a violent manner. He thought again of the cook and duchess in *Alice's Adventures in Wonderland*. He might as well be in a fantasy world. He'd done such a good job of convincing himself that his family was dead that he'd never imagined another life for them.

"I'm proud of you," his mother said. "I knew you'd do some good in the world if you got away from home."

Tom looked down at his mother's calloused hand, clasped in his, and said quietly, "I've done more harm than good, I fear. And I've tried to help strangers while ignoring my family. Tell me how you've been."

"I'm fine. Things were better after your father went to prison—that must have been only a year or two after you'd gone."

"How long was his sentence?" Tom asked.

"Five years." His mother bit her lip. "A man was badly injured during a . . . robbery."

After all this time, his mother was still reluctant to state his father's crimes plainly. Tom took a deep breath. "Did he come back here when he was released from prison?"

"We haven't seen him, but I've heard rumors that he went to America. Or was it Australia? Do you remember, Kate?"

Kate shook her head. "I don't care. As long as 'e stays away."

Tom was of the same opinion.

"When your father went to prison we were poor, but life was easier in other ways," his mother said. "We survived all right for a few years more. Then Kate married Fred, and I moved with them to this house."

"How many children do you have, Kate?" Tom asked, risking a direct address to his sister.

"You've seen 'em. Five. And there's another on the way." The baby in her arms started to fuss again, and Tom rose to approach her.

"May I take him? You look like you could use a free hand."

Kate hesitated, not meeting his eyes, then gave a quick nod.

Tom took the baby, perhaps a year old, and sat down again in the chair by his mother. The baby stopped fussing, and Tom's mother exclaimed, "You're good with little ones."

"The bairn's just startled by the new experience," Kate put in. "He'll start fussing again soon."

"What's his name?" Tom asked.

"Tom." Kate hastened to add, "'E ain't named after you. Fred's father was called Tom."

Little Tom did indeed begin to fuss, but his uncle—it only just dawned on Tom that he was an uncle—took out his watch chain and dangled it in front of the baby. Forgetting everything but the bright, swaying object, little Tom reached for it, fascinated.

"What does your husband do?" Tom asked Kate.

"'E drinks." Her eyes were hard.

"Fred works at the mill," Tom's mother said. "He ain't a bad man, but he does drink too much. He doesn't beat the children, though he's rough with Kate sometimes."

"Mam," Kate said warningly.

"I'm sorry," Tom said.

"That's an easy word to throw around, ain't it?" Kate snapped. "You come 'ere out of nowhere and say you're sorry and you expect us to admire you, the fancy clergyman, the gentleman who 'elps people in London. You can say you're sorry a million times and it won't change anythin'."

The baby started to cry again upon hearing his mother's raised voice. Kate snatched him from Tom's arms and left the room.

"I'm sorry, Tom," his mother said with a sigh. "She takes everything to heart. She'll come 'round eventually."

"I don't blame her," Tom said wearily. "I've apologized to many people in the last couple of months, but it doesn't change their circumstances or the damage I've done. I wish it could." He looked around the room, noticing the makeshift table and chairs, the dirt, the smell of poverty, and he was acutely aware of his clean, well-cut clothing, his polished language. He felt sick. What was he doing here?

His mother rose, beaming at him, and went back to the pot Kate had been stirring. His return had comforted her, at least. For the first time in his life he truly understood what the prodigal son must have felt.

"Mam, how can I help you?" he asked. "I have some money—it won't be enough, but it'll help—and you could stay with me in London if you like."

"London! Good gracious. No, Tom, dear. I like this wild place. The city wouldn't suit me. And Kate and my grandchildren need me."

"Perhaps I could move nearby. I could help you if I were closer."

"What about your work?"

"I don't know if I'll return to the cathedral. I don't think I'm meant to be a clergyman. I've made mistakes—"

"What sort of talk is that?" she said, looking at him fondly. "We all make mistakes, even priests. You still believe in God, don't you?"

"Yes. Yes, I do."

His mother took the pot off the fire, set it on the table, and stood in front of Tom. She reached out to place her palm against his cheek. "I should have protected you better when you and Kate were little. I could have taken the two of you and run away."

"Where would we have gone? You couldn't have done more than what you did," Tom said. "Don't blame yourself."

"Neither could you, love. You were only a boy, and you bore it as long as you could. Don't you think I understand that?"

Tom took his mother's hand and squeezed it, blinking back tears.

"You'd better leave now," his mother said. "Fred will be home soon, and he doesn't like surprises. Can you come back tomorrow afternoon?"

"Yes, I will." He rose and embraced her, then turned to leave.

"Tom?"

He turned back to find her face creased with worry.

"Do you drink?" his mother asked.

"No. The smell of liquor makes me sick."

Her expression relaxed. "Good."

When he left the house, he saw Kate sitting on a rock near where her children were playing. She was holding the baby on her lap, but she was staring out into the distance as if she were alone. Tom didn't know whether to approach her or not, and he hesitated for a moment.

"Leavin' again?" she said without looking at him.

"Yes," he said, "but I'd like to come back tomorrow, if I may."

"Suit yourself."

It was enough for now.

When Tom returned the next day, he found his mother and Kate cleaning the cottage.

He took the children outside and watched them play, thinking how easy it would be to become attached to them, especially little Tom, who liked being carried on his shoulders. After a while his mother came outside to watch him with the children, wiping her hands on her apron and smiling.

"Kate's in a better mood today," she said quietly to Tom. "If you want to go inside and talk to her, I'll watch the wee ones."

Grateful for the opportunity to talk alone with his sister, Tom went into the house. Kate was sitting in the rocking chair by the kitchen window, mending socks. She looked up when he entered the room but didn't speak, her face still wary.

"May I sit with you?" he asked.

She nodded and looked out the window at her children playing. One of the windowpanes was cracked, and the wooden frame was rotting.

It broke Tom's heart to see his sister so worn out. She looked like she rarely slept and hadn't time to do so much as brush her hair. He took one of the kitchen chairs and sat across from her. Studying her face, he saw what looked like a fading bruise on her cheek.

"Kate," he began, "I don't blame you if you can't forgive me for leaving. I didn't understand why you wouldn't come with me all those years ago, but now of course I do. I have no excuse for waiting so long to come back. I just want to know if there's anything I can do to help you now."

"I don't need help." She spoke sharply, looking down to resume her mending.

He looked around the room. "I could replace that window for you, and fix that broken chair."

"No."

"Will you come with me to London, then?"

"What? Me and all five—six—children?" She gave him a challenging look. "Where would you put us?"

"I'd find a place for you. A better place than this."

"This place suits me just fine. Besides, Fred wouldn't let me leave." Her mouth was a hard line.

"He wouldn't have to know."

"'E'd know later, and that'd be worse."

"There are safe places in London for women in your situation. I've worked with them and I could find you something quickly."

"I'm not a charity case." She stabbed the needle with unnecessary force into the sock she was mending.

"I don't think of you that way. I just want to help."

"Some things can't be fixed. Sometimes it's too late. Didn't all your education teach you that?"

"It's a lesson I have trouble learning." He smiled wryly. "I'll leave you in peace now. But you can visit me any time with as many children as you'd like to bring with you."

He took a paper and pen from his pocket and wrote down his London address. Setting it down beside her, he rose to leave.

"Tom?" Her voice was uncannily like that of the sister he remembered, now that he wasn't looking at her.

He sat down again. Her hand was resting outstretched on the arm of her chair, and she ducked her head to hide the tear that was running down her cheek.

"I thought you were dead," she whispered.

Tom took her hand and held it tightly. "I'm so sorry I let you down," he said hoarsely.

They remained that way for a few minutes more before she pulled her hand away and said gruffly, "Go now."

He went, his vision blurred by tears.

Tom returned to his sister's cottage once more before leaving Yorkshire. He didn't meet Kate's husband: she and his mother were united in their belief that it was best for Fred not to know Tom existed. It was clear that Tom didn't belong there. They had lived their lives as if he were dead, just as he had lived the past seventeen years as if they were. He intended to stay in contact and visit as often as he could, but it would take time to get to know them again.

On his last morning in Yorkshire, Tom went for a long walk on the moor and through the fields and woods where he had hidden from his father as a child. Some good memories came back to him, of playing games with Kate, even of his whole family traveling to the seaside on a rare holiday when his father was home and sober. But most of his memories were dark ones, filled with fear and desperation. Even after all these years, he could spot a good hiding place for his child-self behind a bush or in a hollow by the roadside.

As he walked past a grove of trees, he heard a chorus of high-pitched chirps and squawks, and he stopped and looked up. Several finches were sitting on a branch picking at something. The feisty little birds were fighting over the meal, chasing each other away and darting back to snatch the food for themselves. They were too far overhead for him to be sure, but they looked like siskins, and he thought of the bird that had eaten out of Miranda's hand the previous winter.

He could identify with the fighting birds more than Miranda's docile one. Wasn't this who he was? Always fighting, always striving to get what he wanted. What made him think he could fix everything? He didn't even have the answers to simple questions about his own life. He couldn't help himself. He couldn't even forgive himself.

Why would his mother—and Miranda—forgive him? How could they care about someone who had acted as he had? Kate's anger and coldness, especially during his first visit, made more sense to him. But there was a precedent for such lavish forgiveness. God had done the same. No act was so bad that God couldn't forgive it, if the person repented. And what was repentance but sincere sorrow for one's bad deeds and a decision to stop engaging in them?

He felt that sorrow and made that decision now with a silent prayer, bowing his head and leaning his hand against the trunk of the tree while the birds continued to fight in the branch overhead. Being in Yorkshire had clarified his passions. The trappings of the church didn't matter to him. The ritual and the building didn't matter. But the beliefs at the core of Christianity mattered, especially the message of love and forgiveness. His two major passions were still strong: to do some good for people in need, with God's help, and to love Miranda, if she would let him.

23

... that face ... which did not therefore change,

But kept the mystic level of all forms,

Hates, fears, and admirations, was by turns

Ghost, fiend, and angel, fairy, witch, and sprite ...

—Elizabeth Barrett Browning, *Aurora Leigh*

AUGUST 1908

There!" Julia exclaimed. "I told you that dress would be perfect on you, and it is. Turn around and let me see the back."

Miranda obeyed, feeling both pleased and ill at ease. She was in Julia's dressing room, wearing one of Julia's old dresses, a pale blue watered silk gown trimmed with white Valenciennes lace. It was simple and unadorned by Julia's standards, but the rich fabric was so different from what Miranda usually wore that she felt like a little girl at play, dressing up in her mother's clothing.

"It needs some alterations," Lily, Julia's maid, put in, "but you do look pretty in it, Miss Thorne."

"Thank you," Miranda said. She looked at her reflection in the mirror. The woman in the mirror had an uncertain, half-hopeful look on her face.

The pale blue of the dress matched her eyes, and the fitted bodice revealed curves that were hidden by her usual clothing.

"You're not allowed more time to think about it," said Julia imperiously. "There's nothing you can possibly object to about this dress, unlike the others: the décolletage isn't too low, there isn't a bow or flounce anywhere, and the color isn't too bright. Am I right?"

Miranda smiled. "You're right. Have I really been so difficult?"

"Yes, very." Julia smiled back. "Now that we've got you in this dress, I hope you'll let me experiment with others. And Lily has an idea for your hair, too. She's wanted to get her hands on it from the day you arrived."

Lily's hopeful expression corroborated Julia's words.

"Very well," said Miranda.

Lily helped Miranda remove the dress and was sent away to oversee the alterations.

As Miranda changed back into the black skirt and white blouse she'd been wearing before trying on the dress, she noticed Julia watching her with an assessing, thoughtful look.

"Will you ever tell me why you wear such drab clothing?" Julia asked.

"There's nothing to tell."

"I don't believe you."

"I don't dress that way anymore, do I?"

"Not as often, but that, I think, is due to my influence."

"True." It was easier to agree with Julia on this point than to argue, which would only pique her curiosity further. Ever since Miranda had been living with the Carringtons, she was still dressing simply, but she'd stopped wearing the stark, shapeless, black and gray dresses.

"Let's talk about the guest list for the party," Julia said, standing and taking Miranda's hand with a dramatic flourish. "First, promise me you won't be angry."

Although Miranda had grown accustomed to Julia's dramatic behavior, she was confused about whether she was not to be angry about their previous conversation or about something new. "I can't promise until I know what you're talking about."

"I've invited a few more people to the party."

"How many more?" asked Miranda, alarmed. She was still in the process of preparing herself to meet ten new people, and she wasn't ready for more.

"Three."

"Well, it's your house, so you have a right to invite as many people as you choose."

"But I agreed to abide by your wishes regarding the number of guests."

"I suppose a few more won't kill me. Who are they?"

"Francis Wilkinson and his wife—you've heard of him, I expect? He writes for the *Spectator*."

"He's an art critic," said Miranda, instantly anxious.

"Exactly. Don't look like that. You've got to allow people to see your paintings who can say something intelligent about them and promote them to a wider audience. You can still be E.A. and stay in the shadows if you like, just as you did with the Royal Academy. And Francis Wilkinson is a dear old thing, not frightening in the least."

"I suppose it will be all right. And the third guest?"

"Just Tom Cross," said Julia breezily.

Miranda felt a strange little shiver in the region of her heart. Meeting Julia's eyes, she asked quietly, "Has he returned to London?"

"No, he's still in Yorkshire. Charles wanted me to invite him, to show him he hasn't been banished from the kingdom, so to speak, and that he still has friends here. He might not come. In fact, I think it unlikely. You have no objection to the invitation, do you? You haven't said a word about him in weeks."

"I have no objection," Miranda said, removing her hand from Julia's grasp and smoothing her hair.

It was a lie. Miranda believed it was best not to see Tom again. In the days following Ann's shocking accusations, Miranda had done her best to distance herself from him, both physically and emotionally. When she'd had more time to think, she doubted the truth of Ann's story, but she also wondered at Tom's silence. If the things people were saying about him were lies, didn't his silence condemn him further? Didn't he at least wish to explain himself to her? Didn't he owe her that, considering how close the two of them had become? And when no letters came from Yorkshire, she was hurt. But now she realized he had done her a favor. Even if he returned her feelings, which now seemed unlikely indeed, she could offer him nothing. It had been a mistake to tell him she loved him, and she wanted to leave that error in the past where it belonged. She would reserve all her love for Sam, as she always had.

"Surely you don't believe Ann Goode's scurrilous story about Tom being Jack's natural father," Julia said, studying Miranda's face.

Miranda didn't reply. Ann's story had appeared only in disreputable newspapers, as far as she knew. Simon had told her not to read it, so she hadn't, but Ann had said quite enough when she was at the Thornes' house to imagine what the written version would look like.

"Ann made quite a scene at our London house before she left with Jack," Julia added.

Miranda had been dismayed to hear that Jack's sister had come to take him to Scotland, where she had apparently found employment. "So you met her, then?" she ventured.

"Not personally. I just heard a harrowing story from my housekeeper about her barging into the kitchen and terrifying the staff with her demands."

"I wish I knew exactly where she took Jack. I hope she's treating him well."

"From my housekeeper's account, he was happy to go with her. But you haven't answered my question. Do you believe Ann's story?"

"I don't know," Miranda said slowly. She didn't really, but the inappropriate relationship Tom had mentioned was still in her mind, and it troubled her. "Do you?"

"Not for a second," Julia said dismissively. "Tom wouldn't lower himself to so much as flirt with a girl of her class, despite his own humble origins. And she would have been a child at the time. Ugh. Think about it, Miranda. He can have any woman he wants. Do you really think a common girl like that, pretty or no, would attract his notice, much less lead him to risk his reputation?"

Something about Julia's tone, or perhaps the look in her eyes, caught and held Miranda's attention. In their private conversations, she'd noticed a gradual shift in the way Julia referred to Tom, from "Canon Cross" to "Tom Cross" to "Tom," but it wasn't just her use of his Christian name that made Miranda think she knew more than she was letting on.

He can have any woman he wants. The words hung in the air. Did he want Julia? Miranda hadn't the courage to ask.

Julia continued to talk about the party, but Miranda merely went through the motions of listening, her mind spinning with her new realization.

How could she have been so blind? Tom was the lover Julia had mentioned when she told Miranda about her past. And the inappropriate relationship Tom had alluded to during his confession to Miranda was with Julia, not Ann. Every Lancelot needed a Guinevere.

Miranda couldn't condemn Tom or Julia for what they'd done when she'd been in an adulterous relationship herself with Richard. But what an utter fool she'd been to believe Tom could love her when he'd been the lover of the most beautiful noblewoman in England. It was humiliating to remember that Miranda had been the one to push herself on him—the kiss, then her declaration of love—and he had responded with gentlemanly restraint in the first instance and a confession that wasn't even about her in the second.

Before Julia could notice that Miranda wasn't really listening, they were interrupted by a light knock on the dressing-room door and Charles's voice asking, "Is everyone decent in there?"

"Yes, come in," Julia answered.

Miranda remembered the annoyance that used to cross Julia's face whenever her husband appeared unexpectedly, and she was glad to see a neutral expression instead. Perhaps someday Julia would even look pleased to hear his voice or see him, but that might be too much to hope for. Especially if she was still in love with Tom.

Charles opened the door and smiled at both women, his gaze lingering on his beautiful wife. "I've come with exciting news," he said. "Miranda's gallery is ready for viewing."

"Let's have a look, then," said Julia.

The Carringtons had set aside a large room for Miranda's paintings, despite her protests, and Charles had overseen its transformation. As the threesome made their way downstairs towards the gallery, Charles said to Miranda, "I hope you won't regret giving me free rein. We can always change the way the paintings are arranged or the color of the walls, or anything you don't like."

"I doubt very much that I'll regret it. You have excellent taste."

Charles said nothing to this, but he looked pleased. Miranda liked Charles Carrington very much. He was kind to her, as well as surprisingly humble, considering his rank and wealth. She didn't know any other members of the nobility, but he certainly hadn't fit her preconceptions. Although he was nondescript in appearance, he had a deep, sonorous voice to which she never tired of listening.

Charles opened the gallery door with a flourish, beckoning Miranda to walk in first. She went in and moved along in a trancelike state, obeying unspoken instructions to stop and look, then to keep moving, in an expectant silence that suggested something magical. The last painting, and the largest, was the one of Julia, and it was set off to advantage by its placement at eye level and the soft lighting.

The woman in the painting looked obliquely out from her frame, not directly at the viewer but off in the distance, chin raised, as if seeing into the future. She was wearing a blue robe, draped modestly except for one bare shoulder. She held a book in one hand and rested her other on the head of a golden-haired child who leaned against her. She was everything Miranda and Julia had hoped she would be: Madonna, siren, angel, Eve, Lilith, goddess.

Overwhelmed, Miranda couldn't speak. She looked at Charles with tears in her eyes, and he patted her shoulder, beaming.

At dinner that evening, Miranda asked Charles what he thought about the prospects for grouse season. He loved to talk about the latest controversies over different methods of shooting grouse. Charles went on at length about the driven method, which he preferred to walking up, then moved on to the unsportsmanlike practices of netting and traffic in live grouse. Julia had no interest in shooting, and so paid little attention. Miranda herself was not particularly interested in the topic, but pretending to show interest wasn't difficult, and it made Charles happy. It had surprised Miranda at first that Julia didn't see this.

But Julia was centered on her own concerns and would not brook being ignored for very long. At what Miranda felt was the right time, she subtly shifted the conversation from grouse to the party. The guests would be arriving in a fortnight, and Julia had decided to exert herself by behaving like the perfect hostess. Miranda wanted Charles to know how much time and thought Julia had put into the planning and that he could choose to see it as a credit to him.

"Have you told Lord Carrington what you've planned for dinner the last night of the party?" Miranda prompted Julia.

"No. We're having ten courses—I can't remember them all myself. I can show you the menu, if you like."

"I'd be happy to see it," Charles said.

Julia had the menu close at hand in the drawer of a side table. When she presented it to Charles, he looked at it, then at Julia, in surprised pleasure.

"These are all of my favorite foods," he said. "I had no idea you remembered."

Julia glanced at Miranda, who was careful to look only at her plate. It hadn't taken much investigation to find out his favorites—only a talk with the cook, who had known Charles since he was a child and knew exactly what he liked best to eat. Again, it was such a simple way of adding to Charles's happiness that Miranda couldn't understand why Julia hadn't thought of it herself.

"Thank you, my dear." Charles smiled at Julia, but he looked at her too long, and she looked away.

After dinner, Miranda retired to her rooms. She had a bedroom and an adjoining sitting room, both of which were large and luxurious. The sitting room had a large bow window with cushions where Miranda would often sit with her sketchbook. There was enough space to set up an easel as well, and though another room had been set aside for her as a studio, she occasionally worked on her paintings in her sitting room. The bedroom was decorated in shades of plum with mahogany furniture and a huge, high bed that made her feel like the princess in "The Princess and the Pea" every time she climbed into it.

Miranda sat down at the dressing table in the bedroom, unpinned her hair, and brushed it until it shone. Julia had wanted to give Miranda her own maid, too, but a line had to be drawn somewhere. Besides, having her own maid would have interfered with her privacy. Although she didn't need to guard her privacy jealously now that she was no longer living with Simon and Gwen, the impulse to do so was still there.

After Ann Goode had burst into the Thornes' drawing room that fateful night, Simon had become suspicious of Miranda's relationship with Tom. When he found out about Tom's early-morning visits to the studio, he reverted to his overbearing-older-brother role. Gwen had surprised Miranda by taking her side, but the tension between brother and sister hadn't abated. Thus, Julia's invitation to stay with the Carringtons at Rudleigh had come at the perfect time.

Miranda put a hand to the back of her neck and drew her hair forward, watching it fan over her shoulder, silky and straight. She wondered if Tom would accept Julia's invitation, and if so, what it would be like to see him after two months apart. It seemed longer because her life had changed so dramatically. She wondered, too, what he felt for Julia now. Miranda remembered Julia speaking of her lover in the past tense: "He made me happy for a while, but the effects wore off." But even if he no longer made her happy, perhaps they were still lovers. Or in love.

A knock at Miranda's sitting-room door startled her because of the lateness of the hour. It was Julia.

"Come in," Miranda said. "Is something the matter?"

"No, I just want some company." Julia walked in and tucked herself into an overstuffed armchair. She appeared to have been preparing for bed, since she was wearing a wrapper over her nightdress and her auburn hair fell in loose waves over her shoulders. She looked younger than her three-and-thirty years, even younger than Miranda. Although Miranda was only eight-and-twenty, both Julia and Charles sometimes treated her as their elder, which amused her. But tonight all she could think about was how irresistible Julia must have been to Tom.

"Are you happy here?" Julia asked.

"Yes, of course. Don't I seem so?"

"I can't tell."

"I would be ungrateful indeed if I were discontented after everything you and Lord Carrington have done for me."

Julia waved her hand wearily as if to physically brush Miranda's words away. "That's not what I mean. We've made no sacrifices for you and don't expect gratitude."

"You've taken me into your home and treated me like a sister."

"I was on the verge of leaving Charles before you came. Your presence has made it possible for me to live with him. I think we're the ones who ought to be grateful."

Miranda didn't know what to say.

"I asked you if you were happy because I was hoping you'd tell me why you're not speaking to your brother," Julia went on. "You were very anxious to leave home, and he hasn't come here to see you, nor have you gone to London since you've been here."

"We had an argument."

"What about?"

Miranda couldn't tell Julia about Tom. Not now. After a brief pause, she said, "Simon believed I was behaving improperly. That I didn't care enough about my reputation. I'd rather not say more about it."

"Very well. But it seems odd to me that he would think such a thing. You seem overscrupulous about your reputation. I don't understand why you try so hard to fade into the background and why you wear those ghastly black dresses. It's as if you're forcing yourself to do some sort of penance, and it troubles me. I can't believe you've done anything so terrible that it would require you to deny yourself any joy in life."

Miranda had told very few people about Richard. She'd held out the childish hope that if she didn't speak his name, he'd disappear. But of course it had done just the opposite: his presence had loomed over her for many years, restraining her freedom. She sensed that Julia would be a sympathetic listener, and perhaps telling the story would loosen Richard's hold on her.

"When I was very young," she began slowly, "I was seduced by a man named Richard."

24

Even a man who has practised himself in love-making till
his own glibness has rendered him sceptical, may at last be
overtaken by the lover's awe—may tremble, stammer, and
show other signs of recovered sensibility no more in the range
of his acquired talents than pins and needles after numbness.

—George Eliot, *Daniel Deronda*

It had been an interminably long afternoon in the yellow drawing room
at Rudleigh. Tom stood at the French windows, staring out at the garden
and allowing himself to commit the social sin of ignoring the ladies for
a few minutes. For the hundredth time he wished he hadn't accepted the
Carringtons' invitation, or at least that he had invented some excuse to leave
early. Instead, he had agreed to stay out the week. Any gentleman who
didn't hunt or shoot and who had a measure of wit was pressed into service
amusing bored society ladies while their husbands were out shooting. Tom
had fulfilled this social role before at the Carringtons' parties.

Some of the ladies were writing letters on tiny ornamental tables, a feat
that discouraged all but the most determined. Others engaged in desultory

conversation. Tom had exerted himself at first, asking about their children, the theater performances they had seen, the latest gossip about Tyne and Bow. But having lately been the subject of gossip himself, he was less inclined to speculate about others now that he knew with excruciating clarity how such speculation about oneself felt.

It was also difficult to be witty and entertaining when he was frustrated by two things. First, Julia had mentioned when he first arrived that Ann had taken Jack away, apparently to Scotland. Ann had left no forwarding address, and while Tom had no desire to see her, he was dismayed that Jack had seemingly vanished without a trace and anxious about the boy's welfare.

Second, it seemed impossible to find opportunities to talk alone with Miranda. Although he had been at Rudleigh for three days, he had seen very little of her. She had greeted him pleasantly enough when he arrived, but she seemed to be playing the role of the mysterious artist to the hilt: she often slipped away when the others were engaged in conversation, and she retired early after dinner. When she was present, she said little. She had always been quiet in social situations, but Tom couldn't help thinking she was avoiding him.

Julia's clear voice cut into his reverie. "Canon Cross, you haven't said a word about your trip to Yorkshire, though your voice betrays the fact that you were there. Did you find your mother and sister?"

Tom turned from the window to face his hostess, who was sitting on a nearby sofa. Miranda was at her side with a sketchbook, adding shading to a drawing of one of the Carringtons' daughters, but she didn't look up.

"My voice? What do you mean?" he asked.

Julia picked up a book from a side table and held it out, saying in a playfully theatrical tone, "You mun take the bee-yook." Appealing to the others, she added, "You hear it, don't you?"

Miranda was still looking at her sketchbook, but the other women nodded.

"I hardly think my accent is that pronounced," said Tom, trying to hide his irritation. "In any case, I'll lose it quickly enough now that I'm back in the home counties. And yes, I did find my mother and sister."

Now Miranda did glance up at Tom. She was wearing a pale pink blouse with a froth of lace at the neck and wrists. Although her clothing was nothing like the brightly colored, beribboned concoctions on the other women, it was very different from the drab clothing she used to wear. Next to Julia, who was wearing a green dress that made her eyes glow like emeralds, Miranda should have faded into the background. But Tom's perception had altered so dramatically, surprising even himself, that Julia might have been a wilted hothouse rose and Miranda a rare, perfect lily.

"Surely that isn't all you're going to say," Julia said with raised eyebrows.

"He wishes to create suspense," Lady Altwick said from the other side of the room. She had the manner of an ancient dowager but was only in her thirties.

Far from wishing to create suspense, Tom would have preferred not to speak of his trip to Yorkshire at all. Even after a few days at Rudleigh, it was a shock to be in the presence of so much wealth and luxury after being in his sister's dilapidated cottage. But Miranda was looking at him with an interested expression, so he felt encouraged to speak.

He told the story with appropriate modifications for a general audience, dwelling on the wild beauty of the Yorkshire countryside and saying of his mother and sister only that they were poor but healthy and that the reunion had been a success. He regretted the necessity of simplifying what had really happened, but it would be a mistake to say too much to people who couldn't possibly comprehend what he had experienced.

"What an affecting scene it must have been when your mother first saw you!" exclaimed Lady Toynbee, a vapid woman with fluffy blond hair. "It sounds like something out of a Dickens novel."

"Canon Cross's whole life seems like something out of a Dickens novel," put in Lady Altwick.

"I'd say it's closer to the work of Zola or Flaubert," said Julia dryly.

Tom shot her a warning glance.

Miranda was watching him with the penetrating look he knew so well. She knew him far better than did these superficial society women who, behind their polite masks, undoubtedly wanted to know every detail of his life, the more scandalous the better. If he couldn't speak to her alone soon, the frustration would be more than he could bear.

"Have you returned to your regular duties at the cathedral?" asked Julia.

"No." He paused, considering how much he wanted to reveal publicly. "I won't be returning to the cathedral."

A couple of the women gasped. Although Tom didn't want everyone to know about his plans for the future, he had spoken for Miranda's benefit, to see how she would react. He was disappointed to see her head bent over her sketchbook again, as if she hadn't heard him.

He took a deep breath, desperation making him bold, and added, "In fact, I've decided to leave the ministry."

The responses from the others came all at once.

"You can't be serious!"

"Why? The cathedral won't be the same without you."

"What will you do instead?"

But Tom hardly heard anything they said because now Miranda was looking at him directly, searchingly, her beautiful eyes filled with concern. He held her gaze until the silence became obvious and he realized that everyone was waiting for his response.

"I'm still considering my options," he said.

"I hope your decision has nothing to do with those stories that were circulating about you," Lady Altwick said. "I didn't believe a word of it, nor did most people I know."

"It wasn't about those stories," Tom said, "but I thank you for not believing every rumor you hear." He spoke stiffly, hoping nobody would bring up any details about Ann's accusations. "I have other reasons for my decision that are private."

Julia jumped in to change the subject, and Tom wondered if she'd guessed that one of his reasons for leaving the ministry was their affair. Before coming to Rudleigh he had met with Bishop Chisholm to resign his canonry and his license. He'd told the truth about everything, including his relationship with Julia, without mentioning her name. The bishop's disappointment had been difficult to bear, but afterwards Tom had felt a weight lift from his shoulders, despite the confusion he still felt about his vocation.

Now, he was grateful that attention had shifted away from him and uncomfortable that he'd shared so much with people he didn't know. His admission certainly hadn't made it easier to talk to Miranda, who excused herself and disappeared for the rest of the afternoon. He was sorely tempted to ask Julia to seat Miranda next to him at dinner, but he wasn't ready to trust her with the knowledge of his feelings for Miranda.

At dinner Miranda was seated at Charles Carrington's right, and Tom was at the other end of the table, near Julia. He and Miranda might as well have been seated in separate rooms. He was dismayed to see that, not only did Miranda occupy the place of honor next to the host, displacing all the higher-ranked women, but she also seemed to be on friendly, almost intimate, terms with Charles. In fact, Charles and Miranda engaged in several intense little private conversations, almost to the point that Charles was neglecting his duty as the host. Julia didn't seem to notice.

Miranda looked beautiful in a lavender dress. It amazed Tom that he had ever thought her plain and that he had spent so many hours alone with her in the studio without ever having been tempted to kiss her. That one brief kiss they'd shared in the studio months ago didn't count.

"Miss Thorne, when will we have the pleasure of seeing your paintings?"

Lord Altwick asked. He was sitting at the middle of the table and his loud voice interrupted the other conversations. "I hear there is a gallery of your work somewhere in the house."

Everyone turned to look at Miranda. A wave of color came and went in her face, and for a moment she seemed too shy to speak.

"Yes, I, too, have been hearing about this secret gallery," Lady Toynbee put in. "It's all very mysterious."

"It isn't a secret, not really," Miranda said finally. "It's just that I wanted to have some control over who could see the paintings."

"An exclusive gallery!" exclaimed Lady Toynbee. "Now we'll want to see it all the more. I hope we'll be found acceptable?" Her sardonic tone was offensive to Tom, who wanted to rescue Miranda from having to answer.

It was Charles, not Tom, who came to Miranda's aid. "Miss Thorne has her own reasons for keeping some of her paintings out of the public eye," he said. "Julia and I support her decision wholeheartedly."

Julia added, "I'm the one who thought it would be fun to keep the gallery a secret until tomorrow evening. You'll all have a tour of it then."

Mr. Wilkinson, the art critic, expressed his delighted anticipation of this event, and everyone returned to their previous conversations.

After dinner, as the men and women rose to go their separate ways—the men to the smoking room and the women to the drawing room—Tom saw his chance and intercepted Miranda.

"I must speak with you alone," he said in a low voice.

She didn't respond except to glance at him quickly, almost nervously.

When she didn't answer, he added, "Please."

"I'll meet you in the conservatory in an hour," she said in a half whisper.

"Thank you. I'll be there."

He went to the conservatory fifteen minutes before the appointed time. The room was dark except for the light that filtered in from the lamp at the entrance and the moonlight streaming in from the windows. It would be easy to find a private place to talk among the greenery. Tom chose the most secluded spot on a bench far from the entrance, but then he worried that Miranda would think he had ungentlemanly designs on her. He moved to a less private bench closer to the entrance where they would still be shielded from the view of potential onlookers by a tall exotic plant.

She was late. Tom began to pace around the circumference of the conservatory, holding his pocket watch up to the light every few minutes. Finally, twenty minutes after the time they had agreed upon, Miranda arrived, hesitating on the threshold.

"Miranda!" he exclaimed with relief, coming forward. "Come, sit with me."

Two months ago he would have taken her hand. Now he didn't dare touch her.

"I'm sorry I'm late," she said as they sat side by side on the bench. "I had difficulty extricating myself from a conversation with Lady Altwick."

"I thought you might have changed your mind," he said quietly.

"Why would I do that?" She spoke just as quietly, but with a note of defensiveness in her voice. She didn't look at him.

He wished for more light in the room so he could see her face better. Strangely, now that he had the much-coveted opportunity to speak with her alone, he couldn't think how to begin. Tom couldn't remember ever having been at a loss for words with a woman. He felt as awkward and tongue-tied as an adolescent. The unexpectedness of the feeling added to its inhibiting effect, and he sat in helpless silence.

"What do you wish to talk about?" Miranda asked finally.

"It's seems a long time since we've talked," he began. "I've missed that. I've missed . . . you."

She said nothing.

"How have you been?" he asked lamely.

"I've been well, thank you."

There was another awkward silence. Part of the problem was that he had too much to say, and all the words were vying for precedence. Another part of the problem was that Miranda knew him too well. With any other woman, he could act the part of the perfect lover and make her feel as if she were the only woman who mattered to him. The irony was that he could have done this in perfect sincerity with Miranda, but she'd have no reason to believe him.

He was worried that Miranda believed the stories circulating about him. Or that Julia had told Miranda about her relationship with Tom. Either of these possibilities could have killed any feelings she had for him.

"Miranda," he began again, "I'm sorry you had to hear the false accusations Ann Goode made about me. Did you believe her?"

"At first I wasn't certain, but . . . no. I don't believe her now."

"Have the Carringtons said anything to turn you against me?"

"Not at all." She looked down at her hands, which were clasped together in her lap. "Lord Carrington in particular has been very vocal in your defense. He says you couldn't possibly have done . . . all the things you've been accused of."

"Then why are you so cool and distant with me? Were you offended by what I wrote in my letter?"

"What letter?"

"I sent you a letter about a week after I arrived in Yorkshire. Didn't you receive it?"

She looked up at him in confusion. "No."

"Simon asked me to stay away from you. Did you know that?"

"No, but I'm not surprised. That must be why he didn't send the letter."

"One of the things I asked you in the letter was if you agreed with him. If you thought it would be better if I stayed away. Did you?"

Slowly she said, "At that time, I didn't."

Tom didn't want to ask if she had changed her mind in the interim. It seemed clear enough that she had. But if she hadn't received his letter, there was much she didn't know.

"You mustn't think Simon is your enemy," she said. "He was trying to protect me, as he always does, but he's been as much your advocate as Lord Carrington has. He spent the whole day after Ann came to our house going to newsagent's shops, buying every copy he could find of that horrible newspaper so that others wouldn't see the story."

Tom was pleasantly surprised by this evidence of Simon's loyalty, but at the moment all he could think about was Miranda. "The letter I wrote you doesn't matter now. I ought to have told you this a long time ago, but I was an idiot. I didn't recognize what should have been obvious for months. At the very least, I ought to have said it that night in the studio, but I was exhausted and confused, and . . . I'm sorry—I'm making excuses. I want you to know . . . you said something I didn't reply to, and I should have. I didn't realize . . . I hardly knew . . . Confound it! I seem to have lost my ability to speak."

"You had better not say it. Indeed, I wish you wouldn't." She sounded as agitated as he felt. "I regret what I said that night, and you may regret this also."

Her words knocked the breath out of his lungs as if he had been hit full-on by one of Nate Cowan's fighters. They sat in silence for a few minutes, then he slowly rose to his feet.

"I'm sorry to have annoyed you and taken up your time," he said in a voice that didn't sound like his own. He turned and walked stiffly towards the doorway.

As he reached the threshold, there was a quick movement beside him, and Miranda stood there in the light, looking up at him with anguished eyes.

"I can't let you go with the wrong impression," she said.

He waited, hardly daring to hope.

"Tom, I meant everything I said that night. But I regretted saying what I felt for you for many reasons: it wasn't the right time; I hadn't time to think. And now I regret it because . . . things are different. I'm different. I think you can see that."

"I do see it," he said slowly, "but does it mean your feelings for me have changed?"

"I have other ties and other concerns that you don't know about."

"Are you referring to the Carringtons? You seem to have become very close to them, but I hope you don't trust them too much. I fear Julia is manipulating you."

"You needn't fear that," she said firmly. "They've been kind to me. They . . . understand what I need. They don't curtail my freedom."

"Do you think I wish to do that?"

"No, but you'd do it all the same. It isn't your fault. It's simply what would happen. You're not the sort of man who could be content with anything less than a woman's whole mind, body, and soul. You would . . . consume me."

"I'm consumed by you, Miranda, not the other way 'round. I love you." Unable to stop himself, he caught her hands and kissed them, first the backs, then the palms, then the fingers. Her hands were small and well shaped. They smelled faintly of turpentine, and there was a callus on one finger where she held her paintbrush. They were perfect.

She remained still as he kissed her hands, but she looked up at him wonderingly, as if she couldn't believe what was happening.

In a low voice, he said, "I can't stop thinking about that day in the studio when your lips touched mine, and I've been longing to kiss you again. A real kiss. May I?"

"No," she whispered.

"Why not?"

"I am . . . astonished to hear this from you," she stammered. "I need time to think."

Reluctantly he let go of her hands and stepped back. "Of course. I'm sorry if my . . . ardor has frightened you. You needn't fear that I have dishonorable intentions. I won't ask anything of you now. It would be wrong to ask you to share my life when I don't even know where I'll be living or working, and when my reputation is still low in the eyes of the public. But when I return to work and when I prove my faithfulness to your satisfaction, I want to marry you."

His words didn't have the effect he had hoped for.

"It's late," she said. "I have to go." She turned, picked up her skirts, and rushed away.

25

I'm not resign'd, not patient, not school'd in
To take my starveling's portion and pretend
I'm grateful for it. I want all, all, all;
I've appetite for all. I want the best:
Love, beauty, sunlight, nameless joy of life.
There's too much patience in the world, I think.
We have grown base with crooking of the knee.
                              —Amy Levy, "A Minor Poet"

T ell me everything." Julia threw her arms wide in her usual dramatic way before settling back in her chair, an expectant look on her face.

"There isn't much to tell," said Miranda.

"Nonsense. You can play coy with me all you like, but I know you agreed to meet Tom alone in the conservatory last night. Something must have happened."

They were in Miranda's sitting room. It was afternoon, and Miranda had taken the first opportunity she could to get away from everyone else to be alone and think. She hadn't had more than a few minutes to do so before Julia burst into her sitting room as if she were a tardy audience member at a theater. It seemed wrong, with Julia's flair for the dramatic, for her to be the audience member and Miranda the performer.

"Since you are not forthcoming," Julia said, "I will get to the question I want answered most: What was your response when Tom proclaimed his love to you?"

Miranda was startled into meeting Julia's eyes. "What makes you think he did such a thing?"

"I have eyes in my head. Why would he be staring at you the way everyone else was staring at the chocolate cream we had for dessert if he didn't intend to declare his feelings?"

"I didn't expect any of this," Miranda said. "I thought he considered me only a friend. I thought he came here only to see you."

Julia frowned. "Why would you think that?"

Miranda hesitated, weighing her words carefully. "I have the feeling that you and Tom know each other rather better than either of you have let on."

Julia's eyes widened. "How long have you known?"

"I didn't know for certain. I only guessed it from things you've said."

After a brief silence, Julia said, "My relationship with Tom is long over."

Miranda wanted to ask if Julia still had feelings for him, but she hadn't the courage, and Julia's face yielded no clue.

"Whatever Tom felt for me in the past," Julia said briskly, "I think we can safely rule out the possibility that he came here to see me, as well as confidently assume that he thinks of you as far more than a friend. Did you let him kiss you?"

"No." Miranda felt her face grow hot and was annoyed with herself. She was hardly a green girl who couldn't think about kissing without blushing.

"Poor Miranda. He unleashed the full power of his charm on you, didn't he? You don't have a chance."

"I won't see him again. I can take meals in my room and stay here until he leaves."

"That's ridiculous. You shouldn't have to hide from him."

"Then will you ask him to leave?"

Julia looked surprised. "I can't. Such a request coming from me would look suspicious to Charles. He knows nothing of our affair."

"What if I asked Charles to send Tom away for my sake? That wouldn't throw suspicion on you."

"Is that truly what you want?"

Miranda could neither answer this question nor meet Julia's eyes, so she rose and walked to the window, taking a deep breath.

"Tom and I were bad for each other," Julia said. "Even if I wasn't married, it would never have worked. We're both . . . oh, I don't know, like jagged rocks that crash into each other and break. Nobody can enrage me as quickly as Tom can, and I think he'd say the same of me. You're different. You're softer on the outside, even though you're strong in your own way."

Julia followed Miranda to the window and stood in front of her, looking earnestly into her eyes. "Believe me, Tom is nothing to me now. My only concern is that he may hurt you."

Miranda felt a rush of anger. "He shouldn't have come here. It was very wrong of him—unfair to you, and insulting to Charles."

"He obviously wanted to see you badly enough that he was willing to endure the discomfort of coming here. Do you love him?"

Miranda closed her eyes. "I thought I did, but now . . . I don't know. It doesn't matter."

"How can you say that?"

"I don't love anyone more than I love Sam. He is first with me, and I can't allow anyone to interfere with my devotion to him. When I gave birth to him I vowed I would never marry, and I intend to keep that vow."

"My dear friend, you can love your child with all your heart and love a man, too. You needn't choose between them."

"I know that's true for most women, but my situation is different. I can't have both."

"Have you told Tom about Sam?"

Miranda shook her head. "He wouldn't understand. Besides, I won't insult or hurt you by accepting Tom's attentions after what happened between the two of you."

To Miranda's surprise, Julia's eyes filled with tears. "You would refuse him on my account?"

"I'll be guided by you in this matter," Miranda replied.

Julia dashed at her eyes and smiled. "You're worth ten of me. And you're far too good for Tom."

Miranda merely shook her head, but her own emotions were so close to the surface that she hardly knew whether she meant to deny Julia's first or her last statement, or both.

Julia went to the door of Miranda's bedroom and looked in. There were two dresses laid out on the bed—one was the pale blue dress of Julia's that had been altered to fit Miranda. The other was one of Miranda's old black dresses.

Looking back over her shoulder, Julia asked, "Why is the black dress here?"

"I'm thinking of wearing it tonight."

"Absolutely not." Julia went into the bedroom and emerged with the black dress crumpled into an unwieldy mass in her arms. "You may be sorry you promised to be guided by me, because I'm going to take you at your word. Tonight is the last night of the party and I utterly forbid you to wear this monstrosity. I'm not going to ask why you even considered it. I don't want to know."

"But—"

"Just a moment." Julia opened the door that led from the sitting room into the hallway, dumped the dress unceremoniously onto the floor outside, and closed the door again. Returning to Miranda, Julia said, "I have three requests: you'll wear the blue dress to dinner this evening. You'll let Lily arrange your hair. And finally—most important—you'll enjoy the evening. You will do exactly as you please and you won't worry about what Charles or Tom or anyone else thinks of you. Do I have your word?"

Miranda smiled. "You have my word."

"I know you have a backbone. You're stubborn in your own way, and you have plenty of strong opinions, even if you don't express them very often. But your stubbornness sometimes takes the curious form of forcing yourself to deny your feelings or to submit to painful situations when there is no apparent reason for you to do so. Tonight I insist that you act on your feelings, no matter the consequences."

"You would turn me into a hedonist."

Julia laughed. "It would take more than my efforts to effect such a transformation. I would merely like to see you behaving like a normal woman instead of an ascetic."

After Julia left the room and Miranda was finally alone, she sank onto the sofa and closed her eyes. Julia didn't know everything. Miranda was indeed adept at self-denial, but it was based on fear, not discipline. In her mind she could allow herself all manner of fantasies, but she was unprepared for them to be offered to her in reality.

She could live without the plenitude that had been showered upon her, without the Carringtons' wealth and luxury, without being recognized as an artist, without Tom's love. The trouble was she wanted all of these things, and the wanting was frightening. Since she had lost Sam, she hadn't allowed herself to want anything, never to this extent. For several months, Miranda had felt as if she were holding her breath, living indefinitely in a strange, hushed state, an expectant silence just before a storm. It would take so little to bring on the storm, and yet it didn't happen. Good things kept happening instead.

And now Tom had told her he loved her. It was a shock after his long silence to find that, instead of being alarmed by her declaration of love for him, he returned her feelings. Just seeing him for the first time in the Carringtons' drawing room had been overwhelming. He was not hardened or constrained by the scandals as she thought he might be, but humbler, more thoughtful. And more handsome than ever. He'd always filled a room with his presence, but in casual tweeds instead of his clerical clothing, his voice tinged with broad Yorkshire vowels, he exuded a powerful virility. And when they were in the conservatory and he kissed her hands, it had taken all of her strength, fortified by surprise, to resist him.

Why not take Julia's advice and simply enjoy the evening? Surely the sky wouldn't fall in.

"Ah, Cross. I've been looking for you."

Charles Carrington's voice startled Tom, who had been walking in the Carringtons' extensive gardens with his head down, deep in thought. He hadn't seen the other man approach him, but there he stood, less than ten feet away.

"Have you?" said Tom, instantly on his guard. He still had no idea what to make of Charles.

"Yes. Are you on your way back to the house? I'll come with you." Charles fell into step with Tom.

The sun had set, though some light still lingered on the horizon. The Carringtons' gardens were bordered by decorative lamps that lit the pathways, but Tom had walked beyond them and was unsure of his footing.

"I was thinking," Tom said, "if Jack left before receiving his final wages, Ann Goode might write to your butler to ask for them. Will you let me know if you hear from her?" Realizing that his interest could be misconstrued, Tom added, "I just want to be assured of Jack's well-being."

"Yes, of course. I'll talk to Grogan. If we hear anything about Jack, we'll inform you."

"Thank you." Tom waited, but Charles said no more, which made him uneasy. "I also want to thank you for inviting me here," Tom continued, glad he was walking beside Charles and not facing him. "Not many people would welcome me into their homes after the stories that have been circulating about me."

"You're welcome, but I ought to confess that my motives were selfish."

"What do you mean?"

"I wanted to see how Julia would behave in your presence. It was the easiest way."

Tom stopped walking and stared at Charles.

They'd reached the perimeter of the gardens, and the lamplight cast an eerie glow on Charles's face as he turned to face Tom. But his expression was as pleasant and bland as if he had been discussing the weather. "I don't believe everything I hear, Cross, but I'm not stupid. As soon as I realized there may be some truth in the rumors about you and my wife, I decided to observe the two of you for myself instead of flying into a jealous rage, which isn't really my style anyway."

Tom was speechless. He didn't know what he would have done in Charles's place, but he was quite certain it wouldn't be this.

"I'm pleased to say," continued Charles in his smooth, well-modulated voice, "I have no concerns on that score. Whatever may have happened between you and Julia in the past, I don't want to know it. But I have studied my wife as if she were an abstruse branch of science, and I can say with some confidence that I now know her. Certainly, no woman can be entirely known or understood, but I've learned to read Julia's face, and I can antici-pate what she wants before she knows it herself—sadly, all too often what she wants isn't me. But she's given me no reason to believe she wants you. Not now, anyway. I've been watching you as well, and you don't seem to be making a secret of your interest in Miranda Thorne."

Tom didn't reply. His mind was spinning.

"Let's keep walking. I'm sure you don't want to miss the exhibition of Miranda's paintings." Charles spoke in such a companionable tone that Tom had a sudden, bizarre fear that the other man would sling his arm across Tom's shoulders as if they were a couple of schoolboys out for a ramble. Fortunately, this fear was not realized.

"Now, about Miranda," Charles went on. "I wouldn't want to lose her. She's become indispensable to our household, like a small, apparently insig-nificant cog in a monstrously large wheel that, if removed, would cause the whole machine to grind to a halt. She has somehow, magically, made my wife appreciate me again, so you can understand why I want to keep her."

"You can't force her to stay," Tom said, angered by the way Charles spoke of Miranda as if she were a useful pet.

"Do I seem to you the sort of man who uses force to solve my problems?" Now Charles's voice had an edge to it, a subtle but definite sharpness. "That might be the only solution for a Yorkshire blacksmith's son, but it's not mine."

What was the man about? Tom couldn't believe how stupid he had been to underestimate Charles Carrington.

"I don't see Miranda agreeing to be your wife, if that's your object," Charles went on. "Or is your intention merely to seduce her?"

Tom clenched his fists, trembling with the effort of controlling his anger. "If you dare to hurt her, just to spite me—"

"My dear fellow, my life isn't a Shakespearean tragedy, though perhaps yours is. I don't utter threats or plot against people's lives or hurt innocent young women to get revenge on their unworthy suitors. But she is a charming creature, and the truth is we're all a little in love with her here at Rudleigh. She's safe here. I don't think she'd be safe with you. Trouble seems to follow you everywhere."

Something in Charles's tone indicated that he knew more than he was letting on.

"It was you," Tom said. "You hired those men to attack me and leave me for dead in the countryside last year."

Charles raised his eyebrows. "No, I didn't. But I think I know who did."

"Who was it?" Tom asked.

"William Narbridge. He told me he had you followed and that you weren't the paragon of virtue you pretended to be. I chose not to ask what he meant, and he dropped the subject. But he said something to me again just before I left London earlier this summer, something about a 'greedy girl who would say anything for money.' I didn't know about Ann Goode then, but when I found out, the two comments seemed to fit."

Tom remembered the man across the street from the hotel where Tom had stayed with Julia, and the man in the oversized bowler hat outside the Smithsons' house when Tom had first met Ann. There were other times, too, when he'd felt a vague sense of unease as he went about his duties, as if he was being watched. And while Narbridge wasn't Tom's only enemy, he was wealthy enough to hire private investigators and, based on their last conversation, still angry enough about Tom's role in the investigation of his business to gather as much evidence against him as possible. Or even to manufacture it, as in Ann Goode's case.

"Thank you for telling me," Tom said. "But why did you bother?"

Charles shrugged. "I don't like injustice, even when it's perpetuated against someone I dislike. There's nothing more I can do, though. I can't prove anything, and I won't testify against Narbridge in court if it comes to that."

"I understand." Tom hesitated. "Why did you come to see me at the cathedral that time?"

"Wasn't it obvious? I was desperate for help, and I was under the impression you were a respectable, God-fearing clergyman. How you must have despised me then! How pathetic I must have seemed to you."

"No, I—" Tom stopped, feeling dizzy from a combination of anger, mortification, and shock.

"Of course, I understand. You had your position in the church to maintain. You couldn't admit to anything a good clergyman wouldn't do. While I was sobbing like a child you were probably congratulating yourself for playing your part so well."

"No, I was sorry. I *am* sorry."

Charles held up a warning finger. "Remember, I don't want to know if anything actually happened between you and Julia. My God," he said, staring at Tom with contempt, "to think you convinced so many people you were a gentleman when you really belong with the servants."

"I'll get my things and leave at once," Tom said, starting to turn away.

"No, I want you to stay, just for tonight. I want you to see Miranda looking her best and sitting at my right hand at dinner. I want you to see how she hangs on my every word. I want you to see the gallery I created for her paintings and how happy it makes her, and then ask yourself whether she could ever be happy with you."

They had reached the house. Before Tom could speak, Charles said lightly, "You'll excuse me while I find my wife."

Charles walked away, leaving Tom seething with rage. How dare the man speak of Miranda in such a familiar way? Charles had a right to be angry about Tom's affair with Julia, but Tom wasn't convinced that Charles wouldn't try to hurt Miranda somehow now that he knew Tom's feelings for her. It was true that she seemed happy, but Tom didn't believe she would prefer to stay with the Carringtons than be with him. On the other hand, she'd said they gave her a freedom that he couldn't give her. He didn't understand that.

As if he had agreed to obey Charles's instructions, Tom did indeed watch Miranda at dinner as she shared private conversations and smiles with Charles. It was impossible not to watch her—she looked more beautiful than ever before in a pale blue dress that matched her eyes, with her hair swept up into an intricate mass of plaits and curls. Although the gown was hardly daring by the fashionable standards of high society, it was so compared to what she usually wore, showing her delicate curves to advantage. Her usually pale skin was flushed becomingly. Had she become the Carringtons' puppet, or did she know exactly what she was doing?

Instead of going to the smoking room with the other men after dinner, Tom went across the hallway outside onto a balcony that overlooked the back garden. It was a warm evening. The heady scent of roses was in the air and a nightingale was singing. He leaned his arms on the stone balustrade and stared into the twilight.

He was startled by a rustle of silk beside him. It was Miranda.

"What are you doing out here by yourself?" she asked with a smile, gazing up at him. Although the light was fading, he could see her face clearly. Unlike the night before when she had seemed anxious and uncertain, she now looked comfortable, even happy.

"Just thinking."

"May I think with you?"

"Of course."

They stood side by side in silence for a few minutes, both facing the garden.

He felt slow and stupid. His conversation with Charles had numbed his brain, and knowing Miranda was on such intimate terms with both Julia and Charles seemed to open up a great gulf between them.

"Tom, have you ever been frightened by your own happiness?" she asked. There was an undertone of excitement in her voice.

"What do you mean?"

"Have you ever had a moment when you had nearly everything you ever wanted, and you were so happy you could hardly bear it, but at the same time you were frightened to death it would be taken away from you?"

Tom's heart sank. Charles was right. She really was happy here, and Tom's presence was unnecessary at best and an annoyance at worst. "I don't think I've ever felt that," he replied quietly. "Is that . . . how you feel?"

"Oh, yes. I wish I could just enjoy it."

He could hardly breathe, but he forced himself to speak. "Are you truly happy? I mean, are you pleased with your own life, not only pleased that others around you are happy?"

"I'm not selfless. I have what I want right here."

Tom wasn't looking at her, but he felt the glow in her words. The Carringtons really were enough for her. "I'm glad," he choked out, although he was anything but. "I'm sorry if I've intruded or . . . interfered in any way with your life. I didn't understand how much has changed for you."

"You haven't interfered. You surprised me, that's all."

"If you want me to leave Rudleigh at once, you have only to say the word."

"Why would I want you to leave?" She sounded genuinely puzzled, confusing him all the more.

He turned to face her. "Miranda, you're speaking in riddles. Will you please tell me plainly whether I've lost my chance with you? Was I mistaken in thinking you love me?"

She looked up at him with—of all things—amusement. "Didn't you hear me say I have what I want right here? Are you not right here?"

Tom stared at her.

"You were not mistaken," she added softly.

He took her in his arms, lowering his head to hers. Even then he hesitated, and she was the one to press her lips to his as she had in the studio months ago. This time, she didn't pull away.

Intoxicated by the lavender scent of her hair and the softness of her mouth, he kissed her passionately, moving his hand to the small of her back to pull her closer. She returned his kisses with an eagerness that thrilled him. A long, ecstatic, silent interval ensued in which he was aware only of the warmth of her body and the sweetness of her lips against his.

After a while, Miranda drew back and said, "We ought to go inside. Everyone will wonder where we are." But as soon as she had said it, she rested her head on his chest with a little sigh.

He tightened his arms around her. "I'd rather stay here." Yet he was only too aware of being in the Carringtons' house, and not wanting them to find him and Miranda together like this. He didn't know what Charles was capable of; he felt as though he and Miranda were surrounded by wolves.

They remained in a silent embrace for another long moment, then went inside.

Nobody seemed to have noticed Tom and Miranda's absence. They entered the drawing room just as the men were going in, and Lord Altwick immediately engaged Tom in conversation, while Miranda joined Lady Toynbee and Julia at the other end of the room. Tom wondered when the tour of Miranda's gallery would begin. He tried to stay away from her, worried that his face would betray what had passed between them. Tom had never been so overwhelmed by a woman in his life—he felt hungry for as little as a look from her or the brush of her hand against his. Their brief time on the balcony had only sparked his desire for more. And he desired more than her body, unlike what he had felt for women in the past. He craved her opinions, her thoughts, her presence.

When Julia announced that the tour would begin, Tom looked around for Miranda, surprised to see she was no longer in the room. Others obviously had the same reaction, for a few guests asked, "Where's the artist?" and "Won't Miss Thorne conduct the tour?"

"Miss Thorne had to leave momentarily," Julia said. "She'll meet us at the gallery." Although Julia looked unruffled, Tom sensed something was wrong.

He braved the potential displeasure of Charles to fall into step with Julia as everyone made their way to the gallery. "Is Miranda all right?" he asked.

"Yes, of course. She forgot something in her room, that's all." Julia turned away from Tom to speak to Lady Toynbee.

Miranda was waiting for them at the door to the gallery, but she stood in the shadows as she welcomed the guests.

"Thank you for coming to see my paintings," she began. Her voice was very quiet, but Tom was so attuned to her that he heard the slight tremor in it. "Most of all, I'd like to thank Lord Carrington for setting aside this room and designing it so well to show my work. I hope you enjoy the exhibition." She disappeared inside the gallery.

Tom went in with the other guests just in time to see Miranda leaving through the doors at the other end of the room. Instead of following her, he decided to stay and look at the paintings. If she wasn't there when everyone had finished the tour, he would find her.

He had to admit the gallery was beautifully arranged to show Miranda's work at its best. His favorite paintings of hers were there—one of a mother and son, another of a street beggar, and the ones on religious themes: the prodigal son, the poor widow. He paused in front of the mother-and-son painting. He had seen it before, but it struck him now how much emotion was expressed in the mother's eyes as she gazed at the boy, who was half turned away, reaching for a toy soldier.

Tom hadn't expected anything from the portrait of Julia. He didn't particularly want to look at any representation of her—too many people already paid homage to her beauty. But when he saw the painting, he understood why it was Miranda's pièce de résistance: the woman who posed for the portrait didn't matter. It wasn't about Julia. What it was about escaped Tom, but he stared at it along with everyone else, mesmerized by the contradictory expression on the woman's face. How could a portrait of one woman embody so many different, nameless things? It unsettled him. Could any artist paint such a thing without a lifetime's worth of knowledge about human nature? He didn't believe talent alone could account for it. Something about the painting reminded him of the biblical passage, "Be ye therefore wise as serpents and harmless as doves." Who was Miranda Thorne, this woman he loved, and did she have as many sides as the woman in the portrait?

The others exclaimed over the portrait in excited whispers. Francis Wilkinson, the art critic, said, "Miss Thorne has a remarkable eye for color. Not many artists use muted colors in such a powerful way. And the composition is exquisite."

Miranda wasn't there when the tour was over, and the guests asked about her again, some eager to buy her paintings. This time Julia announced that Miss Thorne was unwell and would see everyone in the morning.

Tom intercepted Julia again in the hallway on the way back. "I don't know what all this secrecy is about," he said, "but I need to see Miranda. Will you ask her if she'll meet me?"

"I've just said she's unwell," Julia said impatiently. "Obviously she can't meet you."

"Will you look at me and tell me truthfully, on your honor, that there is nothing really wrong?"

Julia smiled. "On my honor?" She leaned closer to Tom and said quietly, "What do you and I know of that?"

"Julia, I'm serious." He noticed a few people looking at them and tried to speak more calmly. "Tell me the truth."

"The truth? Why, Tom, for someone who has lied to so many people about so many things, it's quite shocking to hear of your interest in the truth." She gazed up at him, clearly enjoying his frustration.

He waited for her to continue, refusing to rise to her bait.

"I've never seen you play the lovestruck suitor before, not to this extent." Lowering her voice, she added, "You might try to hide it to save my injured pride, you know. I'll tell Miranda when I see her to send a note to your room. Will that do?"

He assured her curtly that it would and avoided her for the rest of the evening.

26

Am I proved too weak
To stand alone, yet strong enough to bear
Such leaners on my shoulder?
—Elizabeth Barrett Browning, *Aurora Leigh*

I'm so sorry, my dear."

Someone with Richard Morris's voice was holding Miranda's hand, kneeling in front of her and looking into her face with a solicitous expression, but the sudden dizziness that had come over her prevented her from pulling away or even speaking. All she had been able to do is sit down quickly in the nearest chair. When Lily had entered the drawing room to tell Miranda there was a gentleman in the front parlor asking to see her, she had assumed it was Simon, and she had rushed into the room without asking questions, relieved to have the chance to reconcile with her brother. Never in her worst nightmares had she imagined Richard Morris would find her at Rudleigh.

"I ought to have realized it would be a shock for you to see me," he said. "Shall I call a servant to bring some sal volatile?"

"No." She pulled her hand out of his grasp and sat back in the chair, taking deep breaths, and managed to choke out the words, "Is Sam all right?"

"Oh, yes. Healthy and happy. I truly am sorry for frightening you."

He rose and sat in a chair a few feet away. In the seven years since she had seen him, he hadn't changed except for a bit more gray in his hair and a few more wrinkles around his eyes. He had to be well into his fifties now, but he could easily pass for forty. Richard had always been a distinguished-looking man, not handsome, but with arresting, strong features and an alert look that reminded Miranda of an eagle. His personal magnetism had served him well as a clergyman, especially when he preached.

Miranda thought she had forgiven Richard long ago for the way he had treated her, but some residual feelings—anger? fear?—made it difficult for her to look at him without a twinge of nausea.

"How did you find me?" she asked, wishing the tremor in her voice would disappear. She didn't want him to think she was afraid of him. In fact, she wasn't. She was afraid only of his power over her with respect to Sam.

"A happy chance. I was at a dinner party with an acquaintance of your sister-in-law. She told me you were staying with the Carringtons." He gave her a long look. "You're lovely, even lovelier than you were years ago."

Miranda felt like a wild animal caught in a trap. "Why are you here?"

"Not to make trouble for you, I assure you. Partly I came to apologize for the way I treated you." He looked contrite, but Richard had always been difficult to read. "I meant well, at first—I hope you know that. I only wanted to help you and Simon, to provide a family for you when you needed one so badly. But I allowed myself to think too much about you, to care too much. As a married man, I should never have spent so much time alone with you."

Miranda swallowed and looked away. She remembered how flattered she had been by his attention. Everyone admired him, and instead of considering her beneath his notice, he had praised her, encouraged her, made her feel important. In the beginning, anyway.

"I know I behaved badly towards you when you became pregnant with Sam," he continued. "My actions were cruel, but they were motivated by fear, not hatred. I know it probably doesn't matter what my motivations were at the time. My actions were unforgivable. I was afraid of losing my position in the church and it was easy to transfer my hatred of myself to you. I convinced myself you were to blame, and that's why I was able to act as I did."

She took a deep breath. "You nearly destroyed me."

"I'm so sorry, Miranda. I'm prepared to spend the rest of my life making it up to you."

The twinge of nausea intensified. "What do you mean?"

"My wife died a year ago. It forced me to look at myself and the terrible things I've done. I had blamed her for so many years whenever anything in my life went wrong that it was shocking to realize I was responsible for my own bad behavior and attitudes. I've spent a year searching my soul and apologizing to the people I've misled and hurt." He paused, looking at her intently. "I went back to Smythe and spoke to the congregation of our old church. I told them I was an impostor and that I told lies about you—I confessed my sins publicly to them. I'm here to confess to you also, to ask your forgiveness for casting you off after taking advantage of you."

If he wasn't sincere, he was doing a very good job of appearing so.

"I forgive you," Miranda said, "but you can't expect me to be glad to see you."

"I don't expect it. But I do have something else to say."

A shiver of foreboding went through her.

"Years ago I promised you I'd marry you when Lucy died so you could be my true, legal wife. I'm here to honor that promise. You needn't answer me now—I realize my coming here is too much of a shock to allow you to think clearly. But I still love you, though you'll likely find that difficult to believe. I've changed so much over the years; I could be a good husband to you now."

If he had spoken these words seven years ago, she would have been over-joyed. As ugly as it was to hope for someone's death, especially someone as sweet and good as Lucy Morris, Miranda had hoped for it, imagining her-self as Richard's socially accepted, legal wife until it nearly drove her mad. But that was a long time ago.

The trouble was that part of that fantasy still appealed to her, and he knew it. Not to be Richard's wife, but to be Sam's mother. To see him every day. To be there when he needed her. To watch him grow.

As if he could read her thoughts, he said quietly, "It would be such a relief to see you take your rightful place as Sam's mother. Lucy was good to him, of course, but only a child's true mother can love him as he ought to be loved. How wonderful it would be to see the two of you together. He is very like you, you know: quiet, artistic, intelligent. I live in Birmingham now, and Sam is at a day school there. You could read to him every night, watch him fall asleep—"

"You must go now," Miranda interrupted, suppressed emotion making her voice sharp. She stood up abruptly.

Richard stood also, looking at her gravely. "I'll go. Again, I'm sorry for upsetting you. I'll give you all the time you need to think about my proposal. Will you write to me with your answer when you're ready?"

She nodded, not meeting his eyes.

He pulled a card out of his pocket and handed it to her. "Farewell, then, my dear. Thank you for listening to me. God bless you."

Miranda didn't even consider rejoining the party in the drawing room. She asked the first servant she saw to give Julia a message that she was unwell, then fled to her room.

Tom had spent an hour pacing back and forth outside in the garden, and now he was doing the same in his room. It was past midnight, but there was no hope of sleep. He would be leaving in the morning along with the other guests, and he still hadn't heard a word from Miranda. He had done everything he could think of to communicate with her that wouldn't compromise her reputation. Given the perverse pleasure Julia seemed to have in thwarting him, he didn't press her further, but he'd asked a servant to deliver a note to Miranda. Nothing had come of that. Lady Toynbee had sworn she saw a carriage draw up to the house and a strange man get out of it shortly before Miranda disappeared from the drawing room. Who was he and why would he cause Miranda to suddenly take to her room?

Just when he was considering going to her room, risking being seen and expelled from the house, there was a quiet knock at his door. He flung the door open to find Miranda standing at the threshold with a candle. She was wearing a white silk wrapper over her nightdress, and her hair was twisted into a loose plait from which several strands had escaped. Tom stared at her for a few seconds, then caught her free hand and drew her into the room, afraid she would disappear as suddenly as she had materialized.

He closed the door and took the candle from her, holding it up so he could see her face more clearly. She didn't look ill, but he saw signs of strain and anxiety. Tom set the candle on a side table and took her hands. They were ice cold.

"Are you all right?" he exclaimed.

"Yes, I think so."

"You can have no idea how worried I've been."

"I'm sorry. Something . . . unexpected has occurred, and I had a decision to make. I had to be alone to make it."

"Let's sit down and you can tell me about it," Tom said.

She nodded.

"Come to the window. There's enough moonlight—we don't need the candle."

Tom put out her candle and led her to the window, where there were two armchairs side by side. She sat and waited while he opened the curtains to let in as much light as possible. When he sat down beside her, he regretted the loss of the candlelight. There was a sense of unreality in the atmosphere. Bathed in moonlight, Miranda looked like a ghost, less substantial than ever.

"Do you remember the vicar I told you about who . . . took advantage of me when Simon and I lived in Smythe?" Miranda began.

Tom nodded grimly.

"His name is Richard Morris, and he came here this evening to see me. Apparently his wife died a year ago and he's been looking for me. He came to apologize for the way he treated me. He also asked me to marry him."

Whatever Tom had expected her to say, it was not this. He stared at her in shock for a moment, then said slowly, "Do you mean to tell me you've accepted him?"

She rose hastily and turned towards the window, twisting her hands together. "There are things you don't know about my relationship with Richard. About a year after Simon and I moved into the house with Richard and his family, I became pregnant with his child. I was only nineteen and terrified. When I told Richard, he was angry, as if he had nothing to do with my condition. He threatened to turn me out of his house, but I had nowhere to go.

"Simon blamed me for seducing Richard." She glanced at Tom and added quickly, "You must remember that Simon was as much under Richard's influence as I was. Richard could do no wrong. To my surprise,

Richard's wife Lucy was my savior. She guessed my condition, as I suppose any woman who had children of her own would have, but she didn't guess who the father was.

"Incredibly, Lucy offered to raise my child as her own. Of course, the whole village knew by that time I was a fallen woman, and that fact, taken with Richard's attempts to blacken my character further, ensured that I was shunned. I've wondered many times if Lucy suspected the truth, but as I said, everyone else idolized Richard, and he certainly said and did everything right in public. He spoke of me sorrowfully as a wayward daughter whom he had tried and failed to reclaim. People praised his kindness, his Christian compassion, in allowing my child to be raised in his home." Her voice took on a hard edge that Tom had never heard before. "His other children could have been sullied by the child of a whore."

Tom winced.

Miranda glanced at him again and said, "I must tell you the whole truth now. That's what people thought of me."

"How can you even consider marrying a man who treated you that way?" he demanded. "And how can you expect me to stand back and let you destroy yourself?"

"I would do anything to be with my son," she said. "Besides, Richard says he's changed. Perhaps he'll be kinder to me this time."

"People don't change."

"You don't believe that," she said gently. She returned to the chair beside him and sat down again.

"I've seen so little of Sam," she went on, "and only from a distance—" Her voice broke and she lowered her head.

"Your trip to Birmingham last winter was to see him," Tom said dully.

"Yes." She swallowed hard and went on, "When he was born, I had three months with him before Richard sent me away. He told me that if I ever tried to see Sam again, he'd be sent out of the country. Ever since, I've lived in a blur of longing to be near my child, even just to have a glimpse of him. I've had to fight very hard not to be completely consumed by that longing, to find pleasure in life again. When I met you, I didn't think there was room in my heart to love anyone but Sam. I could see that you didn't return my feelings, so I thought I was safe, that there would never be anything more than friendship between us. But now . . ." She took a deep breath.

"Does Sam know who you are?"

"No. I was afraid Richard would make good on his threat to send Sam away. I've visited his school and watched him from afar. I went there last spring and actually spoke to him. He dropped a ball, and I picked it up and asked, 'Is this yours?' He took it and said, 'Thank you.' That moment kept me going for months." She smiled and shook her head. "Can you imagine? But now I have the opportunity to teach him, to comfort him when he's sad, to find out what makes him happy. After all these years."

"Why did you never tell me about him?" Tom's voice still didn't sound quite like his own.

"Only Simon has known from the beginning. Julia knows now, too. And I thought you'd judge me. You were so critical of Ann Goode, even before she made those horrible accusations, but she and I have more in common than you know."

A realization hit him. "You didn't do charity work at a penitentiary. You were an inmate."

"Yes. Richard convinced me to go there when he turned me out of his house." She raised her chin, giving him a wary look.

"What right have I to judge you?" Tom said quietly, holding her gaze. "You know my past."

"What right has anyone to judge? Yet they do. And women are judged more harshly than men."

"I'm sorry. I've been guilty of that more than once." He hesitated. "Did you think of Richard as your husband? Is that why Simon told me you'll never marry?"

"Did Simon say that? It was true, for a while, but Richard wasn't the reason I felt I couldn't marry. Sam was. I've always thought that if I were to marry anyone but Richard, it would be disloyal to Sam. I must be his mother first. I won't have a divided heart."

"Don't you have one now?"

She didn't reply.

He leaned forward. "If you must go to Birmingham to see your son, I'll wait for you, but don't marry Richard. Don't throw away this beautiful thing that's begun between us."

She drew in a shaky breath. "Tom. Please don't."

He caught her hands, drawing his head down to hers. "Don't what? Wait for you? Love you?"

"If I'm to give Sam a fair chance, I must not see you or write. You ought to forget me."

"You're a fool if you think I could forget you," he shot back, gripping her hands harder. "And you're going to make us both miserable."

A strand of her hair slipped forward, partly hiding her face, but a little sob escaped from her and a teardrop fell on his hand.

Regretting his harsh tone, he said, "Forgive me, sweet. I just can't bear the thought of losing you. I'm sorry I've taken so stupidly long to realize how much I love you."

He stroked her hair away from her eyes, wanting desperately to kiss her but afraid of overwhelming her with his intensity. To his dismay, she pulled away and rose to her feet. He opened his mouth to protest, but she surprised him by maneuvering herself onto his lap, slipping her arms around his neck. When he raised his head to hers, she kissed him, her lips salty-wet from her tears. She seemed to melt into him, and he kissed her deeply, intoxicated by the proximity of her body and the sensual way she played her tongue against his.

One of his arms was around her waist, and his other hand was resting on her bare ankle. The hem of her nightdress brushed his hand. The temptation was too much for him, and he slipped his hand under the soft fabric to stroke the smooth bare skin of her calf, then moved higher to her thigh. She gasped softly against his mouth.

Knowing he was dangerously close to losing control, Tom forced himself to withdraw his hand, but he couldn't stop kissing her. He reached up to the back of her neck and loosened her plait with his fingers. Her hair fell in a silky curtain over her shoulders. He pulled her closer, wanting to bury himself in her and protect her at the same time.

Her hands found the buttons of his shirt and started undoing them.

"Ah, sweet girl, don't," he breathed.

She ignored his words, unbuttoning his shirt, then sliding her hands against his bare chest.

Tom caught her hands in his, breathing hard. "Miranda, we can't do this."

"Yes, we can," she said with an intensity that matched his. "It's our last night together, and I want to be with you."

"One night isn't enough," he insisted. "I want you with me every night—and every day—for the rest of my life. If I take you to bed now, I'll be no better than Richard. And no better than the stories that have circulated about me. I want to do this right."

He pulled her into an embrace, murmuring against her neck, "Do you remember at Gwen and Simon's wedding, when the priest mistook us and those children for a family?"

"Yes." Her voice seemed to come from far away.

"I wanted it to be true. I didn't want to admit it even to myself at the time, but I realized when I was in Yorkshire that I do want to be a father. I know you love Sam, but we'll have other children that you'll love just as much." He kissed the warm hollow at the base of her neck. "Be my wife, Miranda."

"I can't." She braced her hands against his chest and wrenched herself out of his grasp, rising to her feet.

"You don't mean that," he insisted, stung by her flat tone. "Why hang all your hopes for the future on this child you don't even know?"

"I don't expect you to understand." She pushed her hair back and straightened her wrapper. Then she walked towards the door.

He followed her and caught her hand, but she wouldn't face him. "You can't leave like this," he said.

"I'm not the right wife for you," she said in the same flat tone. "I'm going to Birmingham, and I don't want you to follow me, or write to me, or try to see me again. Please let me go."

But he didn't release her hand, and in frustration, he said, "First you say you want to be with me tonight, and now you say you want to leave. Which is it?"

Slowly and deliberately, she said, "I want to leave. Will you keep me here against my will?"

He released her hand, and she left the room without another word.

When she was gone, he returned to his armchair and stared at the door in the faint hope that she might change her mind. She couldn't possibly mean what she'd said. But much later, when the early-morning light began to filter into the room, he was still there, alone.

27

He was conscious of that peculiar irritation which will sometimes
befall the man whom others are inclined to trust as a mentor—the
irritation of perceiving that he is supposed to be entirely off the
same plane of desire and temptation as those who confess to him.
Our guides, we pretend, must be sinless: as if those were not often
the best teachers who only yesterday got corrected for their mistakes

—George Eliot, *Daniel Deronda*

LONDON: OCTOBER 1908

Tom approached the public house in Holborn with trepidation. Simon
had written to ask him to meet at the pub, but it seemed like a bad sign
to meet in public, given that Tom used to visit the Thornes' house whenever
he liked. But he wouldn't turn down a chance to see Simon and try to renew
their friendship. It had been four months since they'd last seen each other.

He was also hoping for news of Miranda. He hadn't heard from her since
that last night at Rudleigh, but he didn't believe she would marry Richard
Morris. She loved him, not Richard, and though it was understandable that
the thought of raising her child would tempt her, he couldn't accept the possibility that she would marry someone who had treated her so badly. Still,
there was room for doubt, and he was worried.

Simon was already there, waving to him from a table. He looked cheerful, though tired.

Tom sat down at the table across from Simon. "How are you?" he asked.

"Pretty well, all things considered," Simon answered. "I'm sorry I couldn't ask you to meet at the house, but we're moving tomorrow and it's chaotic right now. I don't even think there's a chair available to sit on."

"Moving? Where?"

Simon put the cigarette to his lips, inhaled deeply, and turned his head to blow the smoke away from Tom. "Back to the countryside, as it happens. A village called Ingleford. I've found a better position there in a solicitor's office."

"I had no idea you were looking for work outside London."

"I wasn't. I happened to hear about the position and decided to apply. We need a bigger house and can't afford one in London." Looking a little sheepish, he said gruffly, "Gwen's going to have a baby."

"Congratulations," Tom said. "Does Gwen mind leaving the city?"

"Yes, a little, but she understands why we need to go." He stubbed out his cigarette and cleared his throat. "Tom, I didn't ask you here to talk about myself. I've long owed you an apology for the way I treated you the last time we saw each other. I'm sorry I believed Ann's story, and I'm sorry I was suspicious of your relationship with Miranda."

"I forgave you long ago for all that," Tom said. "I understood that you were trying to protect Miranda's reputation."

"I should also apologize for keeping your letter from her when you were in Yorkshire. I shouldn't have interfered."

"That doesn't matter now. I saw her at Rudleigh."

"Yes, I know. She mentioned it in a letter."

Tom took a deep breath. "Is she in Birmingham?"

"Yes." Simon hesitated. "She told me that you asked her to marry you. I think it's best that you prepare yourself for the possibility that she'll marry Richard Morris instead."

The words felt like a physical blow to Tom. "She doesn't love him. And you know better than anyone else how he treated her."

Simon sighed. "Her son means more to her than you can understand. If the only way to be with him is to marry Richard, she'll likely do it. Sam has always been a kind of monomania with her."

"There must be a way to convince her to see reason. If she had more children, surely that would help. They wouldn't replace Sam, I know, but she could still have a family . . ." His voice trailed off when he saw the shock on Simon's face.

"She didn't tell you?" Simon said.

"Tell me what?"

"She can't have more children."

Tom stared at him. "I don't understand."

Simon took another cigarette out of his case and lit it. "She had a difficult birth with Sam. Richard wouldn't even call a doctor until it was almost too late." His voice broke, and he made a swipe at his eyes. "She had to have an operation to save her life, and . . . she can't become pregnant again."

Tom couldn't speak. He pressed his fingers to his temples. How Miranda must have suffered, both physically and emotionally, all those years ago. And he had unknowingly hurt her more when he told her he wanted to have children. He must have given her the impression that children were more important to him than she was. A flood of remorse washed over him.

"I need to see her," he said. "Do you have her address?"

"Yes, but I wouldn't advise you to go there. She's been trying very hard to get to know Sam, and if you interfere or cause any trouble between her and Richard, she won't forgive you." Simon leaned forward. "Look, Tom, I know it's not natural for you to sit back and wait instead of acting, but in this case, it's your only chance of success with Miranda."

"Surely I could write to her," he insisted. But even as he said the words, he remembered her telling him very clearly not to write.

"You need to give her time. If you interfere in her relationship with Sam, even unintentionally, you'll become the enemy." Simon paused, then added in a gentler tone, "If you really love her, let her do what she needs to do."

This wasn't the advice Tom wanted to hear, but he sensed the truth in Simon's words, and the heaviness of that truth weighed him down.

"Say, Tom, did you ever find out who attacked you and left you in our wood? We haven't spoken of it for months."

"I don't have proof, but it's clear to me now that it was someone I angered years ago. I knew he disliked me, but I was surprised to find out he still holds a grudge."

"Are you going to bring charges against him?"

Tom hadn't been sure until that moment what he would do, but now the answer was clear. "No. I think he's had his revenge and won't trouble himself about me again, especially now that I'm no longer a contender for the dean-ship. And I want to focus on my future, not my past." This was easier said than done where Miranda was concerned, but he had no doubt he could put Narbridge out of his mind.

After parting from Simon and leaving the pub, Tom didn't feel like going home. He wandered aimlessly, toying with the idea of going to Miranda's old studio. Perhaps she would magically appear there as she had the night after his father came to the cathedral. But there was no point trying to find her if she didn't want to be found. He turned eastward instead and eventu-ally found himself in Shoreditch.

On a street populated largely by dilapidated tenement dwellings, there was a building that Tom knew well, though he hadn't seen it in many years.

It was a stable, but the first floor had been converted into a makeshift church by Osborne Jay, the man who had saved Tom from his life of fighting and sent him to Cambridge.

Tom entered the stable and climbed the ladder to the loft. He was half expecting it to look as it had fifteen years ago, with a few rows of chairs and an open space at the front. But it was just a hayloft now and there were no signs of its previous ecclesiastical role, though he saw the holes in the floor and remembered how children would gather there to watch the horses during services.

His memories had led him astray: he'd heard more recently that Jay had raised money for a new church building on Old Nichol Street, so he left the stable and walked in what he thought was the right direction. It wasn't easy to find, for there was no church spire to follow, only a maze of lanes and alleyways. Tom knew he was heading in the right direction when the odor of dried fish and decaying vegetables wafted to his nose and the street became crowded with women carrying bundles of matchboxes, men with baskets of boots, and sellers of every type of street food from eels to meat pies.

At Old Nichol Street he paused. Most of the buildings on the street had broken or boarded-up windows, but there was a large redbrick building that looked clean and well-kept, so he headed towards it. On his way, he was assailed by a group of dirty, ragged-looking, but cheerful boys who asked if he was looking for "Father Jay." Trying not to wince at this popish title, Tom replied in the affirmative. The boys accompanied him to the first door of the redbrick building and rang the bell.

Jay himself answered the door. He hadn't changed much over the years, aside from losing a little hair and gaining a little weight. As a youth, Tom had been impressed by Jay's bulk and height. He looked like a prizefighter, even if he'd never put on the gloves in his life, as he liked to tell anyone who would listen. He still had the same air of uncompromising authority, even as his eyes crinkled at the corners and a slow smile spread across his face.

"Well, if it isn't young Tom Hirst," he said.

"Not so young anymore," Tom said, returning the smile.

"Neither am I, more's the pity," Jay replied. "Come in." He took a step back to let Tom enter.

"Father Jay, Father Jay," cried one of the smallest boys, "will there be cake after church tomorrow?"

Jay swept his eyes over the youngsters and said, "Yes, indeed, Dicky. Have you ever known me to break a promise?"

"No, Father."

"Come early so you can sit at the front." He turned to the biggest boy and said, "Johnny, I spoke to Mr. Croft, and he says you can start work at his shop at nine o'clock sharp on Monday. Use that new clock you mysteriously acquired to make sure you're on time." He winked, and Johnny nodded.

"I'm sorry I've taken so long to find you again," Tom said when he and Jay turned from the door into the foyer. "I went to the stable first and was surprised the church wasn't there. How long have you had a real church building?"

"About ten years. Would you like a tour?"

"Yes, very much."

Jay led Tom through the foyer into a large, open room with tables set up on one side and wooden bunks along the wall on the other. In the corner near the bunks was a refreshment stand with bright copper urns.

"We use this room for meetings during the day," Jay explained, "and for a men's club in the evenings. At night we offer a free night's lodging to homeless men."

The church was upstairs, its decor an eclectic mix of Jay's high church taste and more homely touches: the large images of saints gazing impassively at what must be the parishioners' handiwork, a brick wall painted green and red.

When Jay showed Tom into the clubroom beneath the meeting room, there were about twenty men there. A foursome at a table was playing cards. Others were playing dominoes, and in the middle of the room two men were engaged in a boxing match. Save the absence of drink and rough talk, the room could have belonged to any working-class men's club.

"How many men are on the roll here?" asked Tom.

"Over four hundred," Jay replied with a look of satisfaction. "They pay a penny a week."

"What are the rules?"

"No drinking, no coarse language, no gambling. That's essentially every-thing."

"Remarkable."

Jay led Tom back upstairs, and they sat down at an empty table in the meeting room.

"This place is what you used to speak of, isn't it?" Tom said. "Not just a church but a social center for the whole community."

"It's certainly the realization of my early dreams. And you were the inspi-ration for the club."

"I was?"

"Indeed. You needed an outlet for all that youthful energy, and there was nothing for you here but street fights and those illegal boxing clubs. And I doubt Cambridge offered as much exercise for your body as it did for your mind."

"Not the sort I was used to, certainly," Tom agreed.

"I don't know how much you've heard about changes in this parish. Not everything has gone according to my plans. The new housing estate we raised money for was built, but the people who'd been evicted from the slums didn't move in. Just as I feared, the rents were too high. They moved into nearby areas that were already overcrowded, creating more problems there."

"I'm sorry to hear that."

Jay sighed and sat back in his chair. "That's enough about me and my work. Tell me what you've been doing since Cambridge. We saw each other once or twice after you graduated, didn't we? I lost track of you after that."

Tom told Jay about his work at the cathedral, the prison, and the hospital. Then, more haltingly, he spoke of his father's reappearance, his visit to Yorkshire, and resigning his license.

"Surely you haven't left the ministry because of your father?"

"No. I've made many mistakes, especially with women. I've also gone back to the Club to fight from time to time. I don't know what you've seen in the papers, and not everything I've been accused of is true, but I've come to realize that being a clergyman, much less a cathedral dean, is not for me."

Jay had warned him about the temptations of women and fighting all those years ago, and Tom expected a reminder of that warning now. Instead, the older man said gravely, "This is my fault."

"How could it be?" Tom asked, mystified.

"I pushed you too hard. I tried to mold you in my own image instead of giving you the freedom you needed."

Tom shook his head. "It was my choice. You gave me the opportunity I wanted most—to go to university. You never tried to pressure me to enter the church."

"Perhaps, but I didn't blame you for keeping your distance after you left Cambridge. You needed to make your own way."

"I ought to have kept in touch, at least to thank you properly for everything you did."

As soon as he'd been able to save enough money, Tom had sent Jay a check to repay him for the university tuition with a brief note of thanks.

Jay returned it with a note just as brief, telling him to use the money for someone who needed it.

"It doesn't matter now."

"It does." Tom leaned forward. "I'm sorry I resisted your efforts and made your job more difficult. I didn't see at the time what a sacrifice you made: not just the money, but your time and energy, too. You didn't need to do that for me."

"You were too young and too focused on your own survival to notice anyone else. It's just a fact. But I'm sorry, too. You told me often enough that you were just a project to me, and it stung at the time, but I've come to realize there was some truth to it. I was zealous and idealistic, still new to the parish—and to the ministry—when we met, and I was trying to prove myself. You were the first person I felt I had really helped, and I lost sight of you as an individual."

"I hold nothing against you. After all, you inspired my passion for reform. I'm starting to realize that if anything is my true vocation, that is."

"Well, you inspired my club, so let's call it even. Look, Tom, I have an appointment, but if you're interested in returning to the Old Nichol, I may have a job for you. Will you come back another day so we can talk more?"

"Yes, of course."

Tom regretted having kept his distance from Jay for so long. For the first time in months, he was excited about reform work. It didn't matter that someone else had begun it. He just wanted to be part of it. What he had expected in Yorkshire had happened here instead, in the slums of London: he had come home.

28

There are no words to express the abyss between isolation and having one ally. It may be conceded to the mathematicians that four is twice two. But two is not twice one; two is two thousand times one.

—G. K. Chesterton, *The Man Who Was Thursday*

BIRMINGHAM: OCTOBER 1908

"Would you like me to read to you?" Miranda asked her son.

"No, thank you." He was looking through a stereoscope that she'd brought him as a gift a few days earlier. She regretted the gift now because it meant she couldn't see his face.

They were in the parlor at Richard's house. The room, like Richard himself, was sober and utilitarian, all sharp edges and no wasted space. At least she was close to Sam on the hard sofa, and they had a rare few minutes alone.

"May I see the picture you're looking at?" she asked.

Sam reluctantly moved the wooden device away from his face and handed it to her. She looked through the viewer, breathing in the mossy scent of

Sam's hair that clung to it. The photograph was of a terrier standing on its hind legs.

"Is this your favorite picture?" she asked, lowering the device to her lap.

"Yes. I want a dog, but Papa said no."

"Why not?"

He shrugged expressively. It was so like Simon's shrug that Miranda caught her breath. Little things like that were always surprising her, things that reminded her Sam was a Thorne as much as he was a Morris.

He looked at the stereoscope in her lap as if he wanted to take it from her.

She took a deep breath. "Sam, I'm going away today, and I want to tell you how much I've enjoyed spending time with you."

He looked at her wonderingly. "Where are you going?"

"I'm going back home, to London."

She waited for him to say, "Don't go," or "Take me with you," as he had in her fantasies, but he just studied her face, then said, "The boys at school sometimes tease me because I have strange eyes."

"Do they? That's unkind."

"Your eyes are the same color as mine. Do people tease you?"

"No. You and I have special eyes that adults appreciate. You'll see when you grow up."

Richard came in then, and the private moment was lost.

"Say goodbye to your aunt, Sam. The carriage is here to take her to the train station."

Miranda winced inwardly, as she always did, when Richard referred to her as Sam's aunt. She understood the necessity for the falsehood, but it still troubled her. She supposed she should be glad Richard was willing to acknowledge some familial connection between her and Sam, however distant.

Sam stood and offered Miranda his hand. She stood too and took it, resisting the urge to pull him into her arms. Such a small hand he had. It was difficult to let go, to act as if she were saying goodbye to any child of her acquaintance.

"Goodbye," her son said. Then he turned to Richard. "David says he has three new minerals for his collection. May I go to his house to see them? Please, Papa?"

"Of course," Richard replied, smiling and reaching out to ruffle Sam's hair.

Sam beamed and ran out of the room without a backwards glance.

Miranda left the room with Richard hovering at her elbow, his usual place. Perhaps he was afraid she'd try to kidnap Sam. But she had no intention of doing so. Sam was clearly happy. He had all the material comforts he needed. She wouldn't try to take him away from a life he loved.

As Miranda put on her cloak and hat in the front foyer, Richard waved away the maid and said, "My offer still stands. Stay here and marry me, Miranda."

She looked up at the man who had been the cause of so much pain in her life. He had kept his promise not to pressure her into marriage, but she felt oppressed in his presence, as if that pressure was only just being restrained, that desire to control her and make her into his image of a perfect wife.

"I can't," she replied. "Thank you for giving me this time with Sam, but I can't marry you."

His face darkened, but he answered coolly, "Why not? Don't you believe I've changed?"

"I can see that you have. That's not the problem." She hesitated. "I've changed too, but not in a way that would make me a good wife to you."

He sighed. "Perhaps you just need more time."

"No," she said firmly. "I don't."

"I expected that my offer would be too good for you to refuse. To have Sam, a comfortable home, all the freedom you desire . . ."

Freedom, she thought, was exactly what she *wouldn't* have if she married Richard.

"Is there someone else?" he persisted.

She thought of Tom. With all his faults, he'd never made her feel trapped. She never felt she couldn't speak her mind with him. But she couldn't marry him, either. Not if he desired children of his own.

She looked up at Richard and said, "There's no one else." Then she asked the question to which she was afraid of hearing the answer. "May I see Sam again?"

"Of course. Perhaps during the Christmas holidays."

She thanked him and let him escort her to the carriage.

On the way to the train station, Miranda thought about what she would do when she arrived in London. She needed to find her bearings and make a life for herself. She didn't want to live with Gwen and Simon or Julia and Charles, though they'd all invited her to do so. She'd agreed to a temporary stay with Julia and Charles only until she could find a place of her own. She fantasized about finding a tiny studio, a miniature version of Isabella Grant's, where she could live and work, supporting herself by giving art lessons and selling her paintings.

She thought back to her time at Rudleigh. Sometimes she doubted the reality of everything that had happened there. That last week, especially, was such a strange, terrifying, magical time that she sometimes thought she'd dreamed it. An influential art critic praising her work. Two proposals of marriage in the same day when she'd never received a single one before. And most astonishing of all, Tom, whom she'd loved secretly for so long, declaring his love for her. She blushed to think of her own actions that last night, going to his room in her nightclothes and practically begging him to take her to bed. It spoke well for him that he hadn't, but there was still a tiny doubt in her mind about the suddenness of his realization that he loved her. Perhaps he was merely swept away by the strange atmosphere at Rudleigh.

Her mind played tricks on her in many ways. All these years she'd been thinking of Sam as real and nearly everyone else as imaginary. But when she finally had the chance to spend time with him, she'd realized he wasn't real, not in the way she'd expected. Everything Simon had been trying to tell her for years was true. She didn't know Sam, and he didn't know her. The child she'd been longing to raise was a child of her imagination. And Tom, whom she'd tried so hard to relegate to her fantasy world, had become more real than anyone else. It made no difference that she hadn't seen or heard from him in two months. It was too easy—dangerously easy—to remember the scent of his cedarwood soap, the heat of his mouth on hers, his hands caressing her body.

Once at the station, she pushed away thoughts of Tom and found her seat on the train to London, collapsing into it with a sigh. She'd hoped for a private compartment, but the train was crowded. A young couple, perhaps newly married, sat across from her, whispering and holding hands, completely absorbed in each other. The elderly woman sitting next to Miranda alternated between giving the young couple disapproving looks and making loud comments about the sort of people who could afford a second-class carriage in this day and age.

Miranda wondered if she was making a mistake leaving Birmingham. Could she really let Sam go? She closed her eyes and tried to imagine him, but the memory of the real child was already fading. As she opened her eyes again and gazed out the window at the platform, her vision blurred by tears, she saw a boy begging, holding out a dirty cloth cap for coins. He looked familiar.

She blinked the moisture from her eyes and looked more closely. She still wasn't certain, but she jumped up from her seat just as the whistle sounded and pushed past her startled fellow passengers, hurrying to the door as the guard shouted, "All aboard!"

"Please, let me out!" she cried.

"It's too late, ma'am," he said.

But the door was still open, and she flung herself out of it, stumbling on the steps and nearly falling onto the platform. Once she had regained her footing, she approached the beggar child.

"Jack?" she asked. "Jack Goode?"

His face was grimed with dirt, and for a moment she thought she was mistaken about his identity, but gold-flecked brown eyes looked up at her in shocked recognition.

"Miss Thorne?"

"What are you doing here?" she asked.

"Tryin' to get back to London."

"I'm going to London, too. Would you like to ride with me?"

He nodded.

Her train was already pulling out of the station. She had her reticule, but her small trunk was in the luggage van and would arrive in London without her. By the time she wired the Carringtons to send a servant for it, bought a train ticket for Jack, and visited the refreshment room, it was nearly time to board the next train. Jack had a dirty bundle of rags that he told her he'd been using as a bed, and she was relieved that he took her suggestion to leave it behind.

Miranda was aware of the raised eyebrows and whispers as she and Jack boarded the train together, but she paid no attention and hoped Jack didn't notice. He certainly looked much the worse for having spent several days sleeping in the train station, but soap and water and some clean clothing would solve that problem. Fortunately, they found a compartment that was empty except for a sleeping old man. Miranda sat across from Jack and watched him eat the hot roll she'd bought for him, trying to hold herself back from asking the million questions in her mind.

"I've missed you, Jack," she said. "I was living with the Carringtons for a while and was hoping to see you there. They told me Ann took you to Scotland."

"She meant to, but we didn't get there."

"Where did you get to?"

"A town in the north somewhere. I think the name starts with a *C*."

"What happened then?"

"She met a man." He turned to the window and breathed on it, then traced a pattern with his finger that only he could see. "'E didn't want me around, so I left."

"That must have been difficult."

"Nah, I didn't like 'im. I'm going to London 'cause I want to live with Mr. Cross again. Do you think 'e'd let me?"

"Oh, Jack." Her eyes filled with tears again, but she dashed them away quickly before he could notice. "I don't know if that will be possible."

"Do you know where 'e is?"

"No," she said slowly, "but I think my brother does. He'll tell you."

"Even if I can't live with Mr. Cross, I want to see 'im to 'pologize."

"What for, dear?"

"For takin' the cross."

Miranda looked at him quizzically. Jack reached into his trousers pocket, pulled out a cross on a broken chain, and handed it to her. It was the gold cross that had been her grandfather's, the one she had given Tom. There was no other cross like it, with those telltale scratches on its surface. She bit her lip to stop it from trembling.

"I was savin' it," Jack continued, "to sell if I couldn't get to London any other way. But now I can give it back. D'ye think 'e'll be angry?"

She took a deep breath and handed the cross back to him. "I don't think so. Not if you apologize and return it to him."

"I want to 'pologize about my sister, too. She said bad things about Mr. Cross that warn't true. An' she said she was my mam."

"She's not your mother?"

"Nah. I was little when my mam died, but I remember 'er." He looked out the window. "She was nicer than Ann."

Miranda wanted to take him in her arms, grime and all, and tell him everything was going to be all right. For the first time in months, she almost believed it herself.

29

Admired Miranda!
Indeed the top of admiration, worth
What's dearest to the world! Full many a lady
I have eyed with best regard, and many a time
Th' harmony of their tongues hath into bondage
Brought my too diligent ear. For several virtues
Have I liked several women, never any
With so full soul but some defect in her
Did quarrel with the noblest grace she owed,
And put it to the foil. But you, O you,
So perfect and so peerless, are created
Of every creature's best.
—William Shakespeare, *The Tempest*

LONDON: APRIL 1909

Tom didn't have an official title for his employment in Shoreditch. He was partly Osborne Jay's curate, though having relinquished his license as a clergyman, he couldn't claim such a title. He was still doing what he'd always enjoyed most: working with people in need and trying to improve their lives, as he was trying to do now with John Barnes.

"Sally and the baby are real bad, Mr. Hirst. I ain't found work yet, and I can't afford their medicine." John stared at his feet as he spoke.

"Have you gone to the dispensary?" Tom asked.

"No, sir. With all due respeck, I didn't see the point."

Tom hesitated, then reached into his pocket and handed the man six-pence. "Take this, then, and go directly there. Do we understand each other, John?"

"Yes, sir. Thank you, sir. You're a good man." And he was gone.

When Tom had first started working in Shoreditch, Jay had warned him not to set a precedent of almsgiving. Tom knew that Jay himself gave the parishioners money sometimes, but only sparingly and as secretly as he could manage. After only a month of working together, Jay had admitted that Tom was better than he was at discerning when people were deceiving him, so he had relaxed his rule, but still, Tom knew he shouldn't fall into the habit of giving money to these men. More often than not, they would spend the money on drink or gambling.

Later that afternoon in the church when Tom and Jay were setting up for the next day's service, Jay told Tom about an old charity, the Mansion House Fund, that he intended to revive to help unemployed men find work. Tom knew about the charity and listened with interest to Jay's plan, which essentially involved identifying men who were able and willing to work and matching them with employers.

"That's brilliant," Tom said, "but how will you have time to oversee it? You're already run off your feet as it is."

"I didn't say I'd be running it. What do you think about taking charge of it yourself?"

Tom stared at his mentor. "Do you mean that?"

"Unfortunately, I do." Jay set down a chair, straightened up and wiped his forehead with his handkerchief. "I say 'unfortunately' because I don't want to lose you as my assistant, but running the charity will take most of your time."

"There must be others who are better qualified than I am for such a position."

"If there are, I don't know any. I've been watching you, Tom. This work won't be easy, but it's in line with the work you've already done for the Prison Commission as well as your experience as a prison chaplain. You'll need to brush up on Poor Law relief and state programs, but that won't be difficult for you. And I can't think of anyone else whom I'd trust more to make the difficult decisions about who qualifies for the program and who doesn't. Are you interested?"

"Yes, very."

Tom was touched by Jay's faith in him and intrigued by the prospect of running a new charity. He was well aware that his bruised reputation had benefited greatly from Jay, who had been singing Tom's praises often, loudly, and publicly since Tom had begun working for him. He was still on good terms with the bishop, too, despite resigning his license. Jay paid him a small stipend, and Tom was much poorer than he had been as a canon at the cathedral. But he was happier, on the whole. He had enough money to support himself and to pay for the modest rooms he rented in Bethnal Green. He felt both that he was doing useful work and he could be himself for the first time in many years.

Still, he was lonely. Having been educated as a gentleman, Tom had little in common with the people he worked with. Only Jay was Tom's social equal. Partly by choice, Tom had distanced himself from many of the people he'd associated with before Ann Goode's false accusations and the truth about his father came to light, but he craved the society of people he could talk with openly about his thoughts and goals for the future.

All of which made the letter that had arrived from Simon two days earlier very welcome. Only a few letters had passed between them since their meeting at the pub. Such meager correspondence was more Tom's fault than Simon's. Tom had explained his own silence to himself by blaming his work. Certainly he was very busy, and the work had saved him from dwelling on aspects of the past he preferred not to think about. But this time Simon's letter included an invitation to visit him and Gwen at their new home in Ingleford, and Tom decided to accept it, though the visit would inevitably make his longing for Miranda more intense.

As much as he tried not to think about her, Tom was under no illusions about his feelings. No matter how doggedly he worked, how exhausted he made himself with twelve- or fourteen-hour days, Miranda was always there, just beneath the surface of his mind, a phantom who still ruled his heart. Even Tom was surprised by the tenacity of his love, but there it was. Perhaps Simon had news of her.

A few days later, Tom took the train from London to Ingleford. The village was in Surrey, on the same line as Denfield, and he was reminded of the last time he was on this train, going in the opposite direction. He remembered his reluctance to leave the peaceful atmosphere of the Thornes' cottage, and dreading the troubles that awaited him in London. He was not the same man he was then, and he was glad of it.

When Tom disembarked at Ingleford, Simon met him at the station and they walked the short distance to Simon and Gwen's house.

"This path reminds me of the one near your old cottage," Tom said, feeling a twinge of nostalgia for the fairy-tale place where Simon and Miranda had nursed him back to health. It had been autumn then, and now it was spring, but the rolling hills and hedgerows and the little wood in the distance were reminders of that time.

"Yes, I can see how it would."

"Do you have a vegetable garden?"

"Naturally." Simon grinned. "I don't have much time to spend on it, given my work in the village and my family responsibilities, but I put my hands in the dirt every chance I get." He turned to Tom, his expression becoming serious. "I ought to tell you Miranda's at the house, too, and she's brought a guest with her. I'm not allowed to spoil the secret by telling you who her guest is, but I wanted to prepare you a little."

After a pause that Tom hoped didn't betray how shaken he felt, he said, "I see." All he saw, though, was his hope that the guest would be Sam—that Miranda would have her son with her at last—and his fear that the guest would be Richard Morris.

Simon nodded and went on talking about his vegetable garden, or perhaps about his work—Tom didn't hear any of it. After eight months of hearing nothing from Miranda, he would see her in a matter of minutes.

As he and Simon came within view of the gray stone house perched on a gentle slope, with a meadow on one side and a wood on the other, he saw a woman sitting on a blanket on the grass in the sunshine.

It was Miranda. She was holding a baby and smiling down into its face.

Tom's breath caught in his throat as he approached her. He had imagined their first meeting after the events at Rudleigh so many times in so many different settings that the reality was overwhelming. She was wearing a blue dress with a lace collar. Her hair was plaited and pinned around her head like a coronet, the sunlight playing on the gold strands.

Miranda smiled up at him and said, "Won't you sit down?" as if it had been only a week since they'd last seen each other. The baby began to fuss and she looked down at it, holding out her index finger, which was immediately clutched by a tiny fist.

Before Tom could reply, Simon said, "There's no time to sit, I'll wager." At the same time, the front door of the house opened and Gwen emerged.

"Tom! How good to see you," Gwen said with a smile. "And you're just in time. Dinner's ready." She went to Miranda and held out her arms to the baby, cooing, "Come to Mama, darling."

"That amazing creature is our daughter, Mary," Simon said to Tom.

"She's beautiful," he said, a lump rising in his throat.

"There's someone else here you'll want to meet," Simon added. "Where is he, Miranda?"

Tom couldn't look at her.

"I'll find him." She rose and hurried away. It must have been no more than a few minutes before she returned, but it was the longest few minutes of Tom's life.

Miranda appeared from behind the house, holding the hand of a boy. Tom felt such a wave of relief that he didn't look closely at the boy, only at the uncertain, half-hopeful look in Miranda's eyes as she approached. But when he did look at the boy, he was stunned all over again.

"Jack!" Tom exclaimed.

"Hullo, Mr. Cross." Jack extended his hand and shook Tom's solemnly.

Tom crouched down so he and the boy were eye to eye. "Where in the world have you been? And how did Miss Thorne find you?"

"That's a long story we can tell you over dinner," Simon interposed.

In the general bustle of everyone's going into the house and finding a seat at the table, Tom managed to quiet his mind enough to take in his surroundings. The house wasn't large, but it was comfortable, and Gwen had clearly made an effort to make the rooms look attractive. The dining room was more formal than one might expect in a simple country house, with an enormous oak sideboard that displayed a profusion of ornaments, china, and a dessert service that looked like it was never used. They'd brought their servant Jane with them from London, and she looked a little embarrassed to see Tom, given the fact that she'd shut the door of their London house in his face the last time she saw him.

Gwen and Simon did most of the talking as Jane served dinner. The occasional tension Tom had noticed between them in the past was gone, and they were consumed by love for their baby. It was good to see. Miranda then told the story of how she and Jack had been reunited at Birmingham

New Street station and how he was living with the family of one of her art students.

"You're giving lessons, then," Tom said. "Do you have time to work on your own paintings?"

"Yes," she said. "I've been selling them, too. I have a small studio in London. The Carringtons helped me find it. And Jack is my assistant."

Jack beamed, clearly proud of his new job.

Miranda looked at Jack, then across the table at Tom with a light in her eyes that made his heart beat faster. "Simon mentioned you're doing reform work in the East End," she said. "Will you tell us about it?"

Tom began to talk about his work with Jay, hoping he didn't sound incoherent. He talked about the church with the club and games room beneath it. He talked about the way Jay had made friends with his poor and sometimes criminal parishioners and how Tom had begun to do the same. He talked about how good it was to see the men in a safe place, enjoying their free time in Jay's club instead of a pub or gaming house. Miranda listened with the alert stillness that was uniquely hers. He had missed that.

Tom wondered if Miranda would notice that his life in the East End had changed him. Perhaps living there was already making him uncouth in ways he couldn't detect. Was his clothing clean enough? Was his speech and manner still that of a gentleman? Looking down at his hands, he saw calluses on his palms and even traces of dirt under his fingernails. While his duties at Jay's church and club didn't usually involve manual labor, he had lately been helping the men install a new boxing ring.

"Isn't it difficult to live among such rough people?" Gwen asked. "I know you grew up poor, but can you feel comfortable again in such surroundings?"

"It was difficult at first," Tom admitted. "It still is, sometimes. I grew up in the country, and though my family was indeed very poor, the poverty of the East End is certainly very different for me, all overcrowded tenements and constant brawling. But I'm encouraged by the number of people who attend the church and are members of the club. The interest in both gives me hope that my work does something, however small, to improve people's lives."

"I don't think what you're doing is small," Miranda put in quietly. "You and Mr. Jay have given these people a place to go, perhaps the only place that doesn't lead them into a life of crime or drunkenness."

"Thank you," said Tom. He held her gaze until she looked away.

Simon looked up from a slice of bread he was buttering and said to Tom, "Now that you know where we live, you must come to visit us more regularly. It's been too long since we've seen you."

"I know. I've been working so much that I lose track of time sometimes. It's hard to leave London, but I'll certainly do my best."

He wanted to speak to Miranda alone, but before he could contrive a way to do so, Gwen came to his rescue. As Jane began to clear away the dishes, Gwen said, "Miranda, why don't you take Tom for a walk before the sun goes down? The wood is beautiful this time of year. Off you go." Gwen's brisk tone nearly made Tom laugh. Now that she was a mother, she seemed to be treating everyone like a child.

Miranda turned to Tom. Without quite meeting his eyes, she asked, "Would you like to come with me?"

"Yes. That sounds wonderful."

"Can I come, too?" Jack asked.

"Not this time," Simon said cheerfully. "I need your help. There's a plant that's just come up in the garden and I don't know what it is. You can help me identify it."

Simon whisked Jack away, and Tom and Miranda left the house together. The sun was still high in the sky and not anywhere near setting, in spite of what Gwen had implied. They headed towards the wood along a footpath wide enough for them to walk side by side. The air held the fresh, warm scent of spring.

"How long were you in Birmingham?" Tom asked.

"Two months."

"Will you tell me what happened there?"

She paused, as if unsure where to begin. "Richard wanted me to live with his sister at first, but I refused, because I wanted lodgings that were not connected to him or to anyone he knew. I found a respectable lodging-house not far from Richard's home, so I could see Sam every day."

"Was Sam ever told that you're his mother?"

"Richard thought it would be confusing for him and would expose him to ridicule. Sam thought Lucy was his mother. He introduced me to Sam as an aunt."

"That must have been difficult for you."

"It was." Miranda pulled her skirt away from some brambles alongside the path. "Sam was shy with me at first. After a while, though, he became used to my presence, and I would read stories and play games with him, but I was rarely alone with him." She took a deep breath, then continued, "Richard made no demands on me, but he was almost always with us. I think he was trying to prove that we could be a family."

"Did you believe he had changed?"

"Yes. I still do. Losing Lucy really did shake him, and he was kinder than I remembered. He did his best to give me time to think about whether I could marry him. I knew I couldn't, though, almost from the beginning."

Tom couldn't beat down the spark of hope that rose inside him.

"It was difficult to leave Sam," she continued, "but I could see that he's happy there. He has a good life with Richard."

They entered the wood. With the sunlight filtering through the trees and a carpet of bluebells at their feet, it was breathtakingly beautiful. They both stopped to take in the scene.

After a moment, Tom turned to face Miranda, forgetting his surroundings as he gazed at her. She was even more beautiful than he remembered, and it was difficult not to touch her.

"Will Richard allow you to visit Sam again?" he asked, trying to keep his voice steady.

"He said he would," she replied, "but it wasn't good for me to go there. I'm still sad when I think of Sam, but I know his life and mine must remain separate."

"Is that how you feel about ours, too?" he said. "Your life and mine?"

She was silent, looking up at him gravely.

"Why didn't you tell me that night at Rudleigh that you couldn't have more children?" Tom asked.

She blinked. "How did you know?"

"Simon told me."

"I hadn't the courage, not after you said you wanted to be a father. You want your own children—"

"I want *you*, Miranda. You're more important to me than any children." His voice trembled with emotion as he looked down at her. "I need you. You've shattered every category I've tried to put you in. You're the only woman I've ever wanted to marry. Even if you make me wait for the rest of my life, I'll marry no one else."

She remained silent, looking up at him as if she couldn't quite believe what she was hearing. Then she reached for his hand and clasped it between both of hers. Her touch sent a thrill through him, but he was ashamed of his work-roughened hand.

"You know I live in humbler circumstances than before," he said, his words spilling out as if he had only a short time to convince her. "I don't expect you to live in Bethnal Green, but I won't be there forever. Jay has offered to put me in charge of a new charity, and if it works out, we could move to a more suitable neighborhood. We could find a house with a room that you could use as a studio—"

Miranda interrupted him by raising his hand to her lips and kissing it, then pressing it warmly against her cheek. "I've always loved your hands," she said.

Tears sprang to his eyes, but he didn't care. She'd seen him cry before. She'd seen him at his worst, known the worst, and if any woman could live with him, she could. When she looked up at him again, there were tears in her eyes too, but she was smiling.

He swept her up in his arms and carried her into the wood, across the carpet of bluebells. He meant to set her down, but it felt too good to hold her like this, with her arms around his neck and her body against his. And when she whispered in his ear that she loved him, he turned his head to kiss her. The kiss lasted a long time.

When they paused for breath, she said, "Aren't you going to put me down?"

"Do you want me to?"

"No." She smiled. "But I don't think Elaine and Lancelot are supposed to end up together."

"Lancelot!" he exclaimed, laughing. "Is that how you think of me? I don't know what's sillier, my calling you Elaine or your calling me Lancelot. No, you're Miranda and I'm Ferdinand. I'm not a knight but a log bearer."

"I don't know. Ferdinand always struck me as being too agreeable. You're far more difficult than he is."

"True," he murmured, his lips against her neck. "I'm not an easy man to live with."

"I suspect you're right."

"And I can be moody."

"Yes."

"And stubborn."

"Yes."

"And hotheaded."

"Are you trying to change my mind?" she asked.

"No!" He raised his head and tried to give her a stern look, which failed utterly. "Don't change your mind."

And she didn't.

Author's Note

In the nineteenth and early twentieth centuries, penitentiaries were not prisons but rather charities meant to reform "fallen women," a category that included prostitutes, unmarried pregnant women, and women who had been seduced or raped. In theory, women would enter penitentiaries voluntarily, but in practice they often had little choice. The first penitentiaries were run by men associated with the church, but later most were run by Anglican sisterhoods or even by private patrons (famous Victorians involved in this charity work included Christina Rossetti and Charles Dickens). Some penitentiaries treated their inmates kindly, but many were worse than prisons and operated like workhouses. Of course, no such institutions existed for "fallen" or sexually transgressive men.

All the characters in *Bear No Malice* are fictional, with the exception of Arthur Osborne Montgomery Jay (1858–1945). When he began his work in 1886 as Vicar of Holy Trinity, Shoreditch, there was no church building in the parish, so he did indeed hold services in the loft of a stable. Over the next ten years he raised enough money for a church building as well as a social club, lodging house, and gymnasium where boxing matches were held. Jay's encouragement of boxing caused controversy even among proponents of muscular Christianity, but he held firm about its usefulness as physical exercise. Jay also pointed out that there were no fields in

Shoreditch where the men could play cricket or football, so boxing was the main sport.

The Mansion House Fund, the charity Jay puts Tom in charge of at the end of the novel, was real, though it was overseen by Samuel Barnett, the founder of Toynbee Hall, not Osborne Jay.

Acknowledgments

Bear No Malice began, as so many novels do, with a "what if" question: what if I took the villain of *Impossible Saints* and made him a hero? What would Thomas Cross's story look like from his own perspective? This was an experiment, a writing exercise meant to tide me over until I thought of an idea for a new novel, but it surprised me by turning into the new novel. Years of revisions ensued, and I would have given up on it completely if not for the advice and support of the following people:

Christine Thorpe and Joyce Pitzel, who managed to find things to like even in an early draft.

Ruth Zavitz's critique group, an invaluable resource in the early stages. Special thanks to beta readers Ruth herself, for reading to the end despite disliking Tom, and Chris Mazmanian, for the necessary capitalized reminders about Jack.

Andrew Murray, Kelley Armstrong, John Jeneroux, and Bev Irwin, who inspired me to dig up this novel years later and revise it yet again. Without you, the end of the first chapter would still be puzzling and illogical.

Karen Harwood, for much-needed help with the boxing scene.

Jennifer Delamere, for beta reading two different drafts and making excellent suggestions, as always.

Abby Murphy, who was again the bright, clear voice in my dark editing cave. You have a true gift for supportive, insightful critique.

Ellen Winters, for being on Tom's side from the beginning.

Katie McGuire, my editor at Pegasus. Getting to work with you on two books makes me feel as though I've won the lottery. You continue to amaze me with your preternatural ability to cut to the heart of knotty story problems and communicate so clearly and effectively. And to the Pegasus design team, I would buy any book with this gorgeous cover no matter what the story!

Laura Crocket, my agent, who has made so many of my writing dreams come true. Thanks for having my back and being the best agent any writer could hope for. Thanks also to the team at TriadaUS for all your hard work behind the scenes.

Michael Harwood, for helping me fix plot holes, being my PR guy, and tolerating the Richard Armitage photos. You're the best man I know.